ADVERSITY'S GIFT

GIFT

A Story Woven with the Power of Personal Development

Opening Note From

Emmy, Oscar & Tony

Award-Winning Movie Producer Phillip B Goldfine

RITA MONTALTO

Notes

OPENING NOTE

Adversity's Gift by Rita Montalto is, without question, one of the most moving and powerful novels of our time. It is a profound journey that goes beyond storytelling to deliver life-changing insight on resilience, family, and the unbreakable spirit within us all. Set against the breathtaking landscapes of Australia and the vibrant energy of New York, this novel immerses you in Bobby Jo's world, a young woman unwavering resolve to save her family's struggling farm, and a profound calling to uplift and empower others, drives her to bring her ambitious self-development board game to life, an effort that is nothing short of inspiring.

Montalto does not just write; she invites readers to walk alongside Bobby Jo, feeling each triumph and every heartache as if they were their own. Her prose is vivid, her storytelling immersive, and her message clear: our toughest challenges are often the greatest gifts life has to offer. This book is a roadmap to personal transformation, a Gold Mine for anyone ready to harness the strength that adversity awakens within us.

Adversities' Gift isn't just another novel; it's a call to action, a guide for turning life's setbacks into steppingstones toward greatness. I wholeheartedly believe in this book's message, and I am certain it will resonate with readers on the deepest level. For anyone seeking inspiration, courage, or a new perspective, this is an essential read... work destined to become a modern classic.

Phillip B Goldfine
Emmy, Oscar, Tony
Award-Winning Movie Producer

PRAISES FOR ADVERSITY'S GIFT

"Adversity's Gift is a must-read that takes you on a journey alongside a powerful young woman with an iron will to chase her dreams. Elements of familial love, perseverance, and willingness to jump into the unknown, this story captivates you from start to finish."

Adde Murrieta – Author and Of Starter Husband

"Rita Montalto's Adversity's Gift is a powerful reminder that life's greatest challenges hold the keys to our deepest growth. Through the lens of Bobby Jo's unshakable spirit, readers embark on an inspiring journey that ignites self-discovery, resilience, and hope. Rita masterfully combines her creativity, humour, and profound wisdom to deliver lessons that resonate far beyond the page. This book is not just a story, it's a toolkit for personal transformation, reminding us all of the strength we carry within. A must-read for anyone ready to embrace life's twists and turns with courage and grace. And everything is spiced up with her amazing Australian humour! I'm so looking forward to playing the game."

Norman Gräter / Three-Time European Champion in Public Speaking, Multi-Award-Winning Motivational Speaker, C-Level Consultant, and Author

Empowering and Transformative!

Adversity's Gift is a game-changer in the self-help genre. The author masterfully combines practical advice, heartfelt anecdotes, and actionable strategies to guide readers toward achieving their goals and overcoming life's challenges.

What sets this book apart is its relatable tone and clear step-by-step approach. It feels like having a conversation with a trusted mentor who genuinely wants to see you succeed. Each chapter builds on the last, offering insights that are both inspiring and immediately applicable.

Whether you're looking to boost your confidence, cultivate better habits, or simply gain a fresh perspective, Adversity's Gift provides the tools you need to create lasting change. Highly recommended for anyone ready to take charge of their personal growth journey with a twist.

Natasha Brune, Published Author, The Wise Marie Project

"Rita Montalto is such an inspiring writer. She transports you into the tale of a lifetime, on a path toward self-improvement. This book is filled with adventure and emotion that immerses you in awe til the very end."

Kizzy Lee- Singer/Songwriter, Screenplay Writer, and Editor, Kiz Assisting

ACKNOWLEDGEMENTS

To my dear husband Bruno,

I am grateful for your unwavering belief in me, even during our toughest times. Thank you for always understanding and supporting my endless travels to learn more about personal development.

Your understanding and encouragement mean the world to me. I feel incredibly fortunate to have you by my side through it all.

And to our beautiful children, Andrea, Nicole, and Matthew, sons-in-law James and Michael, thank you for bringing immeasurable joy into our life.

To our grandchildren Lewis, Samuel, Mia, Claire, and Lorenzo that bring a special light that nothing else can match.

*"You are **all** my forever love, the eternal flame that guides my heart."*

"To all the incredible individuals I had the privilege of meeting during my travels abroad and across Australia while collecting life-changing personal development knowledge. There are too many of you to name but you know who you are, this message is for you. From the depths of my heart, I am eternally grateful for your friendship and unwavering support. Meeting you has been one of the most impactful parts of my journey, shaping who I've become. You filled it with immeasurable joy, meaning, and memories I'll cherish forever."

A special acknowledgement goes to my publisher, Ava V Manuel, from the Los Angeles Tribune.

Ava, you have been my rock throughout this entire journey, offering encouragement.

and an ocean of wisdom. Your heart of gold has been a guiding light, and I couldn't have done this without you. Thank you!

DEAR READER

Hand on my heart... Thank you for choosing to read this book. I am truly honoured to share Bobby Jo's journey with you.

When I set out to write this story, I wanted to do more than just share a story. I wanted to include universal principles of personal development and combine it with entertainment. My goal was to bring those principles to life through characters you could cheer for, learn from, and connect with. Through Bobby Jo's challenges, triumphs and joy, I hope you'll see how clarity, resilience, determination, action taking, and having a kind heart leads to extraordinary growth.

I have allowed a page with lines so you may write down the key principles as you read so it may teach and guide you in your own unique journey. Please take the time to do that, as it will help you with your learning process.

As you turn the pages, I hope you feel both entertained and inspired. But beyond that, my wish is for you to reflect on your own goals and dreams. If you have ever questioned whether your success is within reach, let this be a gentle nudge: it is. The tools for serious success are not "out there somewhere"; they are within you.

Don't worry about knowing exactly how to get there. The path will reveal itself as you take one small step at a time... consistently, even if that step feels uncertain or imperfect.

Embrace your uniqueness, and remember, you have the power to be wealthy and successful in every area of life... never let anyone tell you otherwise.

With gratitude and belief in you,

Rita

TABLE OF CONTENTS

YOU DON'T GET WHAT YOU WANT

YOU GET ...

WHO YOU ARE BEING.

CHAPTER 1

HOW IT ALL BEGAN

Narrated by Nonna Giovanna

The story I am about to share with you still rocks me to the core. Some things have happened in my life that are buried so deeply that I have never dared tell a soul. Even now, my heart skips a beat when I relive them.

I never imagined such a force could exist; I have never told a soul, let alone begun to unravel how forces beyond our understanding can inexplicably draw people together. The weight of this secret has pressed heavily on me for years; the fear of being judged or dismissed prevents me from ever confiding in anyone. Perhaps my limited cultural beliefs, or the weight of tradition, have kept me from truly accepting such a possibility.

I have made an effort to ignore the memories, but they persist, haunting me with their inexplicable and potent grip.

How were these events even possible? Here I am today, 76 years old, not knowing how much time I have left in this world. But I do know that this story, my story, needs to be told.

Imagine this: endless golden wheat fields stretching under the open sky. In the distance, a flat land so vast you can almost see the curve of the Earth; red soil so red that we never wear white socks, as the stain from the soil does not come off. There is a slight hill rise on our property, adding a touch of majesty to the landscape. Not a green blade of grass can be seen anywhere except for our garden and the sheep paddocks, which we water from the nearby springs. Our place, a modest rendered double-brick homestead my son Alonso built with his own hands, stands proudly in the Australian outback with a shearing shed that could tell a good few stories of its own over the years. Farm machinery rests in a separate shed, parked with pride, neatly inside. This farm is the heartbeat of our family, where generations have poured their strength into the land.

This is where my story unfolds, but it truly began half a world away in the sun-drenched vineyards of Siracusa, Sicily. Every day, my son, Alonso, and my granddaughter, Bobby, worked tirelessly, nurturing the rich wheat crops. Meanwhile, the sheep grazed peacefully, enjoying the wide-open spaces.

This farm is more than just a place. It's a way of life, a testament to the resilience and dedication of those who call it home. I feel privileged to have experienced the serenity and pure beauty of the Australian outback.

Though I now find myself surrounded by golden fields and harsh outback terrain, my story truly begins in a different land, on the island nation of Sicily.

It is there where my family, the Lombardos, had worked the land hard for generations. Farming would become my future instead, in a far-off land some 16,000 kilometers away. I immigrated to Australia in February 1965. Alonso was only eighteen months old.

The haunting voices of Angelo's first cousin Sergio, who eventually moved to New York, rang in my ears at the time; Sergio and his family's disbelief and disapproval of our choice to move to Australia echo through my mind at times. Back in Italy, when they were young, Angelo and his cousins were close. They did everything together back in the early days.

I smile to myself, recalling the conversations. *"Come with us to America instead!"* They would say.

"Australia?! Ma sei fuori di testa cazzo e troppo lontano!" (Are you out of your f*cking mind? That's way too far away).

And yet, Angelo and I defied their expectations and chose the furthest land, the one they deemed insane. But it was not enough to just be in Australia, oh, no, we had to go beyond the main cities, deep into the wild and untamed outback where the most poisonous snakes in the world roamed.

Even as we set off for Australia, the echoes of Angelo's cousins calling us *"Pazzi (crazy), America is closer, safer, and easier,"* they had said. But no, Angelo had made up his mind, Australia, he had decided, was where our future lay.

I loved my husband deeply. Angelo's strength, his confidence, and his courage to forge his path were qualities I admired about him each and every day. I felt lucky to walk down the path of life beside him. His cousins in New York would have been shocked by the difference between their comfortable city lives and the wilderness we chose here. They would never understand the beauty, the thrill, and the risk of making a living in such rugged land. Maybe that's why they never visited us; however, we never visited them either. I am not sure why. In time, sadly, we just drifted apart and lost touch with them.

I guess it was an inevitable reality, one that some of us face at some point in our lives, the slow drift of people away from each other. For some, it may be due to a deep and irrevocable reason, something that time could never heal. But for us, it was simply the distance, the physical separation that came with our decision to wander to opposite ends of the world in Australia. I remember Angelo trying to find their contact details online some years ago, hoping to reconnect, but coming up empty-handed. The thought still lingers in my mind every now and then, wondering if they are still alive, still out there somewhere in this vast world.

If I look back even further, to the roots that run deep in my memory, I see the day I was christened Giovanna Mariella Lombardo, named after my grandmother, born at home and raised on the farm where we worked. The farm where my parents and six other siblings created memories and built a wonderful family foundation for me to model from.

I met my husband, Angelo Russo, at a small-town gathering in Sortino, not far from home. We found common ground almost immediately. I was just 17, and he was 19. Angelo was my first and last boyfriend, and we often joked that we had embarked on a 60-year-long romance.

I lost him suddenly from a burst appendix three years ago, just 1 year short of our dream of retiring. The whole family felt the heavy blow, especially Alonso and Bobby.

To say I was devastated is an understatement. Even to this day, I still quietly speak to him, as if to keep in touch; my intuition says that he is in a good place. Before he passed away, we had planned to move to a small home we had purchased in the township of Sunflower Springs and rent out the farmhouse so we could explore Australia in a luxury caravan.

Now both the farmhouse and the township home are rented, as Melina asked me to move in with them when my husband died.

To this day, Angelo is the only man I have ever loved, and as I sit here twirling my wedding ring, looking out across the fields as the sun goes down, I miss him dearly like I do every day. I know that the years in his arms were years well spent.

We only had one child; his name is Alonso Angelo Russo, and today that man is the absolute image of his father. I often catch myself looking at him toiling in the hot sun under an old-brimmed hat that should have been long retired, and all I see is Angelo, that same cheeky smile that won my heart all those years ago.

I have watched his beautiful wife, Melina, receive all his love and attention in the same way I had received so much love from Angelo.

Alonso reminds me of his father in so many ways, a quiet determination, *un testa dura* (stubborn), always doing things his way, no matter how difficult, always loving deeply, no matter what was going on. He very rarely got angry with anything or anyone.

The decision to start a new life in Australia was not easy to make. I still remember waving goodbye to my father as he remained in the field while my mother held me tight at our front gate. Pappa could not bring himself to see me off, preferring to give his support from a distance. Later, through letters back and forth with Mamma, I learned that he cried for hours the day I left. It would be the last time I would ever see him.

The day we finally docked in Melbourne after a grueling two-month voyage on a passenger ship, our spirits were drained from leaving our families, and our bodies were exhausted and weary.

I will never forget the exact date we arrived in Australia, it was Monday, the 14th of February, 1965, at 10:30 AM. It was a scorching hot day, and it hit me: I thought, *'Oh my god, this is it!'* It was so beautiful, with so many working opportunities here, I thought, *'Where do we start?'*

All we had to our name were the tattered shirts on our backs.

Despite our monetary situation, Alonso refused to sell his farms back in Sortino. Being the beautiful person he was, he did not put his brothers out of their livelihoods; it broke his heart to leave his two brothers, and he never desired to rearrange their lives by forcing the sale of the farm they owned together. So, he walked away from everything, choosing to start anew with nothing but our love for one another, our determination, and our resilience. With those three aspects, anything was possible to achieve, anything!

There was one particular gentleman we met on the ship who was from Venice, Italy. His name was Bruno Strarto.

Bruno was a hard-working, charismatic, and very loving fellow a lot older than us, probably in his mid-thirties at the time. We did not speak English at the time, so we gravitated to the Italian migrants on board. We purposely found a way to make friends with other non-

Italian-speaking passengers on board and communicated in our unique, hilarious way via using hand gestures.

Our friend Bruno Strarto was an electrician from Venice and had a dream of building a big business in Brisbane, Queensland. He was travelling back and forth on his own until his wife was ready to migrate to Australia. That is how he knew about all the working opportunities.

We would joke with him that his electrician job would have been hazardous in Venice with so much water around, and he would be in stitches laughing. He commented that it must be the reason why his hair is frizzy.

Bruno kept us in the know of where to work in Australia in the sixties; some of these places were Queensland sugar cane cutting, the Riverina fruit picking, the Sunraysia grape picking opportunities, and the snowy hydro to help the government build a huge water dam. Our newfound friend, Bruno Strarto, was a man of strong integrity, relationships to him always came first, and it showed by how many people flocked to him.

Let me tell you, Bruno Strarto was no ordinary man. When he looked into your eyes, it was as if he flowed straight through you, and he could see your soul, but always in a non-awkward, beautiful way.

On the last day of the voyage to Australia, although we were so glad our non-glamorous two-month trip was finally over, we were also sad to say goodbye to our true friend Bruno Strarto.

He made us promise never to touch, no matter what we were going through. He made us promise as if our lives depended on it. I could not quite put my finger on what it was about him.

When you spend two solid months on a ship with someone, an unforgettable bond forms, and just as he said he would, he visited us every few years. We exchanged Christmas cards with enclosed photos every year without fail.

As it turned out, his wife never did come to Australia to join him as she promised him, and Bruno loved Australia too much to leave.

I remember Bruno opening up to us, his voice shaking with suppressed anger and disappointment as he revealed that his wife's broken promise to move to Australia had left him deeply wounded. Her words *"semplicemente non posso"* ('I just can't' in Italian) were like knives stabbing into his heart, a painful reminder to him that she does not value or love him enough to make sacrifices for their shared future. His vision of a life together is shattered by her inaction, leaving him feeling betrayed and alone.

In our last conversation with him, he mentioned he wanted to sell his electrician business in Brisbane to retire and live a simple life in the country on his own. We were surprised he never remarried or met another partner.

One Christmas, when we did not receive a card, we called him, but his phone was disconnected. We imagined it was because he was moving house. We did everything possible to find a phone number but with no luck. I remember Angelo suspected he was sick; he may have been right. Because now, sadly, 20 years have passed since we last heard from him, and that is completely out of character. It did not feel right not to attend a funeral; it felt like unfinished business on our priceless friendship. To this day, it still breaks my heart.

I am eternally grateful to have met him. He was a burst of pure sunshine just when we needed it the most. But what I also loved was he kept on shining no matter what life threw at him, and life did throw a lot at him, but he would just shine some more.

My mother used to always say, *"You meet the exact people you are meant to meet, and everything happens exactly when it's supposed to happen; there are no mistakes."* If you truly adopt that philosophy, you are actually at peace with life. I can honestly say I have adopted that philosophy.

I believe that Bruno Strarto entered our lives for a reason. What that reason is, I'm not entirely sure, and maybe we are not meant to know why certain people enter and exit your life. All we need to know is that life is a beautiful thing. A tapestry that gets more beautiful the more you work on it.

Finding work was, of course, our priority. My husband would not even consider indoor work, as it was outside the scope of his personality. He loved the great outdoors and the sense of freedom it gave.

As if it was not hard enough to move to a completely foreign country halfway around the world, we also did not speak one word of English. Oh, hang on, that's not true; we knew four words, *'G'day mate', 'bloody bastard', and 'Sh*t'*. As you would imagine, it helped us none, so we committed to night classes and heavy study every night to learn soon after our arrival.

Alonso had a natural talent for picking up new languages quickly and easily, but I still vividly remember his first day of school. His teacher called me, confused about what *"il gabinetto"* meant. I explained that it meant toilet, and she felt terrible as she had not understood, and Alonso ended up wetting himself. When he came home that day in the spare clothes provided by the school, he told me that he had gotten wet from playing under the sprinkler, instead of admitting the truth.

Fierce pride for a boy of his age. I went along with his story to avoid further embarrassment for him. Deep down, I knew that things would only improve as he continued to navigate through the language barrier.

We decided to work at the snowy hydro first so we could slowly migrate to the hotter Queensland areas afterwards to wean into the heat. We settled close to the New South Wales and Victorian border, as that's where this ambitious hydroelectric power project was underway in the nearby snowy mountains. At its peak, 100,000 men from various countries around the world worked tirelessly to accomplish that magnificent hydroelectric power project.

The Snowy Hydro Dam project was built between 1949 and 1974. The Scheme took 25 years to build and was rated one of the civil engineering wonders of the modern world.

Angelo and I were proud to play a small part in Australia's progress.

While we stayed in the snowy mountains, we met so many lovely, hardworking, genuine, good-hearted people who had also migrated from Europe with dreams of their own.

I worked full-time with the same company, doing less physically demanding work indoors but taking on more responsibilities. I was surprised by how quickly I picked up the English language. Angelo often complimented me for my linguistic cleverness. He would accidentally place some Italian words in a sentence, and we would laugh. I started work every day at 6 a.m. and brought Alonso with me to work. Back in those days, we weren't bombarded with so many rules and restrictions. Angelo, Alonso, and I remained on that gloomy site for five years before we were close to having enough money for a deposit on our dream farm.

The vision of a dream farm pushed us forward every day with excitement, instead of dreading the day's work ahead.

We lived an extremely hard life for years, with no luxuries whatsoever, not even minor ones, like buying treats at the grocery store. What kept us going, day in and day out, was, in a nutshell, that vivid dream of a better life for Alonso.

Living in a tiny space never became a big deal to us. The way we saw it was that as long as we had each other... the rest would come in time.

Exhaustion consumed us each night as we pushed ourselves to the brink of collapse. After dinner, we would crawl into bed, too drained for anything else. But our goal burned super bright in our minds, growing closer and closer with each passing day. We endured the hardships and sacrifices, knowing that delayed gratification would lead to greater rewards, like being our own boss and taking control of our futures. The thought of Angelo's dream manifesting closer each day fueled our determination to carry on with an even stronger purpose and drive.

At this stage, we had not decided exactly what type of farm we wanted, but we knew that, with divine timing, the farm of our dreams would reveal itself.

In July 1975, we moved to Mackay in the far north of tropical Queensland to cut sugarcane, back in the days when it was all done by hand. Now, that was tough by anyone's standards. We slept in our secondhand green Holden Kingswood sedan in an abandoned shed for 12 months, as there was no accommodation available. We later regretted not keeping that green Holden sedan, as we recently heard it has become a collector's item.

I remember how hard it was to fall asleep, especially with the *mozzies* (mosquitoes) eating us alive at night. We had only cold water to shower with and often caught the flu because of it. It was so hot and humid that sweat would pour down your body, leaving you constantly sticky and uncomfortable from the humidity. The poisonous cane toads and snakes among the sugarcane were a constant threat, and I was in fight-or-flight mode all day.

We worked our fingers to the bone seven days a week. I remember feeling so proud of Alonso; at such a young age, he never complained once.

Finally, we had more than enough for the deposit on our dream farm.

Those were the longest two years we had ever experienced. Alonso was eight years old by then, and we were so glad to get him out of that horrid work environment.

At this point, we decided what type of farming we wanted to do: wheat and sheep.

The dream farm we purchased is still the one my family lives on today, in the small community of Sunflower Springs, located midway along the border of South Australia and the Northern Territory. The closest city is Adelaide, some 3,050 road kilometers away. The heat here is hot and dry, but we were more comfortable with this type of heat than the humidity of Queensland's far north. Don't get me wrong, the extreme heat isn't easy at times, as it's not uncommon to reach 47 degrees Celsius (116.6 degrees Fahrenheit) in summer, but somehow, we adapted remarkably well.

The memory of my husband, Angelo, walking out of the Sunflower Springs real estate agency after signing the contract for the farm will always be etched in my mind. The expression on his face was one I had never seen before, a mix of pure excitement, accomplishment, and gratitude. It was heartwarming to see my life partner experience such joy. Our son Alonso was equally overjoyed, his usual energetic self multiplied tenfold, bouncing around like a jumping jellybean as soon as his father told him the good news. On this fine day, Alonso, at this point eight and a half years old, is bursting with excitement and pride for his father's efforts.

We built a home there where we could celebrate life together, overcoming every hardship and conquering every struggle. Our lives gained even more purpose the moment we had Alonso, our carefree boy who sought to explore the wonders of life in his own unique way. Our home became more vibrant with Alonso's presence, and the farm became his comfort zone, shaping him into the man he is today. My eyes beamed with pride as I witnessed the growth of my dear Alonso, a fine young man who truly deserves the world.

Alonso is very social; he often spends his free time with his mates. As the years flew by, Alonso crossed paths with Melina, a tall, stunning young woman with shiny, long blonde hair, piercing blue eyes, and a slender figure. She was the daughter of a friendly neighboring cattle farmer, Ken Dawson, who had become a widower when Melina was 7 years old. Ken sent her to boarding school, so although we lived in a small town, Alonso did not meet her until she finished year 12 in high school at 18 years old.

Melina exuded an aura of unbreakable fortitude and steely determination, her uncanny intuition bordering on the edge of being both surreal and awe-inspiring. Despite growing up in a vastly different culture from Alonso, they were inexplicably drawn to each other, like two magnets with an undeniable connection strong enough to ignite a fire that could not be extinguished. I adore my daughter-in-law, and I see so much of my granddaughter, Bobby, in her.

Although Alonso had a couple of fleeting romances in his early twenties, no one captured his heart like Melina did. I could see the love in his eyes, just as I had with his father. I remember the day Alonso came bounding through the front door to announce their engagement. We could not have been happier for them.

They married a year later, and soon their own children followed: first a son, Carlo, then two daughters, Bobby Jo, and finally, Zoe. They built their family home on the same land, about half a kilometer away from the house Alonso grew up in. I remember the day they named the farm *"Eucalyptus Ridge,"* after the road we live on, Eucalyptus Road. It had been named by the local council because of the long line of eucalyptus trees along the roadside.

Alonso placed a sign at the gate entrance to the driveway that read *"Eucalyptus Ridge,"* featuring a beautiful steel cutout of a sheep. Angelo and I had always hoped and dreamed that all our hard work would be worth it, and it was. We proudly handed them the title to the farm the day they got married, as a gift. I will never forget my husband's watery eyes on their beautiful wedding day. The legacy of the land, the endless cycle of sowing and harvesting, felt like it would last forever. Our family seemed woven into the very soil, our footsteps falling on the paths that had shaped our lives. It was perfect.

But life does not follow blueprints, and the land itself has a mind of its own. Working on this farm was never easy; it demanded everything we had. Many seasons brought their own trials, droughts that cracked the earth, relentless winds that bent the young shoots, unexpected pests that devastated crops in a matter of days, sheep foot and mouth disease, and shifting markets that sometimes made a year's work seem almost futile. Yet we persisted, pouring ourselves into the land because it was more than work; it was our way of life, our connection to one another, and the foundation we hoped to leave behind.

As the years passed, we watched our grandchildren grow with a mix of pride and concern. Carlo, the eldest, was once the dream-holder, the boy who would take over the farm and carry on the family legacy. But as he grew, his spirit sought something different. Our hearts ached through countless conversations, each more difficult than the last, as we tried to steer him toward the path we had laid out. Eventually, however, we saw it in his eyes, his need for a world larger than the rows of crops and open skies. Carlo left for Sydney to study law, choosing a different future, one that would break away from the life he had known.

Letting him go was a quiet heartbreak, a lesson in understanding that we can pour everything into our children, yet they still forge their own paths. Thinking back, I understand how my father felt when Angelo decided to leave Italy and move to Australia. It hurt him deeply, but I was on the journey to my own destiny, the life I was creating for myself with Angelo.

Deep-rooted dreams must always find a way to be released, and I am so happy for Carlo for giving life to his own dreams. Now, as a lawyer with his own law firm, he has flourished not only financially but emotionally. Our hopes for a third-generation farm takeover nearly faded until Bobby Jo, the seventeen-year-old, determined, willful middle child, came forward with a strength that surprised us all. She stood on the land with a fierceness in her gaze, the determination of someone who understood the weight of what she was choosing.

Bobby's decision brought life back into Alonso's weary spirit; it was as though the land had found a new steward who would honour and protect it, someone who understood its value as more than a livelihood. She embraced the struggles, the unpredictability, and the sacrifices that Carlo had walked away from, breathing new hope into the soil her grandfather had tilled.

Bobby took to the land as if she had been born with soil in her veins, just like my Angelo. She felt it in her heart to continue what the family had created with each of our hands. Carlo... ah, che peccato (what a pity in Italian), his heart found other dreams. I adore my grandson and only want what makes him happy.

The farm is where our true story begins, a story of family and the choices we make, of holding on and letting go. In that moment when Carlo left for Sydney, I realized that while the land connected us, it was our resilience, our love, and our acceptance of each other's dreams that truly held us together. The legacy would continue, not bound by expectation, but by the courage to choose it.

Standing open to the steady warmth of the sun from dawn until dusk, from the western veranda, the land stretches flat and vast, an unbroken expanse reaching out until it meets a low-lying hill on the horizon. The view is simple yet endless, with hues of ochre and rust shifting under the vast sky as the sun moves overhead.

Atop the highest point on this distant hill stands a very large, solitary Australian gum tree, its branches weathered and twisted, rising boldly against the deep blue sky. It is a quiet sentinel, rooted firmly through decades of droughts and wild summer storms, a landmark that commands respect.

It is said that a tree standing alone with no other trees around it is extra resilient, just like my husband, who did it alone and came out as a winner.

Climbing the hill reveals a panorama of sunflowers spreading across thousands of acres, their golden faces a patchwork of vibrant yellow stretching under the open sky. The flowers were grown by the very wealthy Hallington family, John and his son, Tom.

Zoe calls young Tom Hallington *"Shallow Hal."* She is hilarious, and she is also right. If Tom were any shallower, he'd be flat.

They own a separate spring water outlet on the other side of town.

The flowers glisten in the early morning light, filling the air with a faint, sweet fragrance that mingles with the dry, earthy scent of the soil. The sunflowers are grown for sunflower oil. Bees hum softly, threading through the blossoms, bringing a gentle, rhythmic life to the vast stillness of the Outback.

As the sun sinks lower, casting an amber glow, the land seems to breathe, each grain of red dust holding memories of those who have tended and treasured it.

In the far distance, you can spot a massive pool of spring water with a beautiful waterfall among a narrow gorge that is connected to a distant mountain. The waterfall does not always flow, but when it does, it's spectacular.

Wheat does not get irrigated; it relies on rain to grow. The spring water is what has made it possible to generate income by having sheep for their wool. For many years, wheat would not grow due to a lack of rain, and the sheep made it possible to stay afloat. The spring water also makes it possible to grow a good-sized vegetable garden and fruit trees for our own consumption. We built a dam to collect the water so it does not go to waste.

A main road separates an adjoining property my son, Alonso, purchased five years ago to increase his crop yield, only months before Carlo declared he was leaving.

I would often see Alonso pause in the field to watch the four-wheel drives, towing caravans and RVs, as they went by on the main road.

Inside, the Grey Nomads, who traverse the country, are free from the bounds and commitments that he and Melina have. It was really sad to see him remove his sweaty hat and hold it up to the sun so he could watch them disappear over the horizon before returning to work. Yes, it would seem he, too, had dreams, none of which he ever shared with any of us.

One day, quietly, he was working in the distance by the roadside, doing what we all thought was repairing a fence. We did not ask, and he did not say why.

What he was actually doing was creating a little roadside-free camp stopover point so the caravanners would have somewhere to rest.

After a few weeks, no one had stopped, so he added a fire pit, stocked it with firewood, and placed a small rainwater tank there. He then built a wooden picnic table and chairs with a tin roof over the top. Weeks later, he added solar panel lights; it looked spectacular at night as well as in the day. If only his father could have seen it. It had such a rustic old charm about it, Angelo would have loved it.

Again, with Alonso, no questions; therefore, no answers. But I knew what it meant.

If he could not go with them, then he would just have to bring those people to him, spending hours in conversation in the evenings, hearing tales of their travels. I just watched quietly without a word. What can I say? I know my son.

Over time, more and more people started to stop at Alonso's rest area, even replacing the firewood so he wouldn't need to.

Sometime later, I stopped there with Melina to see what had consumed so much of his time. On the picnic bench, someone had carved the words *"Alonso's Patch."* I knew it wouldn't have been him, he's too humble for that. I then noticed he had cut down a couple of large bush shrubs that were in the way of the view, but he left the gum tree on the left side of the patch. It was much too magnificent to trim down. What a breathtaking view as the golden sun landed on the branches of that singular tree, on its way to rest at dusk.

The view is truly a beautiful sight, one I never tire of. It's always a pleasure watching the sun land in the tree's fork, above its tall and wide trunk, in front of a huge field of sunflowers bordered by a vivid purple bloom of Patterson's Curse at the base of the hill at certain times of the year. The purple bloom added a majestic touch (Vast Australian low-growing purple weed). This pesky weed may be detrimental, but its beauty is truly alluring, and one would stop to appreciate its enticing purple flowers. Today, Alonso's Patch appears on many camping websites as a must-see place when passing through.

As I mentioned, Bobby, at seventeen, had stepped up to the plate, taking the reins alongside Alonso. She brought with her fresh ideas, and in many ways, more modern and streamlined approaches to running the farm.

Our little Zoe, on the other hand, showed little or no interest in either participating or contributing in any way. Due to her five-year gap with Bobby, she preferred the solace of online communications, expanding her circle of friends outside the borders of Sunflower Springs.

I knew in my heart that Zoe would find her own way eventually, but in the meantime, a growing sense of uncertainty ensued amongst our family. More so with Bobby, who had all but committed herself to the family farm for years, her work ethic admirable, until, of course, other interests would take hold. But that is another story entirely. Bobby had stepped up in ways that none of us fully expected. Where Alonso carried the wisdom of years in his bones, she brought fresh ideas, a new perspective, and the drive to streamline how things were done. The consistent work ethic of father and daughter was truly admirable. This is enough for us, knowing that Bobby is there to continue the dream... our dream.

CHAPTER 2

KEEPER OF BONDS

Narrated by Nonna Giovanna

Alonso and Bobby became an unlikely but unstoppable team. She took on her role not as a duty, but as a choice, and it showed in every decision she made. Bobby was not just helping her father, she was redefining what the farm could become, blending tradition with her vision of something more sustainable and efficient. This was not just Alonso's legacy anymore; it was becoming hers too.

I recall hearing Bobby declare with her usual enthusiastic, zestful way, *"One week till harvest, Dad! Whew, Woo, Hoo!!!"*

The conversation between them would go something like this:

"Dad, we need that harvester running by next week. I burned my hand checking the power steering hose, it's got a hole in it, and the John Deere water pump seized. Dad, we need that harvester back up and available! You know we start our own harvest next week. I don't want to keep reminding you, Dad!"

She would continue, *"We need a new power steering hose, Dad, ASAP! Not to mention what we need for our livestock. If we don't replace those parts, we're stuffed. I called PFG in Glentvale, they have the power steering hose, water pump, and trailer belts we need. If we don't replace those parts, we can't harvest. Seriously, Dad, you know two things are not fixable, and new parts won't be delivered in time before harvest. We have to go pick them up now."*

Bobby and Alonso also worked as contractors for other wheat farmers in the district, creating a lot of wear and tear on their two harvesters. This helped with earning extra income, but it also created extra stress between them this time of year.

"I'll check with the Hallingtons; see if they have spares," Alonso replied, his tone tinged with irritation.

"Let me know by 4:30 p.m. today, Dad. Seriously, I have to call to see if they're in stock before I take the trip to Glentvale... the trip alone will take a day!" Bobby continued,

"I can get Barry O'Connor and Steevo out here on Wednesday to give you a hand getting prepared, if you want."

Alonso, still annoyed at being under pressure, replied, *"Ok, ok, leave it with me. Barry can come and help, but not that other mongrel!"*

If Alonso didn't like someone, there was no way he would utter their name; it was as if that name was forbidden. He was referring to Steven Patterson. Being Australian, we tend to shorten names a lot, so we always call him Steevo. Steevo is our next-door neighbour; his house is roughly 500 meters away from ours.

And well, Barry O'Connor is a very popular.. genuinely nice young man, but let's just say he is not the 'sharpest tool in the shed.' He is the local bartender who hires himself out to farmers needing an extra hand from time to time.

"You know who... will never set foot on this property again, capisce.

"I've told you that, so stop trying to fix things all the time, Bobby!" Alonso stated in a very firm and frustrated tone.

"Dad, you don't know the facts!" Bobby protested. *"You've been friends for 30 years, just talk to him! Capisce?"*

Alonso would always try to fix his machinery himself to save money. In the last few years, he had become tight with funds, which was not like him. If Alonso were feeling stressed, he wouldn't make it obvious, not wanting to burden the family. Melina would always include me in their private family financial affairs so I wouldn't feel like an outsider. She told me that Alonso had overstretched himself five years ago when he bought that extra 1,000 acres, making it now just over 3,000 acres in total with the sheep paddocks, which, even by Australian standards, is considered a sizable broadacre farm area.

The desire to leave a lasting legacy for his children was the driving force behind his actions, just like his father, Angelo.

Little did he know at the time that his son Carlo would soon go astray, shattering his carefully crafted plans.

Alonso's love for family and the weight of his responsibilities drove him to make choices that would change everything. He poured all of his energy into securing a bright future for them, unaware of the impending turmoil and heartache that lay ahead. Now, looking back at it all, I wonder if things might have been different if he had not overstretched his finances to take on that extra land, but his commitment to our family's future was always steadfast.

Alonso often spent a lot of time in his office if he wasn't out in the fields. His office is next to the kitchen, and I noticed he would always shut the door and make it clear he didn't want anyone mucking up his desk.

"How can we muck up your desk, darling?" Melina would say, *"There's nothing on it! You have everything in the drawers!"*

One day, Melina was vacuuming the house while Alonso was in his office. She wanted to vacuum that room too.

"It's okay, love; this room has no dust. Shut the door, please," Alonso said.

Melina would roll her eyes, responding with a smile on her face and a sarcastic remark, *"Oh yeah, that's right, I forgot. The dust mites are all on strike in your office!"* And she moved along to vacuum the other rooms.

She gets it from her father. Bobby is no stranger to hard work and is quite capable of changing out parts of the farm equipment herself, saving them loads of extra expense and the wait time for tradespeople to show up. Her dad had taught her everything, from the tools to use to how best to use them. She knew them all by heart. None of this *"tool thingy"* language would be tolerated. Alonso wouldn't stand for sloppiness in anything.

He had even taught Bobby some carpentry when she was in her teens, which came in handy when you live far from tradespeople. Maybe he had sensed early on that Carlo was losing faith and had decided to invest in Bobby. I'm not entirely sure.

But either way, she knew her stuff and could be relied upon to pull her weight, day in and day out, seven days a week. I have lost count of how many times Bobby has climbed under a tractor or a piece of machinery that Alonso had been trying to fix for hours. She'd carry out the repair in the short space of time it took Alonso to eat his lunch. I think it frustrated him that she could blow in like a breeze, fix the problem, and leave without a word.

He would always be blown away by her efficiency and competence.

"Maybe I'm getting too bloody old for this," he'd say. *"Dad, I was taught by the best,"* Bobby would reply modestly. *"If you'd only put your stupid pride aside and wear your bloody glasses, you'd save yourself hours."*

What this did was give him confidence in her. *"You just can't argue with an analytical, brilliant mind,"* he would say.

But there is another side to my granddaughter that didn't quite match the *'girl on the land'* image.

Her discipline was flawless. Bobby's life ran on a rhythm all its own. Like clockwork, she would rise at 5 a.m., then at 6 a.m., no matter what the weather, she would swim in the farm dam after cleaning the horse dung from the stables. Her discipline was something to marvel at, a trait she'd inherited, I think, from her grandfather and her father. It was only on Sunday mornings that we would take a few hours off to attend church; however, Alonso wasn't so keen. On Sundays, we would play Briscola (an Italian card game). The whole family would play board games with our friends on most Saturday nights, as Zoe had a huge board game collection.

Just before her morning swim, Bobby would sit up on what she called her *'thinking tree,'* a beautiful, large weeping willow tree with the most sensational evergreen cascading branches.

Bobby would meditate daily for 20 minutes, no fail, visualizing in her mind's eye her goals and creating clarity on the next action steps to take.

Zoe, her younger sister, would often send wisecracks while riding her push bike around that area. Bobby thought the tree was situated about 50 meters from the house.

"I see you're off with the fairies again, Bob," she'd say, which infuriated Melina to no end.

"Her name is Bobby! Zoe, how many times do we need to have this conversation?" Melina would yell from the chook pen.

There was always a deep, unbreakable bond between Bobby and her mother, which I just loved to witness, I sometimes wondered if part of that bond was something spiritual, something unspoken but deeply rooted.

I had actually lost a second child during Alonso's birth. Yes, Alonso was supposed to be a twin. His sibling would have been a girl. I had always avoided speaking about our loss, especially with my husband, Angelo, as it was simply too painful.

Looking back now, I realize that we should have spoken about it. I believe it was much worse not to.

The other baby, growing inside me, would have been our daughter. It was already hard enough for my husband, Angelo, to accept that we had lost her. He always blamed himself, saying I had worked too hard on the farm in Sicily at the time.

Back in those days, so few words were spoken when there was a loss during childbirth.

Things took a turn for the worse during the second delivery. I never held her. I hardly even saw her. I only remember seeing the doctors frantically trying to resuscitate her tiny, lifeless body before whisking her away.

My baby girl didn't even have enough oxygen in her to let out a cry, so I didn't hear her beautiful voice either.

I lost a lot of blood and briefly lost consciousness shortly after the delivery. When I awoke, all I heard were faint whispers from behind a curtain: *"La bambina è morta"* (*The baby is dead*).

Quietly to myself, I named her Lilliana.

What I did insist on, however, was that she be buried wearing a handmade gold and ruby-encrusted bracelet that had belonged to my mother. Although it was too long for her tiny wrist, they said they would place it on her.

At that moment, I knew I was never meant to have a daughter of my own. I also knew I couldn't bear the thought of going full term again, with the possibility of losing another child. But that choice was taken from me when I could no longer fall pregnant due to internal damage from Lilliana's birth. The centuries-old mother-daughter history would come to an end in that room that day.

Although Angelo and I rarely discussed the event, I did share the pain of my loss with Alonso, not long after Bobby was born. I think this is part of what has driven the closeness Bobby and I have always enjoyed. I love that girl with all my heart, and she loves me in return.

There was a method to Bobby's daily schedule, a far deeper reasoning behind her routine. She found solace in her meditation, a way to reset and ground herself.

As her grandmother, I had long sensed the restlessness in her, as did Melina. We often wondered how long it would be before Bobby would feel comfortable sharing more with her father. But in the meantime, she continued to soldier on, day after day, week after week, and year after year, giving of herself to all who crossed her path.

A trip to the local library to borrow personal development books was Bobby's weekly event; her thirst to understand how the mind works was an incredible fascination to her. Her father, without realizing it, had instilled a deeper mental fortitude in Bobby than he ever imagined.

And still, after everything, she was resolute in her decision to continue the legacy of the farm. It wasn't just about the land or the livestock; it was about something far greater than any of us could ever imagine.

CHAPTER 3

SAVING BRIAN TAYLOR

NOT NARRATED

Life in Sunflower Springs had a rhythm, one that Bobby had grown into as naturally as the land itself. Her days revolved around the farm, but her world had slowly expanded beyond the family fields. She'd always been curious about people, what made them tick, what drove them, and over the years, that curiosity had drawn her deeper into the lives of others. It was not just the wheat and sheep that kept her grounded; it was the connections she had built with the people in this tight-knit town.

Of all those connections, the one with Brian Taylor was the most unexpected.

Back when Bobby was a teenager, Brian Taylor was the heart of Sunflower Springs, one of the town's most respected farmers, steady, and always the first to help. His land had thrived, his marriage had seemed solid, and he was the kind of man people admired, genuine, reliable, and generous. Bobby remembered attending regular barbecues at Brian and Karen Taylor's farm. So many locals attended those barbecues, making memories and sharing stories. Brian, in his quiet way, made sure everyone had a drink in hand and plenty to eat.

In many ways, Brian reminded Bobby of her father, strong, proud of his land, loved company, and always humble.

But as the years passed, cracks began to show. Bobby, not quite old enough to fully understand it at the time, as she was only 14 years old, saw the beginning of the end of that happy era in the Taylor family. The locals watched as Brian's life slowly fell apart.

Alonso, being the kindhearted and generous person he is, desperately wanted to help Brian but was at a loss for what to do. After much discussion with Melina and consideration, they decided to offer Brian a loan so he could keep running his farm. But Brian, embarrassed, could not bring himself to accept monetary help. He was determined to make it on his own, despite the struggles he faced. And so, with a heavy heart, he politely declined their offer and continued with his work, hoping for a better season ahead.

Soon after, his farm went bankrupt. As if that wasn't enough, rumors spread like wildfire about an affair between his wife and the bank manager. Karen left him, and from that point on, Brian's presence in town slowly faded. He stopped coming to events and stopped socializing. He became a shadow of the man he once was.

They reconnected in the quietest place, the Sunflower Springs Library. Bobby was returning a book on marketing when she spotted Brian sitting in the back corner, hunched over a book on Australian wildflowers, clearly gazing but not reading. His frame somehow appeared smaller than she remembered, his gaze distant. She approached, and when he looked up, the recognition in his tired eyes was enough to break her heart.

"Brian?" Bobby asked, walking over to him. *"I haven't seen you in a while. Is everything alright?"* she asked gently, sitting across from him. He looked up, startled at first, but recognition soon softened his expression. He was happy to see her but didn't show it.

"Bobby Russo, right? Oh my gosh, it's been years!" His voice was quieter than she remembered, hollow in a way that made her heart sink in disappointment.

"Yeah," she said, sitting down across from him. *"Are you doing, okay?"* she asked again.

He smiled, but it didn't reach his eyes. *"Ahhh, you know how it is. Life... doesn't always go as planned. You know, Bobby..."* He paused. *"What your father did, I will never forget; he is a true gentleman, and from what I can see, you are his carbon copy."*

Bobby smiled at Brian but didn't ask what her father had done to earn that compliment. She simply knew that her father would have done all he could.

She saw the weariness in his eyes, the way he clutched that book like it was an anchor, something to keep him from drifting completely. They talked for hours that day. About life. About loss. Bobby found herself sharing things she had not shared with anyone, her doubts about the farm's stability, the pressure she felt to carry on the family legacy, and the uncertainty of farming income that hung over her future like a shadow. Brian, being an ex-farmer, had a lot in common with Bobby. They truly understood each other's way of life on the farm.

That conversation marked the beginning of something new, or something unfamiliar, that Bobby questioned in her mind. Is it friendship? Or does it ignite something else that Bobby opted not to name? She was getting close to naming it, but one thing's for sure... Brian mattered to her.

He was not just another person in town. He was someone who had lost his way, and Bobby couldn't help but feel compelled to reach out to help him find his footing again. She was never the type of girl to ask herself, *"What's in it for me?"* Instead, it would be, *"How can I help?"*

Bobby's connection to Brian deepened over the following months. It wasn't a dramatic shift, more like a slow, steady growth. She started checking in on him whenever she could, bringing him books from the library, especially ones on success principles and emotional intelligence, what most call personal development. At first, it was just an attempt to get him back on his feet, but soon she realized that she was drawn more and more to the same books herself. These books truly resonated with her on a personal level.

She'd always been a reader, but now Bobby found herself devouring books about mindset, motivation, the law of attraction, vibration, and the power of positive thinking. Her thirst to know more was unquenchable.

Early in the mornings, before the farm work began, she'd sit on top of her thinking tree with a book, letting the words sink in as the sun rose over the horizon. She would take notes from the lessons she learned from those books, about thoughts shaping reality, about turning adversity into opportunity, becoming part of her daily life. Her carpentry skills made it possible for her to build a wooden platform high up in her thinking tree, which was a huge old weeping willow tree with a wide trunk spreading upward, perfect for placing a platform. The cascading branches, with millions of tiny green leaves, were so mesmerizing, always offering great shade from the hot sun. To add to the majesty, she placed solar-powered lights all over it, just as her father had done on his stopover patch.

She applied the success principles she studied from her books to the farm, especially during tough seasons when it felt like everything was falling apart. Slowly, those ideas became part of how she lived, her health, how she approached her family, her work, the people in her life, and her relationship with herself. She quickly learned that controlling her thoughts was everything. Once she figured out how to manage the thoughts that weren't serving her, anything became possible.

She became aware of her inner powers: her spirituality, her relationships, her body health, and learning about the rules of running a great business. It was this 'can-do' mindset that drove her to help Brian.

She knew the risk she was taking, Sunflower Springs was a small town, and people loved to talk. Dorothy Blake, the town's self-proclaimed gossip queen, had already spun her web of rumors about Karen's supposed affair with the bank manager. Now, with Bobby visiting Brian, the whispers had started again.

But Bobby didn't care about the gossip. Brian needed someone, and she was determined to be that person. The more time they spent together, the more she saw not just the broken man he had become, but the potential of the man he still could be. And if there was anything Bobby believed in, it was the full-blown power of human potential.

Narrated by Nonna Giovanna

One late afternoon, I was sitting on the back veranda having my afternoon tea when Bobby rode in on her quad bike. I placed my hand over my vanilla slice so the dust wouldn't ruin my favorite sweet as Bobby suddenly slid her quad bike to a halt. Melina always buys one for me each time she shops in town. A furrowed brow suggested something was on her mind.

"Can we watch the sunset together over at 'the patch' tonight, Nonna?" she asked. *"I really would love to talk to you. I'll pick you up later."*

Before I could even respond, she was gone in a cloud of dust, and again, I covered my plate, this time with both hands. If she thinks I am getting on that thing, she can think again, I thought.

The patch turned on its usual stunning display as we trekked up the hill. As we reached Alonso's Patch, the hill was bathed in a golden glow, and Bobby's face seemed lost in thought. She looked out at the land, and I wondered if she'd ever leave it behind. She was a Russo through and through, yet there was something in her gaze that hinted at more, something beyond Sunflower Springs. On this particular evening, we were accompanied by Hillery, the sheep. This sheep follows us just as a dog does. We call her Hillery the hilarious!

Let me tell you a funny story about this sheep of ours. She's from our herd of 9,285 sheep. This particular sheep, whom we later named Hillery, always managed to cause chaos, Hillery, the sheep version of Houdini. Despite our attempts to keep her contained during the shearing time, she would somehow escape and head straight for the hill where Alonso's Patch was, hence the name

Hillery. We still don't know how she escapes the sheep yard come shearing time. She loves to follow us everywhere... and we are so fond of her. What a character!

It was about 5 p.m. when Bobby and I reached the patch. The hill was bathed in golden light, and I found Bobby staring at the beauty of the land. I wondered if it was enough to hold her here forever. I watched her carefully and remember looking at her with the last remnants of the sun on her face, thinking how beautiful she was. She has her mother's blonde hair and good looks combined with her father's skin tone. Both women could have been models.

As the sun dipped low, casting shadows over the patch, Bobby's phone rang sharply, shattering the quiet. Her face shifted, growing somber and serious as she listened. Finally, she hung up, a mix of determination and urgency in her eyes.

"It's Brian Taylor, Nonna! I have to go; I'm so sorry," she said firmly, already heading back down the hill.

Disappointment washed over me as I watched her go. We had been planning an outing to the patch for weeks, and now it seemed like it would have to be postponed. But deep down, I knew that whatever was calling Bobby away was important.

"Be careful, Bobby; don't rush too much. And remember, you can't fix everything, my Bella."

I remained behind, letting the quiet wash over me. A wave of nostalgia hit as I thought about the little girl she used to be, always eager to learn. I thought to myself how I loved the years when she was a toddler, a little girl who had barely just learned to walk but insisted on knowing all the proper names of the farm implements, never settling for baby talk. I taught her how to speak Italian, as it's much easier to learn another language from infancy, and I remember her delight as she said *"gallina"* (chicken) for the first time, repeating it perfectly, as if she were born speaking two languages.

Bobby managed to wrap her tongue around all of the words I taught her. Never once did she shy away from learning something difficult. I knew then that this girl was no ordinary girl.

Now, all grown up, I stood there, staring out at the fields, feeling nostalgic. I had a vivid flashback of Alonso asking her, barely eighteen months old, to hand him a spanner. She corrected him with a straight face: *"No, Daddy, this... shift spanner!"* I remember how Alonso laughed, pride glowing from him like the afternoon sun.

She dreams big, my precious girl. She *always* has, even as a six-year-old, when she would ask her father when problems arose, *"Why hasn't a better way been invented?"*

And though a part of me selfishly wanted her to stay here in little Sunflower Springs forever, I also knew she was meant for something much greater. Something beyond farming and small-town life.

I deeply wished for her to have wisdom, purpose, adventure, good fortune, and most importantly, true love. And I couldn't help but feel that none of these things could be found by staying in Sunflower Springs.

In my heart, I knew that Bobby needed to spread her wings and fly toward the path her heart deeply desired.

Living in a small town like Sunflower Springs had its perks, but it also meant that everyone knew everyone else's business. The chronic gossipers could make life difficult at times, but the tight-knit community also had its benefits. In times of need, neighbors would come together to support one another, just like Bobby, who was always quick to drop everything and lend a helping hand to those in trouble. Even Zoe would help the locals from time to time, but not with the full-hearted dedication Bobby showed. I never did find out what she wanted to say to me that day, never sure if it was about her feelings for Brian or something else.

NOT NARRATED

Bobby sped toward Brian's house, the setting sun painting the sky in brilliant shades of orange and red. When she arrived, the house stood as it always did, tired, worn, reflecting the man inside. She knocked on the door, her heart racing, hoping this wasn't the time things had gone too far.

Gossip spreads faster than wildfire in a dry season. Dorothy Blake strolled through town with her co-conspirator Wendy Hallington, their heads bent in hushed whispers, eyes scanning the streets for their next subject. When they spotted Bobby heading into Brian's home, Dorothy's mouth was off and running.

"Would you look at that?" Dorothy nudged Wendy, her voice dripping with mock scandal. *"Bobby Russo, sneaking into Brian's house during pre-harvest season! I bet she's shacking up with him!"*

"You think Alonso knows?" Wendy smirked, but Dorothy was already pulling out her phone, taking photos and calling people, eager to share her concocted stories with anyone willing to listen.

Bobby knocked loudly and frantically on the door, her heart racing with fear that Brian might have done something desperate. As she waited for someone to answer, she couldn't help but feel a pang of sympathy for him.

Brian had been struggling for a long time. In his mid-thirties, having lost his beloved farm and his zest for life, Bobby had admired him growing up, as he used to radiate pure happiness and empathy for others, but all of that had been overshadowed by financial struggles and personal turmoil. It was as if the successful man she once looked up to had slowly crumbled before her eyes.

The door swung open suddenly, and Bobby stumbled into the room. Brian stood there, his face a mask of pain, a ghost of the man he once was. His once-proud frame seemed to have collapsed in on itself; his face was gaunt and hollow, with the lines of despair etched deep into his features. The house around him mirrored his internal state, dishes piled in the sink, old takeaway containers littering the countertops, and unopened bills scattered across the coffee table.

"*Brian...*" Bobby's voice was filled with relief but also concern. "*I'm so glad you're okay... well, physically, at least.*"

Brian's shoulders slumped at her words; the weight of his struggles was evident in every line of his body. He didn't respond at first, his posture broken, his spirit crushed. "*I'm sorry, Bobby,*" he mumbled, knowing he had inconvenienced her once again. "*I shouldn't have called you. I know how busy it gets with harvest preparation.*"

Bobby shook her head, placing a firm but gentle hand on his arm. "*Don't be silly, Brian. I'm here because I care about you. And you promised you'd get back on your feet.*"

She glanced around the room, taking in the disarray. Her chest tightened as she noticed the hopelessness that seemed to cling to every corner of his home. She turned back to him, her expression resolute.

"Now tell me what's going on," she said, her voice steady but determined. *"We'll work through this together, and your life will thrive again. You've got to believe that, Brian... belief is a crucial ingredient to success in life. Did you know it's a common denominator for all self-made, highly successful people?"*

Brian sat down heavily on the worn couch, running a hand through his disheveled hair.

It was obvious he wasn't listening to a word Bobby was trying to say.

"I don't know if I can do it, Bobby. I'm stuck. Every day feels darker than the last."

Bobby took a seat beside him, her voice steady. *"Brian, did you read that book I gave you, Your Power, Your Perspective?"*

He sighed, shaking his head. *"I just... couldn't."*

She placed a hand on his arm. *"If only you knew how powerful the human mind is!"*

"I can help you," she continued, her tone serious, *"but only if you truly have a strong 'desire' to be helped."*

"You were not put on this earth to suffer. You are here to experience joy, purpose, love... and all the hard bits of life just sharpen your pencil."

"You have an awesome dream of growing unique Australian wildflowers and selling them worldwide. Let's make that happen. Do you want that dream to come true?" Brian quietly said, *"Yes, I do."*

"Well, guess what!" Bobby responded, her tone brightening.

"What?" replied Brian, still wrapped in a dark, negative vibration.

"You don't get what you want!" Bobby said with a grin. Brian looked at her, confused. She continued, *"You get "WHO" you are being!"*

Brian had a lightbulb moment.

"Brian, people are like magnets. You being who you've been in the last few years, what will you attract?"

Brian replied, *"Nothing great, I guess."*

"Sorry, Brian, I'm not going to sugarcoat this, but…" Bobby paused, letting the weight of her words sink in. *"…you've attracted nothing even remotely great."*

"Everything is first created in your mind's eye, your marvelous mind; then, with regular action steps, your dream life manifests in the physical world. It's a proven universal law."

Brian slipped back into unresponsiveness, his face growing distant.

Bobby's eyes flashed with frustration as she locked gazes with him, determined to break through the wall of hopelessness surrounding him. She reached out and gently touched his face, her touch both caring and urgent.

"Listen to me, Brian," she said, her voice taking on a firmer edge. *"I am here for you. Do you have a desire for change, or am I wasting my time?"*

Her words stung Brian like a slap in the face, jolting him out of his downward spiral. He straightened up, suddenly aware of how much energy he had been wasting on feeling sorry for himself.

"You're still young," Bobby continued, softening her tone slightly but maintaining her resolve. *"You have your whole life to look forward to. Maybe a new career and someone new to love. You have a dream! I want to see that dream come true, and I want to be your first customer!"* A small smile tugged at the corners of her lips as she added, *"You're intelligent, honest, hard-working, compassionate, and, though I shouldn't say this, you're bloody good-looking too!"*

Brian smiled faintly, his spirit lifting just a little. He leaned closer to Bobby, their faces now only centimeters away from one another. It appeared like Brian wanted to kiss her. Bobby added with a playful grin, *"And if you come any closer, I'll break your friggin' neck!"*

A small laugh escaped them both, and Bobby felt a glimmer of hope.

"I respect you too much to do that, Bobby," Brian said, the laughter fading but leaving a small light in his eyes.

Bobby realized that what he was truly saying was that being with him romantically would be a *demotion* to Bobby. Oh my god, Bobby thought, this man really is down and out!

"Brian, you are not your farm, and you are not your marriage. You are your soul," Bobby explained.

Brian responded, *"You should put an ex in front of those."*

Bobby replied, *"Well, you can put an X in front of the first two, but you can't put an X on your soul, my friend."*

There was a big pause. Bobby couldn't tell if Brian was deep in thought or just tired of her.

"Listen, Brian, have you eaten yet?"

Brian nodded.

"No," he said.

Bobby said, *"I'll be right back."*

She went to get some takeaway pizza from the local pizzeria and returned to Brian's house.

When she returned, Brian had washed the dishes that had been lying around for days, vacuumed, and tidied the lounge room where they had been speaking.

Bobby returned with a huge surprised look on her face, not expecting Brian to have done that at all. She was planning to help him clean up after the pizza.

"Good on ya!" Bobby said, excited to see some progress. *"You feel better for it, right?"* she asked

Brian nodded yes.

After enjoying the pizza together, Bobby said, *"I better get going."*

Brian's voice trembled with emotion as he looked at her, his eyes pleading.

"I can't do it, Bobby. "Why can't I escape this darkness that consumes me every day? I can't keep going like this. How do I get out of it?"

Bobby's thoughts were, *'Oh Sh*t, we're back to that again'!*

Bobby fell silent, carefully considering her response. She knew the weight of Brian's words and the pain behind them. Finally, she spoke, her tone calm and thoughtful.

"Don't let this temporary defeat define you," Bobby went on, her voice now softer but filled with passion. *"Let it reveal you, the true, beautiful, higher version of yourself… if you persist, the universe has a better plan for you!"*

Brian smiled but said nothing.

"Brian, how do we counteract darkness?"

Confusion clouded Brian's face as he struggled to find an answer. After a pause, he whispered, *"I don't know."*

"You do know!! Brian?" she said, her voice low but clear. Another pause, and then Brian whispered, *"You counteract darkness with light."*

"Exactly," Bobby replied, her eyes softening as she saw a flicker of understanding in his expression. She posed another question.

"So, what could you be doing to shed light on your thoughts?"

Brian was silent, furrowing his brow in concentration. Bobby waited for a response. *"What could you be doing, Brian?"* She pressed gently again.

Bobby's voice took on a more urgent tone as she leaned in closer. *"Your thoughts create your vibration, Brian. That vibration governs your actions and ultimately shapes your life."*

Brian nodded slowly, understanding beginning to dawn on his face.

"See, here's the beautiful thing, Brian, the good news is, we can control our thoughts," Bobby continued, her voice full of conviction. *"Our thoughts shape everything, and we must learn how to take charge of them. If we stay stuck on the negative, we get more of it. But once we start shifting our thoughts only to what we want, amazing things happen.*

Nothing good is ever created from negative energy. Trouble is, if your thought patterns are negative for too long, it starts to set like concrete and becomes a stinking bad habit, and as you know... it sticks, and it sucks, and it's worth zero bucks."

Brian's face softened as he responded, his voice quiet but with a glimmer of hope.

"So, you're saying I could be thinking in those positive, powerful thoughts?"

"Exactly!" Bobby exclaimed; her excitement palpable. *"That's 100% right. It's all about mastering our thoughts and using them to create the life we desire. And whatever you do, don't focus on what you don't want. If you do, you'll attract more of what you don't want."*

Bobby leaned back, her tone growing more reflective.

"Is it easy? Hell no! Not at first. But it's simple. It's not rocket science. People miss it because it's so simple, but it's not easy because we're fighting against a bad set of thought habits. As I said before, those thought habits tend to set like concrete over time. It's called your paradigm. We all have a paradigm, this set of belief patterns that form into a habit of doing things a certain way."

She paused, her gaze intense. *"So, Brian, it starts with awareness. Then comes a deep desire for change. Once you reach that point, it's a beautiful place. You won't go back, I assure you."*

He smiled softly. *"So, we are fighting against my mind's paradigm, is that right?"*

She smiled. *"Yes, Brian. We're fighting against your mind's paradigm. But we're going to jackhammer that pesky paradigm together. It's going to take time, and it requires reading every day for it to work for you. Just like physical exercise, you can't exercise for only 30 minutes and expect to be fit. The same goes for your mind. You have to read every day to be mentally fit to grab life's difficulties by the horns."*

Brian looked at her, still puzzled but with a growing sense of understanding. Bobby threw one last analogy his way.

"Brian, I'm going home now, but one last thing I want to share with you, it's an analogy that I love."

"If life were a ten-story building, and each story in that building represented your vibration, your 'feelings', right now, you're in the basement. Are you going to pitch a tent and stay there for good?"

"If you do, your tomorrow will be the same. The week after, the same. Years after that... the same."

Bobby leaned forward, her voice soft but insistent.

"Here's what I suggest: go up a level at a time. It doesn't happen overnight, but I can assure you that eventually, you'll reach the top floor and have a penthouse mindset. The view will take your breath away, and everything becomes clear from up there. Will you go down

a few floors from time to time? Hell, yes, life happens, and things lower our vibration. But there's always, always a seed of equal or greater good in every adversity you encounter. Isn't that exciting?" *she added in her usual zestful way.*

Bobby could see that she was finally getting through to Brian.

At least she thought she was.

The next morning, Bobby's world fell apart. Brian was gone. Brian had taken his own life that very night of their conversation.

All her words, all her efforts to help him find light again, they hadn't been enough. Her heart was shattered. In the stillness that followed receiving the news, she sat in grief, a cold weight in her chest, wondering what more she could have done to reach him.

She sat in stunned silence, the weight of his loss pressing down on her like a suffocating blanket. All her words and all her attempts to help had not been enough.

She couldn't help but wonder if there was a more effective way she could have helped him, a way to keep him mentally fit on a daily basis. Would it have made a difference?

For a time, Bobby herself sank into the basement of the building she had described to Brian. The grief was overwhelming, and for a while, she too pitched a tent in that dark basement of the analogy she used, consumed by the weight of not having been able to save him.

CHAPTER 4

THE DARKEST DAYS OF HARVEST

NOT NARRATED

The harvest season had always been Bobby's favorite time of year. It was a season of celebration, neighbors helping neighbors, families gathering for meals after long days in the fields, the sounds of laughter, the clinking of glasses, and the shared pride in the fruits of their labor. The rich smell of freshly cut wheat filled the air, the sun bathed the land in golden light, and every sunset seemed to promise a brighter tomorrow.

But this year was different. For Bobby, the harvest had become a relentless routine, one where her hands and body moved as if on autopilot, but her mind, her heart, was lost in a fog of grief and guilt. The death of Brian weighed on her like an anchor. The community celebrations, the camaraderie, the joy of harvest, it all passed her by like distant echoes, too far away to touch her.

Physically, Bobby was present. She worked as hard, if not harder, than anyone else. Her body, conditioned by years on the farm, responded to the demands of the season without hesitation. From sunrise to long after sunset, she pushed herself, sometimes working through the night, the calloused skin of her hands worn raw from constant labor. But inside, something had broken. Every task, every movement, felt mechanical, like a machine operating with no spark, no life.

It was Brian's death that haunted her. In the quiet moments, when she was alone, the guilt gnawed at her, whispering that she had failed him. Her mind replayed their last conversation over and over, dissecting every word she had said and every word she hadn't. She repeatedly questioned, *"Did I push him too hard? Was I too hopeful, too positive, when he was drowning in despair?"*

She couldn't escape the gnawing thought that maybe, just maybe, it was something she had said that pushed him over the edge. The thought twisted inside her, choking her with doubt. And then there were the rumors, the whispers she imagined spreading through Sunflower Springs like wildfire. Dorothy Blake had probably spun her own version of events, telling anyone that Bobby had visited Brian's home the same night he took his life.

She couldn't help but think… *"Did he feel rejected when I told him to back off when he was getting closer? You should have just kissed him, Bobby! You're such a bloody square!"* she told herself. But she knew that would have only made things more complicated. Bobby believed he needed to heal himself internally before merging his life with someone, and that someone was not going to be her.

The thoughts of her advice to Brian twisted inside her, choking her with doubt. Were people blaming her?

Bobby buried herself in work to keep the whispers at bay, both in her mind and in the town. But no matter how hard she tried, the grief found its way to the surface, spilling over in unexpected moments. She would lose her temper at the smallest things. Zoe's loud music grated on her nerves, and one evening, after a long day in the fields, she stormed into their shared room, her face red with frustration.

"Turn that bloody music down, Zoe!" she yelled, her voice trembling with suppressed rage.

Zoe looked up, startled, not understanding the true reason for Bobby's anger.

"It's just music! Can you just relax for a change… you… you… wet sponge Bobby SquarePants!" Zoe yelled back.

Melina started to walk towards their bedroom, wanting to know what all the yelling was about.

But Bobby couldn't calm down. The music was like nails on a chalkboard, an unbearable noise that seemed to penetrate through the numbness she was desperately clinging to. She slammed the door behind her and stormed out of the house, her heart pounding with an anger she couldn't explain.

Isolation became her refuge.

Bobby began avoiding family dinners, making excuses that she wasn't feeling well or that she needed to check on something in the shed. But in truth, she just couldn't bear to be around people. She couldn't handle the weight of their concern, the way they looked at her as if she were fragile and broken.

At night, when the others gathered around the dinner table, Bobby would retreat to the shearing shed with a small lamp and one of the self-help books she had been collecting. The books, once a tool she used to help Brian, had now become her lifeline. She clung to them desperately, highlighting passages, scribbling notes in the margins, and using Post-it notes to mark the pages she thought she needed to remember. Phrases of hope. She got lost in her thoughts, imagining the words on her page as if she were living them out in her day-to-day motions. The words on the pages were her only source of comfort; they were her companions in the darkness.

In the middle of the day, while others were out in the fields, she would run back to the shearing shed to reread a page or a section of the book *Your Power, Your Perspective* by Christopher Lane, as if confirming to herself that the principles she had explained to Brian were indeed correct. You control your thoughts. Your thoughts create your reality; the book reminded her over and over again. But her thoughts were wild and untamable, spiraling into self-blame and doubt. And no matter how much she tried to remind herself of the lessons she had once believed so deeply, the confusion overshadowed it all.

Melina knocked gently on the shearing shed door, the warm glow of a lantern spilling onto the dark path outside.

"Bobby? Dinner's ready. You've been out here for hours."

"I'm not hungry, Mum," Bobby replied, her voice muffled by the walls.

Melina hesitated; the weight of worry etched into her face. *"You can't keep doing this to yourself, sweetheart. Let me help… please."*

Melina's face was full of worry.

"There's nothing to help with, Mum," Bobby replied, her tone sharper than she intended. She heard the soft sigh from the other

side of the door but didn't move to open it. Moments later, the sound of retreating footsteps left her alone with her inner darkness.

The harvest continued, and so did Bobby's isolation.

Bobby worked through the motions, her hands blistered from the constant labor, her muscles aching from overuse. She was harder on herself than she had ever been, pushing through exhaustion and refusing to slow down, anything to keep the grief at bay. But no matter how hard she worked, the pain remained. At times, it consumed each and every one of her thoughts.

People would look at her, her family, the neighbors who came to help, but no one really saw her. It was as if her parents were too afraid to ask how she was really doing, too scared to touch the raw wound she carried inside. And Zoe, well, Zoe had retreated into her world of music, TV shows, and social media, either too unaware or too self-absorbed to notice the depth of Bobby's pain. Bobby felt like a ghost, moving through her life unseen... unheard. The weight of it all crushed her, her mind, her body, and her spirit.

Alonso kept trying to approach Bobby, and so did Nonna Giovanna, only to be almost ignored. Alonso was fed up and frustrated, so one night he said to Melina, *"What the hell is going on with that girl? I have never seen her even remotely like this! Surely, she doesn't blame herself for what happened to Brian?"* He paused and continued, *"Do you think she was... you know... in love with him or something? Because this is just insane and just not like her at all. I want our Bobby back. I miss her zestfulness! I'm tired of talking to a bloody zombie!!"*

Melina, in her gentle yet resolute tone, replied, *"Babe, she wasn't in love with him. You just got to see a side of your daughter, and that is the depth of her love for her fellow human."*

One night, Bobby found herself particularly annoyed with Zoe again as she walked into their bedroom. **"Get your bloody Sh*t off this floor, Zoe!"** Bobby snapped, her voice breaking. Zoe rolled her eyes but hesitated before picking up all her mess. **"You could just tell me what's wrong, you know,"** she muttered, almost too quietly to hear. Bobby froze in the doorway, anger and sadness warring within her. But instead of responding, she turned and walked away. Behind her, Zoe sighed, staring at the screen of her phone, wondering if she should have said more.

The harvest fields stretched out in front of Bobby, golden and nearly empty; the once-tall crops were now cut down, leaving behind stubble that stretched for miles. The long days of work were almost over. Soon, the harvest would be finished.

Bobby stood on the hill, looking out over the vastness of the fields. She'd been so focused on keeping herself busy, so absorbed in the relentless rhythm of work, that she hadn't really stopped to think about what came next. But now, staring at the fields, a thought crept into her mind, one that she couldn't push away.

What am I going to do when the harvest is done?

The question gripped her, squeezing her chest with an intensity that caught her off guard. Panic began to rise inside her, sharp and sudden. Her heart started racing, her breathing quickening. She'd been using the busyness, the hard work, as a way to escape, to keep her mind from spiraling into the darkness.

"What will I do when the work stops? What will I do when there isn't much left to keep me occupied?" she asked herself as she sat at the patch.

The thought terrified her.

It was now getting dark, so she drove the quad bike to the weeping willow tree. She climbed up the tree with her books, her solar lights strong enough to still be able to read.

Her breath came in short gasps now, her chest tightening as if a weight had settled on it, pressing down hard. She could feel the panic building, a sense of dread that seemed to grow with every passing second. Her hands shook as she reached for the pile of books on her lap, desperate for something, anything, that would help her keep it together.

She grabbed the first book, flipping through the pages frantically, her eyes scanning the words but not really seeing them. Her breath came in shallow, ragged bursts, and her hands fumbled as she grabbed another book, flipping through it just as quickly, searching for something, though she didn't even know what. She felt like she was drowning, her mind racing and her heart pounding in her chest. She looked so confused, as if flipping the book continuously would give her the answer she needed... or so she thought.

"What am I looking for?!!!" she yelled out loud.

Bobby's trembling hands stilled; her eyes unfocused as she realized she had no idea. She didn't know what she was searching for or what she needed. Her panic swelled, the tightness in her chest making it feel like she couldn't breathe. Her hands trembled again, this time in a way that shocked her. She threw the book overboard; it landed on the ground, open and face down, almost tearing it as her tree platform was very high up.

She grabbed another book, this one called *There Is Another Way*, flipping through the pages again, desperate to find something, an answer, a lifeline, anything to stop the rising tide of fear that was threatening to overwhelm her. But nothing helped. The words blurred on the page, meaningless and distant. She was gasping now, her breath coming in harsh bursts, her body trembling as the panic took hold. She threw that book overboard, too.

And then, as she sat there, her hands still shaking, her breath coming in sharp, Bobby felt it, the exhaustion.

The panic, the guilt, the grief, it all came crashing down on her at that moment. But with it came an overwhelming sense of weariness. She was so, so tired. Tired of holding it all together, tired of pretending she was okay, tired of fighting the emotions she'd been bottling up for so long.

Oh my God, what is happening to me? Bobby thought. *These feelings are foreign to me. What is this?*

At that very moment, she felt a hand softly touch her shoulder from behind her. It was Brian's hand, with his tattooed fingers, with O (hug) and X (kisses) signs on his knuckles.

The sobs came like a slow, breaking wave, washing over her in fits and starts until she couldn't hold them back any longer. *"I tried, Brian,"* she whispered, clutching the remaining books to her chest. *"I tried to save you. Why wasn't it enough?"* The memory of his hollow eyes and hesitant smile flashed through her mind, and the weight of it drove her to her knees. *"I'm so tired,"* she sobbed, her voice breaking as she pressed her face into her hands.

For the first time in weeks, Bobby allowed herself to feel the full weight of her grief. She allowed herself to break down completely, the exhaustion consuming her. Her body had finally given up the fight, and she released all the pain. She couldn't do it anymore. She couldn't keep pretending she was okay.

"I'm too tired to fight this feeling anymore," she whispered, her voice barely audible over the soft breeze. *"Not today. I'm just going to let myself cry today."*

It was then, sitting under the weeping willow tree, that the dam finally broke.

The sobs came slowly at first, soft, strangled sounds that escaped her lips almost against her will. But they grew louder, more intense until she was crying uncontrollably, her body shaking with the force of her grief. She clutched the books to her chest, pressing them against her heart as if they could hold her together.

The landscape around her remained still, but the sounds of the night began to rise, a soft breeze rustled the dry grass, frogs croaked in the distance, and the occasional chirp of crickets joined the symphony of the evening. But Bobby's sobs echoed through the fields, her cries filling the vast emptiness around her.

"Why, Brian?" *she cried, her voice breaking.* ***"Why'd you do it? Did you even think about me? Did you think about how much I'd hurt? I was the only one who stuck with you, didn't that matter to you at all?"***

Her sobs grew louder, her cries becoming raw and primal, the release of all the pain she had been bottling up for weeks.

"You're bloody selfish, Brian! You didn't care about anyone else!" Her voice cracked with the weight of her emotions.

But as the sobs began to soften, something shifted inside her. She wiped her tears with her sleeve and whispered, **"Of course, you didn't think of me. You couldn't. You were too lost in your own pain to see anything."**

And with that, she let go.

She let the tears come; let the tears completely wet her face; let the grief and exhaustion pour out of her in waves. The tears were hot and endless, the kind of sobs that left her feeling empty but also, in a strange way, lighter.

She cried for Brian, for the weight of his loss, and for the guilt she had carried since his death. She cried for herself, for all the pain and exhaustion she had bottled up inside. And as the tears fell, as the sobs quieted, Bobby felt the weight begin to lift, just a little. The panic had passed, leaving behind a sense of calm that felt strange but welcome.

By the time her sobs had softened, Bobby was sitting still, the pile of books beside her, some scattered on the ground below, thrown from the top of the tree during her outburst. Her breathing had slowed, the tightness in her chest easing as she sat on the tree, the setting sun casting the world in a soft, golden glow. Brian was in the far distance, waving goodbye to her.

"Goodbye, Brian," she said softly as she waved back with her last tear.

She hugged her knees to her chest, staring out at the quiet fields. The stillness was no longer sobbing, it was comforting, like the land was giving her permission to rest. The harvest was nearly done, and for the first time, she let herself think about what came next. She reached for her phone and scrolled through her contacts, hesitating over her mother's name before pressing the call. Bobby called her mother; the phone dialed out, and when Melina answered, Bobby's voice trembled as she spoke. ***"Mum, can we talk? I think I could do with some company."***

Melina looked up at Alonso with a smile; she had her on speaker phone, so Alonso heard Bobby's comment. He put his hands together in a prayer mode and held them up to his chin to signify his gratitude, and Nonna Giovanna was also relieved. Nonna Giovanna said out loud, ***"At last, our Bobby is back."***

Bobby took a deep breath, feeling the cool air fill her lungs. She pressed the books close to her chest, letting herself sit with the quiet, with the stillness. The panic was gone now, replaced by an overwhelming sense of exhaustion, but also something else, a small flicker of peace.

It was in that moment of peace that some clarity came to her. Bobby finally realized she had not been the same.

She had been so consumed by emotions that she hadn't seen the love her family had been trying to show her. She hadn't noticed the way her parents watched her, worried but unsure of how to help. She hadn't heard the small ways Zoe had tried to reach out to her, the silly jokes, the offers to hang out, even if it had been in her own annoying, teenage way. And she had forgotten about Nonna, her gentle, loving grandmother, who had been there all along, offering quiet comfort and understanding, even when Bobby had been too lost in her own world to accept it.

She remembered now, people had come by the house, neighbors dropping by, others checking on the farm, offering help. She recalled her mother telling her that the librarian had stopped by and brought a new book for her to take a look at. *"What book was it?"* she wondered. She had been so wrapped up in her pain that she hadn't noticed any of it.

As the sun dipped below the horizon, Bobby picked up her books, pressing them to her heart like lifelines, the words within them not just lessons but companions that had carried her throughout the years.

But now, she realized it more and more. Her books were tools, like the ones she used to repair whatever broke around the farm. These books would help her problems, unbreak her. They were repairing her mind, body, and spirit day by day. It occurred to her that these words were powerful tools, powerful enough to change lives.

She pressed the books close to her chest again, closing her eyes and allowing herself to feel the quiet peace of the evening. The grief was still there, but it had softened, like a weight she could finally carry without being crushed.

Even as she was beginning to see how much she had missed the people who showed they cared for her, she realized she wasn't really alone in her darkest times. She had her books, which were her mentors, her lifelines, and most importantly, her family. And now, sitting by the trunk of her thinking tree, she recognized she had something else, too, a small, fragile hope that maybe, just maybe, she could get through this.

Hillery's sloppy chewing broke through the silence, and Bobby turned to see the sheep munching contentedly underneath her. *"Oh no, Hillery, don't eat those!!"* Bobby called out as she rescued her books that had been thrown from the top of the tree, quickly retrieving them before Hillery could slobber all over them.

A small, startled laugh escaped her, a real laugh, light and unguarded. She walked by her side and reached out, running her hand through Hillery's wool. *"I guess even you knew I needed someone today,"* she murmured, her voice soft. The absurdity of finding comfort in a sheep brought another laugh, and with it, a fragile flicker of hope. Maybe healing didn't have to start big. Perhaps, it could start here, with a laugh and the quiet company of an unexpected woolly friend.

"And you... even you cared about me, and I didn't see it. Where have you been these days?"

"Barrrrr," Hillery replied.

"Oh, you've been on the hill again... I see," Bobby replied.

After a moment of hugging Hillery, Bobby sat back up, her legs crossed in front of her, the books still resting on her lap. The sun had dipped below the horizon, leaving behind a deep, dusky blue sky streaked with the last remnants of orange and pink. The warmth of the day had faded, replaced by a cool breeze that brushed against Bobby's tear-soaked skin.

The breeze felt like a gentle caress, as if it were trying to dry her tears. She smiled through the last of her sobs, taking a deep breath and feeling the coolness of the air as it filled her lungs. The colours of the sky were fading into twilight, the stars just beginning to wink into existence as they began to emerge, one by one. The weight of her sorrow hadn't vanished completely; it had shifted. It was lighter now, no longer a burden she couldn't carry.

Bobby stood up, still cradling her books close to her chest as if they were old friends. She looked out over the quiet fields; the crops that had once stood tall now harvested, leaving behind stubble that stretched for miles. The vastness of the land mirrored the space inside her, a space that had been filled with pain but was now making room for something new.

CHAPTER 5

COMING HOME

NOT NARRATED

"It's time to go home, Hillery," she said softly, glancing at the sheep, who was still contentedly chewing the last bits of grass.

As she stood up, Bobby felt lighter. She gathered her books into her tote bag, slung it across her body, and began walking back toward the farmhouse.

Bobby's steps were lighter than they had been in almost a month. Hillery trailed behind her at a slow, relaxed pace, her gentle chewing the only sound breaking the stillness of the night. Bobby felt her lips curve into a smile, a small, tentative one, but real. With every stride, her steps lightened, and the night air brushed against her skin. On impulse, she twirled, her arms slicing through the moonlight, a soft laugh bubbling up. Her body felt free; her mind uncluttered by grief. Behind her, Hillery trotted along, her sheepish gaze almost playful, as though mocking Bobby's newfound energy.

As Bobby walked, something stirred inside her, a sense of presence, of being in the moment for the first time in what felt like forever. She realized she could breathe again, breathe, without the tightness in her chest that had been her constant companion since Brian's death.

She felt a skip in her step as she continued walking, and before she knew it, she was smiling. She tried a chuckle, and the sound of it made her laugh even more. The moon had risen, casting a soft glow over the land, and Bobby felt the night air on her skin like a welcome embrace.

She started to move her arms through the air, letting them dance as she walked, the movement freeing in a way that made her want to laugh again. Her feet picked up a rhythm, a soft shuffle, as she twirled her arms in a wave-like motion, her body swaying side to side as she walked. It felt so good. She laughed again as she noticed Hillery was still mocking her, a real laugh this time, and it echoed through the quiet night.

She realized how tight her neck and shoulders were, the tension she had been holding onto for so long. She rolled her shoulders, moving her head from side to side, loosening the muscles that had been locked up in stress.

"Geez, my muscles have gone tight."

And then, as if trying to release the tension she just felt in her muscles, she started shaking her body in different directions, as if trying to whisk away the tightness. Without even thinking about it, she began to dance, even for a brief moment, as she picked up her steps to head back home.

Her body moved in rhythm with the silent music she imagined in her head. She twisted her spine and swayed her hips, letting her body express the freedom she hadn't felt in what seemed like a very long time. She had also stopped swimming in the dam and meditating after Brian's passing, which hadn't helped things. But tonight was different. She shuffled her feet, her arms swaying with the breeze, her laughter bubbling up from somewhere deep inside.

As she approached the farmhouse, Bobby felt something she hadn't expected, excitement. She sensed this flicker of excitement, as though she had been away from home for ages, and now she was finally coming back, not just physically but mentally and emotionally. She could see the soft glow of the house lights spilling onto the ground, and her heart quickened.

The smells hit her first.

The familiar scent of her mother's cooking drifted through the air, wrapping around her like a warm blanket. It was the smell of home, roasted vegetables, garlic, and herbs, mingling with the sweetness of something baking. She could almost taste it: the buttery softness of potatoes, the crisp edges of zucchini, and the rich, savory flavors of meat roasting in the oven. Her mouth watered at the thought, a sensation she hadn't noticed in some time.

As Bobby got closer, the sounds of home greeted her. She could hear the faint clatter of dishes from the kitchen and the soft murmur of her parents' voices as they spoke to each other in the easy, comfortable way they always had. Zoe's music was playing from her room, loud but somewhat not annoying, a background noise that Bobby had learned to tune out over the years. It was all so familiar, yet tonight it felt different, alive, vibrant, like she was experiencing it for the first time in forever.

And then there was the warmth.

The warmth of home was also something she hadn't allowed herself to feel. It radiated from the house, not just from the heat of the oven, but from the people inside, her family, her roots. The people who had been there all along, even when she had been too lost in her grief to see it. Bobby realized, as she walked toward their white picket fence, that she wasn't just coming back to a house, she was coming back to life.

She looked up at the stars, her breath hitching. *"Brian,"* she whispered. *"I don't know how yet, but I'm going to turn your pain into something beautiful."* The words came unbidden but carried a certainty. She was reclaiming her space. She took a deep breath, filling her lungs with the smells of dinner, the coolness of the night air mingling with the earthy richness of the harvest fields. She felt truly alive again.

Bobby said to herself, *"I feel hope again… I feel alive. Life is a gift, and I realize now how much of it we lose sight of when we focus only on our losses."*

That was a lightbulb moment. It was like a light flickering on inside her, illuminating a truth she had been too lost to see before. She had been trapped in her own darkness, unable to see the love, the joy, or the beauty around her. But now, as she stood under the stars, with the soft sounds of home and the night all around her, she understood. She had been so focused on her own pain that she had lost sight of everything else.

Bobby paused in her steps, taking a deep breath and letting the cool night air fill her lungs. She opened her eyes, gazing up at the stars, feeling a sense of relief wash over her. *"Thank you, spirit,"* she whispered, her voice soft and full of gratitude.

She began walking again, her heart open. She was ready to go home, back to her family, back to the people who loved her. And for the first time in what felt like a very long time, she felt like she could truly be with them and be truly in the present moment, without any negative outside thoughts.

She could feel the love from her family the very moment she walked in, the love that had always been there, waiting for her to return.

Her heart swelled with gratitude as she took another deep breath. She could feel the excitement bubbling up inside her. It was as if she had been away for a lifetime, but now she was back, truly back.

And in that moment, she knew, no matter what the future held, no matter what challenges came her way, she would keep moving forward. Because life, with all its pain and beauty, was a gift. And she was ready to live it.

"I'm home," she called out, stepping fully inside, ready to embrace whatever came next. Her family was relieved to see a glimpse of the true Bobby emerging once again.

That night after dinner, as Bobby sat on the porch in the quiet evening, the breeze carrying the faint scent of eucalyptus, her mind raced with ideas. She thought about Brian, about the conversations they'd had over several months, and how close they had been to finding a way through his pain. But something had been missing, a consistent practice, a daily support system, a way to keep the darkness at bay before it consumed him.

Her thoughts turned to the community around her, to the people she hadn't seen while she was in the midst of her pain. So many of them were just like Brian, just like where she was at, fighting silent battles, their struggles hidden behind the facade of everyday life. Bobby knew that if she could find a way to create something practical, something people could use to sustain their mental health, she could honour Brian's memory in the most meaningful way.

Bobby said, *"Nonna,"* as she found her grandmother in her favorite spot on the porch, her silhouette framed by the full moon. She hesitated, then took a deep breath. *"I've decided, I'm going to create something that helps people like Brian, something that'll make sure no one else has to feel so lost."*

Nonna's eyes, filled with both pride and sorrow, met Bobby's. *"Then you must do it with all your heart, Bella Mia."* She paused, then added, *"But remember, even when we give everything, it may not always be enough."* She reached for Bobby's hand, her grip strong despite her age. Nonna Giovanna continued, *"But that doesn't mean we stop giving."*

Bobby nodded, her resolve solidifying. *"I won't stop, Nonna. I'll find a way to honour him, and to help others."*

Giovanna smiled, though there was a touch of sadness in her eyes. Bobby knew her grandmother was right. She had tried to save Brian, and it hadn't been enough, but that didn't mean she would stop trying to help others. The fire burning inside her wouldn't allow it.

As the stars shone brighter, Bobby stood and stretched her arms toward the stars, feeling the weight of the world on her shoulders yet feeling connected to spirit.

She didn't have all the answers yet, but she knew one thing for sure: she would keep pushing forward, keep fighting, and keep building a way to honour Brian's memory, and in doing so, help others find the light in their own darkness.

The urgency to build a more powerful and lasting way to improve someone's mental well-being and live life in the most successful way was now an even fiercer fire burning inside Bobby, driving her forward despite the pain that almost threatened to consume her.

Nothing could have been done to prevent this tragedy. Bobby had a new resolve. She was determined to honour Brian's memory by channeling her intense passion for human potential into creating something powerful, something meaningful, and most of all, something instrumental to the quality of life for many. Bobby's message to humanity would be that with the correct mindset, all aspects of life would dramatically improve, relationships, health, money, but she recognized and acknowledged that it all starts with spirit. The core is always your spirit. The same spirit that snapped her out of her grief over losing Brian.

Giovanna looked at her granddaughter, her face softening with both pride and concern. *"You carry so much on your shoulders, cara mia. But I know if anyone can do it, it's you."*

Bobby nodded, her resolve firm. *"I'm going to build something that lasts, Nonna. Something that makes a difference. I have decided it will be through a mindset board game."*

Bobby poured her heart and soul into designing the game and inserting content.

Every night, already tired from working on the farm, she would work tirelessly on making the game. Often staying up until the early hours of the morning, fueled by passion and determination to create something amazing. But with only a few hours of sleep before having to get up and go to work, she was burning the candle at both ends. Her dedication was relentless, driving her to push through exhaustion and challenges in pursuit of her dream.

It's harvest season again, and the crop was thick, healthy, and ready to rake in some money at last, but fate had other ideas...

The shearing shed had a musty scent of oil and old wood. Dust floated lazily through the single beam of sunlight that cut through the dim interior. Bobby's fingers traced over the weathered tricycles, their rusting metal and peeling paint telling stories of a childhood long past.

She could almost hear the distant laughter and wild races through the farmyard with Zoe. Memories of scraped knees and carefree days swept over her like a gust of wind, but just as quickly, the moment slipped away.

Her phone buzzed, pulling her back to the present. It was her childhood friends confirming their plans for tomorrow. They were meeting by the river in Glentvale, and for a brief moment, Bobby's heart lifted at the thought of their easy company. A smile tugged at her lips, and she turned to head back toward the house.

She walked over to tell Nonna Giovanna that lunch was ready, using the Italian phrase, ***"Ciao Nonna, mangiare è pronto"*** (Hi Grandma, lunch is ready.) In her usual excited voice, they exchanged smiles before Bobby asked Nonna a question.

"Hey, Nonna?"

Nonna responded with, ***"Si, bella mia?"*** *(Yes, my beautiful?)*

Bobby, in her usual enthusiastic way, said, *"Nonna, I'm going to take you to Milan after harvest! I'll have enough money by then. I'm sorry it's taken so long to get you there, and while we're there, can you show me where Nonno proposed to you at the piazza?"* It had been years since Bobby had promised to take Giovanna to Italy, but money was always poured back into the farm, and none was left to enjoy life.

"Nonna, I can't wait to ride a Vespa together to the beach in Milan! Then afterwards, we'll go to Sicily and visit the relatives and stuff our faces with food!!" Bobby said with full-blown excitement. Bobby had never traveled anywhere in her life, but she so desired for that to change. Her vision board said it all.

Laughing with joy, Bobby exclaimed, *"Andremo all spiaggia!"* (*We'll go to the beach!*)

Nonna Giovanna replied, *"Si, bella mia, "Andremo in spiaggia nudi."* (*Yes, my dear, we will go swimming at the beach naked*).

Bobby responded cheekily, *"Oh no way, Nonna, you are much too modern for me!"*

They laughed together as they walked arm-in-arm toward the house.

In the distance, you could hear Bobby yelling out, ***"Love you, Nonna !!!"*** echoing across the field as Grandma Giovanna handed her a hessian sack of homegrown fresh potatoes.

Bobby added excitedly, ***"Oh… patate! (potatoes) Let's make gnocchi on Sunday!"*** Her voice again echoed through the fields as she couldn't contain her excitement for her favorite traditional family dish.

As the sun set and darkness fell, Bobby finished her dinner with her family. After spending a short while in conversation, she would retreat to her room for a night of study. But this was no ordinary studying for Bobby, it was an insatiable thirst for knowledge on success principles, a burning desire to understand the depths of the mind and body and how she could add it to the game she had so meticulously built.

She had even built her bookshelves, perfect for housing the countless volumes that fueled her curiosity. It was a skill she had picked up after growing tired of sharing a room with loud and careless Zoe, who always had her music blaring with no consideration for her sister. Bobby's carpentry skills came in handy one day when she finally couldn't take Zoe's antics any longer.

On her 23rd birthday, Bobby stormed outside to retrieve the tractor, trailer, and all the building materials stored in the shed to extend the workers' quarters. She grabbed what she needed to build a wall that would separate her room, halving the space she shared with her sister Zoe. Their shared room was quite large, and Bobby's idea of placing a wall between them was a good one.

After Brian's passing last harvest, Bobby wanted to create a better space to work on the game. Yet, she couldn't concentrate deeply with Zoe's distractions.

"Mum, Dad, these building materials can be my birthday gift," Bobby declared with a resolve that wasn't asking for permission.

Alonso was annoyed at first by Bobby's self-made decision, but Melina intervened and whispered to him, *"Would you share a room with Zoe?"* He thought about it for a second and suddenly helped Bobby with building the rest of the wall and bookshelves that day. Melina helped decorate Bobby's room with lots of beautiful live greenery, new window dressings, and sleek, clean-lined furniture. Melina had a fine eye for detail; she would have made a great interior decorator.

As Bobby studied the new special space she had created, her mind buzzed with excitement at the thought of expanding her knowledge without interruption from her sister.

That night, Bobby sat at her desk, her mind alight with countless small ideas. Her fingers traced the edge of a blank notebook, and slowly, a great idea began to form. Life, she thought, was like a maze, twists, turns, and dead ends, but always a way forward. There must be a more immersive way to learn success philosophies and the art of happiness beyond just reading instructions, she thought to herself many months ago when the idea struck her; a game, a tangible and digital blend, enabling people to grasp the keys to success across all facets of life.

As the moonlight spilled across her desk, Bobby reflected on the past 12 months. Despite gathering key pointers and creating designs, she had never been happy with them.

Her rubbish bin was always full of unworkable, rejected drafts of the game, and now she finally had a workable design, so she added the idea of the game being a maze. Bobby was excited, as a maze is a perfect analogy for life's twists and turns.

It was as if her new bedroom gave her a powerful energy that very night. She hand-sketched the first draft of a board game she would call **A-MAZE-IIIING**, a game for the world to learn from, a way to grow, reach goals, and love life.

The idea for the game began to take shape in Bobby's mind, and with it came the creation of four unique mascots, each representing a pillar of wealth that would guide players through the journey of life.

First, there was **Spirity**, a gentle, glowing figure symbolizing the relationship we have with ourselves, our souls, and our connection to the creator. Spirity was the foundation, the essence of who we are at our core.

Then, there was **Energia**, vibrant and full of life, representing our physical health and well-being. Energia reminded players that a strong, healthy body was the key to living a fulfilled life, giving them the energy to tackle any challenge ahead.

Contento was the third mascot, a warm and inviting presence embodying emotional wealth. Contento symbolized the love we give and receive, the relationships with family, friends, pets, and even the bond we have with nature. He was the reminder that happiness comes from nurturing our connections with others.

Finally, there was **Cashanova**, the money mascot, a charismatic and larger-than-life character that would add humour and charm to the game. Cashanova represented financial abundance, guiding players through the intricacies of managing money and creating wealth while maintaining balance with the other pillars.

It felt like a lightbulb moment, like an inventor discovering the answer to something profound. She added all the key points she had collected over the years.

Every inch of her bookshelves was meticulously colour-coded, reflecting her organized and focused mind. The shelves were divided into four distinct zones: yellow for spiritual wealth, blue for physical well-being, red for emotional wealth, and green for monetary wealth. Each zone housed a collection of books, from business marketing guides to new-age farming techniques, which fell into the green zone. Bobby's eyes would light up at the sight of her beautiful collection.

Committed to the impact she knew she would create with her new updated vision board, Bobby felt energized. With precise cuts, she skillfully gathered pictures from glossy magazines to create her vision board. It was a collage of her dreams and aspirations, featuring images of exotic destinations like Europe, China, India, Africa, Canada, the United States, and Brazil. But there were also images of beautiful places in her own vast country that she hadn't seen yet.

Amidst the vibrant colours and landscapes, there was a photo of a charismatic speaker on stage, and another picture of two lovers locked in an embrace against the backdrop of a golden sunset. As time passed, and her goals became clearer, she added more pictures to the board, each one representing a step closer to her desired future. With a determined gaze, she touched the smooth surface of the board with her hand, closing her eyes for a few moments, lost in the vivid visualization of her future and all she had envisioned.

As she stepped back to admire her handiwork, a surge of pride flooded through her. Her room radiated love and prosperity. She carefully placed each book, like a scene from a fairy tale come to life.

Zoe was envious but happy that her music could now be played louder, and she could make a mess without being told off.

Lush green plants adorned every corner, while modern, sleek furniture added a touch of sophistication. It was a sight to behold, one that spoke volumes about her determination and abundant mindset.

CHAPTER 6

THE DREAM

NOT NARRATED

Bobby's vision for her successful board game was taking shape, piece by piece, like a puzzle coming together faster and faster. Every action step gave the idea more and more oxygen to come alive. Her prototype sprawled across the floor, while a towering whiteboard covered in sticky notes resembled a mad scientist's blueprint for discovery. Each note, scribble, and adjustment brought her idea closer to life. Late into the night, she pored over her designs, tearing apart the ones that failed and reimagining new possibilities with tireless determination. It was meticulous, what most would consider grueling work, but for Bobby, it was electrifying. Every setback was a chance to innovate, and every breakthrough a spark of life that fueled her passion. Bobby felt Alive!

She envisioned, clear as a bell, the day her board game would launch and be available for the world to enjoy. The end goal was going to be worth it, she thought.

But tonight, the weight of it felt heavier than usual. She sighed and whispered to herself, *"How can I help when there is only one me?"* The thought lingered in the air, unanswered.

Every night before bed, she carefully placed books from her favorite mentors next to her bedside, their worn spines and dog-eared pages a testament to the wisdom within. With a gentle touch, she traced her fingers over the titles and asked permission to call upon their guidance from time to time. This ritual had become a turning point for her, a small but powerful act of seeking knowledge and inspiration beyond what the world could offer.

Tonight, though, as Bobby felt the call to sleep, she sat at the edge of her bed. Something felt different, the room seemed small; the air too heavy. Bobby's eyes scanned the familiar titles, but nothing brought her comfort. She walked to her desk, where her large whiteboard was covered with sticky notes and sketches. Her designs for the board game were constantly trashed because they didn't have a good flow and wouldn't make sense to players. Tonight, the game felt distant. Her goal was starting to feel like a mirage. The excitement felt flat, and the weight of her unfinished work pressed down on her.

Late that night, she climbed into bed, accompanied by the books on her bedside table that had become her closest companions. As she drifted off to sleep, she felt reassured that she was never alone on her journey. As she closed her eyes, she whispered a silent prayer, asking for guidance.

Bobby whispered a line she used every night: *"Spirit, my co-creator, please help me with my ideas. And by the way, thank you for the gift of today."*

Then, she drifted into a magical, vivid dream, so realistic it felt like she was transported to a different time and place. It was a detailed dream, but more than just a dream, it was something she would never forget.

The Grand Ballroom.

The dream unfolded slowly, like a fog lifting over the fields at dawn. At first, it was a blur of soft colours and distant sounds, but as Bobby's senses sharpened, she found herself standing at the entrance to a grand ballroom. Between the windows hung rich paintings of well-known authors from Bobby's books, each one depicting words of wisdom. It was as if the room itself was alive with stories, the very fabric of the place woven with the threads of human potential.

A sign hung above the entrance, proudly declaring the space as the *"Hall of Wisdom."* Bobby couldn't help but feel enchanted by the mystical atmosphere and the soft music welcoming her inside this extraordinary lobby.

Her breath caught in her throat. The space before her was otherworldly, stunning in its grandeur, yet warm and inviting. The ballroom stretched out in front of her, the kind she'd only ever seen in movies. It was vast, a room that seemed to stretch on forever, its marble floors gleaming under the glow of numerous crystal chandeliers. The light was soft and golden, and the air smelled faintly of freshly cut roses and eucalyptus, a strange yet comforting combination.

Rich red velvet curtains framed tall windows that reached from the floor to the ceiling, through which the soft light of dusk poured, casting everything in a golden hue. A scent of mixed fresh flowers mingled with the sweetness of champagne, filling the air.

Soft classical music played in the background, light melodies of violins and cellos. The musicians, though unseen, seemed to float through the space, filling it with an ethereal sound that felt like it was guiding her forward. Bobby took a deep breath, her pulse quickening. She glanced down at herself, embarrassed by her farm clothes and work boots, but she moved forward anyway. She felt as if she had just passed a test and earned the privilege to be there, fitting into this grand world with a natural grace.

In awe, Bobby stepped through the ballroom, her feet gliding across the floor as if the ground itself were moving her forward. Tables lined with sparkling crystal glasses and ornate platters of decadent desserts shimmered in the candlelight. She could smell the sweetness of berries, the richness of dark chocolate, and the faint bitterness of freshly brewed coffee. She almost reached out to touch one of the delicate pastries, its powdered sugar glistening like frost, when she felt a presence all around her.

Still feeling out of place because of her lack of dress code, Bobby looked down at herself and now realized she was no longer wearing her farm clothes.

She was dressed in an elegant gown, the soft pink tulle fabric flowing around her like a river with embroidered roses attached to the lower body. Her hair, usually pulled back in a no-nonsense ponytail, was styled in soft waves, cascading down her shoulders.

There were thousands of fresh roses arranged, matching her dress, surrounding her, and a narrow arch for her to enter.

As she looked down, she saw her completed board game in her arms.

She felt out of place, yet strangely at home, as if this dream world was a reflection of something deep inside her.

As she stepped forward to enter the grand ballroom, Bobby was met by two men in sleek suits who held open the double doors with welcoming smiles. A soft murmur of conversation and upbeat classical music filled the room. She looked around and realized that the figures gathered here were not strangers, they were her favorite authors, the whole lot, all dressed in elegant attire and holding their prized books close to their chests.

"Holy Sh*t," Bobby said aloud, then quickly placed a hand over her mouth, realizing this was not the place to be rough around the edges.

These were the authors of the books she had devoured for years. The authors stood in small groups on colourful carpets that corresponded to the colours Bobby had chosen for the different pillars in her game. Their heads were bent in quiet conversation. Figures were teaching, learning, and sharing knowledge.

Bobby's heart raced with excitement. She recognized them all, these were the voices that had guided her through her darkest and happiest times, the mentors who had spoken to her through the pages of their books. She couldn't believe she was standing among them.

She made her rounds, stopping to engage in brief conversations with various authors as she made her way through the room. One by one, the authors appeared before her, their admiration evident and their expressions curious. They all asked her the same question: *"What key points did you take away from my book, Bobby Jo?"* Their voices were otherworldly, echoing as if from the pages of their stories.

Somehow, the authors knew Bobby had studied and analyzed every word, placing their names on sticky notes with key points scattered across her whiteboard. Bobby's mind raced as she tried to recall all the insights and lessons she had gained from each book. She could feel the weight of their expectations and their admiration, making her heart beat faster with excitement.

She smiled, her heart swelling with gratitude as she approached them. Each author held their book close, almost protectively. Their eyes lit up as she neared as if they recognized her.

"You've come so far," one of the authors said, their voice like a melody drifting through the air. Bobby nodded, a lump forming in her throat.

"I couldn't have done it without you," she whispered, her voice trembling with emotion. *"Your words... they carried me when I didn't know how to keep going."*

Another author stepped forward, their eyes twinkling with wisdom. *"And yet, it was you, Bobby, who chose to read them. You who decided to act. The strength was always within you."*

She smiled, feeling a deep sense of gratitude for their work. These were the conversations she had longed for during her long nights developing her board game. The conversations that had lived in her mind now felt so real, so tangible. She was surrounded by those who had guided her, even though they didn't know it.

As she continued to speak with them, she remembered their names. The authors' faces lit up with recognition and appreciation. They smiled and nodded in agreement with her feedback, and Bobby couldn't help but feel a sense of pride and accomplishment. In this dream world, her love for books had made her an equal among these literary giants.

Each author she spoke to congratulated her on completing the personal development game.

"But I haven't completed my game yet," Bobby said aloud. But it made no difference to the authors.

One author called out to her, *"Remember... act in your mind as if your goal is already done."*

After countless conversations with different authors, they handed her their personalized, autographed books. Bobby now carried a large stack of books balanced between her arms, yet she felt no weight at all.

She captured the hearts of those she met, her contagious zest for life and stunning appearance impossible to resist.

As she continued through the ballroom, the conversations flowed. Each author offered a nugget of wisdom or a reflection on their work, and each time, Bobby responded with gratitude and insight of her own. She felt light and free, as though she were floating in a sea of understanding and resonance. The weight of her struggles seemed to lift with every exchange, her heart growing lighter with each step.

A captivating aroma of fresh flowers, warm tea, and freshly poured champagne lingered in the air, adding to the elegant atmosphere.

Suddenly, she remembered what she longed to experience most at this event, finding Christopher Lane, her favorite author. He was widely regarded as the greatest personal development author in history.

Little did she know she was about to discover so much more.

"Excuse me," she asked one of the authors, *"Have you seen Christopher Lane?"*

The response from the group was unanimous, no one had seen him. Another author chimed in, claiming he didn't even know who Christopher was.

Frustrated, Bobby courteously replied, *"Oh really? You don't know him? He's the pioneer of success principles teachings; nothing has surpassed his work."* Bobby then puts her hand on her mouth, realizing it may offend the others to say Christopher Lane was and always will be the best of the best.

Voices continued to buzz around her as she searched for any sign of Christopher's presence.

As she moved through the ballroom, her eyes kept searching. His words had been the cornerstone of her journey, the anchor that had kept her grounded when the world seemed to crumble around her. She needed to find him to thank him.

There was a person who caught Bobby's attention. Every time she tried to move toward the edge of the ballroom, where this figure in a stunning, glowing long white cloak lingered, someone would pull her back into conversation, and the glowing figure's presence would escape her.

"Where's Christopher Lane?"

As Bobby interacted with the authors at the event, she mostly offered positive feedback and expressed her gratitude. However, one author, Johnathon Bethol, approached her with the same question the others had asked.

"What key points did you get out of my book, Bobby Jo?" he asked eagerly.

"Oh, you," Bobby replied dismissively. *"I got 'nothing' out of your book."*

Taken aback, Johnathon pressed for more information.

"What do you mean... nothing?" he inquired.

"Well," Bobby continued, *"As soon as I found out that you didn't practice the principles you teach, it put me off. Integrity is everything to me."*

A look of disappointment crossed Johnathon's face.

"So, it wasn't helpful at all?" he asked.

Bobby, almost offhandedly, shared, *"Actually... Yeah, come to think of it... your book 'was' useful."*

Johnathon's face lit up momentarily with an eager smile again. But Bobby quickly added, *"I used it to stoke the fire last winter."*

As she turned to walk away, she couldn't resist one final jab.

"Hypocrite much?" she said.

His smile quickly disappeared, but he kept tugging at her arm, clearly annoyed. Bobby opened her hand and made a circular motion as if casting a spell.

"You're as small as a pea!" she quipped.

To everyone's amazement, Johnathon Bethol shrank to the size of a pea at Bobby's feet.

Bobby continued to scan the room for Christopher Lane. As she searched the crowd, her eyes again landed on the mysterious figure in the glowing white cloak to the left side of the room, almost hidden from view. His face was shrouded in shadows, making it difficult for Bobby to get a good look at him. But every time she tried to make her way over to him, someone interrupted her.

Suddenly, a loud, shrill voice broke through the chatter. It was none other than Dorothy Blake from Sunflower Springs, known for her gossiping, rude, and judgmental nature. *"Well, I fancy seeing you here! Don't you have horse Sh*t to clean?"*

In real life, Bobby had a strong filter, but in this dream, she let it rip. Without missing a beat, she retorted,

"And don't you have people's reputations to destroy? This is the Hall of Wisdom, not the Hall of Stupidity."

She couldn't believe she was being so blunt with Dorothy. Bobby lightly placed her hand over her mouth again, wondering what had come over her.

Dorothy shot Bobby a dirty look of disapproval before turning her attention back to the group of authors. Dorothy flaunted her gown and pretended to understand what they were talking about.

But Dorothy wasn't done. She turned to Bobby again and asked, scornful and disdainful.

"What is all this, anyway, Bobby Jo?"

She pointed at the group of authors and continued, her voice dripping with contempt,

Dorothy added, *"Don't you have anything better to do than brainwash your head with all this... this... rubbish?"*

"Dorothy, I use pure, positive, wholesome soap to wash my brain. What negative, selfish, toxic soap do you use?" Bobby said sarcastically, once again lightly covering her mouth in disbelief at her own confrontational words.

Dorothy had no more words left to say. Her silly smirk vanished from her harsh face.

To Bobby's astonishment, Dorothy began storming toward her, preparing to throw a right hook. But just in time, Bobby made her signature hand motion in front of Dorothy's harsh face and declared, *"You're as small as a pea!"*

Instantly, Dorothy Blake shrank down to the size of a pea, joining Johnathon Bethol by Bobby's feet. The two now screamed in tiny voices, running around wherever Bobby went, begging her to restore their normal size.

Bobby refused to give them any more of her attention. She had wasted enough time on distractions and interruptions, there were still important authors she wanted to meet.

Her gaze returned to the mysterious figure in the glowing white cloak at the back of the crowded room. She felt an undeniable pull toward him and was determined to uncover his identity.

But then, her heart skipped a beat as she noticed a dark figure lurking in the shadows, opposite the one in the white cloak. This figure exuded an aura of malice, sending shivers down her spine.

Bobby tried to ignore the dark presence, but its oppressive energy became suffocating. She couldn't take it anymore. Fueled by frustration but always fearless, she raised her voice and demanded, *"What do you bloody want?"*

The entire room fell silent. All eyes turned toward her as the figure stepped closer, its hostile face sneering at her.

"Bobby," the figure taunted sarcastically, he added *"Inventing a game to help humanity? Don't make me laugh."*

He let out a huge, wicked laugh, the sound echoing in the hushed ballroom.

"Humans are lazy, selfish beings who only care about themselves," he continued. *"They don't even control their thoughts and are full of disgusting bad habits! They haven't even learned how to get along with each other yet, and I love it that way."*

His laughter grew louder and more sinister, but Bobby stood her ground, her eyes blazing with defiance.

"Keyword... YET!" Bobby exclaimed with enthusiasm. *"Humanity doesn't know how to improve... YET!"* she added

She refused to back down. With fierce determination, Bobby raised her hand in front of him, conjuring her inner power.

"You're as small as a pea!" she declared with unwavering confidence.

The dark shadow of a man instantly shrank down to the size of a pea, joining the other screaming figures at her feet.

Bobby stood tall and victorious, a beacon of courage and resilience against the forces of negativity that sought to destroy her dreams and beliefs in a better world.

The room erupted into thunderous cheers. The authors and other guests celebrated Bobby's triumph over the malicious figure, their applause and shouts of admiration loudly echoing through the grand ballroom. Bobby felt a surge of pride and hope, knowing she had stood strong and defended her vision for humanity's potential to grow, evolve, and thrive.

She raised her champagne glass high and yelled out, *"Here's to ever-evolving improvement to the beauty of … HUMANITY!"*

The entire room joined her, lifting their glasses in unison and cheering loudly, their voices echoing with celebration. They all replied at the top of their voices.

"To the beauty of humanity!"

At that moment, Bobby finally saw him, Christopher Lane. Her voice rang through the room as she called out his name. Standing before her was a youthful version of Christopher Lane, seated at a desk and signing books for his many readers. His warm smile radiated love and gratitude.

"Bobby Jo!" he said, his voice filled with admiration. *"It's an honour to finally meet you, sir,"* Bobby says in awe of his presence.

Christopher Lane replied in a thankful tone *"Thank you for putting my life's work to good use."*

Her eyes sparkled with admiration, though a tinge of self-doubt flickered in her heart. Bobby replied *"But I haven't helped anyone yet, sir,"* she admitted softly. *"But you can bank on it, I will, I will complete the game therefore your life's work will stay alive sir."*

Bobby opened the board game, only to find it completely empty. Her smile faded, and the game disappeared from her hands.

"Don't trouble your mind, my dear Bobby Jo," Christopher reassured her. *"Allow divine timing to take its place. You're taking the necessary action steps every day. Your highest vibration is where the magic happens. Ideas will flow in abundance, and spirit will work to you and through you."*

He leaned closer, his tone warm and encouraging. *"Success can come in many forms. You are already successful by immersing yourself in what and who you love, a concept you're quite familiar with from my books."*

Bobby nodded, her smile returning. *"So true. Thank you for reminding me, sir."*

Christopher's eyes softened.

Christopher Lane touched Bobby's arm and said *"Above all else, I congratulate you and I want you to congratulate yourself for transforming your own life and being your higher self-first. That, my dear, is success."*

Bobby's voice trembled with emotion as she replied, *"Thank you ever so much, Mr. Lane. And another thing, sir…"*

Before she could finish her sentence, she felt a sudden tug on her leg. Exasperated, she sighed, *"What now?"* Turning to look, she froze in disbelief.

It was none other than Hillery, the mischievous sheep, staring up at her with big, innocent eyes.

"Hillery!" Bobby whispered urgently. *"What the frig are you doing here?! You're a sheep, you don't need to know anything but how to get to the next blade of grass! Go away before someone sees you!"*

But Hillery remained glued to the spot, her gaze fixed on Bobby.

Panic set in as Bobby scanned the room for witnesses. Desperation creeping into her voice, Bobby pulled a pair of electric shearing shears from her pocket and said. *"That's it Hillery… If you don't leave now, I'll shear you right here, right now!"*

The sight of the buzzing blades struck fear into Hillery, who let out a loud bleat, *"BARRRR!"* So terrified, the poor sheep accidentally relieved herself on the floor.

Bobby's face flushed with embarrassment as she glanced around, praying no one had noticed.

But her eyes fell on Dorothy Blake, Johnathon Bethol, and the evil man. At their tiny size, the *"mountain"* of sheep excrement loomed over them like a towering range. Looks of sheer horror covered their faces as the three of them stood completely drenched in the mess.

Bobby, smiling to herself, continued moving through the room, determined to meet more authors. Once again, her eyes caught sight of the mystery man standing apart from the crowd, cloaked in a glowing, long white garment. Curiosity burned within her. Excusing herself politely from the attendees, she resolved to reach him, no matter what it took.

As she weaved through the ballroom, the crowd began to thin, and the mysterious figure seemed to grow closer. The noise of the room faded into silence. Her heart raced as she approached him. *"Hello,"* she said urgently, her voice trembling slightly. Her pulse quickened as she added, *"Who are you? I feel like I know you."*

Now mere inches away, she gazed into his deep, intense blue eyes. His ethereal beauty seemed otherworldly, almost overwhelming. Bobby was stunned; her thoughts scrambled. She finally managed to blurt out, *"Wow... You are so... beautiful!"*

The man didn't respond. He simply held her gaze, his eyes piercing hers with an intensity that felt both comforting and unnerving. Bobby glanced behind her, realizing that the large, vibrant ballroom guests had vanished. Darkness surrounded her, except for the faint glow of a long, narrow red carpet stretching behind her like an endless escalator. It seemed to pull her back with an invisible force, leading to what looked like her bedroom door in the distance.

Panic gripped her as the mysterious man began to grow distant again, the force of the carpet dragging her away. She dug in her heels and ran against it, fighting the pull with all her strength. Finally, she reached him again, breathless but determined. *"Wait, wait! A moment!"* she yelled. *"You didn't tell me who you are!"*

The man turned to face her at last, his voice soft and loving as he spoke. *"Bobby Jo, my child... I am you... And you are me."*

Confusion and fascination washed over her. *"What does that mean?"* she asked, pleading for clarity.

The man remained silent, watching her with a serene expression. Suddenly, the pull of the red carpet intensified, and she was dragged backward at an even faster pace, her feet barely skimming the ground. Her bedroom door loomed closer and closer.

Desperation filled her voice as she called out, *"Can we talk again? Please!"*

The man's figure grew more distant, his glowing cloak blending into the darkness. His voice, gentle yet firm, echoed faintly: *"I'm always with you."*

The words were muffled, carried away by the distance, leaving her straining to hear. She called out again, *"Can we talk again?"* In one final glimpse, she saw him far away, nodding. He sat gracefully in a spectacular, king-like chair, his presence radiating calm assurance.

The dream began to dissolve. Bobby woke abruptly, gasping for air. Her room was silent except for the faint chirping of birds outside.

She sat upright in bed, her heart pounding as she tried to make sense of the vivid dream and the mysterious man's identity. Her eyes scanned the room, landing on the stacks of mindset books piled on her bedside table. As the first rays of the rising sun streamed through her window, the sunlight illuminated the whiteboard where she had spent months planning the game that consumed her thoughts.

Bobby's mind raced, replaying every detail of the dream. Though she didn't fully understand its meaning at the time, she felt an unshakable sense of purpose and clarity.

The rays of the sun intensified, bathing the room in golden light. The whiteboard seemed to glow even brighter, reflecting rays into her eyes and causing her to squint. It dawned on her gently, but with undeniable certainty, she had found it. The design of the game was finally coming together in her mind. Bobby was astounded by this revelation. It was at that moment that she remembered the author who had told her she had come far. They were right, Bobby just needed that reminder.

Christopher Lane's words came rushing back to her about the power of decision-making. He had written about the fact that one would never feel completely ready. The universe, he had said, would always provide exactly what was needed along the way, as long as you took action every day.

Feeling a surge of energy, Bobby slipped out of bed, stretched her arms wide, and took a deep breath. She inhaled the beauty and power of the incredible dream she had just experienced, feeling its incredible energy. She walked to the window, gazing out at the vast land beyond. In that moment, she reaffirmed to herself that her game was the key to reaching a wider audience, people who had the desire to create better lives.

The seed of an idea had now blossomed into a full-blown mission. Bobby was ready to take on the challenge, a calling she couldn't ignore, driven by her unrelenting desire to positively impact as many lives as possible. She saw it clearly: this game would bring all the golden nuggets of wisdom from the authors into one spot, giving players the tools they needed to transform their lives and flourish.

A sense of strength, unlike anything she had felt before, filled her. Even with all her discipline and hard work, she knew she had more to give. There was a quiet resolve settling deep within her bones. The journey was just beginning, and she was ready for whatever came next.

As Bobby thought back to the vivid dream, the mysterious man in the white cloak lingered in her mind. She couldn't quite make sense of who he was, but one thing was certain. She would always call upon him in times of joy and in times of darkness.

CHAPTER 7

HARVEST AND CHAOS

Narrated by Nonna Giovanna

The beginning of the harvest approached once again, and the sun beat down with relentless heat. It felt like the height of a typical hot summer in the Australian outback, even though it was technically spring. But the scorching temperatures didn't slow us down. We stayed busy every day, no matter the season.

Melina took great pride in keeping a meticulous household and cooking meals fit for royalty. Alonso and Bobby were up before sunrise each day, tackling the never-ending tasks around the farm. From maintaining the sheep to tending the wheat paddocks and repairing fences, there was always something that needed their attention.

My role on the farm was to maintain the vegetable patch, a skill my father had taught me when I was just six years old. He'd always said I'd thank him one day for teaching me this important skill, and he was right. Living in the middle of No-Man's Land had its challenges, but one thing we never had to worry about was a shortage of fresh fruits and vegetables. Our garden was essential to our well-being, especially since the nearest large grocery store was a grueling two-hour drive away.

Sunflower Springs, just a hop, skip, and a jump away, boasted a post office that was open for a grand total of two hours each day. There was also a mini-supermarket with questionable produce, a chemist who probably sold more hydrating powder than anything else, a café serving lukewarm coffee, a library, a police station, and let's not forget, a bakery that Zoe joked would make even the ants turn their noses up at its stale bread. Oh, and then there was the pub, which looked like it could crumble faster than a sandcastle at high tide. A true paradise for any adventurous soul looking for excitement... NOT. But despite everything, we love Sunflower Springs. It has its own unique rustic beauty, not to mention unique people.

Then there was Zoe's *"job."* As the youngest in the family, she seemed to think her primary role was beating her high score on Netflix. Maybe it was the result of always being overshadowed by her older siblings, or maybe she was just born with an aversion to effort. Either way, Alonso and Melina had given up trying to inspire her, and now poor Bobby was left to bear the bulk of the farm work.

But it could also be because Bobby was as speedy as a roadrunner, making Zoe seem even more sluggish by comparison. Still, I adore Zoe, her sense of humour always brightened the family, so maybe that was her true job.

The sun was setting on a Monday, just three days shy of the start of harvest. Alonso worked tirelessly, preparing for the long days ahead. He tended to the pigs we kept for salami, shoveling their waste out of the pen and refusing to let us girls do that dirty job.

"You all do more than enough already," he would always say with a smile whenever we offered to help.

Zoe, feeling guilty for not doing her part, avoided his gaze and continued with her own tasks. I couldn't help but feel relieved that she had a conscience after all.

Bobby, on the other hand, was a strict and disciplined soul. Her routine never wavered, regardless of the weather or the approaching harvest. She rose before the sun to fuel her body with a healthy breakfast, then dove into the cool depths of the farm dam for a thirty-minute swim.

Afterwards, she retreated to her *"thinking tree,"* a massive weeping willow on the edge of the shearing shed, about 50 meters from the house. There, she sat in silent meditation for twenty minutes a day. Once her mind was clear and focused, she joined her father on the farm, working tirelessly until the last rays of sunlight disappeared behind the horizon. She was like clockwork, never complaining, and her happy nature was always contagious.

For Bobby, dinner was a simple affair, followed by hours spent poring over books on personal development, health, and business. Bobby was determined to better herself in any way possible. Often, I would catch glimpses of her late into the night, hunched over her book, exhaustion tugging at her eyelids. Meanwhile, her younger sister Zoe lounged on the couch, absorbed in mindless TV shows. But for Bobby, every moment counted toward her pursuit of self-improvement, and the growth she experienced was exciting to her.

This time of year was always chaotic, wheat harvest and sheep shearing happening only three weeks apart, and some years, even simultaneously. Alonso had managed to put together a reliable team of ten workers who had been with us for years. However, this year, he was short two workers.

Lenny and Joseph were immigrants from Europe. Alonso had employed them, understanding how hard it had been for his father to start over in a foreign country, and he wished them success.

Last year, an incident in the wool shed led to Lenny and Joseph being sacked on the spot. Bobby, unsurprisingly skilled at shearing sheep, worked there every day during the shearing season, while Zoe delivered sandwiches and cold drinks. I suspected that Zoe only did it to check out the young men working.

These two particular workers had whispered inappropriate comments about Bobby's slim, feminine figure in denim work shorts and how her body was perfect. Lenny and Joseph jokingly said to each other that they wished they could shear the clothes off her back. They probably thought Alonso wouldn't notice amidst all the chaos and fast-paced work. But my son surprised them all, as he watched their every move. He ordered them outside, erupted in a fit of rage, releasing his inner Hulk, and took both men down effortlessly before ordering them to leave without another word.

My son has always been very protective of his family, a quality I admire, one that truly reflects his father. Alonso threw some cash at their feet to pay what he owed them.

"Here's what I owe you... now piss off... NOW!!" he muttered, sprinkling in a few Italian profanities as he stormed off. The remaining workers pretended not to be alarmed by the altercation. As Alonso walked back into the shed, he wiped the blood off his knuckles with his shirt.

Bobby, completely oblivious to what had happened, asked her father what was going on. Alonso was known as a great boss, treating everyone like family. Every week, he would buy a slab (carton) of cold beer for the team as a treat, especially welcome in our hot climate. But that day was Lenny and Joseph's last on the property. Their belongings had already been angrily thrown into the back of Lenny's ute (pickup truck) by Alonso. The lively atmosphere of the day had shifted to one of quiet tension.

I remember Zoe watching Lenny and Joseph drive off. She walked past her father and asked, *"Oh, Dad, be honest... they were checking me out, weren't they?"*

Alonso and I exchanged a smile but didn't reply. I thought to myself, *Oh, my poor adorable Zoe, little did she know... she wasn't the one under the spotlight.*

Back to where I was again, harvest time.

"Not long now, Dad!" Bobby said with her usual excitement as she helped her dad fix the harvester.

Our border collie dogs, Mozza and Rella, were named after mozzarella cheese because, when they were pups, they pinched a pizza from the table outside and ate only the mozzarella. These beautiful full-breed dogs followed us everywhere. Zoe, with her trademark humour, had given them those unique names. Bobby and Zoe lavished love and attention on the dogs and all the animals constantly. There were only good vibes on our farm, and it showed.

Alonso was frustrated with the harvester; it wasn't starting, and with the harvest just three days away, time was running out. Bobby pulled apart from the engine, replaced it with one from the toolbox, and said, *"Get up there, Dad, and hit the start button."*

Her dad climbed up onto the massive machine and started it, and the harvester struggled at first, but then roared to life.

*"What the f*ck?!"* Alonso yelled out, slamming the tractor door in frustration. *"I've been here all bloody morning, and you do it in seconds! I'm definitely getting too old for this!"*

"Dad, how many times have I told you to wear your glasses?" Bobby said with a grin, holding up the broken wire. *"You would have never seen this one-millimeter wire was broken. You wouldn't have started this beast in a million years."*

She gave her dad a playful pat and added, *"Love you, Dad. Come on, it's lunchtime!"* And off she went. Her father looked at her, still stunned.

Lunch at the table was my favorite time of day, so many memories, so many celebrations and laughter. I hold those memories close to my heart, and I am so grateful that Melina treats me like her own mother; she is truly the salt-of-the-earth kind of woman. The kitchen wasn't very big, but it was tastefully cozy, welcoming, and well-used.

I remember vividly, it was 12:15 p.m. on a Tuesday. Zoe came storming in from grooming her favorite dog, Rella, outside.

"Hey, everyone! Have you heard what's on TV? A possible cyclone in Cattle Park Station on Thursday, only 200 km from here!"

"Don't tell your father; that's all he needs to hear to dampen things before harvest," I whispered to Zoe.

Then I added, *"Well, by the looks of it, old Mr. Davies won't be milking those cows this week at Cattle Park Station."* As we watched the weather map on TV, Zoe replied, *"Yeah, Nonna, the cyclone will create a huge milkshake!!"* She laughed, and I smiled. *"Oh, Zoe"!* But my smile quickly turned into a worried frown. *"We can't afford not to get this crop in this year."*

As always, Zoe brushed things off with a laugh.

Alonso came in for lunch. *"What's for lunch, babe?"* he asked with his usual excitement, always kissing Melina on the lips on his way in, without fail. It was rare for them to quarrel, and when they did, it never lasted long.

Melina called out, "Your boots, Bobby Jo, you know better!"

"I'm sorry, Mum, but I'm annoyed right now!" Bobby replied.

"No excuses, darling. Take those filthy boots off." Melina added.

Melina always insisted on no shoes in the house, they were to be neatly placed outside on a high rack so snakes couldn't hide in them. No one argued because we all knew that if Melina was worried about something, there was a high chance her strong intuition was at work. She also had a strict "no animals in the house" policy, a point-blank, non-negotiable rule.

I asked Bobby, *"What are you annoyed about, Bella?"*

Bobby sighed and answered. *"Well, of all times, our tractor tire is dead flat. Either I accidentally drove over a nail or the tire tube perished with age. Anyway, it's not fixable, but it's replaceable."*

"I made some phone calls, and Glentvale is the only town within a six-hour drive that stocks a matching tire. If we have it delivered, it won't arrive for two weeks because the couriers go all the way to Sydney first. So, I'll have to take a trip to Glentvale tomorrow to pick

it up. What's worse is it's the large back tire that went flat. I'll struggle to fit it in the back of my ute, but I'm sure I'll figure it out."

During lunch at the kitchen table, Melina reminded Bobby, *"Before you leave, check in on Steevo tomorrow to see if he needs anything in town."*

Alonso chimed in, *"You're not his daughter, Bobby; he can make his own arrangements to pick up his own bloody stuff."*

"Oh, stop it, Alonso. You sound like an infant," Melina replied. *"He's your best friend. He said sorry, and it's about time you let go of all that unnecessary anger knotted up in your stomach."*

Without a word, Alonso retreated to the fields, not touching his lunch and slamming the door on his way out. He mounted the tractor and headed through the gate, leaving the girls shaking their heads.

"Don't worry, Mum. Let him sulk and have his hunger strike," Bobby said. I then said *"Where's he going to go anyway? Where else?"* They chuckled as he disappeared in the direction of the patch.

Melina then asked Bobby, *"Darling, did you make that appointment for your father?"*

"Sure did, Mum." Bobby replied happily before heading back out to work.

Later that day...

"Is dinner ready, Mum? I'm going to shower and get an early night. I've got a big day tomorrow, and I want to read before bed."

"You be careful on the roads tomorrow, Bobby. I'll pack your lunch for you," Melina called out.

"It's okay, I'm having lunch with Sabrina and the girls," Bobby responded, excited at the thought of seeing her friends.

Bobby's room was her own space, and everyone respected that fact. Well, almost everyone. Zoe would occasionally let herself in without knocking, only to be met with a heavy cushion to her face, which Bobby always kept ready for just those moments.

"Get out! You know you're not allowed in my room. I don't want your negative energy in here!" Bobby would snap.

"Get stuffed, (get lost) Bobby!" Zoe would yell back.

Bobby didn't bother replying.

Alonso, Melina, and I would sometimes sit at the end of Bobby's bed, admiring her library of books, knowing she'd read each one cover to cover. Carlo used to sit by her bedside often, sharing his dreams of leaving the land before he mustered the courage to talk to his father about it. Many tears were shed between them in that special space. Carlo would never cry in front of anyone, except Bobby.

Now, it's time I shared the story of the Steevo and Alonso issue. They can't seem to work it out themselves, and to be honest, it's a series of misunderstandings that have grown into mistrust.

After Steevo's 3 daughters all left the farm for a more exciting life in Melbourne, his wife Maggie departed soon after their youngest daughter, Lucy, left. Maggie set a path that no longer included life on the land. It's been six years now, and she visits Steevo with the grandkids maybe a couple of times a year. I see her pale blue BMW parked outside for the night, and then it's gone the next day. They never divorced, and I believe they still love each other in some way, or at least he does. She came from Melbourne, always beautifully dressed, with a background in fashion. She gave it all up to live on the farm with Steevo decades ago, but as she neared fifty-five, she felt that life was passing her by, and she returned to the city for some long-desired excitement.

Steevo never spoke ill of Maggie, even after she left, and in fact, he sold a large portion of his property, along with the spring water rights attached to it, to ensure she was well provided for. This is where the problems began.

There's a large natural spring, hence the town's name, *Sunflower Springs*. Those springs have saved both our properties in times of drought, making it possible for us to keep sheep. Steevo's and Alonso's properties share a boundary to the west, and somehow, that spring has never run dry in the forty-plus years we've been here. We call it our little miracle spring.

When Steevo and Maggie sold a section of their farm, the new owners from Sydney could, in theory, prevent us from accessing that water. We don't know them well, but we've seen surveyors out there, pointing and looking our way, which has made everyone nervous. The next thing we heard was that they'd subdivided the property into two and placed a ridiculously high price on it. It stayed on the market for years.

Alonso was furious. Steevo's decision to subdivide and sell that piece of land five years ago had pretty much ruined our chances of accessing the water. Alonso was disappointed that Steevo hadn't offered him the first option to buy or at least warned him about it, not realizing that Steevo had received an offer from the Sydney buyers that he couldn't afford to refuse. Carlo, being a lawyer, was asked to come out and take a look, and he was pessimistic about the chances of the future owner allowing us to access the spring water.

We would look at that *For Sale* sign almost every day, praying either that it wouldn't sell or that we would find a new buyer who would still allow us to use the water.

Carlo said a legal caveat should have been drawn up when Steevo owned that piece of land, Carlo blaming himself for not suggesting it years ago.

As you'd expect, Alonso piled pressure on Carlo to find a solution, unintentionally making him feel as if he was letting us down.

"The law is the law, Dad. I don't make the rules. I just work within them. I'm so sorry," Carlo explained. *"You're lucky, Dad, that the existing owners are still letting the water into the dam for you to use."* he added.

All of this was happening around the same time that Alonso and Melina purchased the other property nearby, unaware that the property with the spring water rights was about to be sold, possibly affecting their access to the water.

Alonso was hurt that Steevo hadn't given him the chance to buy the land, especially since Steevo had allowed him to access the water while he owned it and should have understood the implications of selling it. The uncertainty about our future access to the spring water hung over our heads for years, and in the meantime, Alonso and Steevo's relationship began to sour.

It even got to the point where Alonso put up a fence, seemingly for no reason, that stopped Steevo from driving to and from the local pub without taking the long way around. It became quite a sight, seeing Steevo's huge wheat harvester parked at the side of the pub in Sunflower Springs. Probably for the best, though, as after Maggie left him, he spent more time there than he should have. No amount of reasoning with Alonso would convince him to take down the fence or put in a gate.

I remember Melina saying to me, *"I don't know why Alonso was so upset about not getting first choice on Steevo's farm. We just bought our second property and were completely cashed out. What the hell were we supposed to offer Steevo? Blinky Bill's gum nuts?"* (*Blinky Bill* is a kids' animation show where a koala uses gum nuts to pay for things.)

A pink sky in the distance hinted at the possibility of rain. Bobby was preparing for her long trip to Glentvale the next day, with a grueling 650-kilometer journey ahead, most of which would be on dirt roads. Alonso had already fueled up Bobby's ute, checked the oil, and secured a can of water and a jerry can of extra fuel in the back.

Dinner was being placed on the kitchen table by Melina and me when Bobby called out from the lounge room, *"Mum, do you have that grocery list ready for me?"*

Melina handed Bobby a long list just as Alonso came back inside from his sulking. In a stern voice, Melina said, *"Bobby, do not, I repeat, do not, take the shortcut. You don't need to rush. You're leaving at dawn, and there's no mobile phone coverage on Fredrickson Road if you break down."*

"*Mum, I drive a top-of-the-range Toyota Hilux ute, not a bloody Beetle bomb,*" Bobby responded, rolling her eyes.

"*You know that out here... Sh*t can happen,*" Melina said, her tone higher than usual.

Zoe, in her sweetest tone, chimed in, "*Bobby, I need a new hair straightener, and not a cheap one, okay? I want a salon-grade one.*"

Bobby rolled her eyes. "*That's not coming out of our business account, Zoe!*"

Melina, now visibly annoyed, added, "*Zoe, I gave you a straightener just twelve months ago. How is it already stuffed (broken)?*"

Bobby sighed in annoyance. "*Far out, Zoe. Who the heck is going to see your hair out here? It's too damn hot to wear it down anyway.*"

Zoe pleaded with her, "*Come on, sis... pretty please with sugar on top?*" She flashed her best puppy-dog eyes to try and get Bobby to relent.

Bobby didn't respond, sensing Zoe's sweetness only surfaced when she wanted something.

Alonso re-entered the kitchen after briefly going into his office.

"*Listen, Zoe, darling,*" Alonso said, shutting his office door behind him. "*Just go to Sunflower Springs to get your hair straightener and see what they've got there.*"

Bobby and Zoe burst out laughing at the idea that Sunflower Springs would stock a hair straightener, especially since it barely had simple combs.

Over dinner, Alonso turned to Bobby. *"So, we need that new gearbox for the John Deere and the tractor tire, right?"* He paused and asked, *"What's it going to cost us?"*

Bobby replied, *"Not sure, Dad. I just ordered it and didn't ask because we had no choice."*

"Look, Dad, the urgent thing is the tractor tire, but it makes sense for me to also pick up a gearbox now since it's been playing up. I'm scared it'll break down in the middle of harvest. And at least if it's here, we can…" Bobby didn't get to finish before her father cut in.

"Did you get a quote first Bobby?"

"Um, no… Look, stop splitting hairs, it makes no difference getting a quote, Dad!"

"Bobby, how many times have I told you it's better to ask them? Sometimes they'll rip you off if you don't," Alonso stated, clearly annoyed.

"Okay, sorry, Dad. Yes, I should have asked for a quote. My mistake."

Bobby didn't agree with him, as the people she dealt with were always honest, but apologized to her father just the same.

The pressure of the upcoming harvest was already showing.

"It's fine. So, what time are you leaving tomorrow?" Alonso said and handed the business credit card over to Bobby.

Bobby looked at him. *"You don't need to give me that, Dad. You're coming too. I made a doctor's appointment for you."*

Alonso slightly raised his voice in annoyance. *"A doctor's appointment? What the hell for?!"*

"*Dad, you haven't had a check-up and blood test in five years, and at your age, that's not good. You're coming with me tomorrow, comprende?*"

Alonso, sounding even more frustrated, replied, "*What do you mean 'at my age'?!*"

Everything went quiet. The family knew Bobby's words were likely falling on deaf ears.

"*You know I'm too friggin' busy, Bobby. Maybe after harvest...ok!*" Alonso yelled from the other side of the house. "*And secondly, I don't need to go to the bloody doctor. I feel fine!*"

"*Dad, you only have one body; there's no spare on standby.*"

As Alonso made his way back to the kitchen, Bobby added, "*What you neglect, you may surely lose.*" Zoe rolled her eyes, thinking, "*Oh, another word of wisdom, what's new?*"

Melina, in her soft voice, added, "*She's right, Babe. Just go... please.*"

Alonso looked defeated, an expression they didn't often see on his face.

Its my Life - Bon Jovi

Go to www.ritamontalto.com/songs
to scan song above

Your paragraph text

High Way To Hell -ACDC

Go to www.ritamontalto.com/songs
to scan song above

Great southern Land - Ice House

Go to www.ritamontalto.com/songs
to scan song above

Play when Bobby leaves Steevo's
house to go to Glentvale

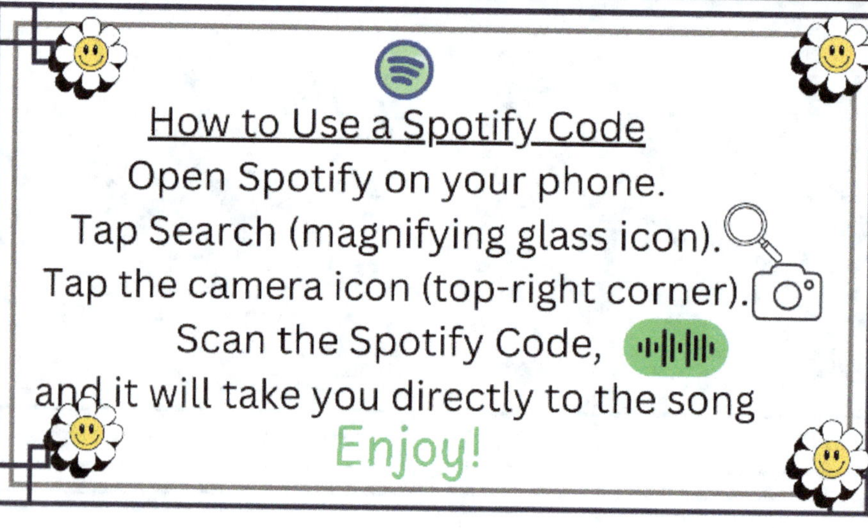
How to Use a Spotify Code
Open Spotify on your phone.
Tap Search (magnifying glass icon).
Tap the camera icon (top-right corner).
Scan the Spotify Code,
and it will take you directly to the song
Enjoy!

TRAVELLING AMONGST THE RED SOIL

NOT NARRATED

6 a.m. the next morning

Bobby stormed off in her ute, her frustration evident as she gripped the steering wheel tightly. Her dad wasn't coming to Glentvale with her to see the doctor, no matter how hard she tried.

"Stubborn old man!" she yelled, her voice ringing out in the quiet cabin. With a deep sigh, she glanced over and caught sight of her dad walking toward the tractor, waving at her smugly.

Alonso watched her drive away, then turned back toward the house, but stopped mid-step. In the distance, Bobby's ute was veering off toward Steevo's driveway.

"Stubborn girl !" he mumbled, an annoyed, almost betrayed look crossing his face. There she was, ignoring his warning not to involve Steevo. Sure enough, Bobby took the turn, kicking up a cloud of dust as she pulled into Steevo's place.

As she stepped out of the ute, Bobby took in the sad state of Steevo's verandah. Scattered shoes, rubbish, and dead flowers in pots, along with overgrown weeds in the garden, are all signs of neglect. Steevo himself looked as worn as the house, his thin frame hunched as he played with his grandkids. Their innocent laughter was a stark contrast to the decay around them.

"Steevo, how are you? Sorry I'm stopping by so early," Bobby greeted him warmly, trying not to let her gaze linger on the mess.

"Nonna asked me to give you these, and she and Mum told me to say hello."

Bobby put down a basket on Steevo's veranda full of fresh, healthy fruit and vegetables of all sorts that Nonno Giovanna picked for him, and a lasagna that Melina added.

Steevo's face lit up at the sight of her. *"No, no, that's okay, it's not too early! So glad to see you, love! Come in, let's have breakfast!"* he said, his tone hopeful. His little granddaughters were busy playing with a pretend shop, and when they saw Bobby, they shouted hello and waved enthusiastically.

"Sorry, Steevo, I can't stay. Just thought I'd stop by and see if you need anything in town today," Bobby said. She glanced over at Lucy, Steevo's daughter, who was sitting nearby. *"I see your daughter Lucy is here. That's great."*

"Are you heading to Sunflower Springs?" he asked, his tone hopeful.

"No," Bobby chuckled, glancing at the girls. *"Your granddaughter's pretend shop here has more stock than Sunflower Springs! I'm heading to Glentvale."*

Little Olivia, just two years old, piped up indignantly, *"This is not pretend!"* She crossed her arms, clearly annoyed.

Bobby laughed, crouching down to Olivia's level. *"I love your shop, baby girl."*

"I'm not a baby!" Olivia protested, crossing her arms defiantly again.

Bobby, smiling, turned around to Steevo, whispering, *"Oopps, I just can't win today,"* as Steevo smiled back.

Bobby smiled at Olivia. *"Oh, silly me! I mean, darling Olivia. You've got a shop now, you're all grown up. Wow."*

As Bobby turned back to Steevo, his expression dimmed.

"Your father hasn't spoken to me in five years now, Bobby… He said if I stepped foot on his property, he'd break every bone in my body… and that wouldn't be hard to do," Steevo said, his voice heavy with sadness, a faint smile on his lips.

There was a pause. The weight of his words sank in, and Bobby felt her heart tug. She hated the rift between the men, but loyalty to both men kept her silent.

"Look, I just wanted to see if you needed anything. Have you done any serious shopping recently?" she asked, sensing he hadn't, and that his daughter wasn't giving a damn about him.

"No," Steevo replied, shaking his head, his disappointment evident as he looked toward Lucy in the distance.

"Hang on, love, if you don't mind, I'll write you a list." Steevo turned toward the door to grab a pen and paper from the kitchen while Bobby waited.

"Make it quick, Steevo!" Bobby called after him, forcing a smile. *"I'm meeting friends for lunch!"* As she waited, she played with the kids, their innocent joy lifting her spirits.

When he returned, he handed her the list. Bobby scanned it, raised an eyebrow, and read out the list. Unsurprisingly, it was long.

"Soap, Milk, Tim Tams, bread, Vegemite, toothpaste... jocks? What?... jocks!!?"

"Yeah, they all had holes in them, love," Steevo admitted, scratching the back of his neck. *"If Maggie were still here, she'd have sewn them up, but I got cranky one day when my... um, well... you know ...my you know what... got stuck in the hole. I got the shits(cranky), so I threw them all out."*

"All of them?" Bobby glanced at his very short blue work shorts, fighting the urge to smile.

Steevo went to grab his favorite outdoor chair to sit down.

"No, no, don't sit down!" she blurted, quickly turning her head away, fearing she might see something she really didn't want to.

Settling into his fold-out magpie's footy chair (black and white popular football team) with a loud *"AHHHHH"* as he winced from joint pain, Steevo was oblivious to the fact that his... fatherhood... was protruding from his shorts.

Bobby left as fast as a slingshot, trying not to make it obvious why. *"Alright then, no worries, Steevo. Bye!"* She waved to the kids at the gate, who waved back with big smiles.

"What about a hug, Bobby?" Little Olivia called out.

Bobby felt awful for not going back to hug her, but justified her rush because she had a lunch meeting with her friends. *"Come over to my place one day, kids!"* she shouted, knowing it was unlikely under the circumstances.

"Oh, Granddad, can we?" Little Olivia asked her grandfather, her excitement shining through.

Steevo's face clouded briefly, and Bobby caught the hint of sadness there.

"Thanks, Bobby! You're a legend, you know that! And thank you for the basket of goodies. Please relay my thanks to your mum and Giovanna," Steevo called out, trying to hide his loneliness. *"Oh, hang on, hang on! Let me give you some money for the grocery list!"* He added frantically.

Bobby, now only meters from her ute, waved off the offer with a raised hand. *"No need, Steevo! I miss you!"* she called back, the words carrying more weight than she intended.

He replied softly to himself, *"I miss you all too."*

Steevo watched as she got in her ute, his voice trailing off. *"Come over again sometime soon, okay?"* he called out, the loneliness etched on his face. Bobby glanced back and gave him a thumbs-up, trying to ignore the pang of empathy in her chest.

Once back on the open outback road, Bobby cranked up the radio, hoping the music would make her trip feel shorter. She flipped through the stations until she landed on a weather report: Cyclone (Hurricane) warnings, tracking inland with torrential rain forecast for the next 7 days.

She shrugged, thinking cyclones never make it this far.

The news shifted to a police report about the notorious Robson brothers, a gang from Darwin in the far north. Normally, Bobby avoids the news because it's always negative, so she cringed and turned the station off. She just wanted loud music. Finally, she found the song "*It's My Life* by Bon Jovi, cranked it up as loud as she could, and sung it out at the top of her lungs. Loving every moment.

"Your gunner hears my voice.

When I shout it out loud...

It's my life...

It's now or never...

I ain't gonna live forever...

I just want to live while I'm alive...

It's my life ...

My heart is like an open highway!!"

She laughed, realizing she didn't see an open highway here, just endless, flat land as far as the eye could see, red soil and dirt roads stretching for miles. A deep sense of freedom and love for the untamed land washed over Bobby. She felt a surge of pride for this magnificent place, fully present in the moment, as if the land itself was alive, pulsing with energy.

Bobby's voice echoed across the barren expanse, the vastness making her feel both small and invincible at the same time. She kept singing, her voice strong against the quiet emptiness,

Singing out the lyrics out loud: *"Like Frankie said I did it my way!!!"*

As she drove on, *Great Southern Land* by Icehouse came on the radio. She got excited and yelled out … *"YES!!"* and cranked up the volume, letting the music carry her, feeling at one with the rugged terrain that stretched endlessly beneath the scorching sun.

At The Beginning of the song *'Great Southern Land'*, there is a distinct drumbeat. Bobby had one hand on the steering wheel and another hand making a beating drum motion in sync with the drumbeat of the song.

An hour into her trip, the radio was starting to get scratchy, so Bobby listened to music on Spotify on her phone instead.

Bobby was relieved to finally hit the sealed road.

Half an hour later, she noticed a car and a caravan pulled over on the side of the road, its hood up, and a family gathered around the engine, showing obvious signs of stress.

Pulling over, she muttered to herself, *"Helping caravanners… holy Sh*t, I'm turning into my father!"*

It was a Hispanic family stranded with car trouble, husband and wife, two kids, and an elderly woman. They looked inexperienced and frightened, isolated in the unforgiving heat with no phone service.

"Gidday, my name's Bobby, allow me to help," she called out, waving at the kids and nodding and saying hi to a concerned elderly man who'd also stopped to assist but didn't seem to know how he could help.

"Hola, my name, Rafael," the man said in broken English. *"Car no work, phone no work,"* he added, then gesturing toward the elderly woman, *"She no breathe."*

Bobby could see the concern in his wife's eyes, but Rafael's indifference made it clear that the elderly woman was his wife's mother. The elderly lady was struggling with an asthma attack, gasping for air.

Bobby quickly grabbed her first-aid kit, pulled out an inhaler, and handed it over. *"Here, use this and keep it, just in case. Don't worry, I have two."* She raised two fingers to show they could keep it. The elderly mother accepted the inhaler gratefully, breathing more easily, and Rafael kept repeating, *"Thank you, thank you, señorita,"* his voice full of deep appreciation for her help.

"No worries," Bobby replied. *"Now, can I take a look at the car engine?"* she offered, walking over to the open hood while trying to gauge their expressions.

"Si, por favor," Rafael responded, and Bobby smiled at the familiar phrase, amused by how similar it was to Italian.

"What happened when the car stopped? Any warning lights?" Bobby asked, peering at the engine for clues.

Rafael's wife shook her head apologetically. *"My name is Edelmira... Sorry, no good speak English... car bang and stop!"*

"Oh... so the car made a noise before stopping? BANG!" Bobby asked, repeating her understanding to make sure Edelmira was clear.

"Si, señorita," Edelmira responded.

As Bobby worked under the hood, Rafael whispered to his wife in Spanish, *"No sirve de nada; ¿qué sabría ella?"* (*It's no use; what would she know?)*

Just then, Bobby asked them to try starting the engine, and to their surprise, it roared to life.

Rafael stared at her, eyes wide in amazement. His wife shot him a knowing smile, as if to say, See, a woman can do it!

"How... you do that?" Rafael asked, still in awe.

Bobby chuckled. *"I'm a farmer from the outback. We have to be our own vets, doctors, mechanics, carpenters, psychiatrists, you name it."* She paused; her tone more serious. And added, *"Only the tough survive out here."*

Rafael turned to his wife, whispering in Spanish, *"¡Qué chica tan buena!"* (*What a hot chick! ...and smart too).*

Bobby, understanding the compliment, smiled. *"Thank you, Rafael,"* she replied, her voice warm but amused. Rafael gave an awkward look, his face flushed with embarrassment.

"Thanks to my grandmother, I speak Italian, it's sort of similar to Spanish," Bobby continued. Rafael then realized he may have given himself away when he doubted her.

"Which town are you headed to?" Bobby asked.

"Hill Broken," he said, pointing to a spot on the map.

"Oh... Broken Hill?" Bobby replied, realizing the mix-up.

Rafael nodded sheepishly, realizing his mistake.

"Oh no! You missed the turn by about 120 kilometers," Bobby said, gesturing dramatically. *"You need to go back and reroute to a different road now!"* She pointed multiple times in the direction they needed to change.

The couple nodded, but their confused looks told Bobby they weren't fully grasping her instructions.

"How much fuel do you have?" Bobby asked, glancing at the fuel gauge. *"Sh*t... you won't make it to Broken Hill on a quarter tank. It's 47°C today, and it's dangerous to be stranded out here."*

The family exchanged alarmed glances, seeing the concern on Bobby's face.

"Here, let me top you up," Bobby said, grabbing her diesel jerry can from the back of her ute. She poured every last drop of the fuel into their tank. *"This should get you there,"* she added.

She looked at them with concern. *"Always carry extra fuel and water when travelling in the outback. This place can turn on you fast."*

Bobby's eyes softened as she continued, *"Please understand, even experienced people have died waiting for help out here. You need to be prepared for the future. Your life depends on it."*

Not sure how much they understood, Bobby pulled out her phone and translated the message for them. The look on their faces when they heard the audio translation spoke volumes.

"A la madre nos tocó suerte esta vez!" (*Holy Sh*t, we got lucky this time!*) Edelmira said to her husband.

Bobby marked the correct route on their map, showing where they'd gone wrong.

Rafael then held out some cash, clearly intending to pay her for the fuel and her trouble.

"No, no, it's okay," Bobby waved it off with a smile.

"Por favor," Rafael insisted, holding out the money again, his voice pleading.

Bobby didn't take the money. As she started walking back to her ute, she called out, *"Thanks, all good. Just follow me to the turnoff that will take you to Broken Hill. We have to go back about 50 kilometers to reroute, okay?"*

Just as Bobby was about to open the door of her ute, Rafael's elderly mother-in-law called out in Spanish, *"¡Espera!"* (*Wait!*)

The elderly lady opened their driver's side car door, leaned in, and unhooked a delicate ornament hanging low from the car's rearview mirror.

Rafael looked at his mother-in-law, a little irritated. *"¿Qué estás haciendo?"* (*What are you doing?*)

The elderly lady responded firmly, *"Esta muchacha nos acaba de salvar el trasero, así que cállate tonto"* (*This girl just saved our *ss, so shut up, fool.*)

She approached Bobby, looking her deeply in the eyes, and with a trembling hand, she offered the small gold trinket she had pulled off the rearview mirror.

"*Oh, you really don't have to,*" Bobby said, taken aback. "*It was no big deal. Todo está bien,*" she added, using the Hispanic phrase she had learned from their shearer, Joseph, wanting to reassure the family that she was helping out of goodwill, not for money.

Edelmira shook her head at Bobby, signaling disagreement. "*Please accept my mother's gift, Miss Bobby. She gives to you with her heart,*" she explained, touching her own heart.

Bobby, not wanting to offend, hesitated for a moment. "*Oh, the last thing I want her to think is that I'm being rude… well, okay then… thank you,*" she said as she accepted the trinket, not paying much attention to its intricate details.

As she held it, she felt the weight of it in her hand, recognizing its beauty and value. "*It's beautiful! What does it represent?*" Bobby asked with curiosity in her voice.

The elderly lady smiled warmly and responded in broken English, "*It's good luck and a message for you, you special girl. God look after you.*"

Edelmira added, "*Your intuition will tell you what it means.*"

Bobby paused, struck by the woman's words and the family's kindness. She felt a deep, quiet connection with them.

"*Thank you,*" Bobby said again, making eye contact with each family member, feeling profound gratitude for that moment in time. "*Muchas gracias,*" she added. They all laughed at her attempt to speak Spanish, and she laughed along with them.

"*It was a pleasure to meet you all,*" Bobby continued, her voice steady. "*Your car's running now, the tank's full, and I'll guide you to*

the right intersection, as you won't have any internet for a few
hours."

As she got into her ute, the elderly male bystander who had stopped
to help waved goodbye. Bobby asked him if all was okay with him,
too, expressing gratitude for his concern.

"Thank you, señorita," Rafael said again, his voice thick with
appreciation, realizing how close they'd come to disaster.

*"You're welcome. Enjoy your holiday, and please travel safely… Now,
follow me,"* Bobby replied.

Rafael stared at Bobby walking toward her ute in her denim shorts,
looking at her with lustful admiration, until his wife gave him a very
hard nudge on the head, breaking his gaze.

To be sure they wouldn't take the wrong turn again, Bobby escorted
them in the opposite direction for 50 kilometers to the turnoff they
needed to reroute to. With no internet, they couldn't use GPS. They
finally arrived at the correct turnoff, and Bobby watched as they
made the turn. All the family's arms stuck out of the windows,
waving goodbye and tooting the horn. Bobby waved back with a big
smile, watching them drive off, and whispered to herself, *"Sh*t…
lucky I stopped."*

The encounter delayed Bobby by almost two hours, as she had to
turn back 50 kilometers in the direction they were travelling.

Little did Bobby know, she'd soon be facing her dangerous
encounter in the outback.

Bobby quickly hung the trinket from the Spanish family on her
rearview mirror, just as they had hung it in their car. She drove off,

but after an hour, she realized she hadn't looked at the trinket properly. She glanced at it for a second but didn't want to take her eyes off the road.

Moments later, the sun glinted off the golden trinket, catching her attention and causing her to take another brief glance at it. Suddenly, she slammed on the brakes, bringing her ute to a screeching halt and kicking up a massive cloud of dust. At that moment, she knew it was more than just a simple decoration. She grabbed it, bringing it closer to her eyes. Lo and behold, it was a mini pavilion with four delicate golden pillars, a roof, and a small crystal dome.

Her hands shook as she held the trinket, feeling its weight and intricate design. *"The four pillars!"* she exclaimed. *"That's what I came up with for my game... oh my gosh, no way! The roof can represent your goals, and the dome on top can be your... your purpose! Oh, wow!"* she said aloud.

It was as if fate had placed this trinket in her hands, and Edelmira's words echoed in her mind, "Your intuition will tell you what it means."

A surge of determination and excitement coursed through Bobby as she thought about the possibilities, this divine message the trinket held. She said to herself, *"If this isn't a sign, then I don't know what is."* She gripped the trinket tightly, her mind already racing with ideas and plans.

"These will be my four pillars of wealth symbol for the game!" Bobby declared out loud with excitement as if she were a scientist who had just made a groundbreaking discovery. This was more than just a gift; Bobby was ready to embrace it with all her heart and soul.

Hoping to call her friends and explain that she'd be late, Bobby checked her phone, but there was no service. She glanced at her watch.

"Great, I'm very late. I have to cancel with the girls," she muttered to herself.

Bobby took a deep breath and set off down the endless road, the rugged, vast outback stretching out before her. The trinket swung gently from her mirror, and as she drove, she couldn't help but feel that this good luck charm wasn't only a sign for her game, it was also a reminder of the universal goodwill that could spring up, even between strangers in the middle of nowhere.

CHAPTER 9

UNBEARABLE HEAT IN AUSTRALIAN OUTBACK

NOT NARRATED

The Trip from Hell

Bobby came to a small wooden bridge that had long since fallen into disrepair, surrounded by witches' hats, a detour sign indicating a 60 km detour to the left, and a warning not to cross the stream in your car. She glanced at the shallow water trickling beneath the bridge, assessing it with a determined eye. The streambed was rocky, but the water didn't look too deep.

"They still haven't fixed this bloody bridge," she muttered to herself, her tone a mix of annoyance and resignation. *"What takes so damn long to fix a pissy little bridge?"*

With a resigned sigh, she navigated her ute through the shallow, rocky stream, weaving carefully between the larger stones, determined to avoid the long detour.

"I've been through worse than this, mate," she reassured herself with a smirk.

For Bobby, this was child's play. But little did she know, as the ute tire slipped over a large rock, it grazed another, causing the edge of her fuel tank to puncture. Unaware, she drove for almost an hour, humming along to the music when her fuel gauge began to drop alarmingly fast. She was still singing when she glanced down and noticed the fuel gauge was nearly empty.

*"What the f*ck!"* she exclaimed, her mind racing. She'd filled the tank up right before leaving, and a full tank always got her to Glentvale. Pulling over, she checked the fuel tank and spotted the leak.

*"Sh*t… Sh*t… what the hell?"* Bobby quickly wedged a stone into the hole and wrapped duct tape around it, but she knew she was in trouble. This was an isolated shortcut, rarely used, especially on a scorching day like this, with the temperature soaring close to 47 degrees Celsius. The air was thick with dry desert heat. And with the blocked bridge, there wouldn't be a soul around to help.

Reaching for her phone to call for help, she realized it had gone flat from playing music during the drive. She plugged it into her charger, cursing softly as she glanced nervously at the dwindling fuel gauge. Desperation crept in as she drove as far as the fuel would allow while charging up her phone. But soon, the engine coughed, sputtered, and died. She was now on Fredrickson Road, an eighty-five-kilometer stretch of dirt road, exactly where her mother had warned her to avoid, as there was no phone service in that area. As it turned out, her mobile phone battery hadn't charged. Normally, when there is no internet service, you can still call 000 (911) to get help, but she couldn't even do that.

Now, Bobby was stranded, no transport, no phone, and only one bottle of water. She had given all her spare water and fuel to the Spanish family, and the scorching heat was working against her, especially with no hat and so little water.

"Oh my god, what have I done?" she muttered in frustration. *"Why doesn't that damn cord charge faster? I shouldn't have played that music."* The phone briefly turned on, and she frantically dialed 000, only to have the phone completely die on her.

Bobby was now talking to herself, and it made her feel a little crazy.

"Well, Bobby, dumb decisions, hard consequences, girl... deal with it. You should have taken the bloody detour." She shook her head. *"Should've kept the phone charged. A phone is a safety tool, girl! You know that"*

Anyone else might have said to themselves, "You shouldn't have given away your fuel and water," but not Bobby.

Out of options, Bobby had no choice but to abandon the ute; she gathered what essentials she could carry: her water bottle, tucked into her Grandma Giovanna's old hessian potato sack, her wallet, phone, charger, a bandage from the first aid kit, and a map. She grabbed the keys, poured a bit of water over her head to keep cool, and set off on foot down the empty, dry road, the red soil stretching endlessly under the punishing sun.

The day was brutally hot, not a cloud in the sky, the kind of desert heat even Bobby, tough as she was, knew could turn dangerous with limited water. A shady tree to rest under became her one small wish, but none were in sight. Knowing direct sunlight on her head could lead to heatstroke quickly, she took off her T-shirt, which she had worn over a crop top, and put it on her head.

Bobby walked for a grueling two hours, with Nonna's potato sack tied around her neck on one side of her body, carrying the few items she had decided to bring. Her shoulders were now red and raw, burning like crazy, and she had to keep her T-shirt on her head to protect herself from the sun. She continued talking to herself, finding comfort in the sound of her own voice.

"At this pace, I'll be sleeping with the snakes tonight," she muttered. *"Just keep walking,"* the voice in her head told her, and she obeyed. I have to get that tractor tyre in time, she said to herself.

Still not a cloud in the sky. Finally, a small old house appeared in the distance, and she headed for it, hoping to find help. Her walk turned into a desperate jog, but when she reached the house, she found it completely abandoned.

Bobby paused, taking a brief rest in the shade of the little house. She kept asking herself, *"What's the next best thing to do?"* Then she spotted a rainwater tank and felt a surge of excitement. She only had about 5 cm of water left in her bottle. She rushed over to the tank, holding her empty bottle under the spout, but much to her disappointment, nothing came out.

Again, she asked herself, *"What's the next best thing to do? "Find something that will help me... anything"* she thought.

Though spooked by the deserted house, Bobby was a girl of great courage. She decided to walk toward the front door, hoping to find anything that might help her situation.

Bobby coughed a few times from inhaling the thick dust as she opened the front door of the tiny house. The layout was simple: one large room with no adjoining spaces.

It was clear the house had been abandoned for many years, the interior stripped of any furniture or cabinets, and webs and large spiders were lurking everywhere.

As Bobby stood in the doorway, something in the far corner of the room caught her eye. She cautiously made her way toward it, feeling uneasy as her feet sunk into the rotted floorboards. After pulling her foot free, she hesitated, unsure whether she should continue exploring, as she sensed a presence but quickly shook off the feeling. Her eyes told her, *"Don't be silly, there's no one here."*

Her strong sense of survival overcame her fear, and she pressed on toward the mysterious objects in the corner.

There, in the dusty corner, sat a very old wooden stool and a wide-brimmed hat, both covered in dust. Bobby felt a wave of relief and gratitude at finding something that would help her cope with the sun. Right next to the hat, leaning against the wall, was an old-fashioned wooden walking stick with a curved end. She gently picked it up, wondering who it had belonged to in the past.

The walking stick had a name engraved by hand into the wood. Bobby blew off the dust to read it aloud: *"Bruno S."*

"Thank you, Bruno S," Bobby said aloud, imagining him as an old man who had once lived there but had passed away. She quickly dusted off the hat and placed it on her head, feeling its weight. She decided to take the walking stick as well.

As she turned to leave, an eerie sensation washed over her, and she felt a presence again, even stronger now. Unbeknownst to Bobby, as she walked toward the door, there sat the friendly ghost of Bruno

Strarto, sitting on the stool, smiling and nodding at her as she walked away.

Outside the abandoned home, Bobby felt a sudden surge of energy. *"That was bizarre! Eww, I got shivers,"* she thought to herself. It felt as though the items had been waiting for her. She shivered again and shook her body as if to shake it off, but the shivers were strangely good, unlike anything she'd experienced before. She started walking back toward the dirt road she had come from.

"I have to get to Glentvale. Great spirit, please help!" she called out, feeling a little crazy but determined. *"Our crop needs to come off as soon as possible..."* The thought of letting her father down by not making it to Glentvale worried her more than her own immediate safety or well-being.

Meanwhile, back at the farm:

Alonso was washing his hands in the laundry when Melina called out to him. *"Has Bobby arrived in Glentvale yet? Did she call you?"*

Alonso wiped his hands on a towel and replied, *"I'm sure she's fine. Probably still chatting with friends before she goes to get the parts."*

Melina's concern deepened. *"I tried to call her this morning to add coffee pods to our grocery list, but I couldn't get through. Maybe she's still on Fredrickson Road and doesn't have the internet, oh no, hang on, I heard that road is closed."*

She paused before asking, *"Where did she say she's staying tonight?"*

"I can't remember, why, babe?" Alonso replied.

Melina frowned slightly but then reassured herself. *"I'll call her first thing tomorrow morning for the coffee pods. I'll also tell her to hurry home because of the weather."*

Alonso nodded, his face showing a hint of concern. *"Yeah, darling, sounds good. She'll be alright."*

Melina glanced out the window, her eyes narrowing as she noticed the thick clouds forming in the sky. A sense of unease settled over her. *Something's not right with Bobby,* she thought, her expression shifting momentarily with worry. But she quickly masked it, knowing that revealing her concern to Alonso would only alarm him. He knew how accurate her intuition was, and she didn't want to frighten him.

With practiced ease, she prepared a plate of fruit salad and handed Alonso freshly baked biscuits, all the while maintaining a smile on her face, though her mind was elsewhere.

Another four hours passed in Bobby's exhausting ordeal. Her vision blurred, her steps growing unsteady as she relied heavily on the walking stick, just like an old woman.

Then, through the haze of heat and fatigue, she saw a tree in the distance. The thought of shade made Bobby's heart leap.

"A tree! A tree, you beauty!" she shouted with joy. She hurried to it, collapsing beneath its shade once she reached it. The small gum tree offered little comfort, but it was enough to give her a brief respite. She leaned back against the trunk, pulled off a leaf, and inhaled its fresh scent. *Mmm, it smells so good.*

Her water bottle was nearly empty, with just two drops remaining.

A faint rustling drew her attention. She froze, her eyes scanning the knee-high dry grass. Something was moving, but the noise was strange, almost like an animal crying. *Maybe an injured animal,* she thought.

With her newfound sturdy stick, she carefully parted the grass, avoiding anything that could be dangerous. As she moved closer to the sound, she found the source: a baby joey, about the size of a human baby, its leg painfully tangled in a barbed wire fence. The infection had already begun to set in, and the poor creature whimpered.

"Oh, little fella, what happened to you?" Bobby whispered, her voice full of sympathy. *"Poor thing, you must've been here for days."*

She gently freed the joey from the wire, and it cried out in pain. Bobby quickly bandaged its leg with the bandage she had brought along for snake bites. *"I hope you're not too heavy, mate. You're coming with me."*

Just then, a rustling in the tall dry grass behind her caught her attention. She turned, her heart racing. Emerging from the dry grass was a large grey kangaroo, likely the joey's mother, drawn to her baby's distress.

*"Ohhh... Sh*t,"* Bobby whispered, keeping her voice low and calm. *"Good Mama, I'm just helping. It's okay."*

But before she could react, the mother kangaroo leaped forward, balancing on her tail to deliver a powerful kick with both of her legs. The force of the blow struck Bobby squarely in the face, sending her sprawling to the ground. Pain seared through her forehead as blood poured down, deep claw scratches marking her face.

Dazed, Bobby lay on the ground, feeling the little joey nuzzling her face. She quickly removed her T-shirt once again and tore it into pieces to create a bandage, wrapping it around her head to stop the bleeding. Her mind was reeling, the pain almost unbearable. Despite it, she gently lifted the joey, tucking it safely into her sack and draping it over her shoulder. She offered her last sip of water from her bottle to the joey. The joey quickly sipping it.

With only her crop top on again, Bobby's shoulders were still exposed to the harsh, unrelenting sun. She did her best to ignore the pain of her sunburn.

Talking to joey to distract herself from the discomfort, she muttered, *"Is your mother always this violent? Ugh... I thought my hangover from my 21st was bad, but this is next level, my little mate."* She chuckled weakly, looking down at the joey with a weary smile. *"You're heavy, little guy. You need a name. Let's see... How about... Fredrickson?"* She chuckled again, noticing the Fredrickson Road sign at an intersection. *"Yes, Fredrickson, it is."*

With Fredrickson in tow, she trudged on, occasionally talking to figures from the books she'd read. Philosophers seemed to keep her company, and her favorite, Christopher Lane, appeared beside her, offering words of wisdom. As the heat bore down, Bobby felt herself lightly drifting in and out of consciousness. The desert landscape stretched endlessly ahead, and she knew something was wrong, she was showing signs of heatstroke, and she was starting to feel ill, and her vision was blurring from walking in the heat all day.

It was now close to dusk, and things were about to get even scarier without light.

Just then, Bobby heard the faint rumble of an engine in the distance. Her heart leapt. *"Hear that, Fredrickson? We finally have help!"* she whispered, glancing down at baby joey's innocent face as if encouraging him to hang on.

But as the sound of the engine grew louder, she turned to see an old, beat-up ute approaching, driven by three wild, loud young men, hoons, by the looks of it. Her smile quickly faded, replaced by a deep unease.

Could this be the group of assholes I heard about on the radio? Surely not. Bobby thought, bracing herself for whatever was coming.

At that moment, the white-cloaked man appeared beside her, his presence calm amidst the chaos. He murmured, *"I detect fear is taking over, Bobby... Focus."*

"How..." she whispered to him in a panic.

The white-cloaked man's voice was steady. "Remain calm and outsmart them. It's out of character for you, Bobby, but it appears intimidating. Quick, they're coming fast."

Bobby quickly removed the T-shirt around her facial wound, causing it to bleed profusely, and with her hand, she smudged blood all over her face, making her almost unrecognizable and appear scary.

The ute rumbled to a halt just five meters in front of her, with Bobby not stopping her walk for one moment. Two of the hoon were perched at the back of the ute, holding onto the bar with beers in hand, turning to look at her with drunken curiosity.

"Eeww! Hey there, did your boyfriend bash you and dump you, sweetheart?" one of them sneered.

"Oh, we can give you another dose of that," another taunted.

Though frightened, Bobby kept her expression hard, showing no signs of intimidation. She could sense these men were dangerous, careless, and looking for any excuse to provoke. But above all, Bobby quickly realized they weren't very smart, and that would work in her favor; she just didn't know how yet.

Heatstroke and exhaustion dulled her senses, and the hoons' voices echoed around her, their taunts blending with the distorted shapes of the white-cloaked man beside her. Suddenly, she vomited from the heat. The hoons let out a heartless, disgusted reaction.

"Eeerrr, yuck! This bitch just had a chunder, mate!"

A surge of determination rose within her as if a burst of genius had struck. She took a deep breath and whispered, *"Great spirit, give me courage."*

The man in the white cloak repeated, *"Focus."*

Bobby never stopped walking, even as the hoon leader slowly drove ahead of her by several meters, trying to intimidate her by keeping a constant, creeping distance.

As she walked, the tail of a black snake hidden in the tall, dry grass caught her eye. She stopped, waiting for the hoons to look away. Then, she turned her hooked walking stick upside down, lifted the snake, and flung it onto the back of the ute tray where the two hoons were standing.

The two men screamed like children, stumbling off the back of the ute and onto the ground in pure terror. The driver, oblivious, stopped the vehicle, got out, and yelled, *"You bloody pansies! What's going on here!!!?"*

"She bloody threw a snake at us!" one of the hoons shrieked, scrambling further away from the ute.

The driver, a sinister-looking man with a redback spider tattoo near his mouth, stormed toward Bobby. His voice was full of menace.

"Hey, crazy bitch! Who are you? And what's in that sack?"

Bobby gave a crazed laugh, deepening the mystery. *"More snakes here, you want?"* she taunted, putting on an odd accent and shaking her grandmother's hessian bag where Fredrickson lay hidden. She pinched the joey gently to make him move, and as he wriggled, it looked like the bag was crawling with snakes.

The hoons backed away, their eyes wide with fear. Convinced that Bobby was mad and had a bag of deadly snakes, they retreated further and further from their ute.

Seizing the opportunity, Bobby leaped into the driver's seat of the ute. She whipped the wheel into a wild 360 donut, flinging the snake off the back tray, landing next to the hoons and sending them scattering in a cloud of red dust, the men choking as they ran away from the deadly black snake.

Bobby sped off, leaving the gang stranded. One of them tripped as the black snake pursued them. She glanced in the rearview mirror and saw the chaos she'd left behind.

"Thank you, Spirit," she whispered, her hands trembling as she gripped the wheel. She took a steadying breath, looking over at Fredrickson, who was curled up beside her. *"Are you okay, buddy?"*

His soft, innocent gaze melted her heart.

"My little mate, imagine what your mother would do to me if she knew I pinched you!" she chuckled, her mind easing as she floored the accelerator, speeding toward safety.

Finally, Bobby reached Glentvale. She parked near the police station and noticed several rifles tucked behind the seat, along with a chilling array of illegal weapons. She shook her head in disgust.

"Such black hearts," she murmured, just before stepping into the station. She needed to alert the authorities before they hurt someone else.

As Bobby entered the station, she collapsed, and they immediately called an ambulance. The paramedics treated her for dehydration and suggested she needed to go to the hospital for her facial abrasion.

Bobby said, *"It's ok, my wound can wait, there are 3 dangerous men out there that could hurt someone else at any time, let me finish here first."* The paramedics treated her dehydration and suggested to Bobby she needed to be on intravenous fluids right away, but Bobby said, *"I need to make my police statement first, it won't take long"*.

Inside the police station, Bobby recounted her ordeal as fast as she could to a concerned officer, who offered to escort her to the hospital as soon as they had the most important details. He took Fredrickson to another officer to ensure he'd be treated by a vet.

"You know it's illegal to domesticate native animals," the officer remarked gently.

"I know," Bobby replied. *"I'll set him free after I pay for the vet bill."*

As she sat with the Senior Sergeant to make a statement, his expression was a mix of concern and admiration. *"You're lucky you kept your wits about you, young lady,"* he said, introducing himself. Bobby noticed his name tag read Snr. Sgt. Jason Willis.

"We identified the ute you drove here as belonging to the Robson brothers," he continued. *"They're wanted for a list of charges as long as your arm, including murder. "We have personnel heading to where you left them on Fredrickson Road."* They assisted her in getting her phone charged and arranged for a towing company to pick up her ute and take it for a fuel tank repair.

Sergeant Jason Willis drove Bobby to the hospital. *"Thank you, Sargent Willis, you have been such a help, I appreciate it very much."* Bobby said.

A friendly, middle-aged nurse carefully analyzed the deep gash on Bobby's forehead.

"This is a nasty one! I'm afraid you'll be left with a scar, my dear. What happened?"

"Oh, a kangaroo attack," Bobby replied with a smile, not going into any detail. She didn't want her ordeal to become public knowledge.

"Oh, okay, animal wound. We need to avoid infection then," the nurse said, reaching for the disinfectant fluid.

"Our lovable kangaroos are feisty, huh?" the nurse added, her concentration deep as she worked on Bobby's wound.

"Yeah, especially when you try and take their joey," Bobby replied.

"Can't blame them. As a mother myself, I'd do the same... only I don't have a tail to balance on while I kick someone in the face with both legs," the nurse chuckled, continuing to place stitches on Bobby's face. Bobby replies, *"Yep, they're amazing animals, alright, I love them, they are true survivors."*

Just then, an ambulance burst into the hospital, nearly knocking Sergeant Willis over as he waited for Bobby. On the stretcher lay the head hoon, the one with the redback spider tattoo near his mouth, severely dehydrated and babbling incoherently.

Sergeant Willis recognized him immediately. *"Well, if it isn't David Robson, the alpha male of the trio,"* he muttered to himself.

He addressed the paramedics who were tending to David. *"This man is under arrest for murder."*

David Robson moaned, repeating like a broken record, *"A crazy lady... bag of snakes."* He sounded delirious. *"A crazy lady... bag of snakes..."* he repeated as if he couldn't shake the image from his mind.

Sergeant Willis raised an eyebrow in disgust. The paramedics gave him a subtle nod of approval to proceed. Willis read David his rights, cuffing him as he lay there, stunned and dumbfounded.

"Now," Sergeant Willis said sternly, *"You're going to tell me where your brothers are, or you'll be taking all the charges yourself."*

In the treatment room, the nurse sewing up Bobby's head wound looked at her in astonishment as she overheard the conversation in the next room. *"A crazy snake lady, huh? Sounds like karma's done its job."*

"Yeah, huh," Bobby replied, her mind replaying the intense events of the day, feeling relieved to be back in civilization.

Later that evening, Bobby retrieved Fredrickson from the vet. She held him close, smiling. *"Okay, Fredrickson, you're not well enough to be set free just yet. You need a week's worth of antibiotics. What a shame, huh?"* She winked sarcastically, glad to have the little guy with her for a while longer.

At her motel late that night, she stared out the window at the traffic, reflecting on the day.

I saved the joey, then the joey saved me... Was it all just a coincidence? A thought crossed her mind, lingering like a whisper: *Is there a reason for all this happening? Was I meant to meet them on that road? Did I save somebody else from getting murdered? Was it karma at work, just as that nurse said? Did it happen to prime me for something more traumatic in the future????*

These were all questions she asked herself, but there were no answers.

Yet, Bobby had a sneaking awareness that there was some kind of beautiful divine flow happening in her life.

To answer her pressing question, her favorite author, Christopher Lane, appeared. His familiar words echoed in her mind: *"Bobby... things happen exactly when they're supposed to happen. There are no accidents."*

She looked at her mentor and smiled. Whatever the reason, she knew she and Fredrickson made a good team.

The next day, after picking up the tractor tire and harvester gearbox, Bobby went to pay with the business credit card, but it bounced. Frowning in confusion and embarrassment, she used her personal account and muttered to herself, *"Dad's been asking me to cut costs a lot lately... something feels off."*

She quickly headed to their accountant's office to retrieve some financial statements.

Sitting in a nearby park, she pored over the financial statements, growing more and more pale as she realized the gravity of their situation.

"Bloody hell, we're hanging on by a one-ply thread!" she muttered under her breath.

Fuming, she dialed her father's number. *"When were you going to tell me, Dad?!"* she demanded, her voice quivering with anger.

"Tell you what?" he replied, caught off guard.

"Our business card bounced today, talk about friggin' embarrassing!" She paused. *"I went to the accountant. I know everything, Dad. And you even skimped on crop insurance? If this storm hits, our crop will be F#%#..."* A passing duck quacked, masking her profanity, and she turned around, muttering, *"Smart ducky."*

Her father's voice softened. *"I didn't want to worry you, Bobby. It's a heavy burden... why put it on you, too?"*

"We could've carried that weight together, Dad. I'm your business partner, not just your daughter!" Bobby's voice trembled with frustration.

Alonso's voice grew firm. *"You're my daughter first, Bobby. I didn't want you burdened with my mistakes."*

But Bobby was still fuming. She let him have it. *"B*lls*t, Dad! I'm not afraid of life's challenges; you know that. You never would've treated Carlo this way. You were always disappointed in me. You would have preferred to work with Carlo. It was him you preferred to work with, wasn't it? Tell me the truth, Dad?"* Her voice cracked, the words carrying years of bottled hurt.

"That's not true!" Alonso shouted back.

"It's bloody well is!" Bobby retorted. *"That's it, Dad!"*

"What do you mean that's it?" Alonso asked, but Bobby had already hung up.

As he sat there, staring at the phone, Melina approached Alonso. The phone was on speaker, and she had overheard everything. *"Babe... You remember what happened last time she said the words, 'That's it,' don't you?"*

"Oh yeah," Alonso muttered, a worried frown creasing his face. *"She said those words to Zoe, and then I helped her build that wall in her room. "I hope this doesn't mean she's going to build a wall between us,"* Alonso said sadly to Melina.

A storm from the distant cyclone was causing clouds to form over Glentvale, and Bobby knew she had to head home soon, but she still had errands to run. She needed to pick up a hair straightener for Zoe, groceries, and purchase Steevo's underwear.

At the salon, where she had been many times before, Bobby noticed the place was nearly empty except for three workers pretending to be busy and one client with foils in her hair waiting for it to process.

"Hi, Sally! How are you? I'll take that black straightener, please," Bobby said, pulling out her wallet.

"Oh, Gidday Bobby! Great to see you again! What happened to your face?!" Sally exclaimed, always happy to see Bobby and her positive vibes.

"Oh, this? It's nothing, just a farm accident." Bobby quickly changed the subject. *"So, how's business, Sally?"*

Sally, always the honest type, sighed and whispered, *"Not great, to be honest... Three other salons opened nearby recently, and I'm struggling to get more clients. At this rate, I'll be closing down and eating two-minute noodles."*

Bobby, ever the upbeat one, flashed her friend an encouraging smile. *"You know, there are a few things you could try to bring more customers in here."* She started sharing ideas about salon marketing and workflow, surprising Sally with her knowledge.

"How do you know so much about business, Bobby?" Sally asked, genuinely impressed.

"I study it every night," Bobby replied. *"I'll email you some info on software that could help with your email marketing, ad copy, and much more."*

Sally quickly jotted down her email address, grateful for Bobby's help. *"Thank you so much, Bobby! Stay safe, I've heard a cyclone is headed toward your town. Are you going to be okay?"*

Bobby's eyes widened. *"What? Really? Damn, I'd better go."* She rushed out, ignoring yet another call and text from her father, who had been trying to warn her about the approaching storm. He'd tried to tell her earlier, but she had hung up in anger.

As she left the salon, she spotted her four friends nearby, heading to the local club. Bobby tried to duck away, not wanting to answer fifty questions about the wound on her forehead, but they saw her.

Sabrina, her friend since kindergarten, gasped. *"Bobby! I got your text late last night. We missed you at lunch! Hang on...what happened to your face?"*

"Long story, guys. Farm accident," Bobby replied hastily. *"I have to go before the weather worsens. Bye, take care!"* She waved, relieved to have an excuse to leave, while her friends remained frozen in confusion.

Bobby could already imagine the incident spreading all over social media if her friends found out the truth. She wasn't one to seek attention or sympathy from anyone, and she certainly didn't want the thugs she'd left stranded to know anything about her. It was the smart thing to do.

CHAPTER 10

THE CYCLONE

NOT NARRATED

Meanwhile, back home, Alonso peered out the window, a worried expression on his face. *"She should be home by now,"* he muttered to Melina.

Melina tried to sound positive. *"She's fine. She had a list of things to do in Glentvale. She'll be here soon."* But deep down, her intuition told her otherwise.

The radio crackled, and the latest report made Alonso tense. The wild category 5 cyclone, the worst type, had changed course and was now heading straight for Sunflower Springs. His wheat crop was at risk, and so was his daughter. He kept glancing out the window, his eyes fixed on the driveway instead of his crop in the fields.

As Bobby got closer to home, the skies darkened more and more, and the radio signal began to fade. She caught fragments of the news: *"Cyclone… Sunflower Springs… tonight…"*

*"Sh*t, not again!"* she muttered, glancing at Fredrickson. *"Sorry, buddy. Looks like we're in deep Sh*t AGAIN."* She gritted her teeth, determined to get home.

"The Sunflower Springs pub is definitely not going to make it. Steevo better not be there." She shot Fredrickson a quick look, and he blinked back at her.

Sure enough, Steevo *was* at the pub, with the bar attendant, Barry O'Connor, urging him to leave.

*"Steevo, mate, you gotta go, the cyclone's headed straight for us. I don't know about you, but I'm shitting my pants, it's a category f*cking 5!"* Barry said, holding up five fingers in fear, and his big goofy eyes glaring at Steevo.

But Steevo was well and truly pissed (drunk) and didn't give a damn about the danger. His heavy intoxication barely kept him upright. He just shrugged and slurred, *"My Maggie gave me no warning, you know, mate."*

Barry groaned. *"Well, I'm warning you… Get out of here now, before I leave you too!"* His property was next door, and he figured he'd just drive his harvester home when he was ready. *"Hey, Barry, do you know if Bobby made it back from Glentvale yet, mate?"*

Barry shook his head and responded. *"I have no clue, mate, sorry. She only comes here in my fantasies."*

Steevo slumped his head down onto the bar, while Barry rolled his eyes in frustration.

Meanwhile, Alonso gathered his workers, who looked visibly nervous. Ben, the young Brit, asked in a shaky voice, *"Is this some kind of outback initiation?"*

Alonso chuckled, trying to keep things light. *"Just another day on the ranch! No, mate, this never happens out here. Now grab only the essentials and follow me to the house! The workers' quarters won't be strong enough to withstand a cyclone."*

The workers scrambled to grab their things, but ignored Alonso's *'essentials only'* advice. They each carried slabs of beer to Alonso's home.

The homestead was built with white rendered double-brick and steel, sturdy enough to withstand the storm.

"Essentials, not slabs of tinnies!" (cartons of Beer) Alonso yelled against the strong wind. *"For God's sake!"* Alonso yelled out

The worker begrudgingly returned the slab of beer back; however, snuck a Playboy magazine under his shirt, considering it an *'essential.'*

Melina watched as her family and their workers scrambled to gather inside, thinking to herself, *"This is all too surreal; we never get cyclones this far inland."*

Zoe's voice wavered as she said, *"I just heard on Facebook that Mr. Davies, the milk cattle farmer, died trying to protect his cows by herding them into the milk shed."*

Nonna Giovanna, without missing a beat, grabbed her chickens one by one and placed them in the bathroom. Melina stared at her in disbelief. *"Really, Giovanna!?"*

"Really," Giovanna replied with a defiant smile.

The scene inside was chaotic. Lorikeets fluttered in from the verandah, while Zoe ushered Bludger the cat inside along with the dogs, Mozza and Rella. To top it all off, Alonso even brought the four horses in.

Melina threw her hands up in mock surrender, but her eyes still held a quiet worry as she continually scanned the driveway. She turned to Alonso, saying, *"Thank you for listening to me about building with steel and double brick."*

Alonso pulled her close. *"Thank you for insisting."* They hugged, both relieved that their home was secure and silently praying for Bobby's safety.

Finally, Bobby's call came through. Alonso answered, frustration evident in his voice. *"Where the bloody hell are you, girl?"*

Bobby sighed. *"What do you care, Dad?"*

"This isn't the time to be angry, Bobby! The weather's angry enough for both of us! Where are you? It's getting dangerous out there. It's raining heavily, and your ute will get bogged for sure. I'm coming to get you."

"I'm almost home, Dad. Stay put. I'll be fine." She hung up, leaving the family to breathe a collective sigh of relief.

But Alonso wasn't taking any chances. The moment she hung up, he moved toward his tractor, with the loyal sheepdog Rella following him as if to offer him protection.

Alonso's plan was simple, he would meet Bobby to help if her ute got bogged if she found herself trapped. *"Get back inside, Rella!"* he shouted, but the loyal dog, eager to stay by his side, refused to listen.

As Alonso was outside, flying debris from the rooftop struck his leg, cutting it deeply. Melina, witnessing it from the window, screamed and rushed outside to tend to his wound.

Just as her father had predicted, Bobby's ute got bogged down in the thick mud, caused by the downpour of rain. The dirt road had turned into an impassable quagmire.

With the cyclone now in full force, Bobby decided it was safest to stay put in the ute. Stepping out would expose her to dangerous flying debris. A rock slammed into her windshield with a loud bang, causing Bobby to scream in shock. Helplessly, she watched as groceries flew out of the back of the ute, scattering everywhere.

Then, to her disbelief, she looked up. All twelve pairs of Steevo's underwear were soaring through the air, drifting like tiny parachutes. *"You've got to be kidding me... this is not looking good,"* Bobby muttered, trying her best to stay positive amidst the chaos.

Fredrickson huddled beside her, shivering but staying put as if trusting her completely. *"Hang in there, buddy!"* she shouted over the howling wind. The cyclone's fury was terrifying, leaving her helpless. *"Don't be scared, little mate. I'll get you out of this."*

At that moment, the cyclone lifted the ute high into the air, and the tractor tire Bobby had purchased in Glentvale flew off the back. The tire soared high before crashing back to earth, and the ute fell directly on top of it, cushioning the impact. Dazed, Bobby lay in the mangled cab, blood trickling from her reopened head wound before she passed out.

Back at the house, the storm tore everything apart. The workers' quarters were totally destroyed, farm implements were scattered, and three-quarters of the roof of the Russo home was ripped away like it was tin foil. Zoe clutched Melina, tears streaming down her face. *"I'm not scared for me, Mum, I'm scared for my sister."*

Melina hugged her tightly, comforting her as she rocked Zoe gently in her arms, as if she were still a child. Meanwhile, Nonna Giovanna whispered a prayer, and Melina watched with gratitude, thankful for the bond between her daughter and grandmother.

Narrated by Nonna Giovanna

As dusk settled, all hell broke loose. By nightfall, the cyclone had become a raging beast, with lightning flashing and rain hammering down, tearing the roof to shreds. The verandah, once our shelter, was ripped away as if it were nothing more than paper. The winds howled, an unrelenting, haunting sound that filled us with terror. I remember looking at my family and the animals, fearing that none of us would make it through.

NOT NARRATED

In the middle of the chaos, Bobby lay unconscious in her battered ute. An old, wrinkled, thin, and hairy arm reached into the wreckage, it was Steevo, bruised and bleeding, his face grim with determination. He gently lifted Bobby out, placing her and Fredrickson in his wheat harvester, which was barely big enough to withstand the wind. Steevo then drove them to Alonso's house.

Inside, Alonso watched the storm's destruction from the window, his stomach twisted in a knot as he saw his life's work being shredded.

He whispered with the weight of the world on his face, *"God... take my crop, but please don't take my daughter,"* as he watched his mother praying silently for Bobby.

He returned to sit on the ground with Zoe and put his arm around her tightly. Everyone huddled together, even the workers, although they didn't want to appear frightened; it was obvious they were.

Suddenly, there was a distant, faint peeping noise outside. They couldn't get up fast enough.

They saw Steevo's harvester pulling up the driveway.

"Is that… Steevo? Is Steevo beeping his harvester horn?" Alonso gasped, rushing outside despite his injured leg.

Steevo stepped out, Bobby's limp body in his arms. Melina screamed, *"Oh my sweet God, is she okay? Please tell me she's okay!"* Zoe looked on with sheer horror at seeing her sister, lifeless, as Steevo carried her into the lounge room.

Steevo laid her down on the lounge room floor gently with a worried look on his face. Bobby's pale face brought back haunting memories for Giovanna, memories of loss she thought she'd buried long ago. Just then, Bobby's eyes fluttered open, and Steevo leaned in close.

"You okay, love?" he asked softly.

Bobby managed a faint nod, to everyone's immense relief.

The family burst into cheers, the workers joining in. There wasn't a dry eye in the house, including Steevo's.

Bobby, dazed and concerned, jumped up suddenly, looked around, and asked, *"Are you all okay?"*

Everyone laughed at her pure selflessness. Even in her pain, she was asking about them.

With a concerned look, Bobby said to Steevo, *"Sorry, Steevo, but I think your underwear has probably flown back to Glentvale by now."* Everyone just looked at each other, puzzled.

Melina whispered to Alonso, *"I think that knock to her head was a hard one!"* Steevo turned to the door to go back home, but Alonso called out, *"Come back here, you stupid bastard! ... Stay here!!"*

Alonso gave Steevo a heartfelt man-hug and said, *"Thank you, Steevo, how can I ever thank you?"* his voice choking with gratitude.

Steevo replied, *"Well, you can invite me over for a beer and get rid of that fence."*

Steevo's eyes were misty. For the first time in years, a bond reignited between the two men, a bond that had survived countless memories and hardships.

Narrated by Nonna Giovanna

The next day felt like a scene from my childhood in Italy after the war, a devastation I'd hoped never to relive. The cyclone had stripped our home bare; the verandah was gone, most of the roof shredded to pieces, and the wheat fields completely flattened. We lost everything. Our beloved sheep, our dog Rella, was nowhere to be seen and was presumed dead, along with over 8,000 sheep, all dead. Alonso and Bobby got their rifles out of the rifle safe and put down the sheep that were lamed. The look on their faces is one I prefer to forget. The sounds of the shotgun blasts silenced our family for days. They then quickly bulldozed a huge hole at the far end of the farm and bulldozed them into the hole, to prevent stench and disease to the remaining few sheep.

We were grateful to be alive, but we faced an unimaginable financial loss. Our community rallied around us, showing up with helping hands and open hearts. People we hardly knew turned up to help clean up the wreckage, to sort through what little could be salvaged. Most of our furniture was damaged by the downpour.

Watching the countless locals help us with the clean-up was soothing to the soul, a reminder of the strength and kindness that binds us.

The second day after the cyclone, the reality of our situation hit everyone hard. The absence of Rella, our loyal sheepdog, cast a heavy silence over the family. The sight of the flattened wheat fields and empty paddocks where our sheep once grazed, no longer there, felt like a dagger to the heart. And to top it off, we had very little insurance cover.

Zoe and Bobby searched anxiously for Rella, and even our human-like sheep, Hillery, was missing. But with the fields covered in debris and lifeless animals wet from all the rain, it was hard to distinguish one from another. Alonso and Bobby probably buried her, not knowing it was her. We later heard of several human fatalities in nearby towns from the cyclone, which saddened us deeply. It rained constantly, day after day, which made the cleanup even more difficult and miserable.

As we sifted through the aftermath, Carlo arrived. He hadn't been around much lately, but his presence now lifted everyone's spirits. He stayed for weeks to help with the cleanup, his calm determination a steady force for the family.

Alonso remained silent for a long while, the weight of everything lost hanging over him like a storm cloud. His home, his animals, his life's work, all of it was gone, shredded in a single night. I watched him, remembering how resilient he had always been, but I could see the toll this loss was taking on him. Even in my own disappointment, I whispered prayers of strength for him, knowing he'd need every ounce of it to rebuild.

NOT NARRATED

Melina called out, *"Where are you going, Bobby?"*

Bobby replied sarcastically, *"Where do you think I'm going, Mum? Where can I possibly go? Either that paddock, the dead sheep paddock, the empty paddock, or Steevo's paddock. Oh, wait... I could always go to that one, or maybe that paddock. They all look the same right now, all bloody flat and empty..."* She then whispered to herself, *"Just like me."*

Her voice echoed as she stormed off toward her meditation tree, now reduced to a mere trunk with branches, with not one leaf in sight; it almost looked spooky.

After that random outburst with her mother, Bobby was aware that her mindset was slipping. It stemmed from a week of not reading and keeping mentally fit. The dam was too muddy to swim in, so even physically, she felt sluggish.

Outside, Bobby was gathering debris from the sheep shed when Alonso approached her.

"Look, darling girl," he began. *"I'm sorry I kept my financial mess to myself. It won't happen again."*

Bobby cut him off, her voice raised. *"Our financial mess, Dad, our mess, not just yours. We share the highs and the lows, remember?"* She continued picking up debris, and Alonso joined her, working silently alongside her.

"You're right," he said after a pause. *"I was wrong. You're a business partner, and you deserve to know every little stitch, the good, the bad, and the ugly... and at the moment, it's the ugly."* Normally, they would have laughed at jokes, but not today.

Bobby remained silent, not wanting to discuss it further. The silence hung heavy between them, stretching on for what felt like forever to Alonso.

Finally, he spoke up, his voice softer than usual. *"You're also right about something else... I do take you for granted. When I thought I'd lost you in the storm, those words you always say came back to me: 'What you neglect, you will surely lose.' I'm the luckiest father alive to have a daughter like you, Bobby. You're a better business partner than Carlo could ever be."* He paused, his voice beginning to break. *"Thank you for being you, Bobby. I'm a better person because of you."*

Bobby kept her head down, still not responding. Alonso stopped, turned away, and sat down on the ground with his head in his hands, feeling the weight of the situation.

"What do we do now?" he muttered, barely audible, not expecting her to hear.

Bobby broke her silence. *"Are you technically asking for my advice?"*

Alonso looked up quickly, a hint of hope on his face. *"Well, technically, yes."*

She paused, then said, *"Give me some time, Dad. I'll come up with something. I promise."*

Narrated by Nonna Giovanna

The cleanup after the cyclone felt endless. We were living in a massive tent that the local council donated until the insurance company could fix our home. It took almost a month just to get the roof back. Inside, it was damaged by rain, and we had to replace nearly everything. By pure miracle, the lounge room and the girls' room did not lose their roofs, meaning Bobby didn't lose her library and all the hard work for her game. What made it worse was that it continued to rain for over a week. Apparently, the Springwater stream was dangerously overflowing.

We all pitched in, even Zoe surprised us with her efforts, adding her usual clever humour, which brought a refreshing lightness, and Bobby's unbreakable spirit was our backbone. By the end of the second week, we were exhausted from the outdoor work, so we started to walk toward the house for a drink, not even knowing what time it was.

"Lunchtime now, let's just bloody stop for a while!" Melina insisted. Bobby and her father still weren't talking much, but things had improved.

So, there we all were, having lunch outside on what was left of our bent outdoor furniture. I stepped back, looking at everyone, feeling nostalgic. Melina must have noticed something in my expression.

"What's wrong, Giovanna?" she asked.

"Oh, nothing," I replied.

"No, tell us, Nonna," Zoe insisted. By this stage, I had everyone's attention.

I hesitated but then said, *"Look at us. What a combination of strengths we have."*

"Elaborate, Nonna," Zoe prodded. I didn't know what that word meant, so I turned to Alonso, looking puzzled. He knew why straight away and whispered to me, *"Mum, it means go into more detail."*

"Oh," I whispered back.

"I want to know my strengths, Nonna, or do I not have any?" Zoe's smile was slowly fading.

"Of course you do, Bella." Then I told her, *"Your strength is your humour. You keep us entertained and remind us of the funny side of things. I believe God gave us humour to help us cope with life."* Zoe had a pride-filled smile, put her finger to her chin, and said, *"Hmm, I'm funny. I'll settle for that."*

"Alonso, you are the workhorse, you make sure things get done. You're our protector; your heart is as big as that horse of yours."

"Melina, your intuition is nothing short of remarkable, almost scary." Everyone laughed. *"It's because of you that this house didn't collapse."* and you're cooking ain't bad either." Almost as good as mine, I said jokily.

Melina reacted with her usual warm smile.

"Carlo, you're meticulous with legal and intellectual matters. You've helped a lot with the legal side of running this farm. I feel complete when you are here."

Alonso then threw in, *"Wish he were meticulous in the house, he leaves his dirty earbuds everywhere!!"*

"Eeeww, are those earbuds yours, Carlo? I've been wondering who they were," Zoe commented.

Carlo's reaction was quick, *"Not my fault! There are no bins in the bathroom!!"*

Then Bobby said, *"After that cyclone, that bin is probably in Timbuktu by now."*

Zoe then put her bit in, *"Well, if our bin landed in Steevo's front yard, hell, we will never find it!!"*

Everyone couldn't help but laugh. We even got a reaction from Mozza

Suddenly, we were all in an unstoppable laughing fit.

Melina cut in and said, *"Shhh, everyone, shhh!! Nonna hasn't finished."*

"Bobby, your inner strength is truly inspirational. Nothing is ever a hassle to you. Your innovation and your discipline are exceptional, and your desire to help and love others is extremely rare."

I paused.

"We could have all easily died the other night, but we didn't. Even though we have a lot of work ahead of us, I could not feel happier or prouder of you all as I do today. I love each and every one of you...

even you, Mozza, and well maybe you Bludger!!" Bludger meowing back at me.

I thought I might've been too dramatic, as everyone stood in silence. But then, all of a sudden, everyone cheered and came toward me, and we shared a group hug, something that had never happened in our family before. We all raised our right arms up to the sky while our hands were touching in the middle as if it were rehearsed. From then on, it became our signature hug for special occasions. My pride overflowed that day. I'll never forget that moment. It's etched in my heart forever.

At that point, little did I know, things in the Russo household were changing fast.

I overheard Zoe say to Carlo, *"I only got one stripe... humour. At least you got two stripes, 'meticulous with legal and intellectual matters.' And surprise, surprise... Bobby got six! Inner strength, nothing is ever a hassle, innovation, discipline, desire to help and love others."*

I felt so horrible that I didn't compliment her more, but I struggled to find more attributes. *"My darling Zoe, I love her dearly. She has her own inner beauty, and I am certain it will come out soon. In the meantime, I have to make sure she doesn't lose her faith in her God-given abilities, which, at the moment, are lying dormant."*

CHAPTER 11

REBUILDING HOPE

NOT NARRATED

Over two weeks after the cyclone, and another long day of fixing damaged fences, Bobby retreated up high in her thinking tree, as she did every day, except for that week after the cyclone. She carried one of her favorite books by Christopher Lane. Her ritual was to sit with her back against the trunk, admire the sunflowers in the distance, only there were none after the cyclone, and hold conversations with her favorite authors.

That day up in her thinking tree, she chose to speak to Christopher Lane.

"Christopher," she said aloud.

"Yes, my dear Bobby Jo," he replied, appearing beside her.

She sighed. *"I'm trying so hard to stay strong. I've studied your principles and applied them, but I feel so deflated, and I hate feeling like this. It's not like me anymore to be in such a low vibration!"*

Christopher Lane replied gently, *"Remember, Bobby, every adversity, every temporary defeat carries with it the seed of equal or greater good."*

They spoke the words together, and Bobby nodded. *"Thanks for reminding me, Christopher. I want to thank you for the years you spent developing your philosophy. I would have loved to know you in your day."*

"You do know me," he replied. *"You read my books, so you know me. You can seek my counsel anytime, my dear. I'm so glad my work found you. And you know, you can bring it to life again in a powerful way with that game you're creating. It has the potential to change lives, Bobby Jo. You have what it takes."*

At that moment, Bobby noticed her father at the base of the tree, calling her name. He looked like he was about to climb up.

"Stop right there, Dad!" she called down. *"You'll hurt yourself. You struggle to climb into the ute, let alone up this tree, it's a long way up!"*

Alonso chuckled, accepting her point but looking a bit disappointed. *"Can you join Carlo and me when you're done up there? We need to discuss a few things."*

A few minutes later, Bobby headed to the tent. Alonso looked grim, and Carlo was frowning over a set of figures that were needed to get back into the business of wheat growing again.

"Dad, every adversity, every temporary defeat carries the seed of equal or greater good. We may not know the reason for all this yet, but we'll find it."

Alonso tried to grasp what she had said, but was too stuck in his way of thinking to let it lift him up.

She placed her hand on his shoulder and said, *"I have a plan."*

Alonso looked at her in surprise. *"What ...Already?"*

"Come with me," she said, leading him to her room, almost untouched by the storm's rain thanks to the intact roof.

Bobby gestured toward her bookshelves, neatly organized by topic: mindset, relationships, health, money, business management, investing, marketing, customer acquisition, and spiritual wealth, all with their colour-coded special place. A massive whiteboard stood nearby, covered with designs for a board game she'd dreamed of releasing. Bobby was so grateful that the cyclone spared the roof over her bedroom, saving her library from irreparable damage.

Alonso took it all in, his eyes wide. *"My darling girl, you really are... dedicated, aren't you?"*

Bobby smiled. *"Now, Dad, you really ...well, you need some personal development, but we don't have time right now. Just grab the green section books, "*

"What ...all of them?" he asked, stunned.

"Not quite!" She laughed. *"Just the ones in the green section on marketing and customer relations for now... I'll give you a crash course."*

Father and daughter spent hours pouring over strategies, making calls to banks and creditors to buy more time.

"We'll need this much to plant the next crop," Bobby explained, *"but there's a new organic variety resistant to disease and drought."* Carlo helped crunch the numbers and offered some ideas for what might be cheap to produce on the farm, but with implements not replaced by insurance yet, that wasn't possible. Unfortunately, not

all implements were covered, and they had very minimal crop insurance, only enough to cover the costs of replacing one harvester.

She continued, *"I had to pick up a straightener for Zoe, and I went to Sally Bedford's salon. She is struggling with her business, so I offered her some marketing ideas. My thought is that we could offer a coaching service to help small businesses like hers and ask only for a commission, so there's no risk to them. As they make a profit, so do we. That way, we can keep up with our farm mortgage, get another crop in, buy some tractors and implements, and lease the second harvester."*

She looked at Alonso and Carlo's blank faces, and she added in despair

"Look, it's going to be hard work to go from salon door to salon door and from town to town, and it's not my dream job that's for sure, but it's a temporary sacrifice that will save our farm."

Alonso looked overwhelmed. *"You're not getting me in a salon. Forget it."*

"Get over it, Dad! You need to do three things to survive: A-K-A."

"What's that?" he asked.

"Adaptable, Knowledgeable, and an Action-Taker!"

Alonso shook his head, a small smile breaking through. *"I'm too old for this."*

Bobby laughed, already making plans and taking action, determined to turn adversity into a fresh start for them all.

"Where are you going, Dad?" Bobby called out.

Alonso, looking tense, replied, *"I just need to get out of here for a few hours."*

Bobby nodded with understanding. *"Yes, I think that's exactly what you need, Dad. Go!"*

Since the cyclone, the weather had been unusually unsettled, with light and heavy rain every day for weeks, making the cleanup incredibly difficult. The region wasn't used to such wet weather, it was as if they'd gone from a bone-dry drought to English weather.

Bobby watched her father as he headed out and smiled to herself when she saw him in the distance, riding off toward the patch on his horse. The quad bikes were too damaged to use.

As he rode, Alonso took in the land, scarred and damaged. *"Wow, this land has taken a beating,"* he thought. *"And yet it's still beautiful."*

When he got to the patch, he sat down on the wooden stool. Just then, he heard a soft noise. *"Mmm... mar mar..."*

Alonso looked around, startled. Where on earth was that sound coming from? He walked over to a yellow wattle tree he'd planted years ago, and there, tucked in the shade, was Hillery.

"Hillery!" he yelled out, grinning. *"...You're a legend!"* He recognized her immediately, she'd been half-shorn when she escaped the last shearing season. Laughing with pure joy, he scooped up her tired body and carried her back to the house on the horse. Finding Hillery was like finding an old lost friend.

Bobby noticed him approaching. *"You're back already, Dad?"* Then she noticed Hillery. *"Well, I'll be buggered; it's Hillery!"* Bobby shouted, her voice carrying through the backyard. *"Everyone, Hillery's alive! Hillery's alive!"* She yelled at the top of her lungs, her joy contagious.

"Here, give her to me, Dad," she said, reaching out. *"We'll look after her, go on, get out of here again; you need it, Dad."*

Alonso laughed. *"Alright, alright. I'll go to Steevo's place for a beer."* he said, heading off on his horse.

"Great idea, Dad," Bobby said, enjoying the fact that Steevo was part of the family's life again.

After attending to Hillery's wounds with her mother, Bobby was curious about the nearby Spring Water Creek. Bobby wondered how it had fared through the cyclone and the constant rain. She decided to go check, concerned about potential flood levels that could be dangerous for caravanners. She quickly prepared her horse, Spunky, with a saddle, as it was a 15-minute ride to get there. She set off, the sky growing darker as another downpour seemed to form.

"Oh no, not more rain," she muttered, urging the horse faster as they made their way toward the creek. Just as she got there, it started to drizzle lightly, forming a rainbow. She reached the gorge where the spectacular waterfall was, and she was shocked. *"Wow, I've forgotten how beautiful this is!"* she said to Spunky. Bobby had never seen the waterfall with so much water. Mesmerized, she stopped for a while to enjoy it. The sound of the water falling was so soothing to her that she closed her eyes and took it all in.

When she reached the creek, she spotted a white dual-cab ute stranded in the middle, its wheels spinning helplessly in over a meter of water.

"Stop! Just stop! Turn around, it's too deep!" she shouted from the bank, waving her arms to get the driver's attention. But instead, the driver turned off the engine and rolled down his window.

What happened next was like a scene out of a comedy movie. Out stepped an Asian man, dressed head-to-toe in brand-new RM Williams gear (The Gorgio Amani of Australian outback attire), complete with the long brown waterproof jacket, the largest brown Australian-style cowboy hat Bobby had ever seen, brown boots, a matching belt, and various accessories hanging off him. He waded into the water and sank down to his waist, which only made things worse as water flooded the inside of the ute, much to the dismay of his wife and teenage kids, who looked horrified.

"Stay with the vehicle! Close the damn door and drive back here, or your family's going to get washed away!" Bobby yelled. As the current pulled at the ute, it drifted closer to the other side of the bank.

Nearby, she noticed her neighbor's son, Tom Hallington, whose family owned all the sunflower fields. Tom was standing by his top-of-the-range Ram 1500 TRX ute, looking completely lost and taking no action to save the family. Bobby quickly asked if she could use his ute, and he nodded yes, still looking shocked but offering no help. Without hesitation, Bobby hit the differential locks on the vehicle and plunged through the creek. She waded into the water, connected a snatch strap to the stranded vehicle, and secured it to Tom's ute. Then, she drove back across the stream.

After several attempts, she finally managed to pull the family's ute out of the rushing water and to safety.

Bobby drove towards Tom to return his ute. She was just about to open the door when she noticed some documents that were sitting above the glovebox. She reached out to place them back when she saw the papers were titled *Hallington's Water Pipe Proposal to the Sunflower Springs Council*, and they contained pictures of the Spring Water area in Bobby Zone with pipeline plans to Hallington's property.

Bobby saw red. She grabbed the document and tucked it into her back pocket, thinking to herself, *"I'll deal with Mr. Hallington later."* Tom wouldn't know his *rse from his elbow, she thought bitterly. (slang for stupid)

When the family's ute doors opened, water poured out as the kids, clutching iPads and other gadgets, scrambled to keep their belongings dry. The wife, though she spoke little English, hugged Bobby so tightly it almost hurt.

"Are you all okay?" Bobby asked.

"Yes," said the husband, *"I bit embarrassed,"* he added with his cute Chinese accent.

"It's okay, nothing to be embarrassed about," Bobby exclaimed. *"I made the same mistake of crossing a rocky creek and damaging my fuel tank."* Tom tried hard to catch Bobby's eye, only to find that she wouldn't look at him at all.

As the water continued to rise, it became clear that Bobby had likely saved their lives. Without her intervention, they could have possibly drowned as the water downstream near the waterfall was extremely deep.

Tom, meanwhile, lingered, Bobby, throwing hints that he could leave now that it was all over. But he stayed, hanging around in awkward silence, showing no interest in the family Bobby had just saved.

The rain stopped, and they stayed by the Creekside, talking while the ute engine dried out. Bobby learned that the family's surname was Wong, and they were from Hong Kong, where they had owned a strawberry farm. Looking to start fresh, they had decided to move to Australia as their new home and were now exploring farm options in the outback.

The Wong children, 14-year-old twin boys, spoke English better than their parents. With a laugh, Bobby suggested to the boys that their father might want to tone down the cowboy look. The kids rolled their eyes and chuckled, clearly familiar with their father's unique style.

Mr. Wong explained that they were going to buy a strawberry farm in Bendigo and sell directly to customers. Bobby wished them well and offered them advice on great marketing. She told them she lived not far from there and invited them to drop by if they were ever in the area again.

Mr. Wong started to take off his brand-new RM Williams gear, the long jacket, the large brown hat, the brown boots, the matching belt, and various accessories. Bobby was relieved that he didn't strip completely naked, as it was frighteningly looking that way.

"Mr. Wong, are you still wet? Is that why you've removed all your beautiful gear?" Bobby asked.

With a strong Chinese accent, he smiled and replied, *"No, Bobby son, me same size as you, Chinese very small. You take, please, a gift from me. Thank you, you risk your life, please take."* He put his hands together in a prayer-like gesture and bowed.

"Mr. Wong, this is expensive gear. You don't have to please …" Bobby started, but then she remembered the Hispanic lady Edelmira's advice that it would be rude not to accept. With grace, she accepted the gift and also put her hands together, bowing slightly in return to show her appreciation for such a gesture.

After a final hug from Mrs. Wong, the family climbed back into their ute, thanking Bobby before disappearing down the road. As they left, Bobby felt a warm satisfaction, knowing she'd made a difference in someone's life.

Bobby smiled as they waved goodbye. Tom Hallington had stayed the entire time, though Bobby couldn't figure out why. Things grew more and more awkward as the Wong family drove off, and it was now just Bobby and Tom alone. She prepared to leave at once, keen to rid herself of his uncomfortable presence.

Finally, words came out of his mouth, although Bobby didn't really want to hear them. Tom furrowed his brow and asked, *"Why did you put yourself at risk to save them? It was their stupid fault for getting themselves in that pickle,"*

Dismayed by his comment, Bobby replied, *"What if it were you there? And someday it WILL be you in a pickle."*

Not wanting to carry the gifts Mr. Wong had just given her, Bobby decided to just put them all on.

And boy, did she look great in that RM Williams gear. But typical Bobby thought *she was like an idiot,* though it was quite the opposite.

Tom, now drooling over how good Bobby looked, plucked out the words with no warning.

"Uh, aarr, how about… we go out on a date tomorrow night?" he blurted, sounding as unappealing as it gets.

Bobby responds sharply, *"Uh, aarr, how about… NO"*

Bobby was on her horse, ready to leave. Even Spunky didn't appear to like him; animals seem to have that kind of intelligence.

Unimpressed, Bobby realized now why Tom had stayed back, so she let it rip.

"You know what gets me about people like you? Do you think your money defines you? Well, it doesn't. This does!" She said, touching her heart several times with her pointer finger. *"This is the only thing that defines you: love and courage. So, until you grow a heart and a set of balls, you've got Buckley's chances."* (Slang for zero.)

Tom continued to insist on a date. He approached her on the horse. *"I'm picking you up at six o'clock tomorrow. I can give you the life of your dreams. Come on, have a champagne lifestyle with me, I can make you happy, Bobby!!"*

Bobby, her face full of disgust, decided to pull out the documents she had found in his ute. She held it up for him to see and said:

*"What's this *rs*h*le?"* Tom's face turned all colours, and he had nothing to say. Bobby made one final statement and said, *"Pay attention because I'm warning you, Tom Hallington. If you so much as place your baby toe on my property, God help you."*

Tom's smirk was completely wiped off his face as he watched her ride off as fast as she could.

Tom yelled out loud in one last attempt to win his point: *"Face it, Bobby! We are only going to buy you out anyway!"*

Spunky could sense Tom's bad energy because he took off like a bat out of hell.

Bobby was convinced her message had been loud and clear, and that he wouldn't bother her again. But Tom's ego was as big as Ben Hur and now bruised. He was used to getting what he wanted. Already plotting another way to get to Bobby's weak spot, not realizing she had none.

Bobby adored her horse. She had an unbreakable bond with Spunky; they could always sense each other's moods. *"Awww, I feel better now being away from shallow Hal. Do you, Spunky? Yeah, I thought so."* Spunky knew when words were directed at him, and his face moved up and down as he made a horse noise.

Bobby was now at the gorge waterfall, but in a different spot than when she rode in. They came to a halt. As always, Bobby spoke to Spunky as if he were human. Ever since he was a foal, she had communicated with him like this. *"Spunky, as much as I really want to stop and be in the moment and take in the view... It doesn't smell too pleasant here. Let's keep going, what do you reckon?"*

Spunky made some more horse noises, but was shaking his head more than normal. Bobby knew her horse's body language down to a tee, and something was bothering him. She got down from Spunky and touched his face. *"Spunky, what's wrong? Take me there to whatever's wrong, boy. Come on."*

Bobby trusted Spunky and knew he would not take off on her, so she let go of his reins. Spunky looked at her, then gently turned back several meters, then turned to the left and kept going for over 20 more meters into a thick, shrubby bush area.

Bobby was starting to think he was just walking randomly and said, *"Okay, Spunky, no more Sunday strolls. Let's get home. There's nothing here."*

Then Spunky made a loud horse noise that echoed in the bushland and took off. *"Wait, Spunky, no, wait!"* And that's when she discovered her dog Rella's decayed body lying next to a tree.

Bobby let out a loud screech of shock. *"Rella!!!"*

Bobby knelt down and whispered, "Oh no, Rella! I'm so sorry this happened to you." She stood there, paralyzed for a while. *"Let me take you home."*

Being so badly decomposed, she couldn't just lift her. She took off her RM Williams coat to remove her white T-shirt to wrap Rella in it. Then, she placed the coat back on herself and started walking home.

Alonso was in the kitchen, looking out the window while having a coffee with Melina.

"Bobby's been gone all day. Where the heck did that girl get to?! Spunky's not here either. She must've gone somewhere with him!"

Melina took a look out the window and said, *"Yes, he is, but why is he loose?"*

As soon as she said that, they both ran outside. They looked around the shed area to see if Bobby was nearby, but saw nothing.

Nonna Giovanna came out onto the verandah and said, *"Who is that in the distance?"* not recognizing Bobby in all the RM Williams gear she was wearing.

They watched Bobby slowly walking closer and closer to the house, carrying something white. As Bobby reached the picket fence, Alonso, Melina, and Giovanna approached her, now well aware of what was in the white clothing she had in her arms, by the look on Bobby's face alone.

At that very moment, Zoe came out from inside the house and saw them all gathered in one spot, and her curiosity was sparked. She walked toward them.

Zoe walked over happily and said, *"Hey, Bobby, since when do you own RM Williams gear, hat, boots, and all? Getting stylish in your old age."* She added jokingly, *"Wow, look at you... what a sexy look with nothing underneath,"* and she wolf-whistled at Bobby. Still oblivious, she asked, *"What have you got there, Bobby? Sh*t, it stinks!"*

But as she took a closer look, her smile disappeared quickly, and she came to a standstill. Zoe, now in a quieter tone, asked, *"Rella? Is it R...?"*

"Yes," said Bobby. *"It's Rella, I'm sorry, Zoe."*

Zoe's face turned pale, and she stormed off toward the sheds, broken-hearted. Alonso had a shovel ready in his hands and said softly, *"Give her to me, love."*

Bobby slowly handed Rella over and just stood there, looking over at Spunky, eating some lawn in the backyard with his bridle hanging down. She walked over to him and stroked his face.

"Did you get emotional, by any chance, Spunky?" Spunky moved his head up and down.

"You're so smart to lead me to Rella. You're so smart," Bobby murmured.

Bobby then went to find her sister. She found Zoe crying in the shearing shed. She put her arm around her and kissed her forehead. Zoe hugged her back.

Two weeks later, with help from a local builder, Alonso had repaired the roof and verandah, though the insurance payout had been minimal. The community held a working bee to help rebuild the sheep shed, and Bobby felt renewed gratitude for their small town.

Bobby finally launched the money-making venture she had promised her father. She'd put together a mentoring program for salon owners, complete with training on customer etiquette, paperwork, staffing, online marketing, outsourcing products to sell, and much more. Her friend Sally was thrilled to be her first customer.

"Dad, guess what? We have our first client!" Bobby announced excitedly.

Alonso raised an eyebrow. *"Oh, really? How much has she paid us?"*

"Remember, Dad? They only pay if we get results. Salons are often cash-poor, just like us, so we structured it to be win-win."

Reluctantly, Alonso nodded. *"Cash-poor, yeah, I know that shitty feeling."*

"Come on, Dad, have a drink with me and stay in good vibes only. 'Operation salon rescue' has officially started," Bobby said as she handed him a beer and one for herself. They clinked their beer stubbies, and Bobby said her signature words, *"To rise stronger, laughing louder, and loving deeper!"*

With Carlo handing them $50,000 to keep the banks at bay for a while, Melina and Zoe worked in the local supermarket to help financially. Nonna Giovanna continued working in the vegetable patch, and as always, it became a team effort, only this time, Zoe actually did something.

Bobby and Alonso hit the road, visiting 65 salons a week, and signing up clients for a six-month online program that transformed their businesses. Over 80% of the salons thrived financially, and some even sold their businesses, earning Bobby and Alonso additional commissions. Along the way, Bobby continued developing her personal development board game while on the road, trialing the prototype with clients and watching their growth and excitement.

Narrated by Nonna Giovanna

We were so proud of Bobby and Alonso's success, and relieved the bank wouldn't sell us out. Weeks turned into months, and we missed them dearly, often not seeing them for months at a time.

After the third month, Alonso returned home to tend to the farm, and Bobby assured us, *"Just three more months, and I'll be back for good. We will reach our target of $750,000."*

I decided to sell the unit Angelo had bought years ago for us to retire in. It didn't fetch much, but after expenses, the sale added $350,000 to our kitty, which, combined with Bobby's and Alonso's earnings, meant we could finally plan to grow a crop again.

NOT NARRATED

With Bobby away, Zoe found herself reflecting more often. She wondered how Bobby managed to work so hard, maintain such positivity, and still find time to develop that 'damn game.' Normally, she mocked Bobby's upbeat nature, but with Bobby gone, Zoe felt an emptiness she had never felt before.

Late one night, unable to resist the curiosity, Zoe snuck into Bobby's room, unlocking the door with a key she'd spotted placed up high at the entrance. Night after night, she'd return, reading for hours on end, absorbing Bobby's world.

One evening, Nonna Giovanna and Melina caught sight of her in the hallway. Melina placed her hands on Giovanna's shoulders and chuckled, *"I know, Giovanna. I know."*

They peeked through the door, watching as Zoe sat absorbed in thought.

"I know you're there," Zoe said softly. *"I've known for weeks. I won't mess anything up, I promise... I miss her, that's all."*

A gruff voice sounded behind them. *"We all do."* It was Alonso, who'd overheard and now stood with them in quiet reflection.

That night, as they lay in bed, Alonso opened up to Melina about his dreams of travelling beyond South Australia. For the first time, they discussed exploring the world's oldest rainforest in Queensland, the Kimberley's wilderness in Western Australia, skiing in Perisher Valley, and visiting the Great Barrier Reef in Queensland, places they'd never seen. They had always focused on providing opportunities for the kids, and now perhaps it was their turn to enjoy life's pleasures.

Over time, Zoe's relationship with the family began to blossom. She had always felt like she lived in Bobby's shadow, but now she spent more time connecting with everyone, even taking lunch with her father in the fields. Her school grades soared as she was finishing up Year 12, and soon she introduced them to Dale, her boyfriend of almost a year, whom she had kept secret. Turns out there was more to Zoe than the family had thought.

Unfortunately, several months later, Dale was involved in a car accident, losing a close friend and ending up hospitalized for three months. The hospital was a two-hour drive. Alonso quietly took Zoe to visit him every few weeks, and on one occasion, went alone. Dale later texted Zoe, *"Your dad was here for hours, chatting and playing cards like we were old mates. I think he actually likes me, he even told me to call him Alonso."*

That evening, Alonso strolled in, looking pleased with himself. *"Oh, Dale says to say hi, Bubba."*

He told Zoe with a small grin before heading to the kitchen. A few surprised looks passed around the room, and Zoe tried to hide her smile.

"Dad, I'm getting too old now for you to call me Bubba."

Alonso yelled out from his office, *"Too bad, you'll always be my Bubba!"*

As the weeks passed, Carlo, who had always felt a bit disconnected after leaving the farm, wanted to start visiting more often. It wasn't easy, as Sydney was a fifteen-hour drive away, and there were no airports anywhere near the place. One evening, during a family meal, he brought up a real estate lead he'd been given.

"Dad, it's Steevo's old block, the second half of the land. It's still up for sale. Ray White in South Sydney has the listing, but the spring water lagoon's ownership is in question. I think I may have found a loophole."

Carlo explained an old common-law clause about necessary water access for adjacent properties if it didn't add strain to the primary landowner. *"It could be a conflict of interest if I mention this to the buyers, but it might be our chance."*

Alonso beamed with pride. *"I think my son's a genius!"* he said, patting Carlo's shoulder full of fatherly pride. *"Let's keep this between us, though, and surprise your mum if it all pans out."*

"Will do, Dad. And hey, speaking of Steevo, how's he doing?"

Alonso sighed. *"He's still on his own. Margie visits him sometimes. I think he lives in hope; his kids are all still in Melbourne. They come up often enough, more than you do, you bugger."*

Carlo laughed. *"Point taken, Dad."*

After a pause, Alonso leaned in. *"When are you going to give us grandchildren? You got someone yet?"*

Carlo chuckled, caught off guard. *"Well, yes, actually, Dad. Her name's Riana. She's in the Air Force, so don't expect grandkids anytime soon."*

Alonso's face lit up. *"No way! Mozza, did you hear that?"* He called out to the sheepdog, ruffling its fur. *"Carlo has a girl!"*

Carlo's grin faded slightly. *"Dad, Bobby told me she found Rella. I felt really sad that she found her that way."*

Alonso's smile wavered. *"I know, mate. Up until that day, we thought just maybe she got lost in all that weather and that she would come back. You know, Mozza fretted for weeks after it happened, making strange noises as if she were mourning her. It was sad to watch."*

They looked at Mozza, and she tilted her head as she sat, sad-eyed, as if she knew what they were saying.

After a quiet moment, Carlo squeezed his father's shoulder. *"I was going to leave today, but maybe I'll stick around until morning. It's a long drive back."*

"Good idea, son," Alonso replied happily, giving him a pat on the back. *"Much smarter to leave early in the day,"* Alonso added.

Narrated by Nonna Giovanna

Almost 1 year to the day, Bobby returned home, three months longer than originally thought, but she was determined to reach the $750,000, and by God, she did! In all that time, she'd only been back home about three times.

Carlo knew Bobby was coming, as they spoke almost every day, so he decided to be there for the celebration of their achievement. We all rushed out to meet her, gathering into a group hug, our special ritual I accidentally started eight months ago when our world seemed to be in a million pieces. I was so glad I'd started that group hug, it had become a symbol of our unity and love.

Bobby looked different somehow. Her skin wasn't so sunburned, and her hands, once rough and calloused, were now smooth, with no dirt beneath her nails. Her long, thick hair was down, and it had grown so long, styled with care. Melina hugged her so tight as we all did.

"You look great, my darling!" Melina said, admiring her daughter.

"Oh, Mum, I 'had' to fuss over myself," Bobby replied. *"My target market was hairdressers, I couldn't turn up looking like a bush pig!"*

"Darling, it's a good thing to look after your appearance, it's not a vain thing."

"Yeah, Mum, how come you never tell me that?" Zoe interjected with a teasing grin.

"Zoe, don't start," Melina muttered under her breath with a smile. Zoe just wrapped an arm around Bobby and said, *"By the way, Christopher Lane is my favorite now."*

"Zoe, you've been in my room?" Bobby raised her eyebrows. *"Mum!"*

"It's alright, Bobby," Melina soothed.

Bobby let out a sigh. *"Oh my God, it's so good to be home! I miss you all."*

"What… did you miss me too?" Zoe asked.

"Yes, you too, you shithead, and I can tell you I will not miss those bloody high heels and wearing uncomfortable dresses." She dashed off to her room and came back in her favorite denim shorts and checkered blue shirt, looking like her old self. *"Now this is more like it,"* she laughed, her face visibly more relaxed.

We all headed to the kitchen, where the aroma of a freshly baked cake filled the air. Alonso took out a bottle of champagne.

"I've been waiting to open this on a day like today," he said, gathering everyone around. *"Alright, I know we're not much of a speech-giving family, but I have a few words."*

Bobby, Carlo, and Zoe watched as Alonso raised his glass, starting with the eldest in the family.

"So, let's start with the oldest family member." Carlo perked up, feigning pride, only for Alonso to laugh and say, *"Not you yet, bonehead!"* Carlo made a sarcastic, sad face, and everyone chuckled.

Turning to me, Alonso continued, *"Mum, you may be the oldest, but you're our rock. You never complain and always keep us steady. Your hard work is endless, and because of you and Dad…"* He paused, his voice thick with emotion, struggling to continue his speech once he heard himself say the word… Dad. He cleared his throat and finished, *"Here's to you, Mum… and Dad, for giving us over 50 years of dedication, we have this beautiful farm because of you."*

A hush fell over the room as Alonso raised his glass, his words full of gratitude. *"Mum, I remember when you worked 12-hour days 7 days a week. You were so tired you'd fall asleep on my bedroom chair after reading me a story, by the way, it was only one book I owned, but somehow, you'd invent a different story each time and show me the same pictures."* Everyone laughed, including me..." Alonso continued, *"Only to wake up and do it all over again the next day. I don't know how you did it, Mum, but thank you from the bottom of my heart. And I love you."* My son's speech directly to me melted my heart.

He turned his head to Carlo. *"Carlo, years ago, when you told me you were moving to Sydney to be a lawyer, it felt like a thousand knives cut through me. But I realized keeping you here would've been selfish. Congrats on all you've achieved, I'm so proud of you. Thanks for visiting more often. I can't wait to meet Riana."* He smiled warmly. *"Thank you. I love you."*

"Who's Riana?" Zoe piped up, earning a shush from Carlo as everyone laughed.

Alonso continued, *"And Carlo's got amazing news about the spring water, he's cleared the way for us to start farming again. Don't ask me how; he won't reveal his secret!"* Everyone cheered, and Melina grew misty-eyed.

He glanced at Melina with a gentle smile. *"I haven't forgotten you, love. I'm saving the best for last."*

Then he turned to Bobby. *"Bobby Jo, well, you're in a league of your own. I've watched you work yourself to the bone. You live and breathe those books, and you'd rather die than let anyone down.*

Please rest for a few days. You truly define success. Thank you for saving our farm!!" Everyone cheered, Alonso added, *"Now, including Mum's money after selling the small house in town, we have 1.1 million, which means we are in business again!!!"* He raised his glass. *"Thank you. I love you."* Everyone cheered even louder.

We all raised our glasses, calling out, *"Here's to Bobby!"*

Everyone called out at the same time while lifting their champagne glasses. Melina popped another bottle of champagne and topped everyone's glass up. It was such a memorable moment.

Bobby blushed and smiled as Alonso turned to Zoe.

"And to our little Zoe! Congrats on finishing your Tafe course in graphic design and for having such fine taste in men. Dale's a top guy, and I hope he's part of our future. You've been great the past 8 months, especially with the housework. Thank you, Bubba, I love you."

While Alonso was giving his speech to Zoe, she had her hand behind her back with her fist clenched, raising one finger each time her father mentioned the good things she had done, with three fingers going up in total. Carlo noticed it and smiled. Zoe turned to him to show her three fingers. *"Three stripes this time!"* she said silently, so he would lip-read her. He lifted up three fingers and said silently, *"Three for me too."* Zoe lip-read him and smiled.

Alonso paused, looking at Melina with loving eyes. *"And finally... you, my love,"* he said as he turned to Melina. *"What can I say? You're the super love of my life."* Everyone was silent.

*"I'll never forget the day I had to tell you we didn't have enough farm insurance after the cyclone. I thought, 'Sh*t, this time she's gunna leave me.' and pictured myself miserable and lonely, sitting on a derelict verandah like Steevo, looking like a skun rabbit with no bloody underwear."*

Everyone burst out laughing, but Carlo was confused about the underwear story. *"Did I miss something about Steevo's underwear?"*

Alonso's voice grew stronger as he wrapped up. *"But today, we've got the funds to start a new-age wheat crop and buy sheep. Now... let's celebrate things going back to normal!!!!!!!"*

Everyone cheered, only to be interrupted by Bobby.

"I'm going to New York on Friday, Dad, and I could be there for a long time!" Bobby blurted out so quickly, almost as if she were afraid she'd lose the courage to say it if she waited.

The room went silent. You could've heard a pin drop.

White Wedding - Billy Idol
Go to www.ritamontalto.com/songs
to scan song

Play when Bobby and Zoe get in the Ute
to leave for Glentvale to go shopping

CHAPTER 12

NEW YORK: THE CITY OF DREAMS

Narrated by Nonna Giovanna

The room fell silent as Bobby announced that she was going to New York. Our joy was replaced with shock.

"Bobby, what are you talking about? You just got back!" Alonso asked, almost pleading.

"Dad, you know I adore this farm, I love Sunflower Springs, it's home and always will be. But I'm ready to launch my game, and I know it can help a lot of people in desperate need of improving the quality of their lives."

Alonso looked at her, frustrated. *"What about your quality of life? For God's sake, go next year, Bobby."*

Bobby replied, *"That's like asking you to plant your crop next year, Dad.*

I've ordered 50 games for publishers to see, and meeting them in person will be the smarter thing to do." Bobby added excitedly, *"You should see it, Dad. It looks amazing. That's what I named it, by the way, A-MAZE-IIIIng, because it's a maze, get it?"*

Alonso was silent.

Bobby, disappointed by his lack of support, said in a somber tone, *"I've got meetings booked with three different publishers, and I'm leaving on Friday. My flight is booked. I will stay in New York until my goal is achieved. It could take weeks, or it could be months or even years. I'm sorry, Dad."* She started walking away.

"I said you're not going, Bobby… We just got back to normal."

Zoe chimed in, *"Dad, hmm, I remember you saying something about realizing it would be selfish to hold your kids back from their dreams?"*

"Stai zitta, (Shut up) Zoe!" Alonso yelled.

Melina placed a hand on Alonso's arm, smiling softly. *"She's set an intention, babe. Don't put a wet blanket over it."*

Bobby looked at her father, disgusted with his reaction.

Bobby turned to me and whispered in anger, *"He knows how much this means to me, and how much work I've put in, Nonna. Why is he doing this?"*

I replied calmly, *"He's just afraid, Bella. You know how he gets. Give him time."*

I attempted to brighten the atmosphere that evening after that family outburst, but even my mouth-watering tiramisu failed to get anyone excited.

NOT NARRATED

Bobby headed to her room that night to plan for the next day's shopping trip.

"Thanks for sticking up for me, Zoe," Bobby said, still in a somber mood.

"It's okay. It's not the first time Dad told me to shut up," Zoe replied.

"Zoe, want to come shopping with me tomorrow in Glentvale? I need clothes for America and a few other things," Bobby asked.

"Do kangaroos jump? Hell yeah!" Zoe replied, all excited. *"Besides …You need me. Your taste in clothes is terrible. You got one good jacket from some Chinese guy with better taste than you."*

"Oh, thanks, Zoe," Bobby replied, rolling her eyes.

"Just saying," Zoe grinned. *"We can take my car if you want, sis,"* she added.

*"Are you kidding? We'd get there quicker on a pushbike than in your bucket of Sh*t, Zoe."*

"Alright, fine," Zoe shrugged.

Bobby couldn't help but smile. She thought to herself how nice it was to actually have an enjoyable sisterly conversation with Zoe for a change. She hoped it would stay that way, it was refreshing for the whole family.

"I'll ring Sabrina and book the motel room for us in Glentvale," Bobby exclaimed.

Zoe, in the background, yelled out, *"We're gunna shop until we drop!!!"* dropping playfully on her bed.

The next morning, as they set off on the six-hour drive to Glentvale, Bobby and Zoe were filled with excitement and actually enjoyed each other's company, which was a dramatic change. Sunlight poured through the car windows, casting a warm glow as they laughed and chatted along the way. Billy Idol's song White Wedding came on the radio.

Bobby put the music up full ball and sung out *"Hey little sister"* and made funny facial impressions of Billy Idol!! Zoe was shocked to see that side of Bobby www.ritamontalto.com/songs

When they finally arrived, they headed straight to Glentvale Central Plaza, where Bobby bought a new large suitcase and some essential clothes and shoes for her New York trip. It was funny because Zoe kept questioning Bobby's choices, Zoe's taste was much more feminine. While Bobby selected a suitcase with a John Deere tractor on it, much to Zoe's horror. Zoe tried to convince Bobby to get one with multicoloured flowers or fun designs. The same clash continued as they shopped for clothes, their tastes clearly opposite. They laughed it off, but Bobby didn't sway.

The next morning, after a restful night at a cozy motel, they met up with Bobby's group of friends, Sabrina, Vicky, Jessica, and Tracey, at a café by the riverside in Glentvale township. Glentvale's spring weather was perfect. There wasn't a breath of wind, and the endless warm sunshine by the mighty Murray River made for a majestic scene.

As Bobby looked out at the river, she thought how wonderful it was to be back in Sunraysia, enjoying the abundance it had to offer. As always, Bobby was in the moment, smiling with deep gratitude to be alive and feel alive.

Bobby looked over to Zoe. *"Zoe, doesn't this river feel so peaceful?"*

However, the peace... didn't last long.

Zoe saw Bobby's friends preparing kayaks for an adventure on the river. *"Oh, Bobby, you didn't tell me we were going kayaking!"* Zoe exclaimed.

"I wanted to surprise you, Zoe, but first breakfast ok?" Bobby replied with a mischievous smile, as they both started running toward the group of friends.

Sabrina, Bobby's friend since kindergarten, greeted them warmly as the others joined in, Jessica, slim but with an ego bigger than a football field; Tracey, a kindhearted, insecure girl with a need to fit in; and Vicky, attractive but rather lazy. Despite their quirks, Bobby valued these girls like family.

As they gathered for a big, fancy breakfast, Bobby asked how everyone was doing and how they were settling in Glentvale after leaving Sunflower Springs after high school.

It had been quite some time since they'd last gotten together, usually with Bobby being the glue that held them together by being the one who organizes events for the group.

"Sabrina, did you enroll in that teaching degree you wanted?" Bobby asked.

"Nah," Sabrina replied, uninterested. *"Can't be bothered."*

"Oh," Bobby replied, trying to keep the conversation positive. *"Well, you know you can achieve anything you set your mind to. What else are you interested in?"*

All four girls went quiet and just looked at one another. Zoe, who understood the dynamic, noticed that while Bobby asked everyone what they had been up to, no one asked Bobby. Not a word was said about Bobby's experience with the farm's devastation after the cyclone. Instead, they talked about trivial things or gossiped about who was sleeping with whom, making Zoe frown in frustration.

Zoe had had enough and spoke up. *"Hey, sis, let's get going. We've still got a six-hour drive."*

"What about kayaking?" Bobby reminded her. *"It'll only take a few hours,"* she encouraged.

Zoe sighed and then turned to the group, prompting Bobby, *"Tell the girls about your new adventure, Bobby!"*

Bobby hesitated, as she wasn't one to boast. *"Oh… okay. Well, I've designed a personal development board game to help people set and achieve their goals,"* she began.

Jessica chuckled dismissively. *"Goals? Who even has goals!!?"*

Sabrina joined in, laughing. *"I have a goal!"* she said, and everyone turned to face her, and she added, *"To go to the pub Friday night and get totally wasted out of my brain!"*

The other girls burst out laughing, except for Bobby and Zoe, who forced polite smiles. Then Jessica said, *"Yeah, my goal Friday night is to pick up"*. Vicky rolled her eyes and said, *"Jessica, you have already achieved that goal numerous times,"* and the girls then had another laugh.

After a brief silence, Bobby continued, *"Anyway, I'm hoping to help people better their lives by improving their mindset, to get unstuck in their business or entrepreneurial journey.".*

Vicky asked, *"What's an entrepreneur?"* struggling to even say the word properly. Bobby was silent for a moment, not sure whether she even deserved an answer, then responded, *"An entrepreneur is…"* she paused again.

Jessica laughed at Bobby and thoughtlessly blurted out, *"She doesn't even know what it means!"* and all of them joined in to laugh. Zoe put her head down with her hand over her face and whispered under her breath, *"Oh, this is painful!"*

Bobby continued, amidst the laughter, *"Entrepreneurs are…"* The girls stopped laughing, curious to hear what Bobby was going to say.

… visionaries with the strength to turn ideas into reality. They practice creativity and resilience and have the ability to take risks while navigating uncertainty. Their problem-solving skills and determination allow them to adapt and thrive, even when faced with countless setbacks. They face challenges such as balancing work and life, overcoming severe financial hurdles, and managing self-doubt and burnout. What makes entrepreneurs truly special is their relentless drive to innovate, inspire, and create value, not just for themselves, but for the world around them."

They shape our future, the very reason you can hop on a plane and be on the other side of the world within the same day, the reason you have that phone in your hands. Their courage to chase dreams even though everyone around them says they can't do it sets them apart from everyone else. The reason we can have this fancy breakfast is that a husband-and-wife team took risks and made it possible." They all looked at the owners working tirelessly serving customers. No one said a word.

Bobby added, "Simply put, entrepreneurs are the reason it's possible you all have jobs!!"

Everyone went silent until Vicky said, *"Well, I didn't ask for an essay!"*

Zoe saw red after Vicky's rude comment and got up at the speed of light from her chair, but Bobby, seated next to her, pulled her arm back down, signifying for her to sit down. *"I've got this,"* Bobby whispered.

Bobby continued, *"Anyway, I'm off to New York on Friday to meet with publishers for my board game."*

Sabrina and the others exchanged looks. Sabrina said, *"New York? Far out, Pluto will be closer!"* They laughed again.

Then Sabrina started, *"Listen, Bobby, what are the chances this will even succeed? Someone's probably invented it already. Stick to farming, and stop wasting time on that silly idea. Why don't you just take it easy and live it up, girl?"* Sabrina said with a smirk while lifting up her orange juice.

Bobby's face went blank, while Zoe, disgusted by their lack of support and airhead mentality, clenched her fists.

When it was time to pay for the elaborate breakfast, Bobby reached for her card, but Zoe whispered to her, *"Don't you dare pay for everyone, Bobby."* She pushed Bobby's hand away from the eftpos machine.

"Girls," Zoe called out, *"FYI, we're all paying for our own."* The group looked disappointed, having expected Bobby to cover the bill as she often did.

As they headed toward the kayaks in front of the café, Zoe pulled Bobby aside, far enough so the others couldn't hear. *"You usually pay every time, don't you? Why would you pay dickheads for giving you a headache? They're not worth your time, heck, they're not even worth 'my' time."*

Bobby sighed, unwilling to admit her friends' faults. *"Come on, Zoe, let's just enjoy ourselves kayaking."*

In an explosive burst of energy, Tracey sprinted towards Bobby and Zoe, skidding to a halt just inches from Bobby's face, her breath coming in ragged gasps. Her eyes wide with urgency, she blurted out, "Bobby, Bobby, I HAVE a dream! Please, where do I start?!" Before Bobby could react, Zoe interjected with an intensity that cut through the air like a knife, "By getting rid of those so-called friends of yours!"

Sabrina shouted out to Bobby and Zoe, *"Wait, you two, wait!"*

"What?" Zoe replied, annoyed.

"The kayaks are for someone else," Sabrina said with a shrug.

Bobby was puzzled and replied. *"But I told you to hire two for us, Sabrina! I even paid you for it."*

Sabrina replied, *"Oh, I forgot to tell you, my friends are coming over in a while to use them."*

Zoe gave Sabrina a dirty look and said, *"So what are we… chop liver!!!"*

This was the final straw for Bobby, but instead of reacting, she turned and walked back to the car with Zoe, her head down, and vowed never to return. Zoe shot Sabrina and the girls a middle finger while Bobby wasn't looking.

When they reached the car, Zoe, furious, said, *"Do you realize that shallow piece of work, you called your friend pulled that stunt because you didn't pick up the bill like you always do?!"*

Bobby replied, *"The one that doesn't get angry is always the winner."*

"Yeah, right," Zoe said angrily, unable to grasp the principle.

Then Zoe added, *"Hang on... that dumb bitch took your money for the kayaks. You need to get it back!!"*

Bobby shook her head, her tone flat. *"Don't worry about it, Zoe. I'm not going back there."*

*"B*lls*t! How much did you pay her?"* Zoe demanded.

Bobby hesitated. *"Two hundred and five dollars I paid into her bank account last week."*

"Wait here," Zoe said firmly, marching back.

Bobby leaned against the car, watching her sister walk angrily in the distance. Bobby smiled at how adorable Zoe looked when she was furious.

As Zoe approached the girls, she overheard Sabrina badmouthing Bobby. *"What New Yorker is going to listen to some farmer from the outback? She's just a delusional wannabe who's going to fall flat on her face. Just watch."* *"Better than a delusional never-be,"* Zoe shot back.

The girls turned around, shocked to see Zoe standing there. *"Give me my sister's money back,"* she demanded, her voice steely. Holding out her hand, she added, *"Two hundred and five bucks, now."*

Bobby watches her sister in the distance, demanding the money. She smiled again and said, *"You gotta love her. She gets so angry and throws hot sparks in every direction."*

Christopher Lane, also leaning against the car, nodded. *"Hi, Bobby."*

Bobby casually responded, *"I know, I know, okay... I plead guilty to wanting to punch Sabrina in the face."*

Christopher smiled, then replied, *"Bobby Jo, you know more than anyone... don't let anger control you. Epictetus once said, 'Any person capable of angering you becomes your master. He can anger you only when you permit yourself to be disturbed."*

Scrambling, Sabrina dug through her handbag, coming up five dollars short. *"I don't have it all."* she exclaimed in a panic.

Zoe pointed to the other three girls. *"Then let your accomplices here pay."*

The others tossed in loose change, frantically coming up with the full amount, feeling intimidated by Zoe.

Zoe pocketed the money, her voice dripping with sarcasm. *"Good luck, ladies. You'll need it, there's not much else going for you."* She turned and walked away, leaving the girls standing in stunned silence.

"Here," Zoe said, handing Bobby the cash she had just collected.

"What did they say?" Bobby asked, her voice soft.

"As expected, nothing of substance," Zoe replied, sparing her sister the painful details.

"You know, I should've known better," Bobby said thoughtfully. *"One of my books says to be careful who you share your dreams with, make sure they're aligned with who you are."*

"Oh yeah?" Zoe replied. *"That was Christopher Lane?"*

Bobby turned, surprised. *"Exactly how much time have you been spending in my library?"*

Zoe just smiled, and together they began the drive home.

The next day, Bobby was working with Alonso, fixing fences to prepare for a new flock of sheep. The funding would only allow for 3,000 Merino sheep for wool, but it was a start.

Late afternoon came, and Bobby went back to the house to start packing. Zoe peeked in and asked, *"You nervous, sis?"*

Bobby, placing her toiletries in her beauty bag and not looking up at Zoe, said, *"Yes, Zoe, I'm shitting myself, but I'm going to do it anyway."*

Seconds later, Zoe said, *"Well, you're gonna need this then,"* and suddenly, Bobby got hit in the head with something soft.

"What is this?" Bobby exclaimed and realized it was a full roll of toilet paper. *"I don't have time for this!"* Bobby added.

Bobby stopped packing, smiled, and reminded herself to seize the moment. She chased Zoe all over the house, throwing the toilet roll back at her. What started as a simple toss quickly turned into a toilet roll fight, with paper flying everywhere. Bobby forced the toilet paper around Zoe's mouth, and Zoe forcefully fought Bobby back to wrap her mouth as well.

Alonso asked Melina with a smile if they'd been drinking his homemade limoncello. (strong liquor)

Melina and Alonso were thrilled to see their daughters finally acting like true sisters should.

Bobby and Zoe laughed so hard they couldn't contain themselves. Zoe yelled out, *"I think I just peed myself from laughing! Oh no, give me that paper, I need it now!"*

But as Zoe reached to grab it from Bobby, the last bit of paper came off, leaving Zoe holding only the cardboard insert. They laughed so hard that tears streamed from their eyes, etching priceless memories of pure gold into their world of emotional wealth.

After they cleaned up the mess, Nonna Giovanna called out, *"Bobby, there's a delivery for you!"*

Bobby yelled back from her bedroom, *"What? For me? It could be the book I ordered from Amazon!"*

"Just open it, Nonna," she added.

Nonna Giovanna said, *"It's not a parcel, come and have a look."*

It was a bunch of Australian wildflowers with a good luck card.

Bobby said, "Oh, how lovely! It's from our shearer, Mason. I miss him; he was my favorite. It's an invitation to an Aboriginal ceremony tonight. This is so sweet." But Bobby couldn't help but think of Brian Taylor; these could have been the Australian wild flowers grown by Brian. Bobby felt a sudden, unexpected streak of sadness.

Bobby turned up at the ceremony and met up with Mason, who had just a white cloth wrapped around his hip and was painted from head to toe for the Aboriginal ceremony. Bobby almost didn't recognize him.

"Hey, Mason, is that you? Wow, you look amazing! Hey, what's the occasion?" she asked.

"Tonight, Bobby, we celebrate YOU," Mason replied.

"What? Me? ... Why?" Bobby asked, surprised.

Mason replied, *"Boof head O'Connor told us you're going to America for the game you created. I played the prototype you gave me, Bobby, I loved it. I feel so proud of what you've achieved."*

In that moment, she realized that apart from her Nonna, Mason was the only one that actually offered encouragement. Luckily, I don't wait for encouragement; if I did. I would not achieve jack Sh*t, she thought.

"Mason, I haven't found a publisher yet, so what's the occasion?" Bobby replied modestly.

"Bobby, you are the occasion. Sit, relax, and enjoy the dance, it's especially for you. It will bring you luck."

Bobby was in awe of seeing a dance and traditions that were millions of years old. She paid attention to every step they took and how they sounded. But most of all, she was touched that her special friend Mason had gone through so much trouble for her.

Narrated by Nonna Giovanna

I remember vividly that it was the 2nd of October, and for the first time, there was no harvest or sheep to shear because of what happened. It felt strange and empty to all of us.

The evening before Bobby's departure for New York, our family dinner was unusually quiet. Alonso clearly wasn't thrilled about Bobby's decision, and while Melina supported her, I could see the worry in her eyes. Zoe, though, kept things light with her usual sense of humour.

"Now, Bobby," she teased, *"Don't bring me back some ugly random souvenir. Bring back that hottie Taylor Lautner!"*

Alonso raised an eyebrow, looking unimpressed.

"Who the hell is Taylor Lautner?" Bobby asked, confused.

"Oh, right, you wouldn't know," Zoe smirked. *"You only know author names, not actors."*

"Exactly," Bobby replied with a grin, gesturing a silent *'checkmark'* in the air.

Turning to her father, Bobby reassured him. *"I'll be back before you know it, Dad. I need to do this. You know me by now."*

Alonso sighed with defeat in his voice. *"So, what's your plan, Bobby?"*

Bobby sprung into her zestful self and said, *"Well, Dad, I've ordered 50 board games straight from China, set to arrive at my motel room in three days. Fifty was the minimum I could order, but it's ok, I will travel all fifty states looking for publishers if I have to. I've transferred $50,000 onto this card for publishing costs."* Bobby placed both orange-coloured debit cards on the kitchen table.

She went on to say, *"The salon marketing venture and Nonna's money from the house she sold give just over $1,100,000, so you can* *start buying sheep and leasing the farm equipment and wheat seeds we need. Later, we'll buy our own equipment."*

"Why are you using the business card? Just transfer that $50k into your personal account," Alonso asked, concerned.

"Because, Dad, my board game profits are your profits too."

Alonso insisted, *"Baby, listen to me. You invented that game. You deserve to keep 100% of the profit."*

"We're business partners, Dad," Bobby replied firmly. *"I can't contribute directly to the farm right now, so let me do it this way,"* she added.

Zoe chimed in, *"You know, Mum, if the publishers like the game, it could end up in stores like Target and Kmart. Imagine Sabrina's dumb face if she saw it there!"* she added with a smirk.

Melina beamed. *"That would be incredible, Bobby. I'm so proud of you, my darling girl!"*

As we gathered in our traditional family hug, Alonso held Bobby close and said. *"Go pursue that dream, girl. I love you."*

The next morning, Bobby loaded her suitcase into her ute and prepared to leave. She hugged Mozza the dog and patted Fredrickson, her beloved kangaroo, who wouldn't leave her side, now all grown up and refusing to leave the farm. *"Fredrickson ... Don't go jumping any barbed wire fences while I'm gone, ok,"* she whispered, smiling as he nudged her hand. She gave him a hug and kissed him on the forehead.

I approached her with a small jewelry box, opening it to reveal a delicate gold necklace that had belonged to my mother; it was two gold hearts entwined. She'd given it to me when I left for Australia, and now it was time to pass it on. Bobby protested, *"Nonna, this is yours,"* but I insisted. She put it on straight away.

Tucking a small roll of cash wrapped in an elastic band into her hand, I added, *"And take this, buy yourself something nice. You're about to give those publishers every last cent you have; you deserve to spoil yourself."*

Bobby shook her head, reluctant to accept the money. *"Nonna, it's okay,"* she said softly.

"Take it," I said, holding back tears. Bobby replied, *"Okay, thank you, but I feel bad. I'm the one that's supposed to spoil you and take you to Milan, Nonna, just the two of us."*

"Don't be sorry, my Bella. I'm happier that you are doing what you have been craving to do for years. I have always known you were destined for much more."

"Have you!! Nonna… Thank you, I love you so much," Bobby replied as she hugged me so tight it almost hurt.

Typical of her, she finally accepted the money, with one condition: *"That their trip to Milan is to happen next year."*

Melina approached, trying to keep her worry hidden as she hugged Bobby. *"Just promise me you'll stick to the safe places, baby. Don't make yourself vulnerable. Someone as pretty as you can't afford to be vulnerable,"* she said, her voice trembling slightly.

"Oh, thanks, Mum, I promise ok … love you," Bobby replied, smiling.

I called Alonso over, knowing he'd been avoiding goodbyes like he always did, reminding me of my father. He stepped out from the shed, where he'd been tinkering, and pulled her towards him into a strong embrace. *"Be careful over there, please don't be 'too much' your usual nice self, okay?"* he said quietly.

I reminded Bobby that she was to call every day, even if it was just brief, so that we would know she was okay, and she told us she would.

We watched as she climbed into her ute, the early morning sun casting light across the farm. The engine rumbled to life, and with a final wave, my sweet Bobby drove off toward Adelaide Airport, ready to take on the world.

We stood there long after she was out of sight, each of us feeling the weight of her absence once again, but at the same time feeling immense pride and love that always bound us together.

NOT NARRATED

Tens of thousands of kilometers away on the other side of our beautiful globe, a group of high school friends, inseparable, found themselves scattered across different corners of the U.S. Reunions had become a rare, cherished event full of laughter and reminiscing about the old days. But now, approaching their mid-twenties, they were all grappling with the same sinking feeling, they hadn't reached the level of success they'd once dreamed of.

Liam, Ethan, Ava, and Kizzy, bound by the chains of their shared past yet scattered by the winds of distance, had converged in the whirlwind of New York for a reunion that was long overdue and brimming with emotion. The high school reunion event was the catalyst, reigniting connections but also starkly illuminating the derailed paths their lives had taken. Liam was a bundle of nerves, pacing his apartment in anticipation of their arrival at precisely six pm, as he meticulously crafted a sumptuous homemade dinner for them. He ensured there was an extra plate prepared for Helen next door, as he faithfully did every night without fail.

Helen, a 91-year-old widow living a solitary life, was sadly forgotten by her three children, who seldom visited or even called. Liam had forged an unbreakable bond with Helen, checking on her daily and bringing her evening meals. Her gratitude was palpable, her eyes radiating warmth, and Liam would downplay his kindness with a modest chuckle, *"Well, I have to cook for myself anyway, what's an extra dish?"* Liam's compassion extended further as he accompanied Helen to her doctor appointments and regularly whisked her away to Central Park for rejuvenating breaths of fresh air and a change of scenery for her. He was the embodiment of selflessness, driven not by the prospect of reward but by an innate purpose and a steadfast commitment to humanity. Helen's attempts at matchmaking him with her granddaughter added a humorous twist to their relationship, with Liam only reacting with a smile.

As the clock ticked to 6:20 pm, Liam's apartment burst into life with the arrival of his friends. Together, they shared an electric magic, a rare and powerful resonance that was rare,

The air buzzed with the intensity of their reunion. Their plan was to spend four weeks in New York with Liam.

As their conversations ran deep, it was evident that life had been unkind to them, each carrying unspoken disappointments.

Despite their best efforts, they all found themselves mired in frustration. Liam had recently lost his job as a TV cameraman because his show got canceled, causing him to look for other work. His dream of becoming a movie producer felt increasingly unreachable. Ava, though financially secure as a realtor, wrestled with a deep void in her heart from a lack of a sense of purpose. And Ethan, harboring feelings for Kizzy, had never mustered the courage to confess, fearing rejection, he would hide a lot about what was going on inside. Kizzy, totally unaware of Ethan's feelings for her, shared her frustrations of not being closer to her goal of being a writer and becoming a mother one day.

As they reconnected and shared their inner struggles, they became painfully aware of the gravity of their situations and the urgency to make serious changes before it was too late. Little did they know that this reunion would eventually be the catalyst for transforming their lives forever.

Bobby was brimming with excitement as she arrived in New York City for the first time in her life. She didn't want to miss a thing, her eyes wide as she took in the towering buildings, the flashing lights, and the endless crowds, so far removed from the quiet vastness of her remote farm life.

She ordered an Uber, and a friendly, energetic, African-American man in his thirties pulled up in a well-kept, sleek black sedan. *"Hello, ma'am, my name is Timothy. Allow me to help you with that,"* he greeted, stepping out to assist with her luggage.

Bobby, being her natural happy self, said, *"Hi Tim, as you know from the app, my name's Bobby. Nice to meet you!"*

Bobby was impressed with the Uber driver's great service. Hearing an American accent for the first time was so exciting for her. Bobby suddenly felt the magnitude of the distance she'd traveled. *"Wow... I'm really on the other side of the world, it's so different here."* she thought, absorbing the city's intensity, the noise, the energy, busy people everywhere.

As she started to get into the car, she instinctively reached for the wrong side, almost sitting on Timothy's lap. *"Oh, I'm so sorry...sorry. Pure habit,"* she muttered to herself, feeling her cheeks flush with embarrassment as she clumsily turned to go to the correct side.

Timothy chuckled and quickly made her feel at ease. *"I can tell where you're from,"* he teased, flashing a friendly smile.

Bobby grinned, trying to shake off her embarrassment, and said, *"Why's your driver's seat on the wrong side? I'm feeling dyslexic right now!"*

The driver laughed. *"England, right?"*

"Oh, not even close, mate! I'm from outback Australia."

As the driver sat back in his seat to settle into the trip, he commented, *"Australia, huh? You're a long way from home!"* He shook his head in wonder. *"So, what's the outback like?"*

She paused, searching for words. *"Simply beautiful,"* she replied, almost to herself. *"Simply beautiful,"* she repeated, lost in thought. *"Sometimes, it can get lonely...,"* she added.

"Believe me, it gets lonely here, too," Timothy replied with a knowing look.

Bobby laughed. *"Lonely? With millions of people around you, are you kidding me?"*

The driver nodded, a hint of sadness in his eyes.

Bobby said, *"Well, Tim, if you spend all your time with yourself, you've got to enjoy your own company, right?"* The driver responded with a nod and said, *"True."*

"So, are you here on vacation?" he asked, glancing over at her in the rearview mirror. *"There's a lot to see,"* he added.

"I'd love to see every stitch of this place, but I'm not here on holiday," she replied, her voice tinged with determination. *"I've got important work to do."*

He raised an eyebrow, intrigued. *"Oh, ok …what do you do?*

Bobby nodded. *"I have a product, do you want to hear about it?*

Timothy replies, "Sure."

I created a personal development learning game that includes mindset principles from authors. It has proven success principles and takes inventory of your blind spots, stopping you from succeeding."

"I've got lots of blind spots!" Timothy said.

"It's designed to make superior knowledge accessible to anyone serious about personal change," Bobby continued.

"Sounds interesting. I could use a serious change myself," he admitted with a chuckle.

Bobby went on, *"Well, change doesn't come easy,"* she said. *"People are extremely attached to who they are, even if they're unhappy."*

"I don't think I'm attached," he replied, a bit defensively.

Bobby smiled. *"What I mean is... it's your paradigm, in other words, your habitual way of thinking that leads to a habitual way of feeling, which drives your habitual actions."*

"Wow, that's a lot of habits in there," Timothy replied.

"Yes, habits rule all of us. We're all on autopilot, without even realizing," Bobby explained.

"Can I buy one of your games?" he asked, genuine interest lighting up his face.

She chuckled. *"It's not on the market yet. But I'll have the professional version delivered to my motel tomorrow."*

The driver handed her a piece of paper. *"Could you write down an author's name and book I could start with?"*

With a smile, she wrote down the title of one of Christopher Lane's books and handed it to him, saying, *"Wisdom applied is progress. Wisdom not applied... Well, that's just a waste of time."*

The driver repeated her words to himself, nodding thoughtfully.

"Thanks, Bobby, nice meeting you... good luck with your game."

"Thanks," Bobby replied, then proceeded to get out of the car and added, *"Tim, and by the way, I love your accent. You're the first American person I've met, you're pretty awesome."*

Timothy smirked. *"Accent? What are you talking about? You've got an accent, not me, and I love it; it's so different!"* Bobby replied, *"Oh really, do you think so? Thank you!!"*

They shared a laugh, each feeling an unexpected camaraderie. Before Timothy drove off to greet his next customer, he handed Bobby his business card. *"If you're in town for a bit, call me directly, if you need anything. I could use more of your wise words, plus I want to buy one of your games when they arrive".*

Bobby took his card with a smile. *"Thanks, Tim,"* giving him a playful wave as she headed into the motel lobby, savoring the moment of connection in this bustling, foreign city.

The hotel's elegance took her by surprise, the polished marble floors, the ornate chandeliers, the hum of conversations in languages she didn't recognize. She walked over to the service desk and said, *"Hi, my name is Bobby Russo. I'm booked in for 7 days."*

The receptionist handed her the keys with a friendly smile. Once in her room, Bobby took off her shoes and placed them neatly up high on the entrance table out of sheer habit.

Then she walks across the room. Pulling back the curtains, she gasped as the vastness of Central Park stretched before her. *"Holy Sh*t, I'm in New York. I'm really here, Wow, and look at the size of that park!!."* she said to herself out loud.

She stared, awestruck, tilting her head from side to side as she took it all in. She grabbed a brochure of Central Park on the desk and read it, *"Central Park 843 acres... holy moly ... Eucalyptus Ridge is 3 and a half times bigger!"* She shook her head, laughing, adding. *"No wonder I get exhausted!!"*

Collapsing onto the bed backward, she felt a wave of relief to be there and finally make some traction with her game. She had allowed herself one day off in case the shipment from China arrived late. With little sleep the night before, she rose at 8 a.m., exhausted as her internal clock was still set to Australian time. Heading down to reception, she made sure they knew to expect a large delivery that belonged to her.

She spent the day waiting in the foyer, popping out for a quick lunch, and taking in the vibrant world outside. People rushed by, everyone on their own mission, their lives so different from the simplicity of hers. Returning to the lobby, she dozed off in the lobby chair around 4:30 p.m., headphones on, listening to an audiobook by Christopher Lane.

When Bobby woke at 6 p.m. and approached the reception again, the lobby was buzzing with activity, as it was peak time. She waited in line, her polite manner intact.

"Sorry, miss," she said to the receptionist. *"I'm expecting a large package. I dozed off waiting, it's the time difference thing, sorry."*

The receptionist checked the records and shook her head. *"I'm sorry, ma'am. I don't see any large package arrivals here."*

Frustrated but determined to keep her composure, Bobby insisted, *"Could I speak to your manager? My app says it arrived."*

The receptionist replied with a sympathetic smile, *"I'm afraid the manager isn't here at the moment. You'll need to come back in the morning."*

The following morning, Bobby wasted no time heading down to the reception desk. She had a sense of urgency, fueled by the frustration of yesterday. The manager emerged from the back office with a warm smile on his face.

"What seems to be troubling you, madam?" he asked politely.

Bobby read his name tag carefully before speaking. *"Hello, Jacob, my name's Bobby Russo, I'm in room 702. A large package was due to arrive here yesterday. My app shows it was delivered, but no one seems to know anything about it."*

The manager's expression grew thoughtful. *"What's the approximate size of the package, ma'am?"*

"You can't miss it," Bobby replied, trying to hold her composure. *"It's an order from China, fifty board games. I need access to them as soon as possible; I'm meeting with a publisher tomorrow, and I need to have one of those games with me."*

Jacob nodded, calm and understanding. *"Let me have a look for you, ma'am. You're welcome to come with me,"* he added.

Relieved, Bobby followed Jacob down the halls, stopping as he checked various storage areas. But the package was nowhere to be found. The manager sighed, turning back to her. *"I'm sorry, ma'am. We'll let you know if it turns up."*

Disappointment washed over Bobby. She'd come all this way, and now she only had her scrappy prototype, the one the publisher had already stated would be unacceptable. She clenched her fists, keeping her cool.

That evening in her motel room, the figure of Christopher Lane appeared, his calming presence resonating. He said, *"This part of your life is called muscle building."* Bobby let out a sigh. Despite her frustrations, she knew he was right. She spent her time thinking of different ways to handle the upcoming meeting. *"How the hell am I not going to look like a disorganized fool from the bush!"* she said to herself in her motel room.

CHAPTER 13

MUSCLE BUILDING

NOT NARRATED

The next morning, she prepared for her 11 a.m. appointment with New Age Publishing on High Street. She fixed her hair and applied her makeup, awkwardly, as she rarely wore any. As she gathered her things, her phone rang with an unidentified number. The caller introduced himself with a strong American accent.

"Hello, this is Ben Calper from New Age Publishing. I understand you have an appointment this morning at 11 a.m.," he said.

"Yes, that's correct!" Bobby replied, her excitement renewed. He went on to say:

"Before we proceed, ma'am, there's a $330 deposit required to secure your booking, refunded if there's no contract."

"No one mentioned anything about a deposit," she replied, feeling her enthusiasm falter. *"How about I pay in person when I arrive there in a few hours?"*

"Sorry, ma'am, protocol requires the deposit in advance. We'll email you the details, and upon receiving the payment, we'll confirm the appointment."

"Listen, Mr. … whatever your name is … I have my own protocol. I will pay you when I get there," she snapped.

"Your appointment is pending then. Have a great day, ma'am," he replied and hung up.

"What the hell was that? I didn't travel halfway across the world for my appointment to get bloody canceled!" she said out loud.

Bobby sat at the edge of her bed, too annoyed to think clearly. Her gut was telling her something felt odd.

She hastily opened her laptop, paid the fee of $330 USD, which was $500 Australian Dollars, with her debit card, and slammed it shut. After taking a few moments to meditate and calm down, she set off to the lobby to see if the package had arrived, but it didn't. As the receptionist gave her the bad news, she smiled at her and turned around towards the outside exit. *"Muscle building huh,"* she thought to herself, still trying to keep calm.

She headed off early for the publishing house, allowing time for possibly getting lost. Navigating New York's maze-like streets, her feet ached from the heels she rarely wore. She muttered to herself, *"Stupid fancy-*ss shoes!"* She removed them and replaced them with thongs (flip-flops) until she found herself circling the block back to where she had started. Even though she was using her phone to guide her, she was well and truly lost. But she still remained calm.

In her wanderings, she noticed a homeless man. Feeling a pang of empathy, she stopped and gave him some money. They shared a meaningful glance before she continued on.

Her phone was not giving her the right directions. She whispered, "Sh*t, what if this publisher does not exist?" Deciding to call the publishing office for directions, she finally arrived at the building, thankful she hadn't missed her appointment and that they actually did exist.

"Hi, my name's Bobby Russo, and I have an appointment at 11 a.m. with Mr. Craig Fellman," she said to the receptionist, hoping she was still expected.

The receptionist checked the computer and gave her a warm smile. *"Oh yes, Bobby Russo. Welcome!"* Bobby exhaled with relief.

"Would you like a coffee while you wait?" asked the receptionist.

"I'm fine, thank you," Bobby replied, nervously clutching her prototype. Soon, Mr. Fellman arrived, greeting her with a friendly smile.

"Hello, Miss Russo. I admire your determination, travelling so far to make this happen."

She chuckled, attempting to mask her nerves. *"Thank you, sir. Yes, I sure flew over a lot of fish to get here!"*

He laughed and said, *"This way, Miss Russo."* directing her to his office.

They both sat down, then he gestured toward her package. *"Is this your game?"*

"Yes, but... the professionally finished ones were supposed to arrive yesterday," she stammered. *"They're missing, and all I have is this prototype. I'm working with the manufacturer to locate the shipment; you will have one in your hands this week, sir."*

Mr. Fellman examined her prototype with interest. *"Tell me about it, Bobby. Take me on a journey."*

Bobby brightened. *"It's designed for people who have goals but not a clear path to achieving them. This game guides them toward success through mindset and personal growth. It has an action plan and the resources needed to get to their destination. This is no ordinary game... sir, it is life-altering."*

He paused, thoughtful, and the silence felt thick with anticipation. *"I like it,"* he finally said after what felt like ages following his examination of the prototype. He nodded with approval. *"So, here's what we'll do for you, Miss Russo. We'll test it for 2 months, analyze the results, and then we'll discuss a possible contract."*

Bobby tried to hide her surprise. *"Thank you for your time, Mr. Fellman. I appreciate the opportunity, but I am not willing to wait that amount of time. I have other publishing agents willing to see my game that will be more respectful of my time."*

"Very well," said Mr. Fellman, not in the least bit flexible.

They both walked back to the reception area, and as she turned to leave, almost forgetting, Bobby said, *"Oh, I'd like my deposit back, please."*

The receptionist looked confused. *"Deposit, ma'am? We don't take deposits for appointments."*

Bobby puzzled, replying, *"What... I got a call from someone named Ben Scalper or Calper or something this morning, asking for a $330 deposit to confirm my slot."*

The snobby receptionist shook her head. *"We don't have a Ben Calper or Scalper on staff, and we open at 9 a.m. Are you sure you're not confusing us with another publisher?"*

Panic rose in Bobby's chest as she opened her bank app on her phone in the entrance area. A charge was showing for $98.50 at Sunflower Springs Supermarket. She stared, bewildered. *"What's Dad doing with this card?"*

She recalled the night before she left home, placing two orange EFTPOS cards with different accounts on the kitchen table. She recalled picking one up, then her father picking up the other, both marked Russo Enterprises, with identical colours. It hit her like a punch to the gut, she'd taken the wrong card.

Bobby took a look at the account with the large amount of money that Alonso was supposed to have, and it was completely drained by an unknown debtor from the U.S. *"Sh*t, Sh*t, no way!!"* she whispered to herself.

If she'd taken her card with $50,000 for the game development, she would've only lost that amount. Instead, the card with a bit over $1,000,000, containing not only farm funds but also $350,000 of Nonna Giovanna's money, had been completely drained.

"Bastards". They added three more zeros and withdrew twice. How can that happen?" Bobby yelled out.

She quickly checked the farm account's balance again, in case she was seeing things, her heart sinking further. A transfer of $330,000 USD, around AUD $500,000 withdrawn twice, had drained the farm business debit card to zero. Bobby clenched her fists, muttering

Italian profanities under her breath. *"Figlio di puttana!"* (*Son of a bitch!*)

She stormed back to Mr. Fellman, who was just about to enter the elevator. *"Someone in your organization is a fraud! I authorized $330, not 1 million Australian dollars from my account! Some scum bucket conveniently decided to add four more zeros! My brother is a mean-*ss lawyer, and you are in big trouble... *rs*h*le!!!"*

Mr. Fellman looked at her, appalled. *"Are you accusing us of fraud?"*

"Abso-figgin-lutely, I am!" she snapped.

Mr. Fellman called security, who escorted Bobby out by literally lifting her up and carrying her out as she protested, yelling out, *"I flew over a lot of fish, alright, and now I've encountered my first shark!"* She had never felt so humiliated in her whole life, standing there in the rain with her prototype soaking wet. She looked up at the building and shouted, *"You call this... MUSCLE BUILDING, Christopher Lane, huh?!!!"* A passerby, an athletic man, flexed his huge arm muscles with a grin. Bobby let out a stressed smile, shaking her head at him.

Back at her motel, she walked through the lobby, soaked, as the manager called out to her excitedly, *"Miss Russo... Miss Russo, we found your delivery! A new staff member accidentally placed it in the cleaners' storage, thinking it was cleaning stock. We'll bring it to your room immediately."*

Bobby just nodded, not even managing to smile, feeling too defeated to care.

She entered the elevator with a family, the warmth of their presence filling the air.

It was evident by the souvenirs they were holding that they were on vacation. Bobby, struggling to keep her voice steady, said, *"Enjoying your holiday?* The couple nodded their heads and said yes, but their 3 children shied away as Bobby smiled at them, *"Good on ya!"* She said and wished it were her own family, realizing how desperately she needed their hugs. *"Where are you heading out to today!"* Bobby asked.

The husband, noticing Bobby's Aussie accent, chuckled and said. *"We're thinking of heading out to Australia in an RV for our next vacation!"*

Bobby managed a smile. *"You do that!!!"* She paused for a second and said, *"When you're there, if you venture to the outback, make sure you see Alonso's Patch,"* waving goodbye as the elevator doors opened to level 7. The couple smiled at her in agreement and thanked her for her suggestion.

The husband and wife remained in the elevator. The husband said, *"Gonzo's what?"*

The wife replied, *"Batch... Gonzo's Batch."* She nodded her head, convinced that that's what it was. The husband then said, *"Darling, put that on our bucket list."*

Bobby entered her room and immediately called Carlo. It was 3.30 a.m. in Australia. Carlo picked up his mobile phone in the middle of his sleep, sounding alarmed. *"Friggin' hell, Bobby, you're scaring me half to death! Are you okay?"*

"Sorry to get you up Bro, yes, I'm... okay," she replied, her voice wavering. *"Well, actually, no, I'm not. I'm in the Sh*t creek, Carlo, and I don't mean a small one either."*

Carlo quickly sat up, giving her his full attention, while his girlfriend Riana sighed in annoyance in the background. *"Slow down, Bobby. I need the finer details."*

Taking a deep breath, she recounted the entire nightmare, down to the last humiliating detail. Carlo's hands covered his face.

"Bobby, there's more... I'm afraid overseas money transactions are impossible to recover, especially from Australia to the USA. Out of ten, with ten being most likely, it's a zero chance of getting your money back."

*"Zero... Sh*t?!"* she said frantically. *"I called the bank, but it was outside hours."*

Carlo explained, *"Look, start there. If you have no luck, I'll contact the Australian Federal Police."*

"Thank you, Carlo. And please, don't tell Dad about this. Promise me."

Carlo hesitated, feeling the weight of her plea. *"Bobby, you're in dire straits, and you expect me to keep this from Dad... He's going to find out sooner or later."*

Bobby replied, *"Yes, but let's make it later... a lot later. He might not even have to know if we get the funds back."*

"What if you don't, Bobby?" Carlo asked.

She paused, steadying her voice. *"Then I'll earn it back somehow while I'm here... I am not returning back home until I achieve my goal of finding a publisher, I already declared that to myself and Mum and Dad!!"*

Carlo sighed heavily. *"What? How? Bobby, this is serious. Just get back home."* But she had already hung up. Carlo stared at his phone, exasperated. *"Stubborn girl!"* he muttered, just as Riana tossed a pillow at his face, grumbling about the noise.

Moments later, Carlo's phone chimed with a message. It was a photo of Bobby, pointing her finger at him with a stern expression, captioned: *Promise me!* With a resigned smile, Carlo replied, *"Okay, I promise."* Sh*t! Carlo whispered to himself.

Five hours later, it was 8.30 a.m. in Sunflower Springs. Bobby's phone buzzed with a FaceTime call from her parents and her grandmother, Giovanna. She forced a smile as their familiar faces filled the screen. They were standing outside in the warm morning sunlight.

Alonso's voice was hopeful. *"So, how did it go with the publisher yesterday, love? We're all hanging out to know!"*

"Oh, yeah, I got carried away," Bobby replied, recalling the scene with security carrying her away. She tried to keep her expression neutral.

"That sounds just like you, love," said Alonso.

Bobby explains, *"New Age Publishing said they needed to test the game for two months, so I declined. I told them I have other publishers waiting and interested."*

"Early days yet, Dad. I told Mr. Fellman I'd be investigating other avenues."

Alonso chuckled. *"That's our girl. Always covering all her bases."*

Bobby gave them a strained smile. *"Look, I have to go. It's been a long day already. Love you all!"* They blew kisses, and she ended the call, her forced smile fading as she looked around her small motel room.

"Yeah, I'm investigating other avenues, alright," she murmured to herself, *"and dark alleys, which might be where I'm sleeping soon."*

Three days passed without progress. The Australian Federal Police were now working on the case, but the stolen funds remained untraceable. Bobby's prepaid stay at the motel was nearly over, with just one night left, and she was running low on the cash Nonna Giovanna gave her. Desperate, she approached the reception desk, spotting Jacob, the manager.

"Excuse me, Jacob," she said softly, trying to keep her voice steady. He looked up and seemed surprised and touched that she'd remembered his name. Bobby had a way of making everyone she met feel special because she genuinely felt they were and appreciated their uniqueness.

"Oh, hello, ma'am. How can I help you?"

"I'm in a bit of a pickle," she admitted, nervously twisting her hands. *"This is my last day here, and... would it be possible to use my bond of $200 for one more night? I know you don't know me from a bar of soap, but I promise I won't trash the place."*

Jacob looked at her sympathetically. *"Give me a moment."* She walked over to the front counter and made a quick call; a housemaid appeared moments later, nodding after a brief exchange. Jacob turned back to Bobby with a smile. *"Apparently, your room has been so clean and tidy that she only had to add towels. Consider the extra night on us."*

Bobby's face softened with surprise and gratitude. *"Thank you, Jacob. You have no idea how much this means."*

Jacob tilted his body in a soft, friendly bow. *"You're welcome. And thank you for taking care of your room."*

With half a day left in the motel, Bobby sat in her room, trying to figure out where she could possibly store the fifty board games. She counted her remaining cash carefully, stretching what her grandmother had given her by eating as much as she could from the free breakfast buffet and skipping meals later in the day.

She pulled out Timothy the Uber driver's business card and dialed his number.

"Hey, Tim, it's Bobby... your passenger from the outback," she began. *"Listen, my card isn't working right now, but I've got $30 in cash to spare. Do you think you could help me out with a ride and maybe find a place to store a large parcel?"*

Tim's cheerful voice instantly lifted her spirits. *"AAAAhhhh My Aussie friend! Good to hear from you. Sure, I'm on my way."*

When he arrived, Timothy greeted her with a wide grin. *"Good to see you, Bobby! I read that book you recommended; by the way, it blew my mind!!!.”* He glanced at the large parcel and whistled. *“You didn't mention I'd need a forklift.”*

Bobby laughed, and together, they worked on squeezing as many of the board games as they could into the car. *“We'll have to come back for the rest,”* Timothy said with a grin.

“No, Tim, I prefer not to,” Bobby replied.

She spotted a homeless man and walked over, handing him a game. *“Here, take this; it can be played solo. Learn from it, apply it to your life every day, and I promise you'll see change beyond what you can imagine.”*

The man nodded and thanked her. As she started to walk away, she added softly, *“The most powerful help is... self-help.”* as she looked him deeply in the eyes.

CHAPTER 14

SELF HELP

NOT NARRATED

Back in the car, Timothy looked at her curiously. _"Where are we going, Bobby?"_

She hesitated, then asked him, _"Do you know where the nearest public dunny is?"_

"Dunny? I thought we spoke the same language," Timothy jokingly replied, confused.

"Toilets!" she clarified, laughing.

Timothy chuckled and pointed to the motel. _"You could just use the restroom here."_

"No, Tim, besides there. Somewhere else," she insisted, sparking his curiosity. As they drove off, they spotted the homeless man doing a deal with a passerby, selling the board game Bobby had just given him. Bobby saw a $10 note being exchanged.

"Oh my god, Tim! That homeless guy just sold his chance at a new life for $10! Look, he is selling it to that random woman passing by."

Timothy sighed. *"You know what they say, Bobby. You can lead them to water, but you can't make them drink."* They both shook their heads, echoing the words at the same time.

Bobby said, *"Well … maybe the game is what that Lady needs right now, we will never know"*.

Timothy was impressed by Bobby's caring nature and gave her a smile and said, *"You really are something, outback girl."*

"Thanks, Tim"

"Do you Aussies shorten everybody's name?" Timothy asked.

"Yep!!" she replied. *"We shorten a lot of words and add lots of o's, i's, and a's at the end of a lot of words. But I wasn't even aware of it till I came here"*.

Amused, Bobby decided to teach Timothy some Aussie slang. They spotted an elderly man crossing the street, and Bobby pointed in his direction and said. *"Watch out for the old codger."*

"Codger?" Timothy asked, squinting. *"Is that a dog breed?"*

Bobby burst into laughter. Next, she spotted a young woman in flip-flops. *"Look at that, Sheila in thongs."*

Tim's eyes widened in excitement, and he said, *"Where? And how can you tell she's wearing one?"*

Bobby laughed so hard she had to wipe tears from her eyes and explained to Timothy that in Australia, they never say flip-flops; they say thongs. In Australia, a G-string is often called a g-banger; it's never called a thong.

"Tim, there is much more slang you don't know about, but I won't go there, some words are pretty cheeky... but harmless". Her laughter brought a warm smile to Timothy's face as he looked at her in admiration.

Her laughter faded as she remembered her grandmother's words echoing in her mind: she said aloud, *"Humour is a special gift from God to help us cope with life."*

"Nonna, you were right," she murmured aloud, a bittersweet smile on her face.

Timothy replied. *"Another slang word, 'Nonna'?"*

"No," she replied with a wistful smile. *"It means 'grandmother' in Italian."*

Timothy grinned. *They communicated as if they had known each other for years.*

As Timothy continued driving, Bobby rejected each public toilet Timothy suggested. Finally, with dusk approaching and the area becoming sketchier, Timothy said, *"Look, I hate to tell you, but I refuse to drive further into this part of town. Not without a Crocodile Dundee knife or a live crocodile on a leash."*

"Okay," Bobby laughed. *"We'll make do right here."*

"What exactly are we doing?" he asked, still confused.

She grabbed the stack of games, and under the cover of darkness, carefully placed them in a female public restroom, stacking them strategically in a toilet cubicle with an *"Out of Order"* sign she had prepared earlier. She locked the toilet door with her suitcase lock, making sure it looked convincing. She placed five games in a black plastic bag to take with her.

Back at the car, Timothy shook his head in awe. *"Why not just ask the next hotel you're staying at to store them?"*

"I did, and they said no," Bobby replied, trying to sound like a convincing liar, but it didn't come naturally to her, and she hated having to lie. Bobby was not one to seek sympathy or impose on anyone, so she kept her dire situation to herself.

Timothy gave a mock sigh. *"Alright, let's go ...where's your motel?"*

"It happens to be just around the corner, but I can't remember the name," she said with another forced lie and a tired smile.

They returned to the random motel she pointed at, where Timothy helped her with the last of her bags. As she handed him $30 and apologized that it wasn't much, he held up a hand. *"The book you recommended has already changed my life. Keep the money, Bobby."*

Touched by his remark, she handed him one of her board games. *"You said your dream was to be an airline pilot, right?"*

"Yes," he replied, *"It would be a dream come true,"* he added.

"Then take this, apply its philosophies, and I promise it'll bring you joy and success in every way possible," Bobby said in a stern tone. *"So glad I met you, Tim, you have such a beautiful nature, and I just know you will achieve all your heart's desires... Good luck and never give up."* Bobby said, looking at Timothy with a loving smile on her face.

He thanked her, waving as she entered the motel. Watching her walk in, Timothy muttered to himself, *"Good luck, my little Aussie friend,"* and he drove off.

She walked inside the random motel that she led Timothy to believe was booked for her. Bobby approached the receptionist, attempting her best smile. *"Oh, hi… I think I'm in the wrong place."* She forced a laugh, feeling the awkwardness.

The young receptionist returned her smile and said. *"This is 124 Hauler St, ma'am."*

"Right," Bobby nodded, retreating quickly and saying, *"Thank you, I do have the wrong place, silly me. Good evening to you."* Bobby quietly walked out.

Outside, the biting wind hit her, the cold, unlike anything she'd felt before. She counted her remaining cash under the glow of the motel lights, what her Nonna had given her was nearly gone after currency conversions and a week of meals. Tempted to go back into the motel she'd pretended to be lost in, Bobby knew she couldn't afford it.

For the first time, reality sank in, she was in serious trouble and totally alone.

Bobby tried so hard to fall asleep as she huddled in the side garden of the motel, hidden behind two massive ornamental pots in the dark corner of the property.

She hid behind a large yellow waste bin. The night was pitch-black, her only light coming from the glow of her phone. Her mother made her promise to call once a day, so she did without turning on her camera, so she wouldn't have to explain, and she kept it short.

After the call, Bobby whispered to herself, *"Mum told me not to make myself vulnerable, and I am. I'm sorry, Mum. I miss you."*

"How can this be happening?" Bobby thought, her mind racing. She felt something trickling on her face. *"What's this?"* she wondered as she turned on the soft light from her phone and noticed it was snow. *"So, is this what snow looks like? Wow. Sorry, Snow"*, she joked and added, *"This is not a good first impression."* She tried for hours to fall asleep, hoping to get out of there before dawn.

In her darkest hours, she always sought comfort from the man in the white cloak. She drew incredible strength from acknowledging he was there for her, and he was. At 2 a.m. that night, completely covered in snow, in the pitch dark and shivering uncontrollably from the cold, she didn't know what had hit her. She was extremely resilient to extreme heat but had never experienced such extreme cold.

The white-cloaked man approached her closely. She had her upper legs curled around her torso in a desperate attempt to keep warm.

"Bobby Jo, my dear child, sleep; I have your back," he said softly. She looked up, and there he was. He wiped the frozen tear off her face and brushed the snow off her head. He took off his white cloak and placed it over her. Instantly, she stopped shivering, feeling the warmth surrounding her. Calmly, she rested her head down again, tilted her body to the side on the ground, and drifted off to sleep.

The next morning, Bobby hid her suitcase behind the large waste bin, covering it with dead branches from a nearby tree. She slung her small black backpack over her shoulder, her laptop safely inside to protect it from theft. Grabbing the four remaining games she had wrapped in a black plastic bag, she set out. With no other options, she decided to try door-knocking, hoping to sell the games and scrape together enough cash to make it through until she could figure out a plan.

Visiting game publishers was out of the question; she didn't have the funds needed to close a deal that would cost tens of thousands of dollars, and she couldn't even afford transport to get there anyway.

Bobby had always been a skilled salesperson with a charming communication style, but as she went door-knocking, she faced one slammed door after another. She was accustomed to rejection from her days in salon marketing consulting, repeated refusals had made her tough. Still, the disappointment stung.

But giving up was never an option. Determined to keep going, she stumbled upon a club that hosted game days. The billboard read, *Board Game Days, Every Friday, Join Us.* She boldly walked in and asked to speak to the manager. To her surprise, the room was filled with elderly patrons, some so frail they barely moved.

The manager approached, looking skeptical as Bobby introduced herself.

"Hi, I'm Bobby, the founder of 'A-MAZE-IIIIng', it's a game designed to help people reach their goals."

The manager interrupted, raising an eyebrow. *"Goals? For seniors?"* He scoffed. *"Do you think seniors really want to set goals? Their only goal is to wake up in the morning!"*

Bobby held her ground, her tone calm yet persuasive. *"The game is designed to spark something in anyone with a pulse."*

She offered him a bulk discount on four games, but the manager sighed, clearly reluctant. *"Fine. I'll try one,"* he said, mostly to get rid of her… but didn't pay a cent for it.

Bobby promised to return the next day, eager for any chance to make a bulk sale. She resumed door-knocking until nightfall, but not a single game was sold.

As she sat in the fading light, exhausted, Christopher Lane's words seemed to echo in her mind: *"Embrace pain, for growth thrives beyond comfort zones."*

Bobby headed toward the public toilets, where she'd stashed the rest of her games, but as she approached, she noticed flashing lights. At first, she couldn't tell if they were from an ambulance or the police, but soon she realized it was a fire truck.

The toilet block was on fire. An elderly woman was speaking with the firefighters. *"I saw them, two young boys. Rotten scoundrels scared me. They went into the ladies' section, lit the trash can on fire, and then ran off!"*

Bobby tried to get closer, but a firefighter blocked her path. *"Stay back, miss."*

"Sir, I had some belongings in there," she protested.

"Not anymore, you don't," he replied sternly.

She waited until the fire was under control, and then she was finally allowed in. Her stomach sank at the sight. All forty-four of her games were completely destroyed. She dug through the ashes, her hands blackened with soot, hoping to salvage something. Her heart skipped when she found one game at the very bottom, the corner of the box was blackened, but it was intact.

She carefully placed it in her black plastic bag with the other items. *"You're staying with me,"* she murmured to the game, almost as if it were a person.

The following day, she tried door-knocking again to sell the remaining three games, but no one bought a single one.

Bobby's footsteps echoed through the bustling street as she passed by a row of quaint shops and trendy cafes. But one particular cafe caught her attention - a fit, striking man in his seventies was setting up tables and chairs in the alfresco area, his muscles flexing with each heavy lift. As they locked eyes for a brief moment, his face looked somewhat sad. Bobby gave him a friendly smile, and he smiled back. His gaze was broken by someone calling out rudely, *"Sergio, hurry up!!* Bobby couldn't shake off the feeling that he looked familiar. But her thoughts were quickly consumed by her mission, and she didn't notice the name of the cafe, it was - *'Russo Cafe'* - unbeknown to her, it was her grandfather's long-lost cousin, the one that called him crazy for moving to Australia instead of New York. Bobby charged forward, driven by an unwavering determination to complete her task and stay focused. Sergio paused, his work forgotten, as he watched Bobby in the distance, her body language portraying she was lost in her mission to get to a certain place. A surge of urgency gripped him, and he was on the verge of sprinting toward her, his instincts screaming to offer assistance. But just then, his overbearing wife seized him by the scruff of the neck, her voice a sharp command to finish moving the chairs, yanking him back to reality with an iron grip.

Desperate, Bobby returned to the club to check in with the manager, noticing the game she'd left was still on the counter exactly where she left it the day before, unopened, the plastic wrap intact.

"Sorry," the manager said, not even looking up. *"We haven't tried it yet."*

"That's fine," Bobby replied, forcing a nonchalant tone, though every bit of her hoped for a sale. She left, still carrying the bag with the three unsold games, their weight dragging her down.

Later, she found a park bench to rest, pulling out a sandwich, the cheapest food she could afford. Taking off her shoes to relieve her blistered feet, she rubbed her sore toes and slipped her socks back on, determined to keep moving. When she passed a hair salon, she paused, glancing inside. She realized if she could land a consulting deal like she had back in Australia, she might afford a place to stay, at least temporarily.

Bobby walked in confidently and introduced herself. *"Hi, I'm Bobby Russo from Russo Salon Marketing Services. We've helped 1,564 salons around regional Australia. I have my laptop here to show you some results."*

As she pulled out her laptop, her heart sank, her battery was flat. Of course, a waste bin doesn't come with a power point, she thought, cringing.

Holding up her charging cord, Bobby asked. *"May I ask where your power outlet is?"*

Embarrassment washed over her as she realized her power point adapter was in her suitcase, the Australian power points were different from the US. The salon owner, visibly annoyed, sighed. *"There's no need. Business here is fine."*

Bobby glanced around at the empty chairs and the staff, idly pretending to look busy. She knew business couldn't be that great.

"May I ask your name?" Bobby continued, hoping to recover the conversation.

"Sally," the owner replied flatly, clearly unimpressed.

"Oh, really?" Bobby said brightly. *"I have a friend back home named Sally. She's a salon owner too, and she was thrilled with the results we got her."*

"Look, I'm not interested," Sally said, crossing her arms.

Bobby pressed on. *"You don't pay a cent until I get your results! I handle everything, email marketing, Facebook ads, and special client promotions. I even train your staff on customer care, how to sell and outsource great products, and much more."*

At that, the entire salon seemed to pause. Even the background music cut off, and a heavy silence filled the room. Sally pointed to the door.

A large man, clearly Sally's partner, appeared from the back room. *He must've been the one to turn off the music,* Bobby thought nervously.

Not wanting to be thrown out again and humiliated, Bobby packed her laptop away and slowly backed toward the door, feeling the weight of everyone's eyes on her.

"Here, take this as a gift," she said, holding out a game. *"Enjoy it, and if you ever change your mind, here's my number."* Grabbing a marker from the counter, she flipped the game over and scrawled, *"May your dreams come true, Bobby Russo",* along with her phone number and a little heart.

Bobby walked out, but as she glanced back, she saw Sally toss the game into a corner. Bobby sighed and muttered sarcastically to herself, *"Well, that went well."*

Christopher Lane was standing outside in front of the salon window. *"You're a fighter, Bobby."*

She replied aloud, *"Well, I'm working that muscle, but I think I just pulled a muscle in there."*

"No, you didn't," he said. *"You're just warming up, my friend."*

Days passed without a single sale. Bobby only gifted the last two games to salon owners who showed genuine interest in her services, hoping for a breakthrough. Her small backpack, with her laptop and the game she'd salvaged from the fire, weighed heavily on her shoulders. But she refused to risk leaving it behind, especially where her suitcase was hidden. It was not a secure place.

Each day, she kept in touch with Carlo, who still had no news about retrieving the stolen funds. She assured him she'd found work and a place to stay, not wanting him to worry that she was on the streets. *"I am not leaving here until I succeed Carlo,"* she said with full conviction. Carlo knew that when Bobby said something, she meant it.

A week dragged by while on the streets, though it felt like months. Sleeping outside in the cold took its toll, and Bobby caught a bad chest cold, giving her a constant cough from a bronchial infection, far from ideal for a salesperson. And as if things couldn't get worse, she ran out of cash, the last bit she'd held close to her heart as a gift from her grandmother.

"Thank you, Nonna. I love you so much," she murmured to herself, grateful for the support. She called her family every day, as promised, but this time, Alonso called her.

"Bobby Jo!!!" he said in a stern voice. *"Oh, Sh*t, he used my middle name. I'm in trouble."* she thought, her heart racing.

"When were you planning to tell me?" Alonso yelled.

"Did Carlo tell you?" she asked nervously.

"No, why? Does he know about this?" Alonso replied, his tone heated. *"I went to pay for our equipment at RM Machinery, and the card bounced! How embarrassing. We're business partners, Bobby, no secrets."*

"I didn't want to stress you, Dad," she said quietly.

In the kitchen, Melina and Nonna Giovanna heard the conversation, as it was on speakerphone. Melina exchanged a knowing look with Giovanna and murmured, *"This sounds familiar, talk about like father like daughter."* It was the same conversation, but in reverse, when Bobby found out that Alonso had kept his heavy debt a secret as she tried to buy equipment for the farm.

*"Love, I don't mind you spending on your venture, but we're a team. I need to know what's going on, "*Alonso said.

"I thought maybe I'd get the money back before you knew," Bobby explained

Alonso sighed; his frustration was audible through the phone. *"What do you mean, Bobby, 'get the money back'? Explain."*

Bobby took a deep breath, then recounted the entire story, how they ended up with the wrong card, her efforts to make ends meet, and the challenges she faced. By the time she finished, the line was silent.

Melina and Nonna Giovanna clued to the phone and exchanged stunned glances. By the end of Bobby's story, their faces softened as they listened. The confusion they initially felt turned into sympathy, understanding the lengths Bobby had gone to.

"Oh, my beautiful Bobby," Alonso finally said, his voice gentler now. *"Listen, I don't care about the bloody money...just get home, please! Your hands are tied right now, so there's no point in staying. You might as well come home."*

"Hang on, where are you staying if you have no money?" he added, his tone shifting to worry.

"I'm fine, Dad. Nonna gave me a bit of money before I left, and I'm figuring things out. You know I always find a way," she reassured him, trying to keep her voice light.

"As I've told you before I left, I'm not leaving here until I reach my goal of finding a publisher."

Melina spoke up, her voice firm yet warm. *"Bobby, that could take years. I'm sending some money for a flight back home, ok, stop it please."*

"No, no, I'm okay," Bobby insisted, her pride kicking in. *"I'll send the money right back if you do. I'll find a way out of this, Dad, I promise."*

"Bobby, listen to reason," Alonso pleaded. *"The monthly bank payments are coming up, and the farm bills too. We're barely holding on. Just come back, and we can do the salon thing again. Whatever it takes, as long as we are together, we are stronger."*

"Dad, we covered most of the salons in Australia. We can't redo it," she firmly responded. *"Dad, the insurance company replaced one harvester, right? Do some contract work with it till we figure things out."* Alonso nodded in agreement.

Bobby's voice was strained but defiant. *"I'm working on salons here, and Carlo's working on getting the funds back. Just trust us, young folk, Dad. Please."*

Before Alonso could respond, Bobby hung up, her heart pounding.

"Stubborn girl!" Alonso yelled, glaring at the phone. He turned to Melina and Nonna Giovanna, his frustration clear. *"She wouldn't even tell me where she's staying!"*

Melina placed a comforting hand on his shoulder. *"You know she's just like you, Alonso...determined to handle things her own way."*

"She's too proud, that's the damn problem," he muttered, shaking his head, not realizing that it's one of his traits as well. *"Young folk, huh,"* he added as he stomped out of the kitchen, the door slamming shut behind him.

Back in the city, Bobby slipped her salvaged board game back into her backpack, holding it like a lifeline. *"Looks like it's just you and me,"* she said softly to the game, almost as if speaking to an old friend. She checked her phone every few minutes, hoping for a message from someone willing to take her up on her offer. But there was nothing.

As her funds dwindled to zero, Bobby faced a difficult decision. The hunger pangs were impossible to ignore, her headaches from not eating growing stronger with each passing hour. She had no choice but to head toward the area where the homeless lined up for free food. It wasn't something she had ever imagined she would have to do, but hunger was a powerful motivator.

CHAPTER 15

RAISING VIBRATIONS

NOT NARRATED

Lining up for food, Bobby took in her surroundings, the tired faces, the worn, dirty clothes, the quiet shuffle of people in survival mode. *"This is definitely not on my vision board,"* she muttered under her breath, a sad smile forming on her lips. She felt so helpless, so wanting to help these people who had lost their way.

Next to her appeared the white-cloaked figure, his presence calm and steady. She looked up at him, her expression weary.

"I can't say I'm thrilled right now," she said, her voice barely above a whisper. *"I miss Nonna's homemade gnocchi...I miss everyone."*

The white-cloaked man touched her gently on the arm. *"What do you think you should do, Bobby Jo? You have free will and control over that brilliant mind of yours..."* He paused, his tone steady and compassionate. *"Remember, the only place of true power is in the light."*

"Light?" Bobby scoffed. *"Yeah, well, some electricity would be nice."* At that moment, she became aware that she was slipping into a negative mindset.

Suddenly, she paused, the weight of her answer to the white-cloaked man sinking in. Her gaze softened, and she nodded to herself. *"I need to up my vibration, MY electricity."* she murmured, feeling a surge of determination returning. The man in the white cloak smiled approvingly, his figure gradually turning and fading away.

She finally received her meal, a simple bun and a small serving of beef, mashed potatoes, and vegetables. The lady serving the food called out, "That's *it for today, folks. There are only 6 portions left. Come back tomorrow"*.

As Bobby grabbed her meal and started to walk away, she noticed a young mother holding a baby at the end of the queue, looking dejected.

Bobby's heart went out to her. *"Why didn't they put you at the front of the line?"* she asked the mother. Without hesitation, she handed her meal to the young woman, whose eyes widened in surprise and gratitude.

As Bobby turned away, a homeless man in his fifties approached her. *"I saw what you did there, young lady; that was good of you."*

She looked at him, noting the kindness in his weathered face. *"Looks like you missed out, too,"* she replied, offering a small, tired smile.

The man introduced himself. *"Name's Raymond. And a pretty girl like you shouldn't be in a place like this. It's dangerous."*

"Nice to meet you, Raymond. I'm Bobby," Bobby replied, shaking his hand. She noticed he was holding a book by Christopher Lane, and her face brightened.

"You're reading Christopher Lane!!!" she asked. *"How are you finding it?"*

Raymond's eyes lit up as he held up the book. *"This book is what keeps me going. I used to be a millionaire, believe it or not."*

"Wow... what happened?" Bobby asked, genuinely curious.

He sighed; his gaze distant. *" I lost everything due to matters beyond my control, and I lost it all. Money's gone now... I'm broke... but I'm not broken."* He smiled faintly. *"I'm just rebuilding... one step at a time."*

As Raymond walked away, he waved over his shoulder. *"See you around, Bobby."*

"May your dreams come true, Raymond," she called after him, watching as he disappeared into the crowd.

To stay close to the food area, Bobby had to move her belongings. She found a nearby park, though it was hardly the kind of place any parent would take their kids to play. Hiding her suitcase under some branches in a thick bush, she tried to camouflage it as best as she could.

As she sat down, she heard rustling nearby. Glancing around, she spotted a raccoon, its curious eyes shining in the dim light.

"Oh my gosh, a real raccoon!" she whispered, grinning. *"I've always wanted to see a real raccoon, and now I've manifested it! Wow! Look at those cute, sad eyes! I wish I could take you home with me, you'd love Fredrickson, Mozza, Bludger the cat... and maybe even Hillary the sheep, though she's in a league of her own."* She paused, a wave of homesickness washing over her.

Suddenly, she heard footsteps nearby. *"I think we've got company, little fella,"* she whispered to the raccoon, which quickly scampered off.

An intimidating-looking, large framed African-American woman approached, her expression hard. She yelled at Bobby, *"This is my spot... get the f*ck out!!!"*

Bobby raised her hands slightly, getting up from where she sat and stepping back calmly. *"I'm sorry, miss, I didn't know, I'll leave."*

The woman's expression softened as she chuckled. *"I was just testing your reaction. You seem like a good kid."* She extended her hand. *"Name's Betsy."*

"Hi, Betsy, I'm Bobby. Nice to meet you." Bobby replied, shaking her hand.

Betsy began setting up several old bed sheets between two small trees to create shelter from the cold, crafting what looked like a backyard fort. Bobby thought to herself that little Olivia, Steevo's granddaughter, would have thought it was a great cubby house.

Over the next few days, Bobby found herself sharing stories with Betsy, reading Christopher Lane's book to her, and recounting tales of her family and the life she had back home.

One evening, Betsy shook her head as Bobby spoke of her family. *"Girl, you're lucky. My family wouldn't even give me a nickel if I begged for it. Why don't you just let your folks send you some money?"*

Bobby looked at Betsy, a faint smile forming on her lips as she replied, *"Because if you gravitate toward EASY, your life will always be HARD."*

Betsy went silent, the words hanging in the air.

Yet another week passed that felt like months to Bobby.

Betsy and Bobby had formed a close camaraderie. Bobby noticed subtle changes in Betsy, she wasn't as harsh towards others, and thanks to the teachings of Christopher Lane, she had finally begun to see her own self-worth.

One night, after they had eaten together in their tent, Betsy handed Bobby a pair of nunchucks. *"Here, take these, girl. You can never be too careful,"* Betsy said.

Bobby was taken aback. *"Betsy, you stole these, didn't you? Please, take them back. It's sweet of you, but I don't need them."*

Betsy turned red with anger and yelled, *"You stupid girl, no, you're not stupid. You're too trusting. You don't understand because this is not your turf. You have no idea... no idea, girl, how dangerous this place is. Just last week, I witnessed a sixteen-year-old innocent boy being put into a body bag, bashed to death, his face unrecognizable. I knew him. He was placid and kept to himself... He's one of many. So shut the f*ck up about taking these back. Take them, and keep them with you at all times! You understand? Always...ok!"*

Betsy frantically tucked the nunchucks into Bobby's trousers, at her backside. Bobby fell silent, saddened by what was going on around her. Bobby was shocked by Betsy's outburst, and she quietly said Thank you.

The next morning, Bobby was preparing herself as best as she could, but it was clear she was showing signs of neglect. Her hair was scruffy and oily, her skin unclean, and her clothes were stained, far from ideal for heading to salons for business deals.

There were 18 remaining salons within walking distance, and it would take most of the day.

Bobby braced herself for another grueling day. With a heavy sigh, she muttered through gritted teeth, *"I am grateful for this new day, Spirit. I'll do my best to endure whatever comes my way."* Every morning felt like a battle cry, preparing her for the challenges that lay ahead.

One morning, Betsy was nowhere to be found. Bobby wasn't comfortable leaving her suitcase without Betsy's patrol, so she waited for her return. An hour later, Betsy came back.

"Where have you been? I hope you're not stealing again, Betsy," Bobby said.

Betsy returned holding a small white plastic bag. *"Oh, I was just getting some supplies at the bra and underwear shop,"* she replied.

Bobby watched as Betsy settled in and pulled out a pair of knitting needles from the bag.

Suddenly, Betsy lifted her dress right up to her bosom, and Bobby, looking away, tried to avoid the awkward situation.

Betsy removed her underwear, but it was layer upon layer of lacey underwear.

"Betsy!! What the hell did you do?! It's a lady's underwear shop, not a 'layer up and leave' shop! There must be at least 50 pairs of knickers here! What the heck are you going to do with them?" Bobby exclaimed.

Betsy settled in, grabbed a pair of knitting needles from the white plastic bag, and began her work.

"I knit roses," Betsy exclaimed as she pulled out a large rusty pair of scissors to cut the lace from the underwear.

"That's clever of you, Betsy. Can I watch?" Bobby asked, fascinated. She watched Betsy, who was clearly excited to show Bobby her skill.

Betsy completed the lace rose. Bobby, shocked at how beautiful it came out and that it was fully made of lace, *"Wow, Betsy! Have you ever thought of selling them to make a bit of extra cash for food?"*

"Oh, I don't know!" Betsy replied in a low tone. *"I don't think anyone's going to buy these."*

"Why not? They're gorgeous! I've never seen anything like it," Bobby replied.

"Nah, it's ok, I just enjoy making them, Bobby stop trying to help," said Betsy.

"Hey, Betsy," Bobby said, thinking of an idea. *"There's a piece missing from your rose; it needs a stem. On my way out today, I'll find some straight small sticks, and you can wrap some lace around them to give your beautiful rose a stem. What do you think?"*

"Yeah, okay," Betsy said quietly.

Bobby nodded and headed out. To improve her hygiene, she entered a motel where the mothers' restrooms had free items like wet wipes, tampons, soap, and talcum powder. She took what she thought she could use. Bobby washed and brushed her hair in the sink and awkwardly dried it under the hand dryer, apologizing to any onlookers. While charging her phone, she looked at herself in the mirror, touching her weary face, and thought to herself with full faith, *"You got this. Just keep going, and you will be rewarded for your persistence."*

Christopher Lane's image behind her smiling in the mirror, as she smiled back at him.

Bobby checked her phone for directions to her next salon. She noticed the shortcut through Central Park, so she headed that way.

She soaked in the sun as she walked, feeling grateful to be alive. *"Today is the day,"* she said to herself. *"I will strike a deal with a salon. I won't let my family down."* As she walked along the path, she noticed many people picnicking and having fun in the distance, families laughing with their children. Bobby smiled at them in admiration.

A not-very desirable-looking man in his twenties suddenly stood in her way.

"Hey, Gorgeous, where are you going?"

She ignored him and placed her arm in front of her, gesturing for him to get out of her way. Before she knew it, another man appeared, and then another, and then another. She knew it wasn't looking good for her, and they obviously had bad intentions.

Bobby looked at the strangers occupying the park around her, wondering if they had noticed and if anyone would get help. She had a flashback to when she was confronted by thugs in the Outback.

No one intervenes to help her.

This time, although people were all around her, she felt just as alone as during that bad experience in the Outback. Bobby was frightened but didn't show it.

Suddenly, one of the men ripped the gold necklace from her neck; it was the golden hearts that Nonna Giovanna gave her.

She looked to her left, and there was the man in the white cloak. Bobby gazed into his eyes, and he said, *"Focus and work with what you've got... you know what to do."*

"I said ...where are you going !!" Repeated by the first man who placed his ugly face in her space the first time.

The four thugs were getting closer and circling her as if she were some sort of baby deer they wanted to catch.

Bobby showed no visible signs of fear to the cowardly men. She looked into their eyes one by one, and they appeared empty and callous.

She approached the man who asked the question and said in an upbeat way, *"Hi... You asked me where I'm going. Bit rude if I don't answer, isn't it? I'm going back to Australia; that's where I'm from."*

There was a pause and signs of confusion on the men's faces.

"Can't you tell from my accent?" she said, looking at their blank faces. *"I'm Australian, of course!"* she added with a smile. *"Don't*

worry, gentlemen, I don't have Mick Dundee's knife, but I have these!"

She quickly pulled out the nunchucks Betsy had made her promise to always keep with her. The men all stepped back.

Bobby said, *"Don't fear, I'm not going to use these on you."* She paused. *"I have something much, much more deadly under my belt than these things."*

The thugs all looked at each other, puzzled about what she could possibly mean.

Bobby was sweating profusely. She looked up at the sky, looking very mysterious, and just like a magic trick, she flicked talcum powder into the air that she had taken from the public bathroom. The powder landed on her face, sticking to her sweaty skin.

Completely covered in white powder, she intended to look just as Mason had during her good luck ceremony.

Bobby continued and said, "Surely you've heard of the Indigenous people in Australia." Still no response from the men, only a shrug of the shoulder. One finally spoke and said, *"Yeah, I have... why?"*

Bobby responded, *"Well..."* She paused to gather her thoughts. *"Back home, my Aboriginal friend Mason, taught me how to cast a spell... See, back in the day, the Aboriginals had a unique prison system... What they did was throw a stick at the criminal's feet and call out a certain curse, and it would cause the certain death of that criminal. But the secret curse he taught me is the cruel, deadliest one you can make."*

One thug said nervously, *"I saw something on TV about that... wasn't it a bone or something that they threw at the victim and they would die!!!?"*

"Yes, you're correct. Sounds like you're the smart one, but they weren't victims, they were criminals." said Bobby, as she slowly pulled out the sticks that she had collected for Betsy's rose stems. One by one, she quickly threw the sticks at the men's feet as they pulled away from them in fear.

Bobby quickly started singing a song that sounded foreign and yet somewhat tribal. She grabbed the nunchucks and hit them together, dancing exactly how Mason had danced the day he performed the ceremony with his Aboriginal clapsticks. The language was something Bobby had just invented, but it sounded authentic. She banged the nunchucks the same way Mason banged his clapsticks.

She made her dance moves the same as Mason did the night of the ceremony, thankful that she had paid attention.

The thugs, now starting to get nervous, stared at the sticks thrown at their feet. One thug, who seemed to be the head of the gang, said, *"What are you doing? Shut up! shut up... You witch!* He yelled to Bobby.

"Can't you see she is fooling us!!" He yelled to his accomplices, but they took no notice of him and could not help but stare at Bobby's scary face covered in white powder while she was looking up and down from the sky to the ground as if concocting a spell. The leader now approached her closely with a large pocket knife. He demanded her to stop.

"Oh," said Bobby, *"Too late. I have just placed the curse of the shemi on you all!"* She explained as she kept dancing, looking up into the sky, then deeply into their eyes, dancing like a crazy tribal woman while hitting the nunchucks together. Some onlookers started to congregate, thinking they were witnessing a special performance. Bobby got even more theatrical.

"Mason told me this curse cannot be undone!" she yelled out.

"What will happen to us, bitch?!" one thug said, panicking, sweating profusely. At that moment, she had a flashback of her bad experience in the outback when the thug said the same injudicious word.

"You don't want to know," Bobby said, trying to buy time while inventing something.

"What! What will happen to me?!" the leader yelled out selfishly. *"Tell me now!"* He yelled again, his knife now touching her right cheek and pressing against her skin so hard that she bled.

Bobby quickly responded, *"If you hurt me, you will never know what is going to happen to you."* The thug dug the knife deeper into her face.

*"Ok...Ok *rs*h*le... here is what will happen to you,"* Bobby replied, *"Slowly, your large toe will turn green. The curse will slowly work its way up your body within days, but what's worse than that is everything else in your body that is round will also turn green and fall off within a week."*

A thug grabbed Bobby and violently shook her. *"How do you reverse it, you f*cken ...piece of ..."* Holding his groin fearful at the thought of his testicles turning green.

"It cannot be reversed," Bobby quickly responded in an urgent tone. Suddenly, they all started heading toward her. *"Okay, okay... there is one way, but I don't think you have time..."*

"What is it? What is it?!" a thug yelled out.

Bobby said, *"You must all totally immerse your bodies in saltwater for 45 seconds in order for the curse to be reversed. Is the ocean nearby? "You only have 17 minutes from when I placed the curse.*

Without sparing a second to respond, all four thugs fled to get to the nearest beach to submerge themselves in saltwater. With no taxis stopping for them, they kept running frantically as if their lives depended on it. But of course, little did they know they had just been conned.

And little did they know, the word *shemi* Bobby used meant "idiots" in Italian. Bobby, looking at them as they fled, thought to herself, *Last time it was the crazy snake lady, this time it's the crazy stick lady.*

A sigh of total relief and gratitude came upon her, and she didn't know whether to laugh or cry. Shaking like a leaf, relieved she pulled it off. It just occurred to her that twelve months later, she understood why that trip from hell in the Outback had to happen. She wouldn't have coped with this situation had it not happened.

There are times when we wonder why things happen, but *'the why'* doesn't make sense until years later.

The thug who tore her necklace off dropped it in his frantic rush to soak in the ocean. Bobby picked it up, not able to put it on as its chain was broken.

Bobby put her hand on her heart and looked again to her left. There was the man in the white cloak. She blew a kiss at him and whispered, *"Thank you," and kept walking toward her destination.*

The next morning.

"Betsy, I'll see you for fine dining again tonight," Bobby joked as she headed out.

She visited more salons, crossing each one off her list after receiving countless rejections. Door after door, the answer was the same, and now she was down to the last salon in the area that had free public transport to get there. Still, she approached each with the same magnetic enthusiasm.

At the final salon, the owner raised an eyebrow and asked, *"You mean, if I don't get results, I don't pay?"*

"That's correct! It's a win-win," Bobby replied, nodding eagerly. *"Would you like to watch a video testimonial from some of my clients in Australia?"*

The owner glanced at her watch. *"No need! I'm in, girl! Come back to sign me up after my last appointment leaves at 6 p.m. today, but don't be late! I have to catch a flight to Tahiti tonight and won't be back for three weeks. I won't be contactable."*

Bobby's face lit up. "I'll be here; I assure you! Congratulations, you've done your business a huge favor. I would have given you a free board game of mine, but this one is special and not for sale. You'll get one eventually!" She added, skipping out the door, her spirits soaring.

Finally, things were looking up. She felt a wave of relief wash over her as she realized this deal could mean she wouldn't have to sleep outside. When this salon owner got results, others in the area might be convinced to work with her too. *"Thank you,"* she whispered while looking at the man in the white cloak, smiling at her in the distance.

With an hour to wait until 6 p.m., Bobby found a spot in an outdoor shopping complex. She struck up a conversation with an elderly Indian blind man with a long white beard and a beautiful yellow turban. He held a long white cane and his guide dog with him. Her curiosity piqued.

"Hi, I'm Bobby Jo, your golden retriever is adorable! He did not reply.

Oh, wow, is that braille? I've never seen braille up close," Bobby said, genuinely fascinated. But the man didn't seem to respond, so Bobby settled into her seat, pulling out her well-worn copy of Christopher Lane's book to read as she eagerly awaited six o'clock to come.

Meanwhile, across town, Georgie Hayes, the extraordinarily successful and famous talk show host in New York City and around the world, was out for the day, hoping not to be recognized. She wore oversized designer sunglasses, a long-embroidered designer jacket, and a convincing wig that made her look years younger, effortlessly blending in as she walked into a jewelry store with her English bodyguard, William.

"I could've gotten that for you, Miss Hayes," William said as they stepped inside.

Georgie smiled, waving him off. *"I enjoy shopping. It's nice to feel like a regular person every now and then,"* she replied, savoring the simple moment away from her high-profile life. *"Besides, I know what I want when I see it. I am gifting some things at a charity ball, so I need to be sure this jewelry is appropriate,"* she added.

William sighed. *"We don't have all day, Miss Hayes. It's getting late."*

"Just give me thirty minutes, please. I'll meet you back here," she insisted, her stubborn streak surfacing. Georgie was used to getting her way, especially after all the hard work she'd put in to build her career. She just wanted to escape the pretentious people in her social circle... and even her bodyguard William.

After wandering around the store, Georgie eventually lost track of time, and her sense of direction. Realizing she was thoroughly lost, she fished for her phone, only to discover that the battery was dead. Panic set in as her mind raced. *"I'll just catch a taxi and hope no one recognizes me"*, she thought to herself.

But as she stepped onto the street, she couldn't seem to flag down a single cab. Meanwhile, her elegance and wealth caught the eye of a nearby thug, who quickly noticed her designer bag and the jewelry store shop bag she was carrying. He decided she was worth robbing and slowly approached her, his movements predatory.

Back at the outdoor shopping complex, Bobby was absorbed in her book, occasionally lifting her head to check her watch. Bobby and the blind man were sitting on a garden bench, and in front of them lay a large potted plant. Even though the large potted plant distorted Bobby's view, she noticed Georgie in the distance, admiring the jacket she was wearing. *"Look at that beautiful jacket that lady has on!"* she exclaimed before catching herself. *"Oh, I'm so sorry, Sir. I forgot,"* she added, remembering her new Indian friend couldn't see it.

"It's okay," he replied, forgiving her slip-up. *"Wow, he does speak,"* Bobby thought to herself.

Bobby looked up again, this time noticing something alarming. The woman in the beautiful jacket was now only about eight meters away, and there was a man with her, pointing a gun straight at her. Bobby's heart raced. *"Holy Sh*t,"* she said to the blind man. *"There is a guy with a gun!"*

Quickly, she turned to the blind man beside her. *"May I borrow these, please?"* she asked, not waiting for a reply and taking his dark glasses and his long white cane with a white ball on the end of it.

She approached cautiously, getting close enough to hear the thug's gruff demand. *"Hand over the jewelry you're wearing. Now, bitch!"*

Georgie was visibly trembling, her hands shaking as she scrambled in her bag to give him what he wanted. Bobby began her act with the dark glasses on.

"Mama? Mama, where are you?" she called out, her voice wavering as she stumbled forward. *"Is that you, Mama? "Bobby continued.

The thug turned, momentarily distracted, his gun now aimed at Bobby. *"Get lost, blind girl,"* he growled.

Bobby continued her act, seemingly unfazed. Georgie, pleading with the thug, *said, "Please, leave the poor girl alone. For God's sake! Can't you see? She's blind?"* Bobby fumbled her way closer, pretending not to notice him as she shuffled toward Georgie.

The thug snarled at Georgie, *"Yeah, well, she can't see. But you can! You've seen my face now, haven't you? Now, say goodbye to your fancy life, lady!!"*

Just as he moved to fire at Georgie's chest, Bobby whipped the cane up with lightning speed, striking his hand and sending the gun flying. The weapon discharged, grazing Georgie's arm but missing her chest by mere inches. Without missing a beat, Bobby swung the cane back, jabbing the thug hard in the stomach, then in the crotch several times, and lastly in the head. Her blows were relentless. Much to her relief, the thug was now unconscious.

The blind Indian man managed to voice-dial the police. In a strong Indian accent, he said, *"A woman touched my stick."* The operator on the other end of the phone responded, *"She touched your what, Sir?"*

Sirens echoed in the distance as police approached. Georgie stood frozen, blood seeping from the wound on her arm, still processing what had just happened.

"Are you an undercover cop or something?" Georgie managed to ask, eyes wide open in shock.

Bobby simply replied, *"Or something."* Trying to catch her breath, Bobby asked, *"Are you okay? Can I get you some water?"*

Georgie, still in shock, could barely register Bobby's question. *"I... I almost... I almost didn't make it... by milliseconds!!"*

Bobby and Georgie stood there staring at the low-life thug who had nearly taken an innocent life. *"Yeah, well, I think his dick will be in a sling ...for a while,"* Bobby remarked dryly.

Georgie laughed lightly and added, *"I think after that... not even a pack of blue tablets is going to get that thing up again."*

"Just make sure this piece of filth doesn't get away," Bobby said firmly, then glancing over her shoulder as the police cars arrived. *"I have to go, I'm late for an appointment."* She gave Georgie a reassuring smile and said. *"I'm so glad you're okay."*

"Wait!" Georgie called after her, fumbling in her purse. *"At least let me thank you properly. For God's sake, you just saved my life! Here, take this ticket to my event tomorrow night at 5 p.m., and afterwards, I want to talk to you. Please promise me you will attend, here it's a VIP ticket. Take it, please."* Georgie paused, then asked, *"What's your name?"*

Bobby hesitated, glancing at the tickets before taking them reluctantly. *"Alright, thank you,"* she said, then disappeared into the crowd without answering Georgie's question.

Georgie watched her go, still dazed as police and paramedics swarmed the scene, tending to her wound. Her mind raced, consumed by the close call and the stranger who had risked her life to save her. *"Who is this girl?"* she murmured to herself, desperate to know more. She turned to a nearby officer. *"Officer, see that girl over there in the blue T-shirt? That girl just risked her life to save mine. Who does that?"*

The officer nodded and said, *"We saw her on Rawson Road yesterday..."*

"You mean she's a homeless girl?!" Georgie exclaimed in disbelief.

"*Yes,*" the officer confirmed. Georgie demanded they go after her, "*Miss Hayes, never mind her, you're going to a hospital.*"

Georgie's frustration was evident. "*But I need to find her! I must thank her, she saved my life!*" she insisted.

The officer gave a firm, yet amused, smile. "*Not now, Miss Hayes. You're getting in that ambulance. But before you do, maybe I can get an autograph?*" he said with a cheeky smile.

Georgie rolled her eyes when the officer wasn't looking. She was tired of people around her being star-struck, desperate to find the stranger who had just saved her life.

Meanwhile, Bobby ran as fast as she could, trying to make it to her 6 O'clock appointment on time. Completely out of breath, she muttered to herself, "*Please, please, please be open.*" Her heart pounded as she reached the salon.

CHAPTER 16

ADVERSITIES' GIFTS

NOT NARRATED

Bobby reached the salon, but the lights were off, and no one was inside. She bent over, hands on her knees, catching her breath. Then, throwing her head back in frustration, she yelled at the top of her lungs, *"WHY?!!!!!!!!!!"*

Dejected, she made her way back to her makeshift hideaway, where Betsy was already eating her dinner from the free dinner service. *"You missed mealtime,"* Betsy remarked, barely looking up.

Bobby forced a small smile. *"Hi, Betsy, how are you?"*

Betsy, in her usual straightforward way, handed Bobby the food she'd saved for her. *"Here,"* she said.

"Thank you, Betsy. That was kind of you," Bobby replied, knowing that she wouldn't have received a meal otherwise. Betsy had halved the meal she received, as they were not allowed two meals.

Bobby sat down beside Betsy, totally exhausted. Bobby handed Betsy the sticks for her roses.

As the night wore on, they settled down to rest. They often talked. That evening, Bobby offered to read *Christopher Lane's* book again by the light of her phone, she had been recharging it at the library during the day. But Betsy shook her head.

"Not tonight, Bobby. I found some free lace today to make more knitted roses!"

Bobby, fascinated, watched as Betsy worked. The roses were the most beautifully knitted items she had ever seen.

Betsy managed to make several dozen of them, all different colours.

Bobby silently admired her skills before speaking up with an encouraging voice. *"Betsy, as I said, you could make a bunch of these and sell them! Can you get more lace?"*

Betsy, not seeming to take much notice, replied casually, *"Well, it depends on..."*

"Depends on what?" Bobby asked.

Betsy shrugged. *"I could get more free lace, but the only free lace I can get is this lace I got today ...donated used ladies' underwear."*

Bobby's eyes widened in shock and said. *"Ok... my idea is no longer valid!"* She struggled to hold back her laughter.

The next day, Bobby went through her routine again, visiting one salon after another; now she had to walk over an hour and a half to find them, on top of free travel. No one accepted her offer, and her appearance deteriorating did not help. Her hair was greasier than ever, her clothes worn, and her backpack, holding her laptop and precious board game, seemed to grow heavier with each passing day as she grew weaker.

Meanwhile, back at Sunflower Springs, the family gathered in the kitchen.

"Did you hear about Georgie Hayes?" Zoe called out. *"You know the famous talk show host?"*

Nonna Giovanna replied, *"I heard some celebrity in the US was shot in broad daylight. But she didn't die, some homeless person saved her."*

"Oh wow, really?" Melina said, her eyes widened as she turned on the TV in the lounge. Security camera footage played, showing Bobby in the distance from behind, fiercely defending Georgie against the thug.

"Wow, look at this!" Alonso exclaimed, his face scrunching as he watched. The footage showed Bobby from behind delivering blow after blow to the thug's groin with the cane. *"This homeless girl is savage!"* Alonso said

It was a new day, and Bobby thought it was time to take a different approach.

She decided to find a regular job to get off the streets while figuring things out. So, she headed out to start her search.

Meanwhile, the four friends, Liam, Ethan, Kizzy, and Ava, were wrapping up their time together. They were having breakfast at a diner close to Liam's apartment.

"Oh, I can't believe our four weeks together are already over," Ethan exclaimed.

Liam then added with a playful smirk, *"I won't miss your snoring, that's for sure."*

"Sorry," Ethan said, a bit embarrassed, causing everyone to laugh. *"Good luck on your new job tonight, Liam,"* Kizzy added.

"Yeah, it may not be producing movies, but it's a stepping stone, I guess," Liam replied optimistically.

Kizzy raised her milkshake and declared, *"Here's to pursuing our dreams!!!"* They all followed suit and clinked their milkshake glasses together.

Liam checked his watch. *"I have to drop you guys off at the airport soon,"* he sighed. *"Back to reality,"* Ava says.

Kizzy smiled. *"We'll make the best of our last day, and by the way, here is a small thank-you gift from us."* They handed Liam a box of chocolates. *"You didn't have to do that,"* Liam said. *"You hosted us for 4 weeks, that's the least we could do."* Ethan said.

Kizzy joked, *"Let's hope our next meal together is somewhere fancier than this dump."* But they all knew that no matter where they were or what they were doing, their bond would always remain strong.

Kizzy looked at Liam, he looked back and knew she was holding back from saying something. He said with a smile, *"Spit it out, Kizzy, what's going on in that beautiful mind of yours"!!* Ethan wished he could talk to her like Liam did. *"Liam, move to LA, that's the place to be if you want to be in the movie business, and besides, we miss you and want you closer."* He picked up her hand in a friendly manner. *"Not yet, Ava, but I will come to see you at Easter if you are all free?"*

They all cheered. Liam got up. *"Sit down, Liam ...let's have a cappuccino before we go,"* Ava said. *"Ok, but let's make it quick,"* Liam replied and sat down again.

Bobby strolled past the diner and spotted a sign advertising an immediate opening for a kitchen assistant. She walked into the diner. Liam noticed her soon as the door opened. Bobby requested to speak with the manager, who arrived shortly after, summoned by a staff member.

"Excuse me, sir," Bobby began, *"I saw your sign for a kitchen hand position outside. I'm available right away, and I'm a hard worker, sir."*

The manager eyed her skeptically. *"What's your address? Are you homeless?"*

Bobby hesitated. *"I, uh… I have a home, but, "*

"I'm sorry, miss," the manager interrupted, cutting her off. *"The job has already been filled."*

Liam and his friends were in a nearby booth and overheard the conversation between Bobby and the diner manager. Liam, in particular, bristled at how unfairly Bobby was being judged, especially when the manager reached out to touch her backpack for no reason and asked abruptly, *"What do you have in there, young lady?"*

Bobby instinctively pulled back. *"It's just a board game I created, a success game,"* she explained.

A woman in the next booth snickered sarcastically. *"Well, that game really made you a success, darlin'."*

Liam stood up, clearly irritated, and confronted the manager. *"Look…Why won't you give her the job!!? We had to wait forty minutes to get this slop served!"*

The manager ignored him; Liam's gaze shifted to Bobby. Their eyes met for a brief, intense moment before she turned to leave.

"It's okay," she said softly to Liam. *"I'll keep looking, thank you for trying to help."*

Liam reached out his hand, introducing himself. *"My name is Liam. And yours?"*

"Bobby Jo," she replied, managing a small, shy smile.

"Do you live around here?" he asked, curious.

She chuckled lightly. *"Nowhere near here, actually,"* Bobby said. *"But for now, I do."*

Before she reached the door, Liam handed her a $100 note, insisting she take it. *"Please, take this,"* he said earnestly.

"Oh no, you don't have to do that. But thank you. It's so kind of you," Bobby protested, though Liam continued heading for the door, following her.

"Please," Liam said, his eyes meeting hers again, filled with kindness.

As they held each other's gaze, his friends looked on, captivated by their exchange. Finally, Bobby agreed. *"Okay, but only under one condition."*

"Name it," Liam replied.

Bobby hesitated before asking, *"Do you have a big dream you'd love to achieve, Liam?"*

Liam nodded, puzzled by her question. *"Yes,"* he answered, wondering where this was leading.

She pulled out her last board game from her backpack, the one with the black edge, singed by the fire, the game she had promised herself would never leave her side. *"Then you have to take my board game,"* she said with a smile. *"It's a special one. Promise me you'll play it, and if the principles make sense to you, apply them every day. Your goals will manifest in time, and your life will shine beyond your wildest dreams."*

Liam was intrigued. *"Well, I want to be a movie producer,"* he admitted, almost hesitantly. *"Can I manifest that?"*

Bobby assured him, *"You can manifest what you truly desire in your heart, Liam. It's only a lack of belief in yourself holding you back."*

Liam was mesmerized by her wisdom and her radiant spirit. He watched her walk away, noticing that her backpack had *"Sunflower Springs, Australia"* embroidered on the back. But before she disappeared, he called out, *"Good luck, Bobby Jo!"*

She looked back and smiled at him and kept walking. A site that Liam etched in his mind.

Bobby continued her search for work. After countless rejections, she finally came across a tacky Chinese restaurant on the far end of town. *"Perfect,"* she thought. *"I can work nights and look for salon marketing contracts during the day. If I get this job, at least I won't be sleeping with raccoons."*

"You ...Start tonight?" the Chinese lady asked.

"Oh, yes! Thank you!" Bobby replied, thrilled at the prospect of stable income.

But just as she turned to leave, she remembered her promise to the lady with the beautiful coat. Her words echoed in Bobby's mind: *"PROMISE me you will attend!"*

Bobby hesitated, turned back towards the lady, and asked, *"Um, could I start tomorrow night instead, please?"*

The lady paused, her expression shifting to anger. *"No. Not okay. No job for you,"* she said firmly.

Disappointed, Bobby walked away, struggling to hold back her frustration. Once outside, she yelled out, *"I'm building some bloody MUSCLE still, Christopher Lane! I should be looking like Dwayne Johnson by now! A friggin lucky break would be nice!"* Her voice echoed down the street. Bobby is well aware from her learning that anger is not the answer.

Later, she pulled out the crumpled VIP ticket Georgie had given her. *"Fifth Avenue... where is that?"* she wondered, quickly looking it up. It was 4:35 p.m., and the event started at 5:00. She bolted, racing through the streets to make it on time.

She arrived at 5:02 p.m., out of breath, as an usher looked at her skeptically. *"Are you sure you're supposed to have this ticket, miss?"* he asked, his gaze lingering on her disheveled appearance, now obvious she hadn't bathed in a while.

Bobby nodded. *"Yes, as sure as that ugly bow tie doesn't suit your shirt."* She winced inwardly, thinking, *'Oh my god, I'm slowly turning sour.'*

The usher hesitated but finally said, *"You're just in time. Come with me, please."* He escorted her to the front row, where two seats were vacant. She sat cautiously, doing her best to blend in, painfully aware of how she must look and smell.

Two cameramen were on stage, preparing for the show. She scanned the seat beside her, looking around to spot the lady in the nice coat, but no one approached. *"Why is she not here?"* Bobby whispered suddenly, one of the cameramen looked her way and did a double-take. It was Liam.

"Bobby Jo!", his voice a hushed excitement as he neared her. Despite the dim lighting, Bobby felt her cheeks burn with a fierce blush; her heart thundered in her chest at the sight of his striking features. *"Liam! Hi … You work here!!!?"*

He nodded quickly, casting a furtive glance over his shoulder to ensure his boss wasn't observing. *"Bobby Jo, it's really great to see you again. Yeah, I just started yesterday. What are you doing here? Did you find a job yet?"* Their eyes locked with an intensity that seemed to hold the world still.

Bobby shook her head, the spark of excitement dimming. She whispered, *"No, no job yet. I'm here because the lady who gave me this ticket insisted that I come. I was unsure if I should, but I came anyway. She hasn't shown up, though, so I should probably go."*

"What no …Please don't," Liam implored, his voice filled with earnestness. *"Let's grab dinner afterwards. My treat."*

"Oh, thank you anyway, but … …"

Bobby hesitated, catching sight of Liam's boss scrutinizing him. *"Don't get in trouble because of me, Liam,"* she said with a gentle yet intense smile. Bobby couldn't understand why Liam would be interested in her, how could he be drawn to someone who felt so disheveled and downtrodden?

Liam's determined gaze remained on her as if pulled by an invisible force. *"Just stay put, I'm watching you,"* he said with a soft, yet intensely serious and caring smile.

As Bobby sat back, she couldn't help but admire how well Liam's suit fit, accentuating his tall, slim, muscular frame. She gazed at every detail, the sharp lines, the shimmer of the fabric under the lights, the polished shoes, added to his magnetic aura. His smile made her heart melt as he turned to her to check if she was still there. At that moment, she thought to herself that she could die happy right there.

The show began, and applause erupted as the host announced, *"Now, please welcome Georgie Hayes!"* The audience went wild and clapped loudly as Georgie prepared to take the stage. Just then, Bobby's phone buzzed. She didn't notice that the lady in the nice coat was the lady starting to walk on stage. Bobby had no idea who Georgie Hayes even was, or the scope of her fame.

All of Bobby's attention went to the incoming phone call. It was Zoe. *"Zoe"*? she thought, confused. *"It's 9 a.m. in Australia, she never wakes up before 10 am!!!. Something must be wrong"*. An usher walked towards her to warn her not to be on her phone.

She answered the call, quickly rising from her seat and making her way up the staircase to leave, worried that something may have happened to her family.

Liam noticed her empty seat, a disappointed look crossing his face as he scanned the room. Then he spotted her, speaking anxiously on the phone as she walked towards the exit. Concerned about the look on her face, he abandoned his post just as Georgie took the stage.

Bobby, now close to the exit, sternly headed out to leave the building. The same blind elderly Indian man Bobby met the day before was in the audience, recognized Bobby's distressed voice, and muttered to himself, *"Bobby Jo."*

The blind man could also hear Liam's boss and Liam right next to him, loud as a bell.

"Where are you going?" Liam's boss hissed, grabbing Liam's arm. *"Take one more step, and you're fired!"*

Liam yanked his boss's hand off in anger. *"Then fire me!"* he snapped, shrugging him off. *"A girl I know is in trouble; that's my priority right now."*

Then you are fired, his boss remarked sternly as he went to grab Liam's arm again.

In an unexpected act of mischief, the blind man stuck out his badly mutilated cane from the day before, tripping Liam's boss to the ground. *"Watch out, mister!"* Liam's boss yelled at the elderly Indian man, wanting to punch him, then realized the man who tripped him was blind. *"Oops!"* the blind man said with a grin.

Outside, rain poured down in sheets, and Liam ran through it, searching desperately for Bobby, yelling out her name. But she was nowhere to be found.

Meanwhile, Bobby's world shattered as she received the news from Zoe that her beloved Nonna Giovanna had just passed away.

The Russo family was in the Intensive Care Unit at Adelaide City Hospital. The Royal Flying Doctors (Air Ambulance for remote patients) had arrived within hours of her collapse from a severe heart attack in her beloved veggie patch. Doctors had warned days before that she wouldn't make it.

"*No… this can't be happening!*" Bobby screamed, the devastating news of her grandmother's death crashing down on her like a tidal wave. In that instant, she shattered into a million pieces. Tears gushed down her face as she grappled with the incomprehensible tragedy. Bobby wailed like someone possessed, "*I'm sorry, Nonna! I should've been there! I lost your money; I never took you to Milan… I'm a bloody joke! A bloody joke!!*" Her voice pierced through the pouring rain, a cry of raw anguish.

"*A JOKE!!!*" she roared again, her voice echoing into the storm. "*Why Nonna?! How could this happen?!*"

The relentless spiral of misfortune over the past month had finally reached a breaking point, and now Bobby was a volcano erupting, unable to contain the molten fury and sorrow any longer.

In a frenzy of rage and despair, she ripped her backpack from her shoulders, the one cradling her laptop, and smashed it against a signpost with all her strength. Again and again, she slammed it, the anger within her propelling every swing. "*I don't care anymore about anything! You hear that, Christopher Lane? Do you hear that, spirit? I don't care, I DON'T CARE!!!*" she cried out, her voice raw and ragged. Sparks burst from the battered laptop, scattering like fireflies in the dark.

Blinded by her inner chaos, she didn't register the approaching headlights until it was too late. The impact was cataclysmic. A truck struck her with brutal force, flinging her body across the road like a rag doll, blood gushing from her head and plunging her into unconsciousness. The rain hammered down, erasing any hope of immediate help. In the shadowy corner of the street, no one noticed the accident, and the cowardly driver, gripped by fear and selfishness, sped away in the truck he had just stolen, leaving Bobby to bleed to death in the dark corner of the street.

Meanwhile, Liam tore through the chaos of the storm, a relentless determination burning in his eyes as he desperately hunted for Bobby. His throat was raw and aching, but he refused to let the storm silence his cries. Suddenly, a bolt of lightning illuminated the night with a blinding flash, revealing a motionless figure in the distance for a fleeting instant, *"Bobby!"* he bellowed, his voice cracking with a mix of fear and hope. Propelled by sheer urgency, he sprinted toward her, his heart hammering wildly against his ribs.

Adelaide Hospital

In a sterile hospital room, chaos reigned. Alonso, Melina, and Zoe stood at Nonna Giovanna's bedside, her frail body unrecognizable under a web of tubes and wires.

An hour earlier.

Alonso had been desperate, pleading with the doctors to save her. *"Isn't there something you can do?"* he asked, his voice frantic.

The doctor shook his head, regret in his eyes. *"She's too old for the surgery she needs. It's too risky."*

"But you're saying she'll die without it! Then why not try?" Alonso shouted, his frustration spilling over.

Meanwhile, Zoe was crying, and Melina gently tried to comfort her.

Alonso turned to Zoe. *"Did you call Bobby? We've been keeping this from her for days."*

Zoe shook her head. *"Not yet,"* she replied, her voice cracking up from emotion.

But just as they were about to grab the phone, the flatline beep from Nonna Giovanna's monitor cut through the air, and alarms blared, filling the room with a sudden, deafening sound. Nurses rushed in, pushing the family back, but Alonso, Melina, and Zoe stood frozen in place, their eyes fixed on Giovanna, who seemed to be slipping away right before their eyes. The doctors and nurses had tried everything, CPR, a defibrillator, and even injections, but with no response.

The weight of the impending loss was unbearable for this close-knit family. The very heart of their world was fading, and they couldn't do a thing to stop it.

The nurses started to read out the time of death. The room had an eerie silence. At that moment, Zoe pulled out her phone, her hands trembling, and called Bobby with the devastating news.

CHAPTER 17

BETWEEN WORLDS

Spirit World

Narrated by Nonna Giovanna

It's me again, Giovanna Russo. I *'was'* lying on that hospital bed, technically dead for about 18 Earth minutes. This is the part I mentioned to you that I've never shared with anyone, fearing they'd treat me differently.

Describing this experience will be challenging. It wasn't something earthly, and words, or even images, would hardly come close to capturing it. But I'll do my best.

Imagine a breathtaking, colourful garden, full of towering green trees, knee-high emerald green grass, and stunning butterflies fluttering around. The peace I felt in this world was so profound and foreign to me.

I walked forward, coming to a narrow path of rich red soil, fully present in the moment, without worry in the world, a calm I have never experienced.

Not a drop of fear, no judgments, nor even remembering what had just happened to my body in my veggie patch, just pure love flowing through me. The beautiful blue sky above gradually turned to night, revealing stars like an astronaut's view of space, yet it remained light around me, as though the magnificent garden was floating in space.

Ahead, I saw two beautifully sculpted wooden park benches facing opposite each other, only about two meters apart, surrounded by lush gardens even more stunning than before.

There were magnificent, glowing flowers all around me. The ground beneath my feet transformed from soil to a clear view of the universe, as if I were walking on glass. It was solid underfoot, feeling inner calm and pure, indescribable peace.

Slowly, people began to appear, silently taking seats on the benches. Some were young, but most were older, and occasionally a child joined. Each person looked serene, many holding a shining gold ball the size of a baseball near their chest, matching the large, spinning golden circle up ahead. I sat down on one side of the endless park benches, now holding the same golden ball in my hands as the others. Again, feeling fully in the moment, with an abundance of gratitude and pure love soaking through me.

As we inched forward on the moving bench toward the massive, softly spinning vortex, I watched as people tossed their golden balls into it.

The huge golden vortex stretched into the distant universe. After they released their golden orbs, their bodies turned to colourful dust, drifting away on a gentle breeze as their souls merged with the swirling golden circle, like paint blending. There was no fear, only peace.

But then my peace came to an abrupt halt as I noticed my granddaughter, Bobby, sitting on the opposite side. She was staring at the large golden circle, dressed in her favorite blue checkered work shirt, blue denim shorts, and brown work boots. She had a small black backpack slung over her shoulders, with one corner of her board game poking out, slightly scorched. My heart stopped, and I let out a piercing scream.

"NO! Bobby! Where are you going, Bobby?!"

She didn't hear me. No one did. In this place, only certain things could be heard. Bobby glanced briefly in my direction and seemed to be looking at my boots.

I looked down and realized I was wearing my favorite gumboots, the ones with the chicken print that everyone used to tease me about.

In this world, it seems that we wear only our favorite clothes and sentimental accessories. I noticed Bobby wearing the gold necklace I gave her with the two entangled hearts before she left for New York.

Bobby's lips moved, and I recognized her words, as I was lip-reading her:

"Nonna, I love you." My frustration escalated.

She was only three people away from the large golden circle, where she would soon toss her golden orb, and her body would turn to colourful dust. She would merge with the vortex, never to return.

I tried desperately to get up, to reach her, but I couldn't. It was as if my backside was welded to the bench, unable to move and unable to be heard. Bobby was now only two people away from the large gold circle, getting closer and closer, holding the golden orb in front of her chest like everyone else.

"Please, someone!" I begged. *"That's my granddaughter, take my life instead!"*

Just then, a gentle, mystical-looking man in a colourful suit approached down the aisle between the benches. His voice was soft and sincere, and he was dressed luxuriously, with gorgeous, dark, glowing skin.

He approached me, concerned, and said, *"Giovanna, I hate seeing you troubled. How can I help?"*

"Oh, you can hear me… That's my granddaughter over there!" I cried. *"Please, save her. Take me instead!"* I looked back, panic rising as Bobby now moved within one person of the large golden circle, the circle twirling into oblivion.

I pleaded again, *"Let me stop her! Let me reach her!"* Still, my body could not rise from the park bench.

The man looked at me sympathetically. *"Giovanna, I know how deeply you love her. I can feel it when I touch you,"* he said gently, as his hand was on my shoulder. *"But I can't help her once she's crossed the white line."*

"What white line?" I looked down and saw a thick white line on the ground marking the boundary. Bobby had already crossed it. I struggled to get up, but it was no use; my backside was firmly rooted to the garden bench.

Then, something unusual caught my attention sitting opposite of me, a very unappealing young man, appearing like a criminal. He had a rifle slung across his back, a hard look in his eyes, and a redback spider tattoo on his face, near his mouth. He appeared to me like the criminal I'd seen in the paper that was arrested in Glentvale some time ago.

In stark contrast to everyone else around him, he did not possess a gleaming golden ball. Instead, nestled in his hand was a small, transparent sphere, giving it the appearance of an empty crystal orb. Much to my shock, the park bench where he was sitting abruptly changed course, heading straight into oblivion, with him screaming, *"No! No!!"* I presumed his destination was not going to be pleasant.

NOT NARRATED

Back in the Adelaide hospital, Alonso, Melina, and Zoe watched as doctors and nurses tried CPR, defibrillator shocks, and adrenaline injections. Their efforts showed no results. They were repeatedly told to leave the room, but they refused. The heart monitor's flatline was deafening.

"I'm sorry," the doctor said… *"We've done everything we can. We warned you it would come to this."*

Melina, fierce with determination, pointed toward the door and yelled at the doctors, *"Get out! The Russo family don't give up… Now, GET OUT!!!"* she screamed.

Alonso's pale face was wet with sweat and tears, looked at Melina in shock and said quietly. *"Darling… what are you doing?"*

Carlo, who had just arrived from his flight from Sydney, was freaking out at the scene unfolding before him.

Nurses tried to pull Melina off the bed. Carlo yelled out to the nurse, *"If you don't want your *ss sued, get out now!!"*

Melina climbed onto the hospital bed, positioning herself on top of her mother-in-law with her knees on both sides of Giovanna and starting chest compressions herself.

"Here, Alonso, take this air pump and use it when I tell you, hurry, get around that side." she instructed urgently, handing him the oxygen bag. Melina's resolve turned savage, her strength fueled by love, as sweat poured down her face. She was relentless, even as exhaustion set in, unwilling to stop.

Zoe, panicking, tried to pull her back as tears washed her face. *"Mum, stop! You're being crazy, stop! "Zoe said in distorted words as she was crying.*

"Lock the door, Zoe!" Melina yelled out. Zoe attempted it, but then replied, *"There's no lock, Mum. Please stop!"*

Just then, a large, built Samoan security guard entered. *"I'm sorry, Mrs. Russo, but you need to get off that bed NOW,"* he said, grabbing Melina's arm.

Alonso's face hardened. *"You have three seconds to take your f*cken hands off my wife!!!"* he warned, holding up his fingers, counting down.

One... Two...

In one swift move, Alonso picked up a metal bedpan and knocked the guard out cold. Melina, though shocked, kept pushing Giovanna's chest. The guard started to stir, but Alonso knocked him down again, determined to protect Melina's mission.

More security guards rushed in, but Alonso puffed up his chest and fists, and dramatically shouted, *"Stay back, or you'll end up like Sleeping Beauty over here!"* referring to the unconscious guard on the floor, pretending it was his mighty fist that had done the damage.

Back in the Spirit World

Narrated by Nonna Giovanna

I was finally able to stand up from that relentless park bench, still searching for a glimpse of Bobby. But the beautiful garden faded away, leaving only vast emptiness.

"Who are you, anyway?" I asked the man in the colourful suit who had been so kind to me.

The man introduced himself with a twinkle in his eye. *"My name is Mr. Tinny, but you can call me Des,"* he said enthusiastically.

"Well, thanks for nothing, Mr. Des Tinny," I snapped. *"I asked you to save my granddaughter, and you didn't!"*

Realization dawned on me, and I repeated the name: *"Des Tinny... Destiny? Oh my...*

He smiled knowingly, and in that moment, I felt an overwhelming sense of peace. The surroundings slowly faded as I caught sight of our beautiful planet Earth in the distance. I turned back, but everything was gone, the garden, the huge golden circle, Bobby, and Mr. Destiny. Reaching my arm toward Mother Earth, I felt an inexplicable pull, but before I could understand it fully, I was abruptly jolted back into my body.

I opened my eyes to the loud cheers of my family in the hospital room, feeling somewhat awkward as my daughter-in-law was on top of me. I was confused, unable to comprehend what had just happened. All I could say was *"Where is Bobby!!!"*? Everyone around *the hospital bed looked at me puzzled.*

For some strange reason, the memory of the spirit world was taken from me as soon as I returned to my body, only to resurface later.

Meanwhile, back in the Physical Realm

NOT NARRATED

Moments before …

Moments before Giovanna regained consciousness, the guards stopped in their tracks, unsure of how to deal with Alonso. And then, the heart monitor beeped, first once, then again, and finally in a steady rhythm. The family erupted in cheers, tears of joy streaming down their faces as Giovanna's pulse returned.

After Giovanna screamed out, *"Where is Bobby!!!?"*

Melina collapsed into Alonso's arms from the top of the bed from exhaustion. Alonso caught her in his arms and whispered to her, *"Just when I thought I couldn't possibly love you more."* and kissed her softly on the forehead.

New York City Hospital

Meanwhile, in New York Presbyterian Private Hospital, Bobby lay lifeless in bed, her body battered and mangled by the reckless driver who had hit her and hadn't even stopped. She had been thrown to the ground and left there to die.

Liam was by her side, praying desperately. The damage to her chest and arms wasn't the main concern; it was the trauma to her head and brain that had doctors worried.

Two doctors conferred quietly, exchanging somber looks. Liam, desperate to protect her, claimed to be her husband. *"Is my wife going to be okay?"* he asked, his voice trembling. He feared that admitting her status as homeless might lead to her being overlooked. *"I'll pay for everything, just please help her. We have three young children."*

The doctor's face was grim. *"Honestly, with head injuries this severe, it's extremely rare to get your memory back, or even to survive."*

Liam squeezed Bobby's hand tightly, whispering to God, begging for a miracle. How could someone he had only just met have such a magnetic hold on him? He didn't know, but he couldn't ignore the pull he felt toward her.

Days passed with Bobby still in a coma, her condition worsening. Liam stayed by her side, frustrated that her destroyed phone and laptop meant he couldn't contact her family. All he knew was that she was beautiful in every way, from the outback of Australia, and that he loved her. He didn't even know her surname, but he remembered when they met in the diner, her black backpack with "Sunflower Springs, Australia" embroidered on it. He frantically searched online for any clue. He called the Sunflower Springs post office, but no answer. He called the pub, but no response, as Barry O'Connor was too busy talking to notice the phone ringing. He kept trying.

Back in Adelaide

Doctors decided to operate on Giovanna after all, as she was fitter than most people her age. She had always eaten healthily, eating homegrown food and staying active on the farm all her life. Now, her body was rewarding her for those efforts. Giovanna came out of surgery days later, weak but alive.

Alonso and Melina were worried, they hadn't been able to reach Bobby for four days now. She had always kept her promises, and she hadn't called since Zoe informed her about Nonna's passing.

"I know what you're thinking, babe!" Melina said to Alonso. *"Leave today. You're in a capital city here, you can be in New York within a day. I got Steevo to express post your passport yesterday, it should arrive today."*

"Far out, woman, how did you know? Yes, I was thinking of going to go find Bobby, I am worried sick!" he replied frantically. *"Carlo got onto the authorities to track her phone, and they found the last time it was active was when Zoe called her with the bad news, but it's been out of service since. I'm really worried about her. It's out of character for her to break her promise."*

"I'm worried too, darling," Melina replied. Alonso could tell by her tone and her facial expressions that her strong intuition was telling her something wasn't right. He immediately took action to get the next flight out, as soon as his passport arrived that day.

NYC Hospital

Liam was resolute in his mission to connect with Bobby's family, so he made the nurse vow to inform him of any updates. He remembered Bobby's response when the diner manager inquired about her address, and she was unable to give one, which led him to suspect she was homeless.

He quickly set out to find Bobby's suitcase, hoping it would hold a clue or, better yet, her passport.

Starting at the homeless camp on Rawson Road, mostly being ignored by people he approached. It took him hours to get someone to respond. Liam described Bobby to anyone who was in his path. An older man finally pointed him to Betsy's camp but warned, *"She might strike if you get too close."*

He cautiously approached Betsy's camp area. *"Hello? Is anyone there?"* Liam called out as his face peered inside. Before he could blink, Betsy punched him square in the face, catching him completely off guard.

"Get out of here, boy! "I have company right now, what do you want!?" she growled. Betsy was with her boyfriend, Charles, a scrawny man she had known for years.

Liam touched his bleeding nose, irritated but persistent. *"I'm not here to harm you, woman! My name is Liam, and I was told you know Bobby. I need her suitcase right now, I'm in desperate need of her passport to contact her family, she is in a bad way."*

Betsy's stern expression softened as she suddenly emerged from her makeshift sheet tent. *"Is she alright, boy?"* she inquired, her tone filled with concern. *"No, she's not,"* Liam answered anxiously. *"She's in a coma after being hit by a jerk on the road who just left her there to die."* Betsy's face registered a mix of shock and sadness upon hearing the news.

"Please, I need her suitcase… Come on, I don't have time to waste, I have to get back to the hospital."

Betsy studied him with suspicion, her fierce protectiveness kicking in. She grabbed him by the scruff of his neck and studied his eyes intently. After a long pause, she relented and handed over Bobby's suitcase, holding onto it for an extra second.

"Is everything in there," he said firmly, eyeing her cautiously.

Betsy nodded yes, Liam taking the suitcase from her hand. *"Thanks,"* Liam said to her. *"I'm really hoping Bobby will pull through, she is special to me,"* Betsy said. Liam acknowledged the comment with a soft nod of the head.

Betsy smiled faintly. *"She's got some pretty snazzy 'g-bangers' in there too."*

Liam smiled, a little surprised. *"G-bangers?"*

Betsy chuckled. *"Yeah, Aussie slang for G-string underwear. She's been teaching me a few things."*

Liam smiled, amused. *"Ah, so you been snooping in her suitcase I see?"*

As Liam walked away, Betsy called out, *"I will pray for Bobby, I sure hope she will be okay!!."*

Liam whispered to himself, *"I hope so too."*

Once Liam was out of earshot, Betsy grinned, unfazed, holding up a pair of gold and red skimpy, lacy G-string underwear she had stolen from Bobby's suitcase.

"I think these might fit me just fine," she quipped to Charles, giving a playful wink. Charles shook his head in amused disbelief, knowing better than to argue with Betsy.

Once Liam was next to his car, out of everyone's sight, he opened the suitcase, frantically searching for Bobby's passport. His heart soared when he found it, he felt like he'd struck gold. He opened the passport to see her photo beside her name and smiled in admiration. He read aloud to himself, *"Bobby Jo Russo, 168 Eucalyptus Road, Sunflower Springs, South Australia ... her surname is Russo. I wonder what origins those are from"*.

He held the passport in his hands, a profound sense of relief flooding over him. Immediately, he scanned a travel insurance document and found a phone number under her family's name. He dialed Alonso's number, but it rang and rang with no answer. Frustration built within him as he tried countless times, but it was no use. Finally, he remembered to call the number for the local Sunflower Springs Pub again, the one he'd tried earlier. Now, at least, he had a surname to go by, he thought.

Dialing, he took a deep breath, hoping someone might know Bobby's family.

"Gidday, Barry O'Connor here... what can I be doin' for ya?"

"ohh...Hello, Barry," Liam said, relief in his voice. *"Sir, I know this is a long shot, but I'm trying to reach a family by the name of Russo in*

your area. Do you happen to know them, or maybe someone else there knows them?"

A tense pause filled the line. *"Do I know 'em!!!"* Barry replied with his broad Australian accent. *"Mate, everyone in town knows the Russos! Everyone, not only knows everyone in town, but also who they're sleeping with, their dog's names, and what they bloody had for breakfast!"* Liam looked at his phone, bewildered. *"What kind of place is this"?* Liam thought to himself.

*"Oh, Sh*t, I heard Bobby is in the US. Is she okay?"* Barry added.

Liam took a shaky breath. *"No, she's not. She was hit by a tow truck and is in a coma. The doctors say she might not make it."*

Barry let out a sharp breath and said. *"Bloody hell! Alonso needs to know."*

Liam added, *"Hang on, who is Alonso?"*

"That's probably the number I've been calling," Liam explained and added. *"But no one's picking up."*

"Alonso is her dad," Barry explained and added. *"He's been trying to call Bobby, but she hasn't called in four days. She promised she would call every day, so he's on a flight now to find her because he's worried."*

Liam quickly asked, *"Do I have the correct number?"* and read it out to him

Barry confirmed, *"Yeah, mate, that's the right number."*

Liam requested that Barry send a message to Alonso, telling him where Bobby was and that it was urgent. He thanked him and hung up.

As Barry hung up the phone, he couldn't help but boast to his customers in the bar. *"He called me sir!"* he chuckled, as that term is not used in Australia. *"Hey, by the way, Bobby's in trouble!"* *catching everyone's attention and concern at the bar.*

Barry, being a bit of an airhead, suddenly remembered that he needed to text Alonso immediately. He quickly typed a message and sent it off: It went like this.

"SOME BLOKE JUST CALLED, BOBBY'S IN NYC Presbyterian *private* hospital, DOCTORS SAY SHE'S GUNNA DIE."

Within an hour, the entire town of Sunflower Springs knew about Bobby's accident. Calls and messages poured into Melina, filled with heartfelt prayers, disbelief, and sadness. The small town, usually bustling at its own pace, fell into a somber stillness. The community held its collective breath, hoping for a miracle.

Back at the hospital in New York, Liam returned to Bobby's side, a renewed sense of purpose filling him. He leaned down beside her, his voice a soft whisper in the otherwise quiet room.

"Your family's coming, Bobby," he murmured, his voice thick with emotion. *"Hold on for them... hold on for me."*

CHAPTER 18

SAVING BOBBY

NOT NARRATED

As Alonso's plane touched down at JFK Airport in New York City, his eyes were bloodshot from lack of sleep over the past few days. He anxiously powered on his phone as soon as he stepped off the plane, only for it to be flooded with missed

calls from an unfamiliar number, Liam's number. Among the notifications, Alonso found a text from Barry O'Connor, whom he had saved in his contacts as *"Barry the Boof Head"* (a term of endearment for idiot in Australian slang). Opening the message, he read the chilling words:

"SOME BLOKE JUST CALLED, BOBBY'S IN NYC Presbyterian private hospital, DOCTORS SAY SHE'S GUNNA DIE."

Alonso's heart dropped as he yelled, *"No... No! Why is this happening to us? First my mother, and now Bobby? Che diavolo..."* (*What the devil! In Italian*)

He clutched his phone, struggling to breathe.

In a panic, Alonso hailed a taxi and handed the driver a hundred-dollar bill. *"Take me to Presbyterian private hospital, as fast as you can, please!"*

The taxi driver looked at the $100 bill and said, *"That's a strong please, alright. I'm on it, sir."*

When Alonso arrived at the hospital, he sprinted to the reception desk, breathless, struggling to get the words out, *"My daughter, she's here, she's dying! Her name is Bobby Jo Russo, spelled R-U-S-S-O!"* he nearly shouted. The receptionist remained calm and typed slowly, which tested Alonso's patience. *"Could you look a bit faster, please?"* he said, his voice rising.

"I'm sorry, sir," the receptionist replied, still typing, *"but I don't see a Bobby Jo Russo here... We do have Bobby Martinez."*

Alonso turned away in frustration, rubbing his forehead. He quickly dialed Barry O'Connor's number, his hands trembling uncontrollably.

"Did that guy who called you say his name or where he's from?" Alonso asked urgently. *"Was he a doctor?"* He added

"I don't remember, and I didn't think to ask where he was from, sorry mate... Is Bobby okay?" Barry replied, sounding concerned.

Alonso clenched his fist, trying to control his emotions, and hung up on Barry, leaving him standing there, puzzled.

Alonso dialed the missed number repeatedly, only to get no answer. Liam, who had been trying to charge his phone, hadn't received any of the calls. He was playing soft music to Bobby from his phone so his phone would get flat often. After constantly checking his phone to see if anyone had tried to contact him, Liam muttered, *"Oh, great. Flat again,"* before returning to Bobby's bedside to continue his quiet prayers. He whispered to her, *"What kind of town do you come from where everyone knows each other's breakfast orders?"* He chuckled softly. *"I'd love to see your world, Bobby Jo."*

Outside the hospital, Alonso continued his frantic calls. He caught sight of a stretcher being rolled toward the morgue next door, covered with a white sheet, and dread washed over him. *"Please, God… not my Bobby,"* he whispered as he hurried inside to inquire further in deep despair and dread.

"My name is Alonso Russo," he told the morgue receptionist, struggling to keep his voice steady. *"My daughter …was… is… visiting from Australia. She had some kind of accident. She may not have had an ID on her, but her name is Bobby Jo Russo, is she here?"*

"Let me check, sir," the receptionist, who reminded Alonso of Morticia from the Addams family, replied. He braced himself, feeling his stomach churn. This time, it was the opposite of the slow receptionist from earlier, he wanted her to take her time, not wanting to hear bad news.

After a few moments, the receptionist said, *"Actually, sir, we do have an unidentified young woman here. Fair hair, in her twenties. We don't know where she is from. She was found with a small backpack, wearing a T-shirt with Australia written on it, but no ID."*

"Come this way, sir, to identify her," she continued.

"No… no… no… I can't… I can't… I can't," Alonso sobbed, trembling uncontrollably, feeling his world crumbling around him. It was the lowest point in his life.

Alonso felt faint, his body nearly giving way under the weight of the trauma. He frantically looked around to find a waste bin, spotted one, grabbed it, and vomited in it. Without saying a word to the Unsympathetic receptionist who was staring at him, he pulled the bin liner out of the bin, coming from pure decency to remove his own mess, and bolted outside.

He looked for the nearest park bench to rest on as he tied a knot on the bin liner and binned his vomit.

As he struggled to keep himself together, Melina's call came through Messenger. *"Holy Moses, woman, halfway across the world and you still know something's wrong!"* he muttered under his breath.

He answered the call without showing his face, but Melina, sensing his distress, urged him to turn the camera on, and he reluctantly did. Melina's heart skipped a beat seeing his ghost pale and stressed.

He told her about Barry O'Connor's text message and how it had shaken him. *"WAIT A MINUTE!!,"* Alonso suddenly shouted. *"The guy that called boof head O'Connor knew our family name. They did not have the surname of the girl in the morgue, but who has been trying to call me? Who was it?!"*

She stared at him, the silence between them unnerving.

His call with Melina was cut short by no charge left on his phone, leaving him stranded in a state of helplessness.

In a renewed rush, his mind raced. He planned to keep trying to call the mystery number, but now his phone was dead, and he didn't have a United States power point adapter.

Alonso spotted a young woman at a nearby coffee cart in front of the hospital, placing her phone on a special charging station while speaking with the vendor to order a coffee. Without hesitation, he approached her.

"Excuse me, miss... Sorry to bother you, but do you mind if I use your charger after you're done?" Alonso asked breathlessly. *"Our power points in Australia are different to here, and I didn't get time to buy an adapter as I left Australia in a hurry to get here. Do you know where I could buy an adapter by any chance?"*

Liam, who was also charging his phone nearby, noticed Alonso's accent. The young woman smiled and said, *"Sure, you can use mine for now. You can buy an adaptor or a whole new electrical cord later from the supermarket about a block away that way."* She pointed and pulled her charger out of her phone socket, even though her phone wasn't fully charged yet.

"Thank you so much, I really appreciate it, darl," Alonso said gratefully, using the Australian term of endearment. He realized, however, that the charger wasn't for an Android phone.

Noticing Alonso's distressed look, Liam approached and handed over his own charger. *"Here, take this one,"* Liam, noticing Alonso's desperate-sounding tone, added. *"This one is for an Android, from my old workplace. Keep the cord, sir. I have another, and I don't want to be reminded of them anyway.* He added with a smile, hoping to lighten the mood.

Alonso looked into Liam's eyes and accepted the charger with a quite grateful nod.

*"I've always wanted to visit Australia, "*Liam added zestfully.

Despite the exchange, Alonso barely managed to smile. His mind was consumed by worry, and he was struggling to hold it together.

Liam's phone now had enough charge, and so did Alonso's. Liam dialed Alonso's number. Alonso's phone buzzed immediately.

*"HOLY SH*T!!... You're Alonso, aren't you?!"* Liam yelled out, his voice startling everyone around him. The young lady, who had been so kind to offer her charger, startled, spilled coffee all over herself.

Alonso's eyes widened. *"Yes, yes, yes, I am Alonso!"* he yelled back.

"Come with me, now!" Liam yelled back like a crazy man, leaving the strangers around them wondering what the heck was going on.

Liam rushed into the hospital entrance, urging Alonso along with his arm pointing to their next turn as they ran frantically. *"Are you saying Bobby's alive?!"* Alonso yelled, disbelief at finding the stranger that had come to his aid, lacing his voice as they sprinted toward the elevator.

"Yes, yes she is... but barely," Liam replied, his voice tight with emotion. Alonso's heart sank, but filled with gratitude, whispered, *"Thank you, sweet Jesus, thank you."*

As they waited in the elevator, Alonso's frantic questions continued. *"Was it you trying to call me, and you that called Barry O'Connor?"*

"Yes, it was me," Liam answered. Relief showing on Alonso's face

Inside the crowded elevator, Alonso turned to Liam. *"Who are you to my daughter?"* he asked, his voice a mix of curiosity and concern.

"Just a guy," Liam replied with a shrug, still out of breath.

An elderly woman in the elevator overheard the conversation and chimed in, *"Best to tell the truth, young man."* Liam returned her a small smile, grateful for the distraction.

When they reached Bobby's room, Alonso's heart shattered. He saw his daughter's fragile form lying on the hospital bed surrounded by countless cords. Tears streamed down his face as he prayed, *"God, you spared my mother. Will I be lucky enough to have my daughter spared too?"* He gently reached out, taking Bobby's hand in his, and kissed her on the forehead.

He sat beside her for hours, praying quietly. As time passed, Alonso noticed how exhausted Liam looked. He hadn't thanked him yet.

Putting his hand out, Alonso finally spoke, *"It's nice to meet you, 'just a guy'."*

"Nice to meet you, sir. My name is Liam Martinez." Liam said as he put out his hand to handshake Alonso. Alonso shakes Liam's hand profusely in gratitude.

"So good to meet you, Liam," Alonso said, his voice thick with emotion. *"How do you know my daughter? I can't thank you enough for what you're doing for her. I'm blown away, I really am, young man."* His eyes started to water as he spoke.

Liam explained how they had met in two different places and how it seemed like fate had brought them together. Alonso, who normally wouldn't believe in such things, found himself agreeing wholeheartedly that it was indeed fate.

Liam heard Alonso mentioning that his mother was spared and asked how she was, and that he watched Bobby have a bad reaction to a phone call when she took off from the venue they were at. Together, they pieced the puzzle of what actually happened.

"Glad your mum is ok, sir. Does she know you're here"? Liam said to Alonso.

Alonso replied, *"No she doesn't know, she is in hospital ICU recovering from a major operation so we are keeping the fact we lost contact with Bobby secret, but Mum is not stupid she has been asking about Bobby and wondering why we won't let her call her".* Liam asked how big the family was and what they did for a living showing genuine interest in Bobby's world. Liam taking it all in with fascination. *"3000 acres, you got to be kidding me, are you saying that Bobby is your business partner!!!?"* Liam said in amazement. Alonso briefly explained Bobby's reason for being in the States and what happened to the funds they had. Liam was blown away by the story and explained that he had one of her board games and that he recognized something special in her the moment he saw her.

Alonso couldn't tear his eyes away from Liam, admiring the young man's selflessness. He was amazed that, after only meeting Bobby twice, Liam was already doing more for her than some people did for those they had known for a lifetime. It was a testament to his remarkable character, and Alonso couldn't help but feel deeply touched by his actions and selfless nature.

Alonso then called the family to break the news once it was a decent hour back in Australia. They decided not to tell Giovanna, the news about Bobby would be too much for her to handle at that moment, or any other moment for that matter.

Zoe broke down, as did Carlo. Melina, though emotional, wasn't entirely surprised, her strong intuition had told her something was terribly wrong all along. She had just hoped she was wrong, not wanting to cast a dark cloud over Alonso's head, knowing how deeply he would be affected.

Keeping the news of what happened to Bobby from Giovanna was only stressing her more, fearing that the worst had happened to Bobby overseas and that they were keeping it from her. So, several days later, they told Giovanni but lied that Bobby was in the hospital and conscious but not allowed to receive calls yet. Giovanna was devastated and prayed for Bobby constantly.

Days passed, and Bobby's condition continued to worsen.

Back in Sunflower Springs, the entire community held its breath, keeping her in their thoughts and prayers. Melina, Carlo, and Zoe clung to one another for support, devastated by the lack of positive progress. Alonso stayed by Bobby's bedside, desperately pleading with the doctors to do whatever it took to keep her alive.

Moments later, the head doctor entered and addressed Liam. *"Sir, I assure you, we're doing everything possible to keep your wife stable."*

Alonso shot a puzzled look at Liam. Liam responded by pressing a finger to his lips when the doctor wasn't looking, signaling Alonso to remain silent. Once the doctor began speaking to the nurse, Alonso leaned over and whispered to Liam with a worried expression. *"I didn't miss a wedding, did I?"*

Liam later explained why he had told the hospital staff that Bobby was his wife. It was just a precaution, he said, in case they treated her differently due to her circumstances and her homelessness.

Alonso, now visibly shocked and upset, yelled out, *"What the f... What do you mean she was homeless?!"*

The doctor entered again, this time accompanied by two specialists. They approached Bobby's bed, addressing Liam, as they still believed he was her husband.

"Liam," the doctor began his tone grave, *"Her heart rate is diminishing. Unfortunately, it's not looking good. We expect by tonight her heart will fail altogether."*

Liam and Alonso's faces sank in despair as they both pleaded with the doctors for something, anything, that could be done.

"We wish there was something we could do," the doctor responded solemnly. *"I'm so sorry. Perhaps you want to bring in her children."*

Alonso gave Liam a sideways glance, clearly confused, knowing he couldn't possibly have become a grandfather.

Frowning deeply with fear and disappointment for his daughter, Alonso glanced at the metal bedpan by the bedside, and in a moment of frustration, picked it up, as if he were ready to strike someone.

Liam, across the other side of the bed, raised an eyebrow in curiosity. *"What's that?.. I mean... I know what it is, but why... are you...?"*

"It's insurance... I'm ready to strike those doctors if they give up." Alonso muttered with a serious face, recalling the tense encounter with the security guards back at the hospital in Australia.

Liam stared at him, clearly confused, but then chuckled awkwardly, feeling a strange sense of kinship with Bobby's father.

Slowly, Liam stood up from Bobby's bedside chair and slowly walked over to where Alonso stood. He placed his hand gently on Alonso's shoulder and said, *"She's going to be okay."* There was a slight pause, and then he added, *"Put the weapon down."*

Alonso slowly put the bedpan back down, still shaking, but the faintest flicker of hope seemed to spark in him.

In the Spirit World

Bobby sat on the same side of the garden bench, where Giovanna had seen her, in her hand, cradling the golden orb that symbolized her spirit. The opposite side of the never-ending garden bench was filled with people from all walks of life, moving swiftly toward a massive, swirling golden vortex. Bobby's side, however, had come to a complete stop.

She gazed peacefully at the ever-changing colours of the golden sphere ahead, occasionally turning to smile at those around her, her natural warmth shining through.

Then, a familiar voice broke the serene silence, gentle and filled with kindness.

Bobby turned her head to see who it was, her eyes wide with recognition.

"It's you!" she exclaimed, recognizing the man in the glowing white cloak.

The man knelt before her, meeting her gaze with deep affection. Bobby's eyes searched his face, puzzled but hopeful. *"I think I saw my Nonna's boots with the chicken print on them, but now I can't see her! Please, can you tell me if she's alright?"*

The man in the white cloak's gentle smile softened even further and said. *"It's rare, Bobby, for someone at this stage to think only of others."*

He tilted his head slightly, noticing the scorched board game sticking out from her backpack. Reaching out, he placed his hand over it, and Bobby felt a warm vibration through her spine for a moment. The man then guided her hand holding the golden orb back to her chest, merging it back into her body. While softly saying

"It is not your time to leave, my child," he said softly. *"Go forth and live your life."*

Back in the NYC Hospital

At that very moment, Alonso and Liam were holding Bobby's hands, praying silently. Suddenly, Bobby's right arm rose toward her chest while Liam was holding it.

Both men erupted in shouts of joy. *"She moved! She moved!"*

"Did you move her hand or did she?" Alonso asked, his voice trembling.

"She moved it... she ... I didn't," Liam answered, his eyes widened with disbelief.

Alonso rushed to call for the nurses, who quickly gathered around in disbelief as Bobby's eyes fluttered open.

The doctor, still cautious, warned them, *"She may experience severe amnesia."*

But Bobby, blinking slowly, looked at Liam and then at Alonso. *"Liam... my Nonna... Please... my phone."*

Alonso gently replied, *"Nonna is okay, sweetheart; she is alive."*

Turning to see her father, Bobby whispered, *"Dad... what the hell are you doing h...?"* She couldn't finish her sentence. Her eyelids grew heavy again, and she fell back into unconsciousness, leaving Alonso and Liam watching over her anxiously. Trying to make sense of what was going on, as it didn't match what the doctors were saying.

Relieved that her memory was intact, the doctors noted that the fact she fell back into unconsciousness was likely just exhaustion. Bobby had lost a significant amount of weight in the past month, reduced to almost skin and bones, looking very sickly.

In the days that followed, Bobby's condition steadily improved, much to the doctors' astonishment. She slipped back into consciousness and stayed there.

Alonso and Liam are ecstatic, Bobby is ready to be discharged much sooner than expected.

One doctor, still in disbelief, declared, *"Liam and Alonso, you are extremely lucky. I can say with total honesty, I don't know how this recovery is even possible."*

Liam smiled, replying, *"As I've said to you before, doctor, Bobby's no ordinary woman!"*

Alonso proudly agreed, and the Doctor responded, *"Indeed she isn't!!"*

Liam, grateful that Bobby was healing slowly, secretly cherished these last few days with her before she would return to Australia.

One afternoon, Alonso entered Bobby's room, looking tired but happy. *"Damn, the next flight out to Australia isn't until Monday,"* he announced, his voice filled with a mix of frustration and excitement.

"That's perfect," Liam said, smiling. *"We have three days. You're both staying with me, and I'm taking you out to see the best of New York City."* He looked warmly at Bobby, who tried to hide her excitement.

The young nurse, overhearing, teased, *"Yes, Liam. I think your wife deserves a special treat."*

Liam chuckled, attempting to deflect the comment, while Alonso gave him a knowing smile. Bobby, slightly confused, raised an eyebrow but didn't press further.

Alonso said aloud, *"Son-in-law… time to celebrate with a beer, mate."*

"Oh, sorry, sir, I don't drink, but I will make an exception," Liam replied.

"Will ya stop calling me 'sir'?" Alonso demanded with a smile.

Liam's apartment was tasteful, cozy, clean, and very neat, a true reflection of who he was, always striving for excellence.

Bobby, still mostly covered in casts, still in pain but not showing it, smiled as she looked around. *"Nice place. Amazing plants, Liam. You have great taste. Wow, I love this."*

"*Are you sure it's okay for us to stay?*" Alonso asked, ever considerate.

Liam replied, "*It's a pleasure and an honour to have you both here.*"

"*You haven't worked in weeks,*" Alonso whispered to Liam, hoping Bobby wouldn't hear him.

"*Actually... they sacked me on my second night,*" Liam replied, shrugging. "*But I didn't want to work for people like that anyway. Everything is a transaction to them... they have no soul.*"

"*It's because of me, isn't it?*" Bobby asked, her voice full of concern.

"*No,*" Liam reassured her. "*I chose this, and I'd do it again.*" He paused, smiling. Bobby and Alonso looked at him in quiet admiration.

"*Anyways, we have three days, and we're going to make the most of them,*" Liam added in an excited tone.

"*Bobby, are you up to it with casts at all? ... because if you're not, we'll just stay in.*"

"*I'm up for it,*" she said with a sparkling smile. Alonso nodded his head in disbelief and said to Liam, "*Outback farmers are tough cookies, aren't they, love?*" as he kissed her on the forehead. Bobby turned to her father, smiling at him and replied, "*I learned from the master himself, the unstoppable Alonso Russo.*"

Liam was true to his words, escorting Bobby and Alonso to every tourist spot he could think of. Making her laugh constantly despite her crutches and body pain, she managed just the same.

Alonso tried many times to offer cash to Liam to cover costs, but Liam point-blank refused to accept it.

"You're in my country; you're the guests. I pay, capish?" Liam would say.

Somehow, with Bobby in a full arm and leg cast, they managed, laughing at the awkward hustle through crowds and snapping photos at every possible landmark. They attended a live Broadway show and the New York Zoo.

Liam and Bobby sat together at a quiet corner of Central Park on some single swings, while Alonso was ordering pizza for lunch from a mobile food wagon. Bobby took a deep breath and gazed at Liam.

"I don't have the words to thank you enough for literally saving my life." She paused. *"For God's sake, Liam,"* she whispered. *"Why did you run after me? You hardly knew me."*

"I do know you, Bobby. I manifested you to a tee..."

She looked at him, confused. *"You are the exact girl I knew I would meet someday."*

Bobby, shocked by what he just said, reacted by softly adding,

"But..."

Liam replied, *"I know... I know... there is a 'but'... a huge 'but'."*

At that moment, Alonso came back with excitement, carrying enough pizza for an army. Overhearing what Liam had just said, Alonso asked curiously,

"Whose huge butt?" as he looked around while eating his pizza. Bobby and Liam just smiled at each other.

Passing by a souvenir shop, Liam suddenly stopped and disappeared inside, leaving Bobby and Alonso to wait outside. When he emerged moments later, he held out a large stuffed raccoon and handed it to Bobby with a sly smile.

"Here, this is yours. A little memento from America."

Her heart skipped a beat as he handed it to her, realizing that Liam had been closely observing her during their visit to the zoo. He had paid attention when she told him about her encounter with the cute raccoon that dared to enter Betsy's sheet tent. Liam was fascinated by how much she knew about raccoons, more than he did, especially since they were native to his country.

"Oh, wow, I love it. Thank you," she managed to choke out, trying to hide her growing feelings for him.

As the day of Bobby's departure for Australia loomed like a storm cloud on the horizon, it was Saturday night, Liam organized tickets to a lavish fancy-dress ball. Despite Bobby being encased in cumbersome casts, they somehow managed to pull it off. The trio dressed for the occasion, transforming themselves with an elegance that left onlookers speechless. Bobby, a vision of beauty that took Liam's breath away, Bobby was almost unrecognizable. Liam gazed at her with fierce adoration, murmuring with a playful grin, *"Lucky for those casts, or I would have walked right past you."*

In a display of raw emotion and strength, Liam lifted Bobby to dance, as her movements were limited, a captivating spectacle that drew every eye in the room. The scene was as amusing as it was enchanting, each step a testament to their bond. Alonso, despite his best efforts, found himself unable to tear his gaze away, caught in the magnetic pull of their tender, romantic display. A stunning, flirtatious woman approached Alonso and asked him to dance. He complimented her with a polite greeting, but then explained that he could only think of one woman he wanted to dance with - his wife. The disappointed woman then walked away. His only dance partner in his world was *always* his wife, Melina.

Leaving for Australia.

It was Sunday night. Bobby and Alonso were set to fly back to Australia the next morning at 11 am. It was late at night, and Alonso had gone to bed. For the first time, they finally had quiet time alone, as they sat on the couch.

"Nightcap?" Liam called out excitedly as he handed her a hot chocolate.

"Oh yum, thank you," Bobby said as she accepted.

Liam enthusiastically asked Bobby, *"Can I sign your leg cast?"*

"Of course," she replied with a smile.

He reached for a marker and wrote the words **Always IN my Heart**, then circled the words with a heart. Outside of the heart, he signed it: *Liam.*

A heavy pause hung between them before she said, *"I can't stop thinking about... if it weren't for you, I would've..."* Her voice trailed off, caught somewhere between her usual lightheartedness and something deeper. *"I would've bled to death out there, on that road, looking like some kind of animal roadkill! My game creation and everything I'd ever worked on... all reduced to dust. And my family..."*

She stopped, breathing in a shaky breath. *"They'd be inconsolable. Just like I would be if I lost one of them."*

"Liam," she started, her voice barely a whisper. *"Thank you... for all of this... how do I even deserve it?"* Her words caught in her throat as she looked up at him. Liam gently placed his pointer finger on her lips, signaling her to stop talking.

A small smile played on Liam's lips as he replied, *"My gut feeling about someone is never wrong, Bobby. I knew you had something special the minute I looked into your eyes at that diner."* He paused for a moment. *"And I knew there was something wrong when you took that phone call. I just wanted to be there for you."*

There was a heavy pause. Bobby, trying so hard to hide her feelings, she hugged Liam tightly, overwhelmed by his selflessness. They both chuckled, as it was awkward for Bobby to hug anyone in such a restricted cast on her leg and arm.

At that moment, Liam's heart was beating faster. He wanted nothing more than to close the space between them and kiss her passionately. As difficult as it was for him, he pushed the thought away, respecting Bobby too much to complicate things.

They held each other tightly, enveloped in a profound silence that neither had ever felt before. Completely immersed in the moment and appreciative of the bond they shared, all the while aware that they could never be together.

Alonso walked into the kitchen to have a drink of water. Both hid what was going on. When Alonso was out of sight. Bobby said.

"Liam... can you do me one last favor?"

Liam responded, *"No… because I don't want it to be my 'last' favor."*

Bobby smiled and reworded it. *"Can you do me yet another favor, please?"*

Liam smiled and said, *"Of course."*

Bobby said, *"Can you take me to Betsy's place tomorrow? I want to say goodbye and thank her."*

Liam took her there early the next morning before her flight and watched from a distance as they hugged and spoke for a while. Liam admired every bit of Bobby's persona and was dreading saying goodbye to her.

In the bustling airport, Liam walked ahead, leading Alonso and Bobby through the crowd. Alonso's playful commentary faded, replaced by an appreciative silence as he watched Liam's mannerisms. There was something admirable about this young man who had done so much for mere strangers, Alonso thought to himself.

It was time to depart.

As they entered the airport, Bobby said, *"Thank you again, Liam, for everything. I really enjoyed being a tourist with you, I loved every minute, and I will never forget it."* Bobby said, locking eyes with him, feeling a mixture of gratitude and something more that she couldn't quite name.

Liam nodded and walked on, but Bobby couldn't help sneaking glances at him, her feelings for him stirring in ways she hadn't anticipated.

Then, with a burst of energy, Liam whipped out the instant camera he had used for the last three days. *"Come on, let's take one last selfie!"* he called, grinning widely.

Alonso hesitated, feeling this moment belonged to the two of them, but Liam grabbed him playfully, forcing him into the frame. The picture snapped just as Alonso pulled a hilariously startled face, and Bobby burst into laughter. The three of them shared a final, genuine laugh together. He took two photos and gave Bobby one.

As the PA announced boarding, Liam pulled Bobby in for one last hug. Alonso noticed the prolonged embrace, sensing a subtle bond he hadn't seen before. This wasn't just friendship; there was something deeper, unspoken.

"We've got to go, we're late," Bobby said, her voice bright despite the emotions brimming beneath the surface.

Alonso shook Liam's hand, pulling him in for a quick man-hug. *"Thanks again, son,"* he said sincerely. *"You've got a big heart. Keep chasing that dream of becoming a movie producer. I do not doubt at all your ability to get there and much more."*

Liam smiled back, gratitude lighting up his eyes. He waved goodbye, watching them disappear, a pang of longing rising in his chest. As he turned to leave, he shook off the feeling, setting his focus back on his dreams, determined more than ever to make them come true.

Back in his apartment, now void of love and laughter. Liam glanced at the photo they had just taken, marveling at how life had twisted and turned so unexpectedly in just a few weeks. He asked himself what had changed inside of him, sensing something but unable to pinpoint it.

Bobby's zestful, enthusiastic voice saying, *"To rising stronger, laughing louder, and loving deeper!"* when she would make a toast, echoed in Liam's mind. "Yes, here is to rising stronger, laughing louder, and loving deeper!" he whispered to himself as he raised his glass of water.

He headed to the kitchen, eyeing the cookie jar as he went to put his hand in. He pulled out a stack of cash Alonso had left as a gesture of thanks. Liam had refused Alonso's money repeatedly, but he had sneakily found a way to give it to him anyway, knowing Liam could not give it back once they were gone.

"Stubborn man," Liam whispered, a smile tugging at his lips.

In flight

Meanwhile, Bobby and Alonso settled in for their long flight home. Alonso placed a comforting arm around her, pressing a kiss on her forehead. They sat in companionable silence, both reflecting on the whirlwind of events that had brought them here.

"I can't wait to see everyone," Bobby said softly. *"They must be stressed, running the place on their own."* There was a pause. *"Dad… I didn't accomplish anything I set out to do on this trip."* Her voice grew small. *"The game I planned to launch, reaching a million users to help people…"* She shook her head and sighed. *"None of it happened, Dad. All I managed to do was lose all our money. I'm so sorry."*

Alonso looked at her, eyes wide with disbelief. *"Sorry?"* he repeated, his voice rising. *"Bobby, you don't owe me an apology! If anything, I owe you one. I know how much this game means to you, and all those success principles you want to teach the world…"* He sighed. *"I let my fear get in the way of supporting you fully… I AM sorry."*

Bobby's throat tightened. *"It's more than that, Dad. I lost everything. The $750,000 we worked for, plus Nonna's money from selling her investment home, all the hard work Nonno Angelo put into it before he passed…"* She paused, fighting back tears. She continued, *"I couldn't even sell one game, not one. I had to give them away! And then… there was this woman in a diner. She laughed at me, and for the first time in my life, I felt five seconds of doubt. It felt awful, Dad!!"*

"Five seconds of doubt?" Alonso repeated. *"I wish my doubt would last that long!"* he added.

"And then… I almost got myself killed." She gave a bitter laugh. *"Run over by a bloody tow truck, how careless!"*

She looked at her father, the question hovering between them. *"Why did all of that happen?"*

Alonso let her words sink in, his own emotions simmering beneath the surface. Finally, he replied, his voice soft but steady. *"I remember a wise girl once told me… every adversity carries with it a seed of equal or greater good."*

A small smile broke across Bobby's face, and she rested her head on his shoulder, feeling comforted by the familiar words.

"And that the universe has a better plan," she added.

Alonso chuckled, lightening the mood. *"But for now, Bobby, let's just say…well, we're BROKE!"*

"But not BROKEN," Bobby replied, a line that was engraved in her mind when she met Raymond at Rawson Road.

Bobby's mind couldn't help but drift to Liam's face.

Alonso looked at his daughter, placed her head on his shoulder to rest as she slowly fell asleep, feeling like the luckiest man alive.

CHAPTER 19

HOME IS WHERE THE HEART IS

NOT NARRATED

The New York night was wrapped in rain, each drop bouncing off the pavement as Liam trudged through the downpour. The city lights reflected in ripples along the streets, and his paper bag of groceries grew heavier with each step, soggy and fragile.

It had been two weeks since Bobby and Alonso flew back to Australia.

As Liam approached his apartment building, he noticed a sleek black Mercedes-Benz idling at the curb, its mysterious tinted windows masking the scene within. He slowed, instinctively wary, the hair on the back of his neck prickling.

Brushing it off, he continued toward the front door of his building, trying to shield his groceries from the relentless rain, but the bag was beginning to sag under the weight and wetness, and all his oranges fell out. *"Oh, Sh*t,"* he said, annoyed with himself.

"Shall I pull closer, ma'am?" William offered, watching Georgie's expression tighten. She shook her head, insinuating no.

"That stubborn boy won't answer my calls," she muttered, her gaze locked on Liam. *"Drop me here. I'll walk the rest of the way; otherwise, he will take off on me."*

William, sensing her intention, interjected, *"Ma'am, it's not wise for you to go alone, especially given what happened last time."*

But before he could protest further, Georgie slipped out of the car as it slowed, her steps firm despite the lack of an umbrella or any shelter from the storm. *"I'll be fine, William. Just be ready when I call."*

As she walked through the rain, she called out to Liam, her voice nearly lost in the wind. *"Liam! Liam!"*

As he reached his building's front door after awkwardly picking up all his oranges that had hit the pavement, Liam turned. He froze, his expression shifting from confusion to exasperation.

"What are you doing here? You crazy woman, you're getting wet!!" he exclaimed, moving toward her. Without hesitation, he wrapped his jacket around her shoulders, guiding her into the lobby.

"Georgie, go home... Why are you here?"

She replied, *"Same reason as always, Liam!"*

He sighed heavily and headed to the elevator, leaving her behind. As the elevator door opened, he turned his face to see her just standing there, looking rejected.

"Come on, get over here!"

Once inside his apartment, Georgie glanced around the sparse but neatly tasteful kept space. *"Nice,"* she said.

"I've added a few personal touches since you saw it last," Liam exclaimed.

"You've done a lot with it in twelve months," Georgie added.

Liam's expression remained tense. *"It's not my birthday, so what are you doing here?"* he asked pointedly. *"And don't tell me you convinced that control-freak manager of yours to rehire me. I'd rather starve than work for a narcissist like him."*

Georgie paused, absorbing his words, her face softening.

"Georgie… you know how I feel about letting you help me. I'll find my own way. Thank you, but no thank you."

Silence settled between them, the soothing sound of rain against the building's windows faint in the background.

Finally, Liam broke the silence, glancing at her soaked clothes. *"Let me get you some dry clothes. You can't stay wet like that. Go use my hairdryer."*

"It's alright," she replied, holding up her phone. *"I just texted William. He'll drop off some dry clothes for me that will fit."*

Liam rolled his eyes, a half-smile tugging at his lips. *"I forgot… luxury at its finest."*

Georgie managed a small chuckle, but then her gaze turned serious. *"Liam, you've gotten so much harsher with me as you've gotten older. Why?"*

His face tightened, and he decided to just let it out. *"Tell me, Georgie. I was only seven years old, for god's sake. Why did you let me stay with you for 6 months, promising you'd adopt me, and then drop me like a frickin' hot potato? You said you'd be back."* His voice cracked slightly. *"You're no different from my parents. For you, work comes first, second, and third."*

Georgie took a breath, visibly shaken by his words. *"Liam… I…"*

"Look," he interrupted, his voice softer. *"You don't owe me anything. Really, you don't. I'm sorry I said anything."* Georgie froze in silence.

"No," Georgie replied firmly, emotion brimming in her eyes. *"I am sorry things turned out how they did, but you have to know this. When I applied to adopt you, state law required a six-month trial period before you could be legally mine…"*

"Just before the 6 months were up, I had to go to Malona, a war-torn country at the time. This small country was desperate for aid. Live Aid needed the promotion, and I had friends there who were in parliament, pleading for my help."

Georgie took a deep breath, her gaze fixed somewhere far beyond the rain-streaked window. *"It wasn't safe to take you, and if I left you alone with a hired caretaker, I knew you'd be at risk because you belonged to me. So, I told the adoption agency to place you in foster care for a few months, just until I returned. Then, you'd be with me for good."* Her voice softened, the weight of her words seeming to settle between them. *"They agreed to give you back to me. I even had it put in writing."*

Liam, leaning against the kitchen counter, folded his arms tightly across his chest, his gaze wavering between the floor and her. His silence wasn't encouragement, but it wasn't rejection either.

"When I came back from the war in Melona, I went straight to the agency," she continued, her voice trembling slightly. *"I remember how badly I missed you…"* Her shaking fingers brushed her necklace absently, twisting it as she spoke.

"But they… they told me I couldn't take you back. They said I was now over the legal age of 40." Her voice dropped. *"I was furious. I even offered them an insane amount of money, but then, "* She shook her head, a bitter smile crossing her lips. *"They twisted it around. They wanted money to stay silent about me, even suggesting such a thing."*

Liam's jaw tightened, a mix of anger and something else flashing across his face. *"Sounds like a circus."*

Georgie sighed, staring down at her hands, the memory feeling raw. *"I tried everything, Liam. My lawyers said there was no way to change the law or challenge the agency."*

"So, that was it?" he muttered, barely a question.

"No." She lifted her eyes to him, her gaze steady. *"I didn't truly leave you. I visited you at a foster home, even if it was from a distance, sometimes without you even knowing I was there. I needed to be sure you were okay. They moved you from state to state every six to eight months."* She looked away, her eyes misting as she gathered herself. *"Every birthday, I'd arrange to see you, but it was all… quiet. I had to pay off your foster parents so the press wouldn't ruin it for you."*

Liam looked down, letting out bad feelings he hadn't realized he was holding. *"So that's why it all felt… random. I do remember you coming for a brief time for some of my birthdays and your gifts. They were always pretty great. Georgie, thank you."*

"Being famous has its perks, Liam, but it also makes ordinary things that should be a pleasure... a nightmare."

"When you finally aged out of foster care, I couldn't keep track of you anymore. It broke my heart," she said, her voice almost a whisper. *"When I heard you'd moved to New York last year, I... Well, I was stoked."*

Liam couldn't help but say, *"You didn't 'hear' I moved to New York. I'm a nobody. You paid to have me spied on."*

"Don't EVER, EVER say you're a nobody, Liam! EVER!!" she snapped, unintentionally sounding like a mother.

There was a brief silence between them until a knock at the door cut through the tension. William stood there with Georgie's dry clothes and a neatly packaged dinner in white bags.

"Are you okay, Ma'am? Can I get you anything else?" William asked with his strong British accent.

"No thanks, William. Just make yourself available when I call," she replied.

"Yes, Ma'am," William said before quietly leaving.

She slipped away to change, leaving Liam alone in the kitchen, wrestling with the flood of emotions her words had stirred up.

When she returned, they sat at the kitchen counter, unpacking the meal. Georgie picked up where she left off, her voice softer this time. *"Liam, I didn't reject you. I just... chose to save 'many lives,' and*

I made the mistake of thinking you would be okay." She looked at him, her expression almost pleading. *"Well… Are you okay?"*

He glanced at her, eyebrows raised. *"Georgie, I'm almost 25 now. Of course, I'm okay."*

She studied him, her gaze lingering. *"Hmm. I don't know. My gut tells me something's bothering you."*

Liam shook his head, his tone clipped. *"Nothing's bothering me!"*

She let it go with a resigned nod, reaching into one of the takeout bags. *"Fine. Let's eat."*

Liam added, *"Fine."*

As they dug into the meal, Liam tried not to show how hungry he was. Funds were running low, and he still hadn't found a job. He pictured himself at the diner he loathed, serving greasy plates with a forced smile. Meanwhile, Georgie was doing her best not to let on how lonely she felt, how much love she wanted to give but had nowhere to place it.

After a long silence, she spoke up. *"Take your old job back, Liam. I'll fire that miserable excuse of a manager. I looked at your work history, your credentials are strong. You'd be a valuable asset to us."* Her tone was businesslike, but her eyes softened. *"Strictly a professional decision,"* she added, almost as though trying to convince him it was just for business.

Liam put his fork down, a look of realization dawning. *"So… you were the one behind that job offer the whole time, weren't you? They said you'd be working there temporarily. It was all a setup. My God,*

Georgie, it's too late. Why are you still trying to wedge your way back into my life?"

She paused, the silence stretching between them before she finally murmured, *"Isn't it obvious?"*

He didn't respond, and the conversation drifted back to lighter topics as they finished the meal. They swapped stories about colourful characters in the industry, laughing at the quirks of mutual acquaintances and mimicking the accents of some well-known celebrities they knew. For a moment, it felt almost normal.

There was a pause. Liam looked at Georgie, a glimpse of admiration in his eyes.

"Tell me something, Georgie!"

"Yes, anything," she replied.

"I'm curious... What would you say is responsible for your outstanding success?"

"Well..." She paused to gather her thoughts, making sure she explained it in a way he could understand.

"Firstly, to be one hundred percent honest with you ... I don't feel like a success at all. Sure, I'm wealthy and famous beyond anything I expected, but I have a void in my life... I don't have a sense of true purpose and belonging. I gained wealth from giving value to the world ... money and fame were just a by-product of that value I give."

Liam was shocked to hear Georgie's statement and replied

"I see… well, I will rephrase the question …what key points got you to where you are now?". Georgie, feeling the weight of the question, replied,

"Well, let me give you just five main points to success."

"One: Desire! Without pure, piping hot desire, you won't force your way through all the obstacles. And believe me, there are never-ending obstacles. But after a while, you become thick-skinned, and no obstacle or challenge is too big."

"Do you want more?" she asked.

Liam replied, *"Heck yes! Keep going."*

"Two: Doing what you genuinely love doing, and what you're in resonance with."

"Three: You must have a great team. No one who's achieved great things has done it alone. You need to allow certain people with better skills than you to handle certain things, while you focus on your own strengths, surround yourself with like-minded people on the same frequency as you, and stay clear of negative, toxic people that will surely tarnish you."

"Four: Clarity for what you want. For your dreams to actualize, you must first create a vivid image in your marvelous mind. Then comes motion … action will make those dreams manifest in the physical realm. Massive action, every day."

"And five: Prime yourself every day. Stay fit and healthy. Your body is your vehicle, and you only get one."

She smiled, her voice growing more passionate.

"And… An unrelenting belief in yourself and in the value you put out into the world."

"Use your beautiful, creative imagination."

"Intuition is important, so you don't stray in the wrong direction. We're blessed with so many gifts, and what a shame that the majority are so pinned down by everybody else's crappy mindset."

"Be grateful every day for your blessings and keep expanding those blessings."

"Wow… thanks… and by the way, that's nine," Liam said with a smile.

Georgie continued, *"I have another one that very few people do: study every day for an hour."*

Liam was mesmerized. *"Study? Study what?"*

"I study personal development, and work on my mental toughness constantly." Georgie replied.

"Which, in a nutshell, is learning how to be more emotionally intelligent so you're not bogged down by petty things. It also teaches you the laws of the universe and the laws of growth and how to use your higher faculties."

"It takes years to truly understand it, but if you don't apply it, it means you don't truly understand it." And if you don't apply it, you will remain stuck in the mud.

"Wow!" Liam said again. *"Thank you, Georgie. That was interesting. It's funny because you've just confirmed what a friend of mine was saying about the power of personal development and thought leaders' material. She even created a learning game about it."*

"Really? That's impressive! It's very clever of her to teach it in a unique way that isn't a book or seminar."

Georgie looked at Liam and said, *"You know, you can achieve anything your sweet heart desires, my darling. Don't wait till you feel the time is right because it will never come. Start right now to make your dream a reality."*

"I will," Liam replied.

"I'm loving this," she admitted softly. *"Thank you for letting me stay."*

Liam looked at her, deadpan. *"I had no choice, you were soaked."*

She smiled, savoring the simplicity of the moment. It was getting late, and she started to gather her things. *"I should go."*

Liam leaned back, a mischievous glint in his eyes. *"Let's have a nightcap. How about a cappuccino?"* He grinned, nodding toward the coffee machine. *"Machine's over there, milk's in the fridge, make me one, Mum."* He let the word hang in the air, teasing, but with a warmth that softened it.

Georgie went silent, his voice lingering in her mind. Her heart longed to hear that word, Mum. She lowered her gaze, swallowing hard, feeling the sudden weight of it. That single word, so simple, yet it shattered the years of distance, silence, and longing. She could barely keep her voice steady as she whispered back, *"Fine."*

But she couldn't move, not just yet. Her mind whisked her back nineteen years, to the few precious months when she was his mother, and he was hers. She could almost see him at seven years old, his small hand in hers, his giggles ringing through the air as she chased him around the yard. How they'd made pancake breakfasts, batter streaked on his cheeks as he laughed; how they'd baked cookies, his fingers pressing dough into crooked shapes, their kitchen filled with the sweet scent of sugar and warmth. They'd sat on the couch, side by side, watching cartoons and coloring together, his little fingers clutching crayons, smudges of colour ending up everywhere, on the walls, his clothes, his face.

And then, those quiet nights, when she'd tucked him into bed, her voice soft as she read stories, his eyelids fluttering as he drifted to sleep. She could still remember his head on the pillow, the peaceful rise and fall of his chest, and how he'd murmur, *"Goodnight, Mum,"* just before falling asleep. In those months, she had everything she'd ever wanted; she was the happiest she'd ever been.

But then, almost as quickly as it had begun, it ended. She'd spent years chasing that feeling, watching him from afar, following him from foster home to foster home, glimpsing birthdays and school events like a stranger, always on the outside, never close enough to be part of his world.

Tonight, though… Tonight was different. The years seemed to dissolve with that single word. It was a long shot, a small step, but he'd called her mum again.

With newfound resolve, she lifted her head, letting out a smile while he wasn't looking. Her fingers trembled slightly as she turned, walking to the kitchen with her head held high, each step filled with a hope she thought she'd lost. She could feel peace settling within her, a moment she never expected to have again. She allowed herself to let go of the decades of waiting. Tonight, she was no longer a stranger. She was *"Mum."*

CHAPTER 20

AN UNUSUAL CHRISTMAS

NOT NARRATED

It was nearing Christmas, and the Australian summer sun blazed with an intense sting. Zoe had driven herself to Glentvale on her own for some last-minute Christmas shopping, navigating the crowded shops. She was on her final stop, exiting the mall before heading back home. As the automatic glass doors opened, Zoe nearly collided with Bobby's ex-friends: Sabrina, Tracey, Jessica, and Vicky, who were about to walk into the mall.

The girls froze, exchanging uneasy glances as Zoe approached. They shifted backward, clearly unsure of what to expect from Zoe, almost bracing for a punch. Zoe gave them a wide, friendly grin and said in an enthusiastic tone, _"Hey, girls! Good to see you!!!"_

Sabrina managed a forced, confused smile. _"Oh, um… hey, Zoe."_

Zoe leaned in closer, her voice dropping to a low, conspiratorial tone. _"Sabrina, you were right about Bobby, you know. She did fall on her face, just like you said she would!"_

Sabrina's face lit up with a smirk, clearly pleased to hear it. _"Told you, girls,"_ she remarked smugly as she looked at them.

"Oh, yeah," Zoe continued, keeping their attention closely.

"She lost every last penny from the farm account, bled us dry. Her publicist rejected her game, 50 copies went up in flames, and she ended up completely broke, stuck overseas, sleeping on the streets, and in the hospital for weeks."

Sabrina sneered, her smirk widening. *"Hospital... Really? Looney bin, I bet?"*

Zoe leaned in even closer, her tone almost a whisper. *"You know what's crazy, though?"*

The girls huddled closer, eager for more gossip, only inches away from Zoe.

"What?" Sabrina asked, hanging on to hear more.

Zoe smiled and revealed, *"Bobby's never thrived more in her whole entire life. Now, she's successful in all four pillars, money, health, inner peace, love, and family... So put that in your pipe and smoke it !!!"*

Zoe straightened up and gave a cheerful wave, abruptly bringing the conversation to a halt. *"...Merry Christmas, girls!"* she called out, leaving them stunned as she walked away.

As Zoe headed to her car, she couldn't help but laugh to herself, recalling the look on their faces.

"Well, that was awkward. Glad that's over," Tracey blurted, as she led the group into Kmart, where they were about to spend money they didn't have.

Once inside, they were greeted by a display at the entrance. Bobby's board game sat in front and center, surrounded by festive Christmas decorations. A life-sized cardboard cutout of Bobby, dressed smartly and smiling with confidence, stood beside it, Bobby's eyes bright with pride.

Sabrina froze, her smirk vanishing as she stared at the display in stunned silence. Her friends exchanged bewildered glances. Sabrina clenched her jaw, trying to hide the pang of regret gnawing at her. The others scrambled to purchase the game, except for Sabrina.

"What the hell? She did it…" Sabrina muttered under her breath, her face a mix of disbelief and embarrassment at her behaviour toward Bobby.

Sabrina had sold off a true friend just because her ego couldn't accept someone else achieving more than her. The other three girls filled their shopping trolley with Bobby's games as Christmas presents, while Sabrina shot dirty looks at them, turning green with envy of Bobby's achievement.

Carlo had arrived for the holiday break days before Christmas, and everyone was thrilled. He'd barely sat down before Bobby cornered him, cast and all, asking, *"Do you mind driving me into town later? My cast snapped in half when I tried climbing the tractor."*

"What were you thinking?" Carlo chuckled, shaking his head. *"Climbing a tractor with that thing?"*

"I'm going nuts doing nothing, Carlo," she replied with a grin. *"Anyway, now that some funds are coming in from the game, we've got work to do out in the paddocks. And besides, it's been six weeks, I can take this bloody thing off anyway!"*

The mood was light, filled with an underlying sense of celebration. There was an unexpected weight lifted from their shoulders, knowing that there was some money coming in. It wasn't a lot, but enough to plant a crop again and buy some equipment. Bobby's game was on display and available in all Kmart's in South Australia and Victoria, with Bobby working hard to get availability in all states in Australia and in schools. Bobby's hard work had just begun.

The stolen money was never fully retrieved. Mr. Fellman's fraud had rattled the family, but thanks to more digging by Carlo, the authorities had found the money stashed away in an overseas account. Mr. Fellman himself was now behind bars, having been caught trying to flee the country. Bobby's story had even made the news, her face broadcast across screens, warning others not to fall for scams. The money they found was distributed to 23 people that had also been scammed by Mr. Fellman. Ninety percent of the money was spent by Mr. Fellman, and by the time all funds were distributed among 23 people the Russos' only received $125,000 but they celebrated it just the same.

In the coming months...

Amidst all that chaos, her board game, the dream she thought had gone up in flames, was suddenly resurrected. An LA publisher visiting New York had stumbled upon it after his Uber driver, Timothy, had called them and told them how a modest Aussie girl changed his life forever by playing her game.

What made the LA Publisher decide to move forward was hearing it had already been a hit in Australia. They contacted Bobby, eager to publish it in stores throughout America. Bobby's project became a hit almost overnight, quickly gaining interest in Europe. She reworked every detail, refining it day after day, deep in thought at her thinking tree. Soon, she had an even more amazing version. Bobby planned to go digital as soon as she had the funds available, hoping to help even more people.

Christmas Day

Christmas at Sunflower Springs was simple but filled with little rituals. As usual, Bobby was awake before daybreak and had started her morning meditating and swimming in the dam.

Now, as the soft morning light shone through the kitchen window, she found herself lost in thought. Her mind drifted to Liam, who'd left his mark not only on her cast but in her heart. She'd even saved the piece of the cast that broke off where he'd drawn a heart and written, *"Always in my heart, Liam."* She placed it in her room, near the soft toy raccoon he had given her.

He kept in light touch with her over the six weeks since leaving the States, but not as much as she had hoped. Bobby decided to get him out of her mind and just enjoy what was, for that fleeting moment.

Rarely did Bobby have negative self-talk, but today was different. Her thoughts were harsh, speaking to her in ways she usually didn't entertain.

"Well, he didn't kiss me, so what makes me think he even wanted me? Face it, girl, he just felt sorry for you because you were homeless."

You live on the other side of the planet; how the heck is that ever going to work?

You're just dreaming, girl!" The negative voices went on and on.

"Shut up," she said aloud, cutting off the relentless thoughts. *"Just shut up!"* she said to herself in frustration.

A few days earlier, Bobby had tried calling Liam to wish him a merry Christmas, only to be met by a woman's voice on the other end, saying that he was out with his girlfriend. *"Oh,"* Bobby replied, trying to sound casual, *"...just tell him I called to wish him a very merry Christmas."*

The news stung more than she had expected.

But today, on Christmas Day, Bobby raised her head with a smile, masking the ache in her heart. What she did was feel gratitude for what she had right now.

She said to herself, *"I am happy that he is happy. Then she said aloud, "Here's to rising stronger, laughing louder, and loving deeper!"* the mantra she always used, she raised her coffee cup in front of her sister.

Everyone was waiting for a BBQ breakfast, bacon, eggs, mushrooms, grilled tomatoes, and hot toast, as they lounged around, content and soaking in the warm, peaceful morning sun. Bobby and Zoe were having fun squeezing fresh oranges for breakfast, while Zoe was her usual playful self asking her sister,

"So, what did ya get me for Chrissy?" (slang for Christmas) Bobby teased her saying, *"I got ya jack Sh*t !! Nahh, just kidding, sis. How old are you? I'll give it to you in a minute."*

Melina set up a table and chairs in the large gazebo outside, the one Alonso had built after the cyclone, so they could eat outside in comfort while the builders repaired the house. Melina had decorated the gazebo from top to bottom with Christmas lights and soft, colourful roses hanging from the ceiling. She had decorated the table and chairs with class, using gold cutlery, black plates, and crystal glasses. It looked like something from a magazine, welcoming, warm, but still functional.

Alonso looked at Melina's creation with pride, but then stepped back and said, *"Bit fancy for a Barbie (BBQ), don't you think, babe?"*

She answered without missing a beat, *"Never too fancy for my family, darling. Well, the plan is a BBQ lunch, then dinner will be a formally cooked meal, Steevo and my dad are coming, remember?"*

"Far out, babe, stop cooking or I'm gunna look like him," Alonso said, pointing to a life-size, extra-fat belly Santa decoration next to him.

Bobby had made each family member a Christmas ornament, a sparkling round bauble with their names hand-painted in gold script. She even made one for Steevo, who turned it in his hands and said, *"I don't even have a Christmas tree… Margie took it… along with my magpie shirt (popular black and white AFL football team), the best footy(football) shirt I ever had. I don't know why she took it; it wouldn't even fit her in one arm…"* He whispered to himself under his breath.

After over six long years of Margie leaving him, Steevo finally saw things for what they were, and he knew he deserved better. He shrugged his shoulders and decided to go give Alonso a hand outside with the BBQ.

Alonso smiled at Steevo, feeling grateful that he was there to share in their joy. He clapped his hands and yelled out. *"Right 'o', everyone, let's crank up that Barbie again for lunch!"*

Steevo, struggling to untangle the sausages, lost a few to the ground, and Mozza the dog wasted no time in snatching them up for a feast. *"Merry Christmas, Mozza! Enjoy,"* Steevo said, laughing. Everyone wandered over to the grill to help.

"Give it here, Steevo," Alonso said, taking the sausages off him in fear that Mozza would end up eating them all.

Meanwhile, Bobby stayed inside with her Nonna, sharing a quiet moment in the now-empty lounge.

Narrated by Nonna Giovanna

"Nonna, you haven't opened your prezzie (slang for the present) yet," Bobby said, nudging her grandmother's arm.

"Oh! Sorry, Bella." I smiled, unwrapping the gift Bobby had handed me. It was a custom-made Christmas bauble ornament. Bobby held the shimmering round bauble up to the light.

Bobby smiled brightly and said in her usual zestful way, *"I made one for myself too, see? Now we'll have all our names together on the tree."*

I held the Christmas ornament up high to observe it. Bobby went still, her eyes distant. Bobby, noticing my silence, asked, *"Nonna? Do you... not like it?"*

The Christmas ornaments were about the size of a grapefruit, covered in gold glitter with initials on it, just like the ones she had given to everyone else.

Melina stormed in, and in her usual obsessive-compulsive way, quickly cleaned up the stacks of Christmas wrapping scattered across the lounge room carpet. She then left the room. Bobby and I were sitting on the couch opposite one another.

"Nonna, are you ok? You look pale?" Bobby asked, holding her ornament in front of her chest, just as I was.

Then, suddenly, I froze. *"You don't like it, do you?"* Bobby asked again, sadly, her head lowered. She continued, *"Hmm, ok, Zoe always says I have crappy taste?"* The room filled with an eerie silence.

Just as we both simultaneously held up the Christmas baubles, something strange happened. A wave of memories rushed back to us, triggered by the ornaments. Both Bobby and I were suddenly flooded with a vivid flashback to our shared experience in the spirit world.

That experience, which had laid dormant deep in our subconscious, was now reawakened by the simple touch of the baubles. It all came back in a rush, as if in slow motion, detailed, beautiful, and overwhelming.

The fact that we had shared nearly the same experience in the spirit world blew us away in ways that words could hardly explain.

My heart was beating a hundred miles an hour, and Bobby went white in the face, just as speechless as I was. Almost no words were needed between us; we already knew what was going on. It was as if all the events of the last twelve months had led us to this exact moment in time. My heart was filled with joy that something like this could exist.

"Nonna, you probably won't believe me, but I had this vivid dream. I don't even know when I had it," Bobby said, her voice shaky as she began to describe what she had experienced. It was almost exactly what I had gone through.

"Nonna, I saw your stupid gumboots, the ones with the chicken prints, and you were getting angry with a man in a mixed-colour suit. But I couldn't hear anything." She paused, frozen, her eyes wide.

"I believe you, my precious. I believe you," I said softly, placing a hand on her arm. *"It 'was' me, my Bella. It was me pleading for your life to be saved!"* Tears welled up in my eyes, so many tears rolled down my face that I could have dehydrated myself."

Bobby whispered, *"Oh my God, Nonna... Was it real?"* while placing a hand over her mouth.

I nodded slowly. *"My darling, you know as well as I do... just because something isn't physical doesn't mean it's not real."*

Bobby, still whispering, said, *"Wow, Nonna, we're talking about... the spirit world here. That's a huge thing to grasp. And you know what's crazy?"* She added, *"We've been there. But most don't come back!"*

"Yes, my Bella, there must be a reason we got sent back, God must have more plans for us to complete." There was a brief pause as we both sat in awe of what we had just discovered. Then I added, *"And now it is time to do more work, but above all, enjoy our physical existence, just as we are supposed to enjoy it.*

Let us savor every last drop we can squeeze out of life, just like you squeezed the living daylights out of those oranges this morning, my darling girl!"

We snapped out of our shock mode and into celebration mode. Bobby cranked up the music nice and loud, and we danced with complete euphoria in the lounge room, just me and her.

Need You Now - Lady A
Go to www.ritamontalto.com/songs
to scan song
Play on Christmas Day morning just after Bobby
prepares fresh orange juice

Bobby yelled out her famous toast line, *"Here is to rising stronger, laughing louder, and loving deeper!"* as she raised her orange juice in the air. I will never forget it, and I dare say she won't either. We were two crazy girls dancing and singing around the lounge, promising to keep our experience to ourselves.

"Hey, my Bella!" I yelled out over the loud music. *"Do you remember seeing Mr. Des Tinny at all? You know, Mr. Destiny?"*

Bobby yelled back, *"Nope! Des, who, Nonna?* Bobby then added, *"No, I went straight to the top!"*

"What do you mean?" I yelled back, then turned the music down a bit so I could hear her properly.

That's when I remembered that, in the spirit world, Bobby had passed that crucial white line Mr. DesTinny had mentioned, saying it was out of his jurisdiction.

Bobby shouted, *"I spoke to the boss!"*

I froze again in total shock.

At that exact moment, Alonso entered the room with a smile and turned the music off.

"Yes, I am the boss." Totally oblivious to what we had just experienced and thinking that we were talking about him, Bobby and I smiled at each other as she threw a bauble at her father's head for interrupting us.

Alonso added, *"Have you girls been drinking or something?"* noticing the glasses in our hands and the bauble in the other. *"Come on, you two... we need your help out there setting up a game of Bocci."* He had a beer in one hand and a large pair of BBQ tongs in the other.

"*We were celebrating life, Dad!*" Bobby said with a grin.

"*Yes, I'll drink to that,*" he said, lifting his beer, feeling extremely grateful for having everyone at his home, safe and alive.

NOT NARRATED

They all made their way back outside, gathering around the long table as the aroma of charred meat filled the air. Melina's beautiful setup gleamed under the late morning sun, the flowers and dishes arranged so thoughtfully they could have come from a magazine spread.

As they prepared, placing the cooked food on the table, Carlo emerged from the sheep shed, grinning. "*You wouldn't believe it, but the pigs got out!*" The Russo family kept four pigs for homemade salami. "*We're going to have to herd them back before they get too far.*" Zoe, being her usual clown, sung aloud, "*Who let the pigs out WHO WHO WHO*"

"*Let's go, Mozza!*" Carlo called out, and the sheepdog jumped up, eager to help, her eyes sparkling with excitement.

"*How the heck did the pigs get out?*" Melina asked, laughing in disbelief.

"*This way,*" Carlo motioned, winking at Bobby.

The whole family followed Carlo, including inquisitive Steevo.

"*SURPRISE!*" Carlo yelled out.

Everyone's eyes widened in amazement as they saw a brand-new, top-of-the-range caravan parked behind the shed, a huge red bow on top.

"Merry Christmas, Mum and Dad!" Carlo said, his voice soft with emotion. *"I love you... and I want you to be the caravanners, not just the caravan guides."*

Melina covered her mouth, her eyes misting over, while Alonso shook his head in awe. *"Carlo, you didn't have to, mate…"*

Carlo's gaze was serious, full of gratitude. *"Don't think I forgot, Mum. All those years you and Dad sacrificed everything for us kids… Now it's your turn, go have some fun, ok."*

The family exchanged emotional glances, the weight of Carlo's words filling the air.

"Well, that's not good enough!" Steevo said, breaking the mood with his usual humour. *"Is there a second bed for me in there? I don't take up much space, you know!"*

Melina replied jokingly, *"Sure …As long as you pack your undies, Steevo."*

Alonso cut in, *"Of course, there's room for you… on the roof rack…!"* He grabbed Steevo playfully, and they both scuffled like schoolboys. Everyone burst out laughing.

Just as the laughter bubbled back, Steevo squinted at the horizon. *"Looks like we've got a dust storm coming in, people,"* he said, gesturing to a distant shape on Alonso's dirt driveway.

Alonso shaded his eyes, frowning, replying to Steevo in a friendly banter. *"That's no dust storm, you galah."* (term of endearment for idiot)

"Ohhh no!! I bet it's lost caravanners again," Zoe said, rolling her eyes.

Bobby added, *"Ahhh, they'll see the sign for Alonso's Patch and turn left."*

Zoe warned her father, knowing his tendencies well, and said firmly. *"Dad, don't go gasbagging (talking) to them, lunch is ready, it will get cold! Okay!"*

"Ok, ok." Alonso responded as they all walked towards the front driveway.

But the RV didn't turn on the *'Alonso's Patch'* sign and kept coming towards the house.

As it pulled up to the house, everyone's attention turned to the large vehicle that was parked directly in front of the picket fence. Bobby stepped forward, curiosity piqued, and called out in her usual, genuine, and pleasant manner, *"Hello! Merry Christmas! You may have taken the wrong turn. Can we help at all?"*

Through the dark passenger window, she saw a middle-aged woman, and beside her, in the driver's seat, a man she could barely make out through the glare of the strong sun. But as the door opened and the woman stepped out in a black and white blouse, Steevo's eyes widened.

"Margie, is that you?!" he blurted in excitement, almost drooling.

Alonso, right next to Steevo, said, *"Mate, sorry, but... it's not Margie, and that's not your footy shirt either."*

But Bobby's gaze drifted past the woman as the driver stepped out of the very fancy, huge black RV into full view, now slowly walking in front of the vehicle.

Her heart stilled...

...It was Liam.

CHAPTER 21

COMING FULL CIRCLE

NOT NARRATED

As Bobby caught sight of Liam standing beside the front of the RV with cool Aviator sunglasses on, her face lit up like a Christmas tree, her voice breaking with nervousness. *"Liam!"* she shouted, disbelief and excitement tangling together. *"Oh my God, no way! Is it really you?"*

Zoe, who had been casually leaning against a veranda post observing the visitors, was annoyed as she just wanted to dig into the food they'd spent so long preparing. Zoe quickly slipped off the veranda pole in shock as she noticed how good-looking Liam was, scrambling upright again.

"Best Christmas ever!" Zoe whispered to herself.

The blazing sun reflected in their eyes as they stared at each other, unable to believe this reunion. Then, as if spurred on by the same heartbeat, they quickly ran toward each other, with Liam sweeping Bobby off her feet in a dizzying embrace, spinning her around as the family and friends around them erupted in cheers and laughter.

"Hello Bobby Jo …I'm on your turf now!" Liam said with a huge smile, trying to say the word G'day, but it didn't sound right, making her laugh.

"Ohh wow, I don't believe it …Well, welcome… welcome to MY world! Hope you don't get too bored out here, my friend," Bobby replied.

"Never," he answered.

Alonso raised his beer in the air, calling over the crowd, *"How's that for an insane surprise, everyone?"* He chuckled, relishing the atmosphere, while Carlo looked on with a grin at the impressive RV.

"Yeah, great surprise, Dad," Carlo smirked, glancing at the massive black Mercedes-Benz RV, then back at the modest caravan he had gifted his parents. *"Guess 'my' surprise… just got a bit overshadowed,"* Carlo whispered to himself with a smile.

Alonso moved forward, eager to introduce Liam to the rest of the family.

Carlo looked at his father and couldn't remember seeing him this happy and excited for a long time. *"Do you realize who this is, Carlo? It's Liam I told you about from the US, remember? The American guy who saved your sister's life!"*

Carlo was thrilled to meet Liam and so grateful for what he had done, thanked him, and gave him a firm, heartfelt handshake. *"Welcome… What you have done will never be forgotten, mate. I hope you can stay a while."* Carlo said

Giovanna, addressing Liam and Georgie, said, *"Hello, benvenuta (welcome) to Australia! Is this your first time?"*

They both replied, *"Thank you, yes, it is."*

As the introductions began, Liam shook hands with each family member, gave Alonso a big man-hug, and kissed Giovanna and Melina on the cheek.

Zoe had her face in a position to receive a kiss from Liam as his irresistible good looks took hold of her, but was only disappointed with a handshake instead. She turned to her boyfriend, Dale, for a passionate kiss in spite of it. Alonso remarked with annoyance, *"Hey, hey, enough of that Zoe!"*

Alonso turned to Georgie with a warm smile. *"And you must be…"* he began, only for Georgie Hayes to slip off her designer sunglasses, flashing a charming smile.

"Well, aren't you a handsome devil!" Georgie exclaimed with a twinkle in her eye, instantly charming Alonso, while Melina smiled from the sidelines.

"Are you Liam's mum?" Alonso asked Georgie, looking to Liam for confirmation. Georgie went silent, not knowing what to say.

Liam glanced at Georgie and smiled warmly. *"No,"* he said,

"But I love her like a mother."

For a brief moment, Georgie's eyes softened, a glimmer of emotion crossing her face as her heart filled. It had been decades since she longed for Liam's love to bounce back to her. In the most unexpected place, on the other side of the world, at this magical place called Eucalyptus Ridge, she felt she had finally earned it.

Steevo suddenly placed himself right in front of Georgie's face, almost startling her. *"G'day, my name is Steven Patterson, Alonso's best friend,"* he said with pride. *"I live next door,"* Steevo added, putting his hand out. Georgie, eloquently, said, *"Nice to meet you, Steven. Merry Christmas!"* She then asked him where his house was, and he pointed in the direction. Georgie, puzzled, took a glimpse at where he pointed and squinted her eyes, but couldn't see anything, expecting to see a house within meters. Georgie walked directly to Bobby and gave her a heartfelt hug. Bobby went along with it but had no clue because she received such a huge hug.

"Merry Christmas …Come join us, lunch is ready!" Melina insisted, her enthusiasm contagious, as Zoe darted off to set up extra plates, stealing shy glances at Liam whenever she thought no one was watching. Dale, noticing, gave her a nudge.

Zoe whispered to Dale, *"Did you see the brand-label clothes that lady is wearing? Wow."* Dale pretended he knew the clothes labels, but in reality, he had no clue.

As Liam was guided to the back yard from the side fence, "Oh my, quite the setup you have here," Georgie marveled, admiring the outdoor table setting in the pavilion. The cascading grapevines from the verandah looked like a touch of European charm. There were Christmas decorations everywhere, shimmering in the sunlight.

"And you have such a beautiful family. I am in absolute awe right now, Melina," Georgie continued.

Melina replied in her warm tone, *"Only thing is, we don't have the mystical Christmas snow you're used to, Georgie."*

"Believe me, these surroundings are more than mystical to me," Georgie replied, in a heartfelt manner. Everyone feeling her genuine warmth.

There were beautifully placed Christmas decorations in the backyard everywhere. Alonso would argue with Melina in the past, saying they weren't necessary and that they are only in the way.

But today, he said to his guests, *"Do you like the decorations I put up? My wife tells me they're in the way and unnecessary,"* he said it as a private joke and smiled at the family as Melina rolled her eyes at him.

They all finally sat at the outdoor table, with an array of food fit for a king.

Alonso, beamed with pride for his wife's efforts, he lifted his glass to make a toast, calling for everyone's attention.

"To Liam," he began, his voice sincere, *"because of this fine young man, our Bobby is here with us today. Liam, the only thing that makes sense to me is that you were sent by God."* Alonso's words, though simple, carried a weight that silenced the crowd, even prompting Liam to look away, touched by the rare sentiment. Then all of the sudden everyone cheered.

Breaking the silence, Liam glanced over at Georgie, catching her eye. *"It's too hot for wigs here,"* he said with a grin. *"Take it off, Georgie. You don't need that disguise here."*

Georgie had been wearing a very different wig the day Bobby saw her, so Bobby did not recognize her. With a weary smile, Georgie hesitated but finally reached up, pulling off her long brunette wig to reveal her natural hair beneath. Zoe, mid-sip of her champagne, promptly spat it out and said. *"Wait a minute… no way! Are you… Georgie Hayes"* Zoe's eyes were wide open, paralyzed with disbelief.

Giovanna said to Georgie, *"You are so beautiful."*

"Thank you, Giovanna," Georgie replied modestly.

Zoe and Carlo were the only ones who knew who Georgie Hayes was. The family looked around in confusion, glancing between Zoe and Georgie, who laughed at their bewilderment. Alonso leaned closer to Steevo and whispered. *"Who the heck is Georgie Hayes?"*

"Stuffed if I know," he replied, chuckling.

Giovanna couldn't help but stare at Georgie and said, *"May I ask why you wear a wig when you have such beautiful hair?"*, totally oblivious to the reason why. As Georgie stood and raised her glass to start to make a toast, Bobby said to her, *"Wait a minute, I recognize your voice!"*

Meanwhile, Georgie got up and topped up her glass of white wine and said. *"And if it weren't for this young lady right here,"* Georgie announced, nodding at Bobby, *"I'd be pushing daisies myself."*

Alonso and Giovanna said *"WHAT?"* at the same time.

Bobby's eyes widened. *"Wait… you're the lady from that day,"* she whispered. *"The one in the nice long coat? You were supposed to meet me at the Georgie Hayes show… oh my God, YOU'RE Georgie Hayes! Please excuse my ignorance, ma'am. I don't watch TV."*

Zoe found it strange to hear the word *"ma'am"* used, as it was never used in Australia. *"Bobby, please call me Georgie,"* Georgie said.

"Now, you have no idea how badly I needed to find you, Bobby, to say thank you. And by a pure twist of fate, I am here."

Georgie started to get emotional and gave Bobby the most heartfelt hug, leaving everyone moved and captivated as they clapped, and left puzzled about what had actually happened in New York.

Bobby, being Bobby, hadn't told anyone the story of distracting that thug away from Georgie. Now she felt everyone's eyes on her, curiosity piqued at full throttle from the family, including Steevo.

Georgie went on to say, *"My life was only milliseconds from being over. Meanwhile, Bobby over here borrowed a blind stick and dark glasses from a blind Indian gentleman. She approached the man who had just stolen my jewelry and was about to shoot me in the chest, as I had gotten too good a look at his ugly face."*

Zoe interrupted Georgie's speech. *"Oh my God, that's right! Didn't some homeless chick bash the Sh*t out of him? I saw it on the news..."*

At that exact moment, everyone turned their heads to Bobby in disbelief.

Georgie, smiling, continued,

"This... 'chick,' as Zoe so eloquently puts it, completely risks her own life to knock out this piece of filth who had a gun to my heart. She asks me if I'm okay, offers me water, tells me she has to go because she has an appointment, and rushes off without telling me her name. I gave her a ticket to my show so I could thank her properly, and she ran away, not even expecting to be thanked. Now... who does that?"

Every single person turned their heads to Bobby again, this time in a serious but proud manner. Bobby smiled modestly.

"So, Bobby, are you going to allow me to say thank you this time?" Georgie asked.

Bobby nodded her head slowly.

Georgie became watery-eyed, her face full of so much gratitude, longing to give her thanks. *"THANK YOU, my dear friend. When I get changed every day and see my wound on my arm, I am reminded that this world is wonderful. A kind stranger put herself in harm's way, not expecting anything in return. And that's a huge contrast to the people I have allowed to surround my life."*

Everyone froze in awe at that moment.

Bobby added, *"You didn't need to travel so far to tell me, but I'm glad you did."*

Georgie replied in shock, *"Are you kidding? Girl, you're so worth it! I love being here. I don't care if I have to travel to Pluto to thank you properly! Oh my gosh, you have no idea... I have not felt this relaxed and alive in... never!!"*

Georgie felt at ease with the Russo family. There were no pretenses, no ulterior motives, and no expectations or judgments.

Melina was getting emotional and grateful that her girl had survived the ordeal. Alonso and Giovanna were blown away by what they had just learned, but at the same time, they weren't completely surprised that Bobby would do such a thing.

Nonna Giovanna turned to Bobby. *"Tell me you weren't homeless, Bobby!"*

Bobby just had a blank stare, and Nonna made the sign of the cross.

Carlo, already tipsy, found the whole story hilarious.

Nonna Giovanna asked Carlo, *"Did you know about this?!"*

"No, Nonna, I didn't," he replied, and then Nonna made the gesture Italians do when they don't believe you, flicking her hand under her chin.

Nonna Giovanna, eager to make Dale feel included, shouted in her usual loud style, *"Dale Sweetheart, you're the only one in this family who hasn't lost their marbles!"* Dale nodded, feeling a bit like the only cucumber in a fruit salad, wondering what kind of circus did I join? Yet, he reveled in the chaos and love of this wonderfully wacky bunch. Carlo, joking along, said to Dale, *"You're still in time to do a runner from the cuckoo's nest, mate!!"* As he poured himself another wine, and as Dale says, smiling and handing over his wine glass saying, *"I'll have some of that to ease the pain, thanks."* The laughter filled the air, everyone savoring each moment.

Bobby, still confused, said, *"I didn't tell Liam about you, Georgie, so how did you find me?"*

Liam took the opportunity to explain to the family, recounting their unexpected reunion at his apartment and the events that had connected their lives once more. Everyone leaned in to listen intently, even Mozza the dog as he tilted his head ever so cute.

Here's what happened when Georgie was at Liam's apartment three weeks ago on that rainy night.

"What are you having, tea or coffee, Liam?" she called out, feeling so good to be doing something that everyday people do. It was now getting late, but time passed so quickly as they genuinely enjoyed each other's company.

"How is your wound healing? Let me see," Liam asked. Georgie took off her cardigan to show him. Things went silent, and Georgie opened up.

"You know, when I saw that gun pointing straight at me, there could have been a million things I could have been thinking about... but I only thought of you. And through a stroke of luck, I heard the words, 'MUMMA! MUMMA! Where are you?" Liam stood still, deeply touched by her words. For the first time in his life, someone had expressed such deep love for him. His parents had given him away at infancy to pursue their careers, and he had never been exposed to true family connections. He longed for that just as much as Georgie did.

"Liam, it's driving me crazy. I have to find her!" Georgie said, her voice urgent.

"You mean you still don't know who flicked that bullet away from your chest?" Liam asked, disbelief in his voice.

"No, the surveillance camera only caught the back of her, and I don't have a picture of her face," Georgie replied.

"Well, what have you got so far?" Liam asked.

Georgie explained, *"Well, she was of average height, slim, with long natural blonde hair."*

Liam responded sarcastically, *"Well, that narrows it down."* He paused, then asked, *"What did she say to you?"*

"She said something about the guy's testicles being in a sling for a while," Georgie replied.

Liam laughed. Georgie added, *"And she was late for some appointment... when the police came, she fled."*

"Oh, maybe this girl was in trouble with the law, and that's why she fled!"

Liam suggested. *"Any normal person would probably want to financially gain from saving your life... hmmm, or maybe she was an undercover cop!"* He added with a grin, *"It's a bit bizarre, huh?"* he added.

Georgie, perplexed and frustrated, said, *"I pleaded with her to take a VIP ticket to my show so I could see her again, but she didn't seem keen and she didn't even show up."* Georgie leaned into Liam and whispered, *"Guess what? Even more bizarre..."*

"What?" Liam replied, leaning closer to her.

"She didn't know who I was," Georgie continued, her voice filled with disbelief. *"She called me 'miss'."*

Liam chuckled, *"Maybe she lives in the Amazon, cut off from the world. Lucky girl!"* There was a brief silence.

"What I'm getting at is, this girl risked her life for a complete stranger. At first, I thought she saved me because I'm Georgie Hayes, but to her, it made no difference! Wow," Georgie added, still in awe.

Georgie made herself a black coffee, and made one for Liam just how he had asked. He stood at the kitchen bench, staring at his coffee. *"I take milk, thanks,"* he said. *"This isn't good enough,"* he joked, looking at his incomplete cup.

"Okay, okay, I'll get you some milk," Georgie replied.

"You're not used to serving others, are you?" Liam teased.

"It's okay, it's refreshing to do mundane things," she replied, smiling.

Liam was amused. As a joke, he said, *"Well, it doesn't sound like she's a New Yorker."*

Georgie chuckled, *"Well, yeah, she didn't sound like a New Yorker either, that's for sure. I actually couldn't tell if she was English or South African. I'm not sure; she didn't talk enough for me to pick it out."*

"Give me an impersonation! You were doing some great ones earlier. But my coffee's getting cold, so get me the milk while you do that, please," Liam said with a smile, eager to hear her impersonation.

Georgie headed for the fridge, preparing to do an impersonation.

"Ok, now this is her, Liam..." she said, in her best effort to fake an Australian accent. She said, *"I think his dick will be in a sling for a while."*

Liam burst into laughter. He was laughing so much at her impersonation, but suddenly his face slowly turned serious. *"That sounds Aussie!"* he said, his tone changing as he realized something.

Liam started to suspect it might have been Bobby, but he wasn't sure. After all, Australians love to travel, and it could have been someone else. Surely, she would have told him if something like that had happened, he thought. *"Georgie, did this girl happen to have a slight scar on her face between her hair line and eye, and has the most beautiful…"* But Liam didn't get to finish his sentence.

As in that very moment, Georgie opened the fridge door to get the milk for Liam's coffee and suddenly let out a huge scream.

"AHHHHHHHH!" she shouted.

It startled Liam so much that he got out of his chair from the kitchen bench. *"WHAT the hell? What's wrong? Did you see a mouse or something?"* he asked, his voice a mix of shock and concern.

Georgie stared at the fridge as she saw a picture of Bobby. *"It's HER… It's her, the girl that saved my life!"* she cried, holding up the photo that Liam had taken at the airport. *"It's her! Oh, I can't believe this!!!"* she said, completely hysterical.

"NO WAY! I think you're mistaken," Liam said, his voice filled with disbelief. *"She was in a coma for weeks! Hang on."* Liam replied.

"Did you say you gave her a VIP ticket?"

"YES!" Georgie yelled out.

Liam stood up, his face lighting up with realization.

"OH my god, it must have been her! Oh my god, she was at your opening event! I remember now, she said a lady gave her a ticket, but she got stood up. She must've thought you were going to be among the spectators. She didn't know who you were! I told her to stay anyway, and then she got a call. By the way she reacted, I knew it was bad news. Long story short, she had an accident and was in a coma, but now she's back home in Australia!"

The word *"Australia"* was said heavily and softly by Liam, reminding him of the vast distance between them.

"Hang on, how do you know her?" Georgie asked.

Liam told her the story about how they met at the diner and how Bobby had made such an impact on him.

"I need to see her again, Georgie!" Liam leaned in toward Georgie with a desperate tone.

"Ahhhh! I told you earlier you had something on your mind! I was right, huh? I was right!" Georgie exclaimed.

"Mother's instincts," Georgie said, nodding with a glowing smile.

Georgie said, *"Look how fate wants us to be together. I can't believe it! It's so crazy, isn't it?"*

Liam replied in a serious tone, *"Yes, it is so surreal..."* He paused for a moment before continuing, *"It's Christmas in three weeks. I plan to surprise her on Christmas Day."*

Georgie, with conviction, said, *"I'm coming TOO! "* their excitement was palpable.

Back to Present, Christmas Day at Eucalyptus Ridge...

In the warmth of the late afternoon, as laughter and conversation filled the air, the group gathered around the outdoor table, savoring the unique ambiance. Bobby and Liam couldn't seem to stop exchanging glances, though both tried to be discreet.

As they prepared to head out to *"The Patch"* for a post-dinner walk, Georgie took a deep breath, exhaling in satisfaction as they all walked together.

"This environment," Georgie whispered to Alonso as they strolled, *"it's unlike anything I've ever known. I feel… like my true self here."* Her gaze lingered on Alonso, who walked beside her, taking in the serene surroundings.

Melina, noticing Georgie's gaze, smirked as she nudged Alonso. *"Seems she's taken with the place. And with… you."* Alonso raised an eyebrow but said nothing, his faint smile betraying his pleasure.

Ahead, Bobby walked with Liam, feeling an odd vulnerability rise within her. *"Glad you found someone, Liam. How long have you been dating?"* she asked softly. *"I'm happy for you. What is she like?"*

Liam looked at her, confused. *"Found someone? What do you mean?"*

Bobby explained, *"I called a few days ago to wish you a merry Christmas. A woman picked up and said you were out having dinner with your girlfriend."*

Bobby's tone was light, but Liam could sense the hint of sadness beneath it.

Liam's expression darkened as he glanced over at Georgie.

"Hmm, what is she like? Let me think..." he paused for a moment, collecting his thoughts. Then he gently pulled her by the arm and whisked her away from the small walking crowd, guiding her behind a tree. Her back was against the trunk, while he leaned on a branch protruding from it. Bobby didn't know what to think.

Liam went on, describing her,

"She is like... well..." He paused again, searching for the right words as Bobby stared deeply into his eyes, but not close enough to touch him.

Liam started...

"Around her, I feel the pull to be more,

To rise to the best of who I am,

I'm looking at life with the thrill of exciting beginnings.

With her, there's a connection,

One I never imagined, deep and steady,

Like finding a part of myself I didn't know was missing.

She opens pieces of my heart I kept guarded,

And suddenly, the world feels brighter, richer,

Full of colour I hadn't yet seen.

In her presence, I'm drawn forward,

Aspiring to be the man she sees in me,

Excited for every moment."

There was a pause.

With a slight smile, Bobby replied, *"Oh wow… She sounds like a keeper, Liam."*

She was happy for his happiness, but disappointed for her own.

Bobby was interrupted by her Nonna calling out, *"I better see what my Nonna needs, we better go!"* Bobby took off, leaving Liam still leaning on the branch, the palm of his hand in his face, thinking to himself, *"Why doesn't she realize it's her? I thought my little verse was obvious. That's it, Georgie, you're in for it."* he thought.

He ran to catch up with Georgie and whispered, *"Georgie, Bobby thinks I have a girlfriend. You didn't tell me she called a few days ago!"* "You don't have to whisper, Liam," Georgie said. *"Haven't you noticed the enormous space around you?"*

Georgie added, *"You would have wrecked the surprise. Then I forgot to tell you after I got some business calls I had to attend to."*

"Why didn't you just say I was out with friends?" Liam said in frustration.

Georgie answered, *"Why does it matter? You can't be with her anyway. Sorry. I'll tell her later it was me and explain that I made it up."*

"Okay, fine," Liam whispered in an annoyed tone. The words Georgie said stung and echoed in his mind, ***"You can't be with her anyway."*** He tried so hard not to feel down.

They all arrived at The Patch, enjoying their walk there on such a beautiful day, there wasn't a breath of wind. Georgie and Liam looked around in amazement, captivated by the wide-open land, with the glow of dusk settling over the horizon. Alonso saw it through their fresh eyes as he studied their faces, noticing their awe at the breathtaking view.

As Alonso lit the fire pit and everyone gathered in camping chairs, laughter and warmth spilled over the group as Dale clumsily drove over on the tractor, the trailer packed with more comfortable fold-out chairs, drawing both laughter and a few gasps as he swerved and struggled with the controls. Dale was so clumsy that it was hilarious. By the time the fire was crackling, everyone had settled, and the evening felt like something out of a dream, filled with a rare sense of unity that none of them would forget.

Under the vast Australian sky, night fell, and one by one, stars began to blink awake, casting a soft, silvery glow over the outback. The warm summer breeze swept gently across the yard, bringing with it the earthy scent of eucalyptus and sunbaked soil, the unmistakable freshness of the outback air.

It was Christmas, but here, far from the chill and frost of northern holidays, the air held a comforting warmth, wrapping around everyone like a soft, invisible blanket.

After several hours, everyone hopped on the tractor-trailer with Alonso's more trusted driving, and they all gathered back to the house in the backyard near Georgie and Liam's RV. Their fold-out chairs were scattered around another fire pit that Alonso had meticulously set up earlier. Alonso fussed over his guests nonstop.

Melina enjoyed watching her husband so excited and yet so relaxed at the same time.

Melina had laid out a generous spread on the outdoor table, inviting everyone to fill their plates with a pavlova dessert that made you cry out for more.

Slowly, they all drifted back to the fire to enjoy the evening in its simple beauty. With their dessert plates nearly empty now, the family lingered around the fire for hours, listening to Nonna Giovanna's stories of the old days in Italy, with music playing softly in the background. Zoe turned it down low for a change. Their gazes were drawn to the mesmerizing dance of flames and embers. Even when no one was talking, it didn't feel awkward.

Suddenly, a shooting star crossed the night sky. *"Woooow! Did you all see that? Make a wish, folks!"* Steevo yelled out as he sat next to Georgie, offering her a cappuccino, her accepting with a smile.

Across the fire, Giovanna quietly noticed Georgie, Alonso, and Bobby with the same body language. For a moment, an unspoken harmony fell over them. They each leaned forward, elbows resting on their knees, chins propped on their hands, close to the flickering light and the warmth of the fire.

"What a day!" Georgie said to everyone. *"I just want to say thank you, Melina, Alonso, Giovanna, and all of you, for your amazing hospitality. I can't tell you how special today was. I am so stoked to be here. I have to say, it's the best Christmas I've ever had!"* Everyone was surprised that someone of her caliber would say such a thing, not knowing what was truly going on inside. They thought she was just being polite, but she was telling the truth.

Alonso replied, *"Thank you for coming so far to see us. I hope you can stay for a while. Please don't rush off, our farm work can be on hold this time of year!"*

Georgie replied, *"Well, I have to be back home to start my show on the 3rd of January. Liam is now my cameraman, so can we stay until New Year's Day, if that's okay?"*

"Absolutely, we would love that, Georgie !" Melina shouted. *"We'll take a trip to a country town called Glentvale. Sorry, it's probably not very exciting for you, but it will be a low-key, relaxing outing."*

"Low-key is great, I love low-key," Georgie said. *"Yes, let's do it."*

Liam saw a side of Georgie that he admired. He had no clue how fed up she was with her empty, superficial world. He felt bad for judging her wrongly. She had success, but it seemed she didn't have any relationships of substance, not even with her parents, only with her business team. They never spoke their minds or truly cared about her well-being. Her life was truly unbalanced.

It was well past midnight. They all had a nightcap, and everyone went to bed exhausted from such a huge day. Steevo fell asleep on the lawn, and Georgie placed a blanket over him. Alonso, making his usual wisecracks, said, *"I'm sure he'll wake up when Hillery comes along."*

"Hillery...is that his wife?" Georgie asked, curious.

Alonso replied, *"No, but he would have been better off with Hillery."*

"Oh," said Georgie, having no clue who Hillery was.

There was a beautiful full moon that was admired by all.

Everyone said good night to each other, including Bobby and Liam. Finally, everyone went to bed.

Bobby went to her thinking tree, also adorned with Christmas lights. It looked spectacular as the cascading soft white mini lights hung above her.

Bobby was meditating, and before her stood the white-cloaked man.

"You are troubled, my dearest Bobby Jo," he said.

"I guess I can't pretend with you, can I?" she smiled.

She asked him, *"What should I do? Georgie told me the truth today, he doesn't have a girlfriend. Does that mean what he said today was about me? But we can't be... you know... together!"*

The man in the glowing white cloak replied, *"And why can't you be?"* He gave her a loving smile and slowly disappeared.

"Come back... you know why!" Bobby whispered.

And at that moment, she realized that maybe, just maybe, it *could* be possible.

Bobby heard a bang from underneath the platform. She opened her eyes from her meditation but saw no one there.

"Hillery, is that you?" Bobby called out.

Her heart was racing. She quickly got up from the tree's wooden platform to look down, but there was no one to be seen.

She got up from the platform and headed for the ladder to see what the noise was. As she prepared to climb down, much to her shock, she saw Liam on the opposite side, clinging desperately to the ladder, not expecting anyone on the other side.

"Liam, that's the wrong side!" she laughed with her heart skipping a beat as their hands accidentally touched.

He chuckled and said, *"Yeah, I figured that out when I hit my head."*

Now, their faces were inches apart, the ladder separating them. The full moon added to the mysticism of the evening and illuminated the beautiful weeping willow tree.

Liam admired her so much that he could burst.

Bobby's heart felt like it was going into cardiac arrest, but she masked her excitement, pretending to be unaffected, worried that she might reveal her feelings.

"So, this is your secret hideaway," Liam said, almost out of breath. *"It's very high up here and very beautiful."*

Bobby said to Liam," *Yeah, it used to have lots of leaves, it hasn't fully recovered yet from the cyclone last year that gave this poor tree an unwanted Brazilian."*

After the laughter settled, a quiet, comfortable silence fell between them.

Liam whispered, *"Oh Bobby ... as if being smart, loving, and beautiful wasn't enough, you're funny too!"* Bobby, trying to bring it down a notch, said.

"Hmmm, Zoe doesn't seem to think so. She thinks I'm too seri..." In that unexpected moment, Liam kissed her gently from his side of the ladder. Though the ladder kept them apart, their lips still brushed

together. Bobby froze, thinking to herself, *This moment is better than anything I could have ever imagined in my mind.* She finished her sentence, *"...ous!"*

Liam chuckled, *"Yes, I like the word us."*

Bobby, nervous, stammered, *"Ah, what I meant was, Zoe thinks I'm too... serious." By this stage, they were both in shock mode, that such a mesmerizing experience had just taken place.*

The full moon and Christmas lights cast a soft glow, just enough to highlight their facial expressions. Their eyes were locked on one another.

Liam smiled softly. *"Do you know, this ladder is like a metaphor for our situation?"*

Bobby raised an eyebrow. *"It is?"*

"We're divided by distance," Liam continued, *"Now it's up to us to figure out how to remove this ladder between us."*

Bobby hesitated, then quietly replied, *"I'm not sure we can."*

Liam leaned in slightly. *"My question is, do you desire to remove this ladder between us?"*

Bobby didn't immediately respond. She tried to change the subject. *"Liam, do you want to sit up top for a while?"*

Liam sighed, *"Yes, I'm tired of always having something between us."*

She smiled at him. *"Well, you can't enter the treetop from that side of the ladder. You'll have to go back to the ground and climb up from this side."*

Liam grinned mischievously. *"You mean like this?"* He swung on one arm and flicked his body to her side, landing right behind her.

Bobby felt her heart race as he gently moved her hair aside to kiss her neck. *"You're so beautiful,"* he whispered as he took a deep breath, *"Mmmmm, you smell so good."* he added.

With a steadying hand on a branch, he lifted her onto the tree platform, his eyes never leaving hers.

Liam's expression was warm, his gaze full of something almost unspoken that made Bobby's heart flutter. In the soft glow of the fairy lights, she felt the magic of the moment envelop them. This was the moment she had longed for but had forbidden herself to feel... and now it was here.

Their bodies seemed to move in perfect synchrony as if guided by instinct. The electric connection between them was undeniable, unlike anything either of them had ever experienced before. He touched her soft face gently with the back of his hand, and without a word, sat down with his back against the tree trunk. Bobby sat in front of him, and it felt natural as if they both knew exactly how to move.

He wrapped his arms and legs around her, pulling her closer. She adjusted herself in his arms, feeling the weight of the moment settle between them. He gently slid her T-shirt off, kissing her bare shoulder inch by inch, trailing his lips down to her hand, then inside her palm.

Bobby raised her arm behind her to rest on his head, pausing for a moment. She turned her head. Their eyes met in a long, intense gaze. The world around them blurred as a warmth spread between them. Slowly, Bobby turned her body around. Their lips touched in a kiss, tender, full of promise, and the start of something neither of them had expected but both deeply desired.

The moment was perfect. The full moon was shining, creating a beautiful glow around the tree.

Moments later, a loud scream pierced the air. At first, it sounded like a woman, but it quickly became clear it was Steevo, who had suddenly been awakened by the Mozza licking his ear.

Liam and Bobby, having a bird's-eye view of the incident, couldn't contain their laughter.

"What kind of family is this?" Liam said, his voice soft with wonder.

"What do you mean?" Bobby asked, a small but curious smile playing on her lips.

He looked away for a moment, gathering his thoughts. *"I'm not used to so much…"* His words trailed off as he glanced back at her, eyes sincere.

"So much what?" Bobby asked, her voice barely above a whisper.

"… Love," he finished, almost shyly. The quiet confession took Bobby's breath away, as they kissed softly again and again.

"Well, you better start getting used to 'a lot' of love this week," Bobby replied, as they enjoyed their entangled legs and arms around each other.

Hours later, they came down from what had become Bobby's unexpected kissing tree. They walked back to the house, ready to get some sleep, crossing the lawn with nothing but moonlight to guide them. The only sound was the soft chirping of crickets.

That is, until a loud *"BAAARRR!"* shattered the silence, making Liam nearly jump out of his skin. He turned, startled, and saw Hillery the sheep staring at them from the edge of the lawn, her big eyes reflecting the twinkling moonlight.

"Oh my god!" Liam shouted, clutching his chest. *"I think I just wet my pants! What the hell was that?!"* He fell over in shock. "Haven't you ever seen a sheep before?" Bobby teased

Bobby doubled over in laughter, collapsing onto the grass beside him. They both laughed uncontrollably as if they were drunk on joy. He scrambled to his feet, nervously checking the ground. *"Are you sure there's no sheep poo on this lawn, Bobby!*

"Not entirely sure," she managed, wiping tears of laughter from her eyes.

"Well, I'm not risking it!" he said, laughing as he brushed himself off, while Bobby's laughter rang out, carefree and pure.

She looked up at him, her heart so full of admiration. Teasing, she said, *"Stop being such a city slicker!"*

And in that light, in that joy, they both felt a happiness they had only ever dreamed of, surrounded by a love they could finally call their own. But deep down, they were both avoiding the inevitable.

As the laughter faded, they lay side by side under the blanket of stars, not wanting the night to end. They rested on the cool, damp lawn, with nothing but the sound of their soft breathing and the distant hum of the Outback sound. A Christmas Day to remember forever. A sense of peace settled over them, and they both prayed that somehow... This could be the beginning of something beautiful.

THE NEXT DAY'S EVENTS WERE TOTALLY UNEXPECTED

Early the next morning, Georgie and Liam were still asleep in the RV.

It was 8 a.m., and Bobby had already gone for her swim. She tried to meditate in her thinking tree, but the memories from the night before consumed her thoughts. She skipped her usual 20-minute meditation due to a lack of concentration. She couldn't believe what had happened the night before; it felt like some kind of dream. She couldn't stop smiling and couldn't wait to see him. Her mind was buzzing.

The weather was perfect, another glorious day that Bobby couldn't wait to begin. She quietly made herself a cappuccino in the kitchen to avoid waking anyone up. Afterwards, she took it to the front porch to sit on the swing chair. But when she stepped outside, she found Steevo still sleeping there from the night before, completely out of it from drinking too much. Bobby smiled at him and didn't have the heart to wake him. He was so deep in sleep that not even loud sirens would stir him.

She took her first sip and looked up, noticing someone driving up toward the house. As the car got closer, she recognized it. Bobby stood there in pure disbelief.

It was a red Chevrolet Camaro. *"Oh no,"* she whispered to herself, the smile vanishing from her face. *"Figlio di puttana"* (son of a bitch in Italian), she muttered under her breath.

It was Tom Hallington. He pulled up to the house, parked his car just outside the white picket fence, and got out smugly, dressed in a fancy suit and holding a huge bunch of expensive flowers. *"G'day, Bobby! Merry Christmas for yesterday. Sorry, I couldn't make it yesterday…"*

Bobby cut him off, her voice full of anger. *"What part of 'don't step foot on my property' don't you understand?!"*

His face was full of disappointment, but he persisted. *"Look, Bobby, all I want to do is take you out!"*

Bobby paused, a smile forming on her lips. She nodded her head up and down and sighed heavily. *"You're a persistent little prick, aren't you? Okay, Tom. You win. But let me take you out."*

Tom's face lit up, his grin widening. *"I have my farm clothes on, hang on, let me get changed, I'll be back in a moment,"* she said, heading inside.

Tom turned to his car as if it were a person. *"Told ya, money wins every time,"* he said, stroking the shiny hood with his finger. Minutes later, he turned around to see if Bobby was ready.

And ready she was. Bobby emerged from the house, holding her 22-caliber shotgun, aimed straight at him. With one shot, she blasted the bunch of expensive flowers he was holding into smithereens. His smile quickly faded, and his face expressed pure fear.

"Here… I'm taking YOU out, you stupid bastard!" Bobby yelled out sarcastically as she laughed. Tom shouted, *"What the hell?! No, no, okay, okay, you bloody crazy girl!!"* He scrambled to get back in his

car to leave, but in his panic, he tripped and copped a face full of dust.

The loud blast of the shotgun made Steevo fall off the swing chair, hitting his face flat on the cement, but somehow, he was still out cold.

In the meantime, inside the RV, Liam in his deep sleep, suddenly jolted upright in fright from hearing the gunshot. Confused, he yelled out, *"Are we back in New York?!!!"*

Georgie, still half asleep, woke up and replied, *"Arrrm, I don't think so..."* They quickly rushed out of the RV to see what was going on, Georgie in a skimpy green silk nightie and Liam in just his black boxer briefs. They were met with the sight of Bobby holding the shotgun and Tom, covered in dust, picking himself up from the ground.

Tom looked back one last time and spotted Georgie on the front porch. *"Oh my god.. That looks like Georgie Hayes?"* he whispered to himself before getting in his car.

Tom decided to have his last say by doing an angry wheelie, knowing it would leave a cloud of dust towards the verandah. Bobby, still calm, shot out his rearview mirror.

Liam watched in total shock as Bobby casually remarked, *"Got his rearview mirror... there's no looking back for him now."* as she let out a laugh.

She walked toward the front door to put her rifle away and said to Liam, *"Mmmm...nice knickers."*

Liam stood frozen, still in shock, too stunned to realize he was only in his underwear until she pointed it out.

Georgie was attending to Steevo, who had a slight bleed from the fall. *"Are you okay, Steven?"* she asked gently.

He replied, *"Yeah,"* but then paused and added, *"Oh no, I'm not. I've got such a headache. I think I need some help!"* He said it on purpose in the hope of getting some attention, and it worked.

She said, *"Come on, let me help you up. I have a first aid kit in the RV. Come with me."* Steevo smiled and followed, his eyes wide open, gazing at her skimpy nightie. Georgie looked at Steevo's eyes and said, *"Are you sure Hillery won't object to this?"* Steevo just returned a very puzzled look and nodded no as he excitedly proceeded to follow her to the RV.

Meanwhile, everyone congregated in the kitchen. Melina entered, shocked, and Alonso followed behind her in his Christmas boxers. He was frantic and yelled, *"What the hell is going on? Bobby, was that your gun?! Holy Sh*t, what have you done?!"*

Zoe stumbled out, rubbing her eyes sleepily, and said, still half asleep, *"What's going on here? I saw Shallow Hal's car leave."*

In perfect unison, everyone shouted, *"Go back to bed, Zoe!!"* Still in zombie mode, she turned around to go back to bed, not questioning it.

Carlo and Riana were in the kitchen to see what the commotion was about. Riana rudely remarked to Carlo, *"Told you we should've stayed in a motel, your family is strange."*

Nonna Giovanna overheard and was not impressed. The words *"staying at a motel"* when you are family, and the word *"strange?"* Well, that was like serving pineapple on her pizza... unacceptable.

She shot Riana a sharp, disapproving look. Although Carlo was aware of the inappropriate words, he said nothing.

Liam, not wanting to get caught up in family drama, stayed in the background as much as possible. Georgie and Steevo walked into the kitchen, giggling like teenagers.

"Steevo, look at you, you're a mess… Did you even go home last night?!" Alonso asked, eyeing the pair of them.

Melina, the calming presence, spoke up. *"Okay, everyone, we all need a hit of coffee. Breakfast will be served in half an hour. Meet you at the gazebo after you all get showered and changed… Steevo, you know where the bathroom is".*

As always, Melina delivered what she promised: a first-class breakfast, served with a warm smile, and coffee brewed from a commercial coffee maker using only top-quality coffee beans.

"Okay," Melina said, *"It's a beautiful day. What's the plan today, everyone?"*

Bobby replied, *"Mum, I'm going to check the water at the springs today. Can we go to Glentvale tomorrow?"*

Alonso called out, *"Okay, is everyone okay with Glentvale tomorrow? We can rest today since yesterday was a big day. Let's take a vote: YES, or NO?"*

Simultaneously, everyone shouted *"YES,"* including Steevo, who had refused to go home. Mozza barked right after Alonso, as if to respond. *"Sorry, Mozza, you're outvoted,"* Alonso said with a grin.

Liam, curious, asked, *"Why's the dog named Mozza?"*

Zoe explained, *"We named her Mozza because as a pup her sister pup and herself grabbed hold of a pizza together and ate only the mozzarella."* She explained that Rella, the sister dog, died in the cyclone. Liam expressed his sadness as he looked at Mozza and patted her.

Liam was still watching Bobby's every move, still in awe of the family that had captured his heart, but he couldn't shake the fear that it might be short-lived.

Bobby glanced at Georgie, who was still having breakfast across the table, and asked her, *"Georgie ..do you remember if that Dickhead saw you?"*

"Which dickhead?" Georgie replied.

Alonso, Steevo, and Carlo all laughed. Carlo said, *"What do you mean, which dickhead? Have you met more than one here already?*

Alonso added, *"There's only one in Sunflower Springs, and that's Tom Hallington. With Barry O'Connor a close second."*

Georgie shrugged and replied. *"Oh... I don't know if he saw me... why?"*

Bobby continued, *"Well, Georgie... just so you know... that Dickhead's mother, Wendy, everyone calls her 'the Wicked Witch of the West,' and her sister-in-law is Dorothy Blake, also known as 'the Mouth of the South.'"* Liam chuckled as he sipped his coffee.

Giovanna smiled to herself, thinking how much Bobby was like her father, someone who would never utter a person's name if they didn't like them.

"Anyway, I'm just worried that he may have recognized you, that's all," Bobby added. The family exchanged concerned glances, hoping Georgie hadn't been recognized for the sake of their peace.

"Ahhh," Georgie replied casually, *"They wouldn't know who I am anyway... half of you here didn't know."*

Zoe, ever the bold one, blurted out, *"Yeah, but we're not normal."* The family gave her a look as if to say, *Yeah, very funny.*

Zoe continued, *"Georgie, it's likely they will know who you are. They're couch potatoes, like, seriously, potatoes that have been sitting in the same spot for so long they've sprouted!"* Everyone laughed.

"I'm sure it'll be fine," Alonso added, trying to keep things light.

After breakfast, they scattered around the house. Bobby and Liam, however, still didn't want anyone to know about them, though it was becoming more obvious by the minute.

"Bobby, can we go for another walk?" Liam whispered.

Shushing him, Bobby whispered, *"I have something better planned. Have you ever ridden a horse?"*

"A horse? No!!!" Liam said in total panic. *"Can't we just take the quad bikes?"*

At that moment, Steevo and Georgie came racing toward them like maniacs on the quads. Georgie is having an absolute blast.

Liam sighed. *"I guess that idea's out... Can we just walk wherever we're going?"*

"*It's too far to walk. It's okay, Liam. Spunky won't mind, He's so placid, you'll love him,*" Bobby said, taking hold of his hand and pulling him toward the horse barn.

"*Who's Spunky?*" Liam asked, his curiosity piqued.

"*Follow me,*" Bobby whispered, a sparkle in her eye.

After a few awkward attempts, Liam finally managed to get on the horse with Bobby. He put his arms around her waist to hold on. Bobby closed their eyes, relishing the touch between them, a touch that felt undeniably strong. They were so in the moment, each second spent together making them forget about everything else. Being together was now the epicenter of their newly discovered world.

Off they went to the springs. They passed a billabong with countless flamingos that took Liam's breath away.

A Touch Of Paradise - John Farnham

Go to www.ritamontalto.com/songs
to scan song

Play When Bobby takes Liam to the Gorge
waterfall

When they arrived, they hopped off the horse at the gorge. Liam stroked Spunky's face gently, admiring him.

"Wow, that ride was amazing, Bobby," he said, looking around. *"A waterfall in the middle of nowhere? You didn't say anything about a waterfall."*

Bobby looked at him deeply, her eyes locking with his. She moved closer, yearning to touch him. *"Sorry, I didn't mean to say 'in the middle of nowhere… no place is more special than another,"* Liam said.

"It's okay," Bobby said cheerfully. *"It is 'in the middle of nowhere,' that's what makes it extra special."* Her voice echoed off the rocks.

Liam, smiling, ran toward her and kissed her deeply and passionately. They stopped for a moment, gazing at one another. Spontaneously, he grabbed her and pulled her toward the water, her scream of surprise echoing in the gorge. They laughed like teenagers as they soaked in the cool water from the waterfall. The scenery was simply breathtaking.

As they stood in the water under the waterfall, Bobby felt a deep sense of gratitude for every moment. In the distance, she saw the white-cloaked man. *"Thank you,"* she whispered as she watched him wave and disappear into the distance.

"Thank you for what?" Liam asked, noticing Bobby's eyes were focused on something far away.

Bobby turned back to him and smiled. *"Thank you, universe, for bringing me YOU."* They kissed again, long and gentle this time.

"It's nice to be alive, huh?" Liam said, his voice soft.

"Yep," Bobby replied. Then, she yelled out, *"Here is to rising stronger, laughing louder, and loving deeper!"* Her words echoed as she playfully tackled him in the water.

Liam, finally catching his breath, spotted something in the distance. *"LOOK, a kangaroo!"* he exclaimed, excited to see his first one. *"Wow, they're so cute!"* he added, his eyes wide with wonder.

Bobby looked at the kangaroo and said, *"Did you know that if a kangaroo feels threatened, their survival mechanism kicks in, and they'll dunk your head underwater to drown you? Their looks are deceiving. They're strong and pretty smart, but cute little buggers."*

Liam looked nervous.

"But ...Don't worry, that's only Fredrickson, our Eastern Grey kangaroo that refused to leave my side. He'll love you to death."

"How did you get friendly with a kangaroo?" Liam asked, still a bit unsure.

"I saved his life," Bobby replied with a smile.

"Gosh, Bobby," Liam said in awe. *"You save animals, you save humans... You're ..."* He didn't get to finish his sentence before Bobby grabbed him, and whispered, *"Shhhhh,"* she said as she playfully tackled him.

After some time in the water, they climbed out to dry off before heading back. They didn't want anyone to suspect they had gone swimming together. Laying down on the soft, green grass, the air was still, and the sun scorched the earth, but the coolness of the water kept them refreshed. They enjoyed the warmth of the sun as they lay together, often staring into each other's eyes and smiling, meanwhile, much to Liam's delight... Fredrickson was casually sitting beside them.

It didn't take long to dry off on a typical summer day, much to Liam's shock.

Liam picked Bobby some wildflowers. *"Please don't shoot my flowers,"* he pleaded with mock seriousness, and Bobby laughed, recalling what she did to Tom's poor flowers that morning.

It was like a scene from a movie, but an even more perfect day Liam would hold dear for the rest of his life.

Late that afternoon, Bobby and Liam then rode back to her home.

Liam headed off to the RV to change, and Bobby went to put Spunky back in his stable.

Just as she shut the horse barn door, Alonso startled her.

"Bobby Jo!" he said in a firm voice.

*"Sh*t, Dad! You scared the bejesus out of me!"*

"You know this isn't going to end well, love, "Alonso says with a crim look on his face.

Bobby gave a heavy sigh. "What do you mean, Dad?" Bobby replied, knowing exactly what he meant.

"You both live in different worlds, and neither of you can exactly meet halfway," Alonso said. *"Unless you want to live in the middle of the Pacific Ocean!"* She laughed. *"Haha, Dad,"* Bobby responded, trying to lighten the mood. *"Look, nothing is going on anyway."*

"B*lls*t, Bobby!" Alonso's tone turned serious. *"It takes a man to know a man, and he's totally love-struck with you. He wouldn't have traveled halfway around the world to be here if he wasn't."*

Bobby went silent for a few moments before saying, *"You know, I love this place too much to ever leave. Dad, there's nothing going on".* There was a heavy pause.

*"What are you 'truly' worried about, Dad … what losing this bloody farm that does nothing but stress the f*ck out of us both year in and year out. We are nothing but stubborn farmers working our fingers to the bone getting deeper and deeper into debt, and for what… why do we do it to ourselves, Dad… why?"* She yelled with a fierce look on her face

There was a pause. Alonso looked Bobby in the eyes, but was too stunned to speak at first, then added sternly, *"Russos are not quitters, Bobby!!!"*

Bobby continued in a calmer tone and said. *"I didn't say anything about quitting, Dad, look. You know I don't have a problem with hard work, I adore this farm, but… everything we've got goes back into this farm… we give and give and give. We need to see a return. Our lives are imbalanced …when was the last time we actually enjoyed ourselves on a holiday or even a weekend to see a concert in the city? Carlo has gifted you the caravan; I bet it will just sit there gathering dust."*

It is time for us to live a balanced life, Dad.

She walked away, leaving Alonso to ponder her words.

Later that day, there was a buzz around the outdoor fire pit. The sweet smell of roasting capsicums on hot coals filled the air, adding to the warmth of the day. Alonso and Melina were preparing for a wood-fired pizza night.

Carlo called out to everyone, *"Hey, everyone! Be prepared early tomorrow, we are going to the big smoke!"* What the hell

Georgie, a bit confused, asked, *"Is Glentvale a city?"*

Steevo laughed. *"You don't know Aussie dry humour yet, love. He was being sarcastic, it's just a large country town. But to us, Sunflower Springs folk, it's the big smoke."*

Georgie nodded, now understanding. *"Oh,"* she replied.

"Melina!" Alonso called out. *"Keep that dog away from the pizza!"* He was referring to Mozza, but it was too late, Mozza had already managed to grab a pizza when no one was looking.

It was party mode again, with Zoe blasting music as usual.

"Hey Carlo, I need your help," Alonso shouted from the kitchen, scanning the room for any trace of Riana. *"Where's Riana?"* he demanded, urgency in his voice.

"She left this morning, Dad. We ended things. I told her to leave," Carlo responded, his tone firm.

"Oh, Carlo, I'm really sorry," Alonso said, his voice heavy with concern and empathy.

"Don't be, Dad. She didn't have what it takes to be a Russo. The warning signs were glaring, but I was blind, ignoring them for far too long. I was too much of a coward to confront her, and it was a toxin,

eating away at me. I feel liberated without her," Carlo declared, a newfound strength in his voice.

Alonso's face broke into a proud smile as he embraced Carlo tightly. *"I'm proud of you, son, for always having the courage to stay true to who you are."* Alonso's eyes shone with pride as he grabbed Carlo for a man hug.

As evening came around after everyone had consumed a piece of every type of pizza imaginable, Steevo couldn't move. He approached Alonso and said, *"Mate. What can I do to help? "Sorry, I haven't been helping you much. I have been trying to entertain your guests.*

Alonso replied, *"Yeah, one guest in particular I see."* referring to Georgie, *"Okay, Steevo, can you stoke the fire, please? The logs are over there. Then we can all play Bobby's board game together, and then play briscola."* (Italian cards)

But that wasn't to be.

Typical of rough-nut Steevo, he over-stoked the fire. Alonso, noticing the growing flames, yelled out, *"Whoa, whoa, that's enough, Steevo! It'll get too hot! We are in the middle of summer, you know!!"*

A sudden spark from the flames illuminated a dazzling glint on Georgie's jewelry, a flash of gold that caught Giovanna's eye.

There stood a bracelet, the unmistakable bracelet, resting on Georgie's wrist, worn and familiar in its delicate gleam.

The sight of it sent a jolt through Giovanna's spine, and she felt faint as years of suppressed memories crashed down on her. She swayed slightly in her chair, then collapsed to the ground. Alonso rushed over, alarmed.

"Mum Mum!" Alonso's voice cut through the air that had overtaken the moment. His eyes were wide with concern as he leaned toward her. *"Are you alright!!!? What happened?"*

Everyone turned, confusion and worry written across their faces as they watched Giovanna's reaction. Her breath came in shallow gasps, her gaze locked on Georgie's wrist. There, glinting in the dim light, was the intricate gold bracelet she hadn't seen in over fifty years, one she had believed lost, buried with memories she'd long tried to forget.

Giovanna hated being the center of attention, surrounded by the worried faces of her family. She tried to steady herself as she turned her eyes to Georgie. Her voice trembled as she asked, *"Where did you get that bracelet?"* Alonso said, *"Mum, stop it."* embarrassed that she was sounding rude.

Georgie glanced down at her wrist, absently turning the bracelet, unaware of the depth of the moment. *"This?"* she said casually, confused. *"I've had it for as long as I can remember. My mother gave it to me when I was little. Why?"*

Giovanna's face went ashen, her eyes widening in shock as the flood of memories rushed in. *"That bracelet,"* she whispered, barely audible. *"My mother made it... there was only one. It was meant..."* She paused, her voice cracking as emotion overwhelmed her. *"It was meant for my daughter. For my baby girl."*

Suddenly, Giovanna screamed in disbelief. *"Where did you get that bracelet?! That was meant for my baby girl! Bastarda infermiera (that bitch nurse) must've stolen it and sold it!"* Her voice was frantic, the pain and anger seeping through her words.

A deep, heavy silence fell over the night air, its weight suffocating. The family stood frozen, embarrassed and uncomfortable by what had just happened.

Liam moved toward Giovanna, trying to comfort her. Bobby's face, filled with shock and disappointment, horrified at how quickly the evening had soured.

"I'm so sorry, Liam," Bobby muttered, her voice small, as Liam kissed her on the forehead and said, *"It's ok".* Alonso, watching them, Liam couldn't help but notice the pain in Bobby's eyes.

Alonso, visibly uncomfortable but trying to hold the family together, spoke softly. *"Mum,"* he began cautiously, *"maybe... maybe your memory isn't as clear as it once was? I mean, it's been such a long time."*

His words felt like a blow, and Giovanna's head snapped toward him, hurt flashing across her face. *"Are you saying I'm losing my mind?"* Her voice was sharp and defensive.

Alonso's gaze softened, instantly regretting his words. *"No, I didn't mean that, Mum. It's just... maybe things aren't what they seem?"*

But his words offered no comfort; the doubts and fears still clawed at Giovanna's heart.

Melina stepped forward, her voice calm and steady. *"Giovanna, maybe it would help if you tried to remember... When did you last see the bracelet? Did you actually place it in the nurse's hands?"*

"Yes, I did," Giovanna whispered, her voice breaking. *"She promised me she would place it on my baby girl, she promised me..."* It was all too much, and she broke down in a deep cry. There was not a dry eye around. Everyone was deeply touched by Giovanna's outburst.

Giovanna closed her eyes, breathing deeply as if summoning the memory from its hidden place, raw and vivid as the day it happened.

"The day you were born, Alonso. It was the happiest day of my life..." Her voice wavered, fragile as she struggled to continue. *"...and the most heartbreaking."* She paused, emotion thick in her throat. *"I lost your twin sister that day. They told me... she didn't make it. I never got to see her. But I made them promise... I made them promise to put that bracelet on her."*

The air hung heavy, no one daring to break the silence.

Georgie looked down at the bracelet, her fingers unsteady and shaking as she slipped it off. Faint lines marked her wrist, a subtle testament to years of wearing it as if the bracelet had become a part of her. She studied it, as if searching for answers in the delicate engravings.

Georgie said "Giovanna..." she began, her voice quiet, trembling. *"Do you remember... Was there something engraved on it?"*

Giovanna's voice was barely above a whisper. *"LL,"* she said, each letter heavy with meaning. *"Lilliana Lombardo. My mother's initials. She gave it to me... and I wanted to pass it on..."* Her voice trailed off as she met Georgie's gaze.

Georgie gently handed the bracelet to Giovanna and said, *"I am so sorry I caused you grief that certainly did not draw my attention. I'm determined to get to the bottom of this surreal confusion."* and then Georgie walked away slowly.

Georgie's face drained of colour, her fingertips tracing the engraving as though feeling its history, her hands trembling. Bobby and Zoe stood in silence, each of them piecing together the impossible.

"Hell," Zoe muttered under her breath, her voice a reverent whisper. *"Who needs Days of Our Lives?!"* She shook her head in disbelief, eyes wide with wonder, as if afraid to shatter the fragile moment with a louder voice.

The mood was somber, to say the least.

Bobby nudged her gently, her smile soft. *"Come on, Zoe,"* she whispered, leaning in. *"Help me with the clean-up, yeah?"* Bobby gave Carlo a nod. *"You too, Carlo. Mum can use some help."*

Carlo got up faster than anyone, feeling the awkwardness of the moment. He announced, *"If you'll excuse us, we'll help Mum in the kitchen for now and take Nonna inside. I'm sure we'll be back out again shortly. It's still pretty early."*

Zoe felt the gravity of the moment. She nodded; her cheeks flushed. *"Yeah... yeah, sure, Carlo."* She turned, casting one last glance at the guests gathered there in quiet revelation, before following Bobby and Carlo inside.

"Come on, Mum. Let's get you inside," Alonso murmured, guiding her gently back into the house. Alonso apologized to their guests. *"My mum is still recovering from a heart attack six weeks ago. I'm pretty sure it's been a big day for her. I'll take her to rest for now."*

Liam said to Bobby, *"Georgie and I will head back to the RV. I don't think you need us hanging around right now."* Bobby asked him to stay, but she realized that some space might help her get some clarity somehow.

Giovanna moved silently, her legs unsteady, her mind a whirlpool of questions and disbelief as they walked into the house. Alonso helped her into a chair in the living room, giving her some water to drink. She sat, trembling, the same thought pulsing through her mind over and over. *"Can it be? Could this really be happening? Did they fool me all those years ago?"*

She could hardly breathe as she recalled the sorrowful day of Alonso's birth. The joy of holding him in her arms was tempered by the overwhelming grief of losing his twin sister.

CHAPTER 22

HOLIDAY OF UNEXPECTED GIFTS

NOT NARRATED

Alonso began pacing the room, his frustration clear as he ran a hand through his hair. Finally, he stopped and turned to her, his voice edged with anger and confusion.

"What were you thinking, Mum?" he burst out. *"Why would you bring that up tonight, of all nights? After all these years, after refusing to talk about it, you shut me down every time I asked about my twin, and suddenly, you're throwing it out there in front of everyone, including strangers, how embarrassing?"* He paused, his expression softening just slightly, though still pained. *"Did you see how uncomfortable you made them feel? That nurse, or someone else, would've sold it, and somehow Georgie's mum ended up with it!"*

Giovanna opened her mouth to speak, but only a shaky exhale escaped her lips. She looked down at her hands, clenching them tightly, trying to find words for something that had remained silent inside her for so long.

Outside, Georgie and Liam remained by the fire, the conversation from earlier lingering heavily between them. Liam watched Georgie in quiet support as he grabbed her hand, Liam could see the hurt in her eyes, a mix of pain, confusion, and something almost like hope. He didn't know what to say, didn't want to break the delicate moment, so he simply waited, giving her space.

After a moment, Georgie spoke, her voice low, as if she were talking to herself as much as to Liam. *"My mother put that bracelet on my wrist for as long as I can remember,"* she began. *"When I was a teenager, I didn't want to wear it anymore. It felt like something out of place, a piece of someone else's life."* She let out a small, bitter laugh. *"But my mum, she wouldn't let me take it off. She said she'd made a promise to my godmother when I was born, that I'd always wear this."*

"Liam, what if ... what if she lied to me?"

Liam listened, his face softened by the firelight, unsure what he could say to comfort her.

"It was one of the only times I ever saw my mother show any true emotion." Georgie continued with a far-off look in her eyes. *"She was always so cold, so distant. I think I was more of an accessory to her, something that made her look good, something that got her more attention, something that made her husband stay with her."* Her voice caught slightly, a knot in her throat, but she pushed on. *"But that day, she was real. She had real emotions. I don't know why, but I held onto that. Even after she was gone, I kept it on. It was the one thing that felt grounded, real, in a world that was always... fleeting, always so fake."*

Liam nodded slowly, feeling the depth of her introspection. He placed his arm around her. He wanted to say something meaningful, something that would help, but he hesitated, feeling her words needed their own space.

Georgie took a deep breath, glancing at him briefly before placing a hand on his knee. *"Would you excuse me, Liam? I need to make a few calls."*

He nodded; his gaze steady. *"Don't wander too far, Hillery might get you,"* he murmured, a small smile tugging at his lips, just wanting to break the somber mood.

Georgie managed a faint, weary smile in return. *"I'll just head by the RV."* She rose, moving slowly away.

Inside, Giovanna watched Alonso pace across the room, her heart pounding as the words finally came to her, the layers of pain and memory unfurling within her like a long-lost story. She cleared her throat, her voice a trembling whisper.

"I was told... I was told she didn't make it," she began. Alonso paused, turning to look at her, his face tense with conflicting emotions. *"When she was born... they said she wasn't breathing, and I saw her lifeless body in the doctor's arms. No baby was crying. They took her away so I could focus on feeding you. Your father was away working, and... back then, husbands weren't allowed in the delivery room. They kept me there, waiting, and a different nurse came in... she told me my baby girl didn't survive."* This nurse specifically said, *"Mi dispiace, ma tu bambina sei morta, signora."* (I'm so sorry, madam, but your baby has just died.)

I remember it clearly;".

Alonso's eyes started to water. It was only the two of them in the room, but the family heard everything being said, sitting there quietly with their heads down.

She took a shaky breath, her hands clenching the arms of the chair. *"I made her promise to put that bracelet on her... it was my mother's, Lilliana Lombardo, LL, her initials. I wanted her to have something... something that connected her to us."* Her voice broke, tears welling in her eyes. *"They wouldn't let me see her. They told me... they said it would 'make the breast milk sour' if I saw my dead child. That's how they thought back in those days."* She let out a bitter chuckle full of regret, shaking her head. *"I was so young, so naive... I believed them. And I've regretted it every day since."*

The words hung heavily in the room, and Alonso's face softened, his anger melting into something gentler, more understanding. He opened his mouth to say something when he realized Georgie had been standing there by the door, looking shaken but resolute.

Georgie uttered shakily, *"I made some overseas calls,"* she said softly, her gaze darting to Giovanna. *"I talked to my Aunt Ivy... my mother's sister."* She took a deep breath, glancing down at the bracelet before continuing.

"She said... she said she never saw my mother pregnant. My mum had left for a 'vacation' in Italy to visit a nurse friend and returned a few weeks later with a baby... me." Her voice wavered, but she steadied herself, glancing between Giovanna and Alonso, unsure how they would feel or what they would say.

"My aunt said that when she finally saw me, years later, she knew something wasn't right. The timing didn't match up... she even

confronted my mother about it so My mother shut her out of our life."

After a moment of strained silence, Giovanna, still lost in her regrets, uttered with a pained whisper, *"I didn't get to see her. They wouldn't let me hold her."*

Melina stepped forward from the kitchen, and Carlo, Bobby, and Zoe quietly gathered just behind her. They had been listening in from the kitchen, all in tears, hearing about their lost aunt for the first time. It was something Giovanna never wanted to speak about.

Melina, in her quiet but resolute way, finally spoke. *"Giovanna,"* she said softly, *"Today, you get to see her."*

Giovanna gasped. Her confusion and doubts were replaced with the certainty in Melina's voice. In the Russo family, Melina's words carried weight. When she spoke, everyone listened. Her voice filled the room, and a peaceful stillness settled over them all, as though her words were the answer they had all been waiting for. Giovanna's eyes softened, a flicker of realization sparking in her gaze.

Giovanna's breath hitched, her gaze fixed on Georgie, her eyes brimming with a mixture of disbelief and raw, aching hope. Georgie met her gaze, the familiar spark of recognition lighting between them.

Georgie, coming into realization of herself, felt tears trail down her cheeks as the growing years that didn't make sense suddenly fell into place. The puzzle pieces aligned. She took a step closer to Giovanna. *"It's possible, isn't it?"* Georgie's voice was barely above a whisper, filled with tentative hope. *"It's possible that you're... that you're my mother?"*

The room was silent as the weight of her words settled over them. Giovanna reached out, her hand trembling as she leaned forward to meet Georgie's, the years of loss, hope, and disbelief melting away.

Alonso stepped forward to help his mum stand, gently assisting her to her feet and steadying her. Giovanna took a tentative step forward, her heart racing as she reached out, her hand trembling as it moved toward Georgie's hand.

Giovanna looked at everyone, and with shaking hands, she placed the bracelet on Georgie's wrist. It was like a symbol of a new beginning, a reset from the past, a letting go of what was and moving forward.

"My daughter," she whispered, her voice filled with years of lost love and quiet, unyielding grief. *"You came back to me."*

Georgie's face crumpled, and in that moment, all the years of distance and separation melted away. She reached for Giovanna, and they fell into each other's arms, holding on as if letting go would mean losing each other all over again.

Alonso, standing off to the side, held his breath with his shaking hand over his mouth as Giovanna and Georgie finally embraced, his face mirroring the mixture of hope and disbelief that coloured the air.

Alonso was one who never liked to show anyone he actually cried, even through all the hardships. But not today. He broke down in tears and wrapped his arms around both of them, holding them in a tight family embrace, the Italian way, strong and proud, like the true head of the Russo family.

Then, breaking the silence with a grin, Alonso looked around the room, his voice filled with both joy and humour. *"Hey, everyone, I have a twin! She came back! And she's as gorgeous as me!"*

Everyone broke into laughter and clapped furiously. It was a side of Alonso they had never seen before.

For the first time, Giovanna felt whole, her heart complete after years of emptiness. And as Alonso watched his mother embracing his newfound sister, a feeling of peace washed over him, the long-standing ache of questions left unanswered finally finding its resolution.

Zoe, caught up in the moment, piped up, *"I can handle being related to someone famous, but can you handle us hillbillies, Aunty Georgie?"*

Georgie shook her head in disbelief, her eyes wide. *"As if I would think that, Zoe... I adore you. I adore all of you!!"* She smiled, *"Come here, hillbillies, I need a hug!"* she said, hugging everyone one by one, the feeling so surreal to her as her past finally started to make sense.

Carlo, standing beside her, couldn't help but smile, reaching over to gently ruffle her hair. *"You're something else, sis. You made all this possible."*

Bobby nudged Carlo and Zoe with her elbow, leaning on her with a playful grin, sharing in her sister's excitement.

Then Bobby's eyes lit up with sudden energy. *"Oh, wait!"* She turned to the other side of the kitchen with a quick step.

Grabbing Liam, she continued, *"And this man right here also made all this possible!"*

"What, me?" he replied.

"Yes, YOU," Bobby said with a grin.

The gazebo was glowing with warm, white Christmas lights, casting a soft, magical aura over Bobby and Liam as they sat together quietly under the starry sky.

"Oh my god, Bobby," Liam exclaimed, still in awe. *"Meeting you… it's always felt like divine timing, but this, this is on a whole different level!"* He was raking his hair in pure nervousness from it all.

Bobby smiled, her eyes dancing with excitement. *"I know. I still can't wrap my head around what just happened there."* She glanced back toward the house as if still seeing the echoes of the evening's revelations.

Liam shook his head, almost laughing at the sheer improbability of it all. *"Neither can I… and your dad,"* he added with a grin. *"You should've seen his face when he realized Georgie is his twin sister!!"*

Bobby chuckled. *"Did you see Steevo practically frothing at the mouth every time he looked at Georgie today?"*

"Let's just say Steevo has a very specific type."

Liam added, *"Oh, and did you hear what your dad whispered to him?"* He teased, grinning. *"'You have Bugger all chances of getting with her, mate.'"* He mimicked Alonso's accent, raising his eyebrows.

Bobby burst into laughter, unable to contain herself. *"Oh my gosh, that's Dad for you, always keeping Steevo on his toes!"*

Liam said, *"Can you imagine if Steevo turned into his brother-in-law?!"*

They burst out laughing again.

"Georgie and Steevo together, that's pretty unlikely, Liam!" Bobby said.

Liam replied, *"You realize the pure miracle that we just witnessed tonight? You should NOT be saying the word 'unlikely' ever again."*

It dawned on Bobby as Liam said those words. *Maybe, just maybe, there is hope for a future with Liam if she never uses the word 'unlikely' again.*

After the laughter settled, a quiet, comfortable silence fell between them. Liam was staring at Bobby with an expression so warm.

"Come here, girl," Liam said. *"I miss not touching you. It's been 22 long hours."*

"That bloody crazy sheep better not be here!" Liam said.

"Oh my god! I've converted you into an Aussie! You said the word 'bloody!'" Bobby teased as she laughed.

Liam jokingly replied, *"Oh, I did too! What are you doing to me, Bobby? I'm in the Outback, HELL! Somebody! Anybody HELP ME!!!"*

They fell to the ground in laughter as they wrapped themselves around one another.

The next morning...

They all traveled to Glentvale together to enjoy a full day on the Murray River on a luxury houseboat. Not surprisingly, Steevo was there too.

Giovanna filled Georgie in about their life in Italy and when they made the move to come to Australia. She had Georgie's undivided attention as they walked arm-in-arm, just as they do in Italy.

They stopped the boat for a while and fished by the river. They laughed, shopped, dined, and laughed some more.

All the while, Georgie had to wear a heavy disguise.

"Let's go for a swim," Bobby said.

"No crocodiles, right?" Liam asked.

Bobby replied, *"Absolutely not, they live in the far north of Queensland in the tropical areas. You have nothing to fear. But keep an eye out for snakes, they also enter the water."*

"WHAT?!" Liam exclaimed as he had already entered the water.

Bobby laughed. *"It's okay, it's okay. They don't chase you. They're more scared of you than you are of them."*

"Well, I think my fear of them outweighs theirs..." he muttered. As he got closer to her in the water, he whispered, *"You are fearless, Bobby,"* with a smile, deciding to put his fear aside and enjoy this perfect day.

"Fearless, maybe, but not careless". Bobby responded.

"Now, come here." Liam jokingly demanded.

They cuddled in the water for a few moments, then noticed the others walking onto the houseboat balcony, feeling saddened that they had to quickly separate.

They all headed to the bushland several hours away. Alonso insisted his guests should see wild koalas in their natural habitat.

Finally, they found a koala and her joey. Liam and Georgie were fascinated and loved every minute of it.

Bobby, having a deep love for koalas, said, *"Georgie and Liam, let me introduce you to someone who sleeps up to 22 hours a day."*

Carlo stepped in and said, *"That's not nice, talking about Zoe like that!"* Everyone laughed in amusement.

"Hahaha... so, sue me, Mr. Bigwig brother," Zoe replied sarcastically.

"I wonder why they sleep so much?" Georgie commented.

Bobby replied, *"Because they eat eucalyptus leaves, and they are toxic. Their bellies need help to process it, so they sleep. She is sleeping now because they are nocturnal. I think this one has a joey."* They all looked in awe.

"Wild koalas get stressed if humans get too close, so let's be mindful of these cute little things."

"G'day, cutie!!" Liam said to the koala with a loving smile and deep fascination for the fluffy animal that lived in a tree.

They also got to see some large red kangaroos while in the bushlands. Georgie and Liam were having the time of their lives. Although what they were doing was simple, it was a meaningful and profound experience.

The next morning, they headed back to Eucalyptus Ridge. Georgie decided to remove her heavy disguise.

Only to find the paparazzi at the Eucalyptus Ridge homestead front door, in a frenzy to spot Georgie. There were people everywhere.

"What the hell is this?" Alonso yelled out from his car.

Zoe said, *"It looks like the whole bloody town is here!"*

Carlo and Steevo were driving Georgie's massive RV, and it was obvious that it was once owned by someone wealthy. The RV was swarmed by cameramen and journalists.

They couldn't believe their eyes, this peaceful place had suddenly turned into a circus. They all sat in the car for several minutes, trying to think of a plan of action.

Liam spotted Wendy and Dorothy Blake together, folding their arms with sour looks on their faces. *"Are those two the 'sprouted potatoes?"* he asked.

"Yes," Bobby replied, and Zoe added, *"I'd love to make mashed potatoes from them right now!"*

Bobby replied, *"They're not worth it, Zoe."* She looked at them, as they were both giving her dirty looks, most likely for what she did to Tom.

Alonso got out of the car, looking extremely furious.

*"Sh*t, what's Dad doing? He looks agro!"* Zoe said with a worried look.

Bobby knew exactly what he was doing, as they thought alike. They were all in shock. Melina, in disbelief, whispered to herself, *"Mama mia!"*

It took a while for Alonso to fight his way to his front door, as journalists from every direction asked him questions. One question was, *"Is it true that you're holding Georgie Hayes hostage?"*

They got to the car Georgie was in and noticed she was hiding, then forcefully tried to open the door, but it was locked, so they broke the window with a nearby rock. There, they saw Georgie lying down so she wouldn't be seen.

"She's here! She's here!" a young journalist called out, and they all flocked to her like bees to honey.

All of a sudden, there was a gunshot, and everyone froze. It was Alonso firing a shot in the air from the top of a journalist's car.

*"My f*cken sheep have more brains than you lot! Leave my family alone!!"* he yelled as he had never yelled before, almost hurting his throat.

But after five seconds, they started again, like a loud bunch of selfish beasts.

Giovanna, horrified and disgusted by the so-called professional behaviour and what Georgie had to put up with in her world, said, *"And this is the price she pays for being successful? It makes no sense. "Giovanna whispered to herself.*

Georgie got out of the car gracefully, under her own accord. You couldn't hear a pin drop.

Alonso, from the top of the car, noticed Georgie get out. He whispered to himself, *"No, Georgie…"*

She yelled out, *"It's okay, Alonso."* What she said echoed through the landscape. Liam got out to protect her, and so did Bobby. The whole family formed a circle around Georgie, and things started to get frantic again, with journalists asking stupid questions. Georgie completely ignored their absurd questions. She hugged Bobby, then Giovanna, and whispered in her ear, *"Sorry to have to leave this way, Mum. I love you."*

Hearing the word *"Mum"* from her daughter filled Giovanna with indescribable joy. *"I love you too, Lilliana Russo,"* Giovanna replied.

Georgie smiled at her and stumbled, trying to get to Alonso to say goodbye. He tried to reach her in the crowd. Georgie finally made it next to him, looked him in the eyes, and said, *"As long as they know I'm here, they won't leave you alone. I must leave. Thank you. Goodbye, Alonso,"* being careful not to say the word *"brother"* in front of the journalists. Their hands let go and she quickly headed to the RV.

Liam, with a look of sorrow, glanced at Bobby and said, *"I'm sorry, Bobby. I have to go. I'm sorry it ended this way."* He kissed her on the forehead and headed for the RV's driver's seat. They drove off, almost running over Dorothy Blake, who had started all the trouble. Mozza and Hillery followed them behind the RV, Liam noticing them and smiling to himself. Hillery then returned to chase the very frightened Dorothy Blake back to her car.

That night at Russo's house, everything felt quiet and empty.

Steevo hadn't gotten to say goodbye to Georgie and had the same look on his face as when Maggie left him, only worse.

No one had any clue when they would see them again.

Zoe said to Dale, *"Hmm, I wonder if Georgie wants to keep the fact that she's related to us a secret?"* Dale jokingly said, *"I would"*

Melina overheard and said, *"We are going to keep it a secret until Georgie decides. Capish?"*

"Capish, Mum," Zoe said with no enthusiasm.

Zoe calls out, *"Has anyone seen Bludger? I haven't seen him for a while!"*

For Bobby, it felt like her fantasy had just ended, and the words Liam had said echoed in her mind: **'Sorry it had to end this way.'** Maybe Dad was right. She threw herself on the bed and grabbed her stuffed raccoon. She tried to read but just couldn't concentrate. Then she thought of what Liam had said, *never say the word 'unlikely' again.*

Two long days passed, and no one heard from them, nor did they answer their phone. They presumed they would head for Sydney, as that was where their flight on New Year's Day would leave from.

Alonso was cleaning the car when he discovered that Georgie and Liam's phones had been left behind in the mad rush that day.

Alonso called out as if he had just found gold. *"They forgot their phones! They forgot their phones! That's why they didn't call!"*

Bobby was happy that it wasn't for any other reason.

They sat down to have dinner together.

"No one these days remembers phone numbers, thanks to today's technology," Giovanna commented as she placed photos on the fridge taken on Christmas Day, looking at them nostalgically.

"I miss them so much… at the risk of sounding mushy, Mum, we really did feel complete when they were here, huh?" Zoe said.

"We really did, Zoe, you're right," Melina added.

Bobby didn't say much so as not to make it obvious, but the family knew there was much more going on between Bobby and Liam.

Alonso whispered to Melina as he looked at Bobby from a distance. *"It's obvious, isn't it? She's missing him like mad. She won't admit they're together, she is so stubborn… what do we do?"*

"Niete (nothing)," Melina replied. *"Things have a way of working themselves out, you know that. Be patient. She will be fine."*

Alonso sarcastically said, "Gosh, I taught you Italian so well!"

She replied, *"Cr*p on, babe! If it wasn't for your mum, I would know 'niente'."*

Just then, Alonso's phone rang. *"Unknown number! Is everyone curious about who it might be?!"* he yelled.

Alonso put it on speaker. *"Hello?"* he paused. *"Hello! Who is it?"*

He heard a meow.

Alonso, puzzled, almost hung up. *"Alonso, it's me, Liam."*

Bobby almost dropped her plate while taking it to the sink. *"Liam!"* she whispered.

"We have Bludger here!" Liam exclaimed.

Carlo, trying to be funny, said, *"We have a bludger here too!"* (Australian slang for a bum) as he pointed to Zoe. Zoe just pushed his arm away, unimpressed but taking the joke all the same.

Liam continued, *"Bludger must have crept up in the RV when everyone got out, but no one noticed because of all the commotion.*

Alonso replied, *"Look, mate, we discovered your phones here today. How did you get my number? Did you call Boof Head O'Connor again?"*

"Yes, and that was a painful ordeal, believe me," Liam said.

And added *"Can everyone hear me?"*

"Yes, we are on speaker," Alonso replied.

"Georgie and I just want to say thank you so much for the best Christmas of our lives. It will stay cherished in our memories forever. And our sincere apology for the paparazzi invading your home. We feel so bad for creating that trauma for your family." Liam paused.

"What are you talking about? We are a family. We go through the good, the bad, and the ugly together," Alonso smiled, and you could hear Liam and Georgie chuckling.

"How is Bobby?" Liam asked.

"She's good," Alonso said.

"Can I talk to her?" Liam asked

"Of course," Alonso responded

Bobby got on the phone. *"Liam."*

"Hi, Bobby. Am I still on speaker still?"

"Not now, you're not," she whispered.

"I miss you," Liam said, but Bobby didn't reply as everyone was listening. All she said was, *"I'm glad you're okay. I have a pen; give me your new number."*

"Bobby, I will call you a bit later. We're just checking into a motel in Sydney. We just got here, and we're exhausted."

Bobby and Liam spoke for hours that night.

She left the following morning to see him off, collect Bludger, and give them their phones. She traveled all day to get to Sydney, arriving at 8 p.m. on New Year's Eve. New Year's Eve came with the spark of fireworks in the distance, echoing the excitement and the quiet promise of a new beginning for each of them. They went on an hour-long night cruise.

They enjoyed the spectacular fireworks and had the time of their lives. Georgie is in awe of the party atmosphere. It was another magical night. Bobby and Liam tried so hard not to think about tomorrow as they danced.

"Okay, now tomorrow it's my turn to take you around like a tourist," Bobby said to Liam and Georgie.

Play when Bobby is with Liam on News Years Eve for Sydney Fireworks

Their flight back home to the US wasn't until late at night on New Year's Day, so they covered the town, taking photos and laughing hysterically with Georgie in heavy disguise again, adding to their fun. They visited the Centrepoint Tower, went to the Opera House, climbed the Harbor Bridge, and then sat at the beach. They had the time of their lives. It was almost the reverse of New York, but instead of her father, it was Georgie with them. They yearned for time alone.

Early evening came, and it was time for Georgie and Liam to catch their flight. A bittersweet farewell lingered in the air as they packed their things. Georgie, with misty eyes, hugged Bobby and blew a kiss to her newfound family, one by one, over FaceTime, Georgie making a promise that they would always be close, no matter the miles between them.

"Well, Bobby, this is it. What a week, huh? You have no idea the impact it had on me... and I'm so glad you came to see us off in Sydney."

"Well, the cat doesn't have a passport, so I had to get her," Bobby joked.

Liam laughed. *"Bludger could have come with us to the US. Just think, next time we come over, she'll have an American accent!"*

They both laughed.

"Will there be a next time, Liam? For us, that is?"

"Yes," he replied, and they left it at that.

Liam remembered the day she left New York and how emotional he had gotten. But this time, it was different, it was deeper. They kissed and shared a final embrace, both of them weeping. She watched him and Georgie walk off, disappearing into the crowd.

That night at the motel in Sydney, Bludger kept her company. She called upon the man in the white cloak.

"What do I do now? It wasn't as if I didn't know. I knew it would come to this because it has to. And now all it's done is increase our longing."

The man in the white cloak replied, *"Everything happens exactly when it is supposed to happen if it is meant to happen at all."*

She placed some wine in a tall glass and milk in a saucer for Bludger and made a toast. *"To rise stronger, laughing louder, and loving deeper!"* she said, raising her glass. With that, she found the courage to smile again.

CHAPTER 23

ROOTS AND LEGACIES

NOT NARRATED

For Georgie, it was a time of discovery, learning about her roots, her family, and the life she'd unknowingly left behind. And for Giovanna and the family, it was a chance to piece together Georgie's life, her journey from a little girl to a world-famous figure. They shared their stories over barbecues, sunlit picnics, and starry nights while FaceTiming each other. Each moment deepened the bond they had longed for but never expected to find.

Georgie sat beside Giovanna by the fire on FaceTime, her face softened in the glow. The conversation drifted to stories of Sicily, and Giovanna's voice grew warm as she recounted their father's charm and fierce spirit. Georgie loved every minute.

"He was a proud Sicilian," Giovanna began, her eyes misting with nostalgia.

"Oh, and handsome too, cheekbones like chiseled marble. When he looked at you, it was like he could see straight through to your soul." She paused, her gaze distant, as if she were reaching back through the years to pull him closer. *"He moved us from Sicily to Australia*

with nothing but his heart full of dreams and his fierce determination."

Georgie listened with rapt attention. She ran her fingers absently over the bracelet on her wrist, feeling its history in a way she hadn't before.

"So that's where I got it," she murmured, a soft smile touching her lips. *"My skin tone... it comes from Sicily."* Her eyes were fixed on the horizon as if in deep thought. *"I always felt like I was... different. And now I see why."*

Georgie leaned into Giovanna, curious. *"What was father like on a day-to-day basis? You've told me, but I want to hear it again,"* she asked, her voice gentle, respectful of the moment.

Giovanna's face lit up. *"Oh, he was as stubborn as the mountains of Sicily, but with a heart as big as the sea. He could charm anyone with just a look, but his heart belonged to his family."* She paused, glancing at Georgie with a mixture of pride and awe. *"And you, Bella, you've got the same spark."*

Georgie laughed, her laughter rich and warm. *"Guess I'm like dad, and Alonso too,"* she said, a newfound sense of connection sparking within her.

Georgie soaked up every story of her heritage, from tales of her ancestors in Sicily to the resilience of Giovanna's journey as a young mother in Australia. And as each story was told, she felt pieces of herself falling into place.

Giovanna, overcome with emotion, would blow kisses over FaceTime. *"I always imagined what you might be like if you had lived. And here you are, so much more than I ever dared to hope for. You're beautiful, smart, and overflowing with love to give my darling girl, never to forget your worth.*

Georgie's eyes glistened as she whispered, *"And I always wondered if I belonged somewhere. I've spent my whole life searching for belonging and connection, and now I realize... I had it all along, waiting for me."*

The family knew that no matter where they went or how far they traveled, they would always carry this time they had at Eucalyptus Ridge with them, stitched into the fabric of their lives forever.

As Georgie ended her call with her mother on FaceTime, Giovanna said what she always says, *"See you soon, Lilliana Russo."*

Georgie grinned, repeating the name to herself, *"Lilliana Russo,"* a name she was beginning to feel as deep as her skin.

Finally, getting to Milan...

It had been 6 long months since Liam held Bobby in his arms. Their feelings for one another were intact and stronger than ever, but they had to wait a little longer.

The sun began to rise over the Italian horizon, and Bobby's heart raced with anticipation. She pressed her face against the narrow window of the plane, feeling the warmth of the sunlight casting its first rays.

This wasn't just any morning. It was the start of something bigger than herself, the fulfilment of a dream Bobby had carried for so long. She'd finally done it. The board game, once a wild idea scribbled on seemingly endless Post-it notes and countless cutout design changes, was now a success and changing lives just as she dreamed it would.

It had grown legs of its own, being sold in more and more stores, expanding to more and more countries, and paving the way for the journey she'd promised herself and Nonna.

She took a deep breath, feeling the warmth of the Italian sun on her skin, a warmth so different from home. This wasn't her homecoming, but standing there with Nonna at her side, it felt like coming full circle. This journey had begun in the whispers of her grandmother's stories and in Bobby's own determination to bring those stories back to life.

Giovanna's eyes glistened, her face soft with memories as she took her first steps back into her homeland. Bobby couldn't help but smile, feeling that, somehow, in this moment, they had both found their way back to where they were meant to be.

Bobby had worked tirelessly to bring her board game to life, and with its success, she had finally earned enough to bring Nonna Giovanna back to the place she had longed for, her homeland.

Bobby planned to travel around Europe together for 4 weeks.

After they got to their motel room, they rested overnight and then went walking through the narrow, cobblestone streets. Bobby couldn't help but laugh at Nonna's delight, her eyes bright as she took in the familiar sights. This wasn't just a trip; it was a gift, a way to bring Nonna Giovanna back to her roots, after so many years away.

Bobby glanced over, watching Giovanna close. She noticed her eyes as she took in her first breath of Italian air in decades, a look of reverence softening her features.

Riding together through the narrow, cobblestone streets of Sicily on a Vespa, just as she had envisioned. Bobby felt so much joy and laughter bubbling up inside her. Nonna clung to Bobby's waist on a hired Vespa, her delighted squeals echoing off the ancient stone buildings as they zipped past old trattorias, vibrant markets, and the pastel facades of sun-washed homes.

Giovanna's gaze flicked from side to side, her eyes bright with recognition, her cheeks flushed from the wind. Here, in the streets of her youth, she was alive, radiant, a glimpse of the young woman she once was.

"This is where I learned to love," Giovanna whispered as they passed a small piazza where couples strolled hand in hand. She leaned forward, her voice trembling with emotion. *"It's where I met your grandfather, Bobby. Where we had dreams of our own."* She paused; her gaze fixed on a park bench in the piazza.

"And do you see where that couple is sitting? "Yeah," Bobby replied in anticipation. *"It's the exact spot where your grandfather proposed to me."*

"Oh wow, Nonna," Bobby replied, her heart swelling with the depth of her grandmother's memories.

Giovanna beams with a smile and says, *"Do you want to know something funny?"*

"What is it, Nonna?" Bobby responds, her own smile matching hers.

Giovanna confesses, *"I feel I can't speak English properly and at the same time forgotten Italian... It's kind of weird how my first language has slowly faded, not realizing it till I came back here."*

Bobby bursts into laughter and reassures her, *"Your English is just fine, Nonna."* There was a pause. Bobby puts her head down and then raises it again to look her grandmother in the eyes.

Bobby said to Giovanna...

"You know... You have no idea how much I admire your incredible bravery. The sheer courage it took to abandon everything familiar and venture to an entirely new country, halfway across the globe, during an era when you had nothing but blind faith to guide you. You had to embrace an unfamiliar culture, endure a foreign climate, and face the heartbreaking reality of never seeing your family again, with nothing in your pocket but a dream. Nonna, I adore you. I cherish everything you represent, and I am profoundly grateful for your endurance and the path you've created for all of us."

...I really am."

Giovanna looked deeply into Bobby's eyes. They got teary and gave each other a long, tight hug. All the while Bobby asked herself the question if she would have the same courage to adopt another country and abandon her own, and the answer she gave herself was No.

"Come on, Bella, let's grab a gelato." Giovanna said excitedly.

They stopped by a small café, Bobby watched her grandmother, her heart joyous as she saw Giovanna reconnect with a piece of herself.

"Italy's changed, Bobby, but in all the right ways," Giovanna said as they pulled up to the piazza. She pointed toward the quaint little park where her family had gathered in the past.

Bobby looked to where her grandmother was pointing and saw a grand picnic laid out, checkered tablecloth fluttering in the breeze.

Giovanna sat down to rest.

Giovanna said, *"I am going to give… riding my own Vespa a go, is that ok, Bobby?* Bobby chuckles and says, *"Of course, Nonna, good on you for not being too fearful to do something new!!"* And off they went, all the way to the nearest beach, two hours away.

Riding the Vespas had a deeper meaning than just getting from A to B. It was the long-time promise Bobby made. It was a symbol of perseverance, a symbol of promises kept, and a symbol of unity between grandmother and granddaughter, an unbreakable bond, a memory Bobby would cherish forever. They finally got to the beach, and the weather was perfect, even though it was in the middle of summer, it was neither too hot nor too cold, but almost cold by Russo standards.

"Nonna, are you up for a dip in the water with me, just like we envisioned so many years ago… but not naked, ok !!?" Bobby said laughing

Giovanna paused and thought about it. *"Yeah, why not? Let's go. Andiamo!"* she said with a smile.

Bobby always enjoyed her grandmother's joyous company and was glad she was a fun type and gave almost anything a go.

When they arrived at the beach, they headed toward a colourful umbrella on the sand.

Unlike Australia, Italian beaches have umbrellas for hire.

"Come over here, Nonna, I like this one. Let's hire this umbrella," Bobby called out.

Nonna Giovanna replied, *"What do you mean you like this one, they are all the same, Bella …besides that one looks broken, it's fallen over!!"* An umbrella was still open but lying down.

"SURPRISE!!!"

Suddenly, out popped Alonso, Melina, Zoe, Carlo, Dale, Georgie, Liam, and yes, Steevo in his infamous blue extra-short shorts showing off his skinny hairy legs. They all cheered as Giovanna almost jumped out of her skin.

They had all been hiding behind the umbrella, lying on the ground. Bobby had staged the surprise; their voices rose with laughter. Giovanna nearly had a second heart attack from the shock, but then she burst into tears of joy, making everyone else get emotional. A memory is hard to forget.

"WHAT …Oh my God, my daughter is here too!" she yelled out loud, hugging everyone tightly. *"This is just the best. Bobby, you are so naughty keeping that from me! I love you all so much, wow, I don't believe this."* There wasn't a dry eye between them as they all merged into a laughing fit.

Bobby could hardly wait to see the look on her grandmother's face when they popped out of the umbrella, but she also couldn't wait to get her arms around Liam. They locked eyes, hugged, and spun around so much that they fell in the sand. They weren't in a hurry to get up as they kissed while lying down.

Alonso was so happy, not only to see his sister Georgie again but also to see Liam. They had met at the beach only moments before Bobby got there, texting her to say that they were hiding behind the sun umbrella and ready to yell out *'surprise'*. Bobby constantly checks her phone, trying to look inconspicuous.

That day, Liam and Bobby didn't hide their love for one another, the family saying, *"It's about time they come out clean about it."*

Melina had ordered a feast, with plates brimming with bruschetta, pasta, and freshly baked bread. The scent of ripe olives and tomatoes filled the air, while a guitar played in the background from a nearby street musician, adding a nostalgic Italian warmth to the scene.

Bobby noticed two teenage girls at a distant park table playing her game. She didn't want to appear to stare, so she looked away, but the girls noticed her looking and recognized her from the photo on the game and went up to her, asking if she was the inventor, Bobby Russo.

Bobby replied with a friendly smile and said *'Yes, I am Bobby Russo. What were the key points you got out of it?*

Bobby suddenly had Deja vu and realized that the statement she used was ***What were the key points you got out of it?*** She experienced the vivid dream she had all that time ago when the game was incomplete.

They told her that their grades had soared at school and that they started up a savings account and had $2000 saved in a short amount of time. They asked for their game to be signed, and Bobby was touched that they had asked.

Bobby stood there looking at how thrilled the two girls were to meet her as they walked away.

Bobby took a moment to acknowledge her uniqueness, her greatness, and the turbulent journey that led her here with Liam and Georgie.

Having that short encounter with those two girls was exactly what she needed to remind her of the tremendous achievement that she tends to downplay.

At that moment, it hit her that she never actually celebrated the fact that she succeeded in her goal of reaching over 1 million people. Why didn't I celebrate? she asked herself.

I will acknowledge my greatness from now on, she declared to herself as she saw the man in the white cloak sitting on the beach smiling at her as she gave him a gentle wave. I will celebrate my wins right here and now with my beautiful family and Liam, she told herself.

"Hey, Zoe!!!" Bobby called out, waving to her sister, who ran up with a wide grin, putting her arms around Bobby. The sisters had their arms around one another, walking towards the rest of the family.

Melina placed a tablecloth on the sand and lunch upon it. They were all having a ball reconnecting with Liam and Georgie.

"I can't believe we're all here!" Zoe yelled out to everyone.

Zoe laughed, catching her breath.

Carlo remarked, *"Well, not all of us."* *"What do you mean?"* Zoe replied as everyone listened in.

Carlo responded, "All of us accept for Hillery …I'm half-expecting that bloody sheep to show up, baa-ing her way through the piazza!" Everyone burst into laughter.

Melina wagged her finger. *"Let's not speak her name into the ether, Carlo. Knowing her, she'd find her way here somehow!" she said jokingly.*

Just then, Alonso came striding over with a large stuffed toy sheep he'd picked up at a nearby stall. He snuck up behind them, let out a loud *"BAAARRR!"* and threw it high in the air. Everyone nearly jumped out of their skin and let out a huge laugh. Giovanna looked at him with an exasperated but playful scowl, muttering under her breath, *"Testa di melda!"* (shithead).

The family erupted into laughing fits, the sound echoing across the beach as if the universe itself were joining in. In that golden Italian sunlight, they toasted to newfound connections, old promises, and the healing power of family. Georgie and Steevo stood to announce their engagement, Steevo pulling her close as he raised his glass.

"To Georgie… and the luckiest man alive," Steevo announces. Georgie and Steevo, the unlikely couple, were unexpectedly connected, their happiness standing out. Giovanna could not be prouder of her finding happiness at last and to find a love she could finally call her own.

Although Steevo still had on his daggy shorts, he looked different, like the weight of time had lifted from his face, softening the years that once etched themselves there. And Georgie, oh Georgie... she wasn't just glowing; she radiated pure warmth and resonance with Steevo. Alonso joked that if she shone any brighter, they would get zapped touching her.

Alonso shook his head with a chuckle. *"Oh wow... you've upgraded yourself to Brother-in-law status now, huh!?"* he quipped, grinning from ear to ear about their engagement. Alonso pulled Georgie into a bear hug, then shook Steevo's hand firmly. *"Just a warning, Georgie,"* he said with a wink, *"Steevo likes the idea of going commando."* Alonso knew very well she would have found that out by now, but his mind didn't want to go there.

"We're all going to Sicily tomorrow!" Melina declared, and everyone cheered.

"Salute!!" Alonso called out as everyone held their champagne glasses up.

Bobby, raising her glass, called out, *"Here is to rising stronger, laughing louder, and loving deeper!"* Everyone yelled in unison and repeated, *"To rising stronger, laughing louder, and loving deeper!"* all cheering at the same time.

It was the happiest Giovanna had ever felt, surrounded by her family, both new and old, her long-lost daughter beside her, and memories stretching as far as the horizon.

Giovanna then declared to everyone that she wanted to take them to the spot in Milan where she had been proposed to by Angelo.

Everyone cheered in agreement as they were eating their oversized gelato.

NOT NARRATED

Later that evening, as the sun dipped below the Italian coastline, casting a soft pink glow over the water, Bobby slipped away to find Liam sitting on a nearby bench, gazing out over the sea. She walked over and joined him in silence as they took in the view. The lights from the town reflected in the waves, shimmering like tiny golden fireflies dancing on the water.

"What a family," Liam murmured, a smile on his lips. *"I don't think I've ever seen so much love in one place."*

Bobby leaned her head on his shoulder as Liam embraced his whole body around hers. Liam continued, *"It's more than I ever thought I could have. And it's all here, in the most unexpected ways."* She looked up at him, eyes sparkling. *"So… do you think you could get used to this?"*

He wrapped an arm around her, pulling her close, and smiled as he said. *"I think I already have."*

There was a pause, and he added, *"I miss not touching you. I was going to spontaneously combust if I had to wait another second!"* Liam continued. *"Being away from you was harder than eating a Tim Tam without going for a second one"*. They both laughed, then kissed softly, gazing into each other's eyes.

Bobby stood still, not saying a word; they both felt at ease in the silence.

As they sat on the sand that evening, Liam asked her if she was happy with how her dream for the game panned out.

Bobby's voice grew softer and more introspective as she confided in Liam about her dreams. *"You know, the games... They were never just a way of teaching for me. They're a piece of me.*

I guess. I put so much of myself into them that sometimes it feels like they're the only way I know how to make sense of things. But most of all, it pains me to think that there are people out there suffering in silence when they don't need to, All I want is for the players to become aware of a better way of being."

Liam nodded, gazing at Bobby deeply as she spoke, intrigued by the way her face softened when she talked about her work. *"I can see that. You've got this intensity about you when you talk about it."*

She laughed softly. *"Well, I used to have this whole vision, you know? I used to imagine myself signing with a publisher in New York, flying out, meeting with executives, shaking hands, and watching my games hit the shelves in stores all over,"* she said, with a nostalgic smile.

Liam smiled. *"I presumed that's what you were up to when I met you in New York."*

"Yeah," she said, a wistful edge in her voice. *"But it didn't quite happen that way."*

Liam raised an eyebrow. *"Wait, how did your game end up in stores just before Christmas, so quickly then? I thought a publisher finally came through?"*

"Oh, you haven't heard the story?" Bobby laughed, shaking her head.

"Let me tell you: this wasn't some corporate deal I brokered myself. Nope. Turns out, I have Zoe to thank for my big break. And it all started as her crazy, petty way of getting back at Sabrina."

"Zoe? As in, our Zoe?" Liam grinned, intrigued. *"Oh, I have to hear this."* he added.

Bobby leaned in conspiratorially, her eyes sparkling with amusement, trying hard not to laugh. *"So, you know how Zoe can hold a grudge? Well, after she witnessed Sabrina tricking me into paying for meals, telling me I was doomed to fail my project, and even pulling me out of a kayak trip to make me feel like Sh*t, Zoe decided to get even. She somehow tracked down the company I ordered the first batch of games from, used her own savings, and then roped in Steevo to help fund the first big batch. Then she worked out a deal with our local Kmart."*

Liam burst out laughing, picturing Zoe's fierce determination, and said. *"Oh my god, that's so Zoe. How did she do it?"*

Bobby went on to say, *"She actually convinced the Kmart manager to take them on consignment,"* Bobby said, eyes wide with disbelief. *"She told the manager that my game was on the verge of being released in New York and that Kmart would be missing out on a huge opportunity to feature a local inventor first before it became a sensation in New York. So, they made a deal, no risk for Kmart, nothing for them to pay in advance, just a cut if they sold. And apparently, it worked. By Christmas Eve, they'd completely sold out."*

"Oh my gosh! Zoe!!!" Liam laughed in disbelief. *"Zoe, the unlikely business genius. So, the whole time you were in New York, you didn't know she'd done it?"*

"I had no clue. On Christmas Day, she gifted me a copy of my own board game, wrapped beautifully and tied with a bow. 'Surprise!' she exclaimed when I opened her gift. I thought it was the only one. Turns out, half the whole town has it in their homes, and she'd been my unofficial manager, publicist, and distributor all in one."

Bobby and Liam laughed until they couldn't breathe.

"As you know, when my laptop was destroyed, she corrected herself and spoke.

"...When 'I' destroyed my laptop... I lost all my designs. I was wondering why she asked for access to Google Docs. She said Mum's recipes were on there, the sneaky bugga! Oh, the things that Zoe's spite can do," Bobby roared, her voice full of pride and acknowledgement of the unexpected cleverness and kindness in Zoe's actions.

"And you know the crazy part? That little spiteful stunt caught the attention of stores and led to other stores across the state, and eventually, the *country, ordering my games. It just kept spreading from there. New York publisher? I didn't need one. Zoe's one-woman crusade got my games everywhere. So, two months ago, I was approached by a publisher in LA. I have no clue how they found out about me. I told them that the games were completely sold out in Kmart locally, and they signed the deal. BINGO."* They both laughed, letting the humour of it settle over them.

But after a moment, Bobby grew quiet, her expression thoughtful. *"I guess it's funny, right? We think success is supposed to come a certain way, with all these steps lined up neatly. I had this vision of how it would all happen, but the reality was... messier but even better. I didn't get the fancy publisher, I ended up homeless in New York, and I went through all kinds of unpleasant things. But I met you!!!"* There were a few seconds of silence as they both took it all in. Their heads touched from the forehead.

Liam's gaze softened as he took her hand, his thumb tracing a gentle line across her knuckles. *"Bobby, you've been through so much to get here. But sometimes, the things we don't plan for end up being the best parts, don't they?"*

She nodded, with a smile on her face, and said. *"If going through all of that was what it took to meet you, I'd do it all over again. Every difficult, messy part of it."*

Their laughter faded into quiet, and in the warmth of that moment, they leaned in, closing the distance between them. This time, the kiss was inevitable, a meeting of two people who had come to understand that life's best surprises sometimes arrive through the least likely people, in ways they would never have imagined.

Liam topped up the conversation with *"You could say that the universe had a better plan, right?"*

Bobby nodded, her eyes reflecting the glow of the fading sunset.

And in that perfect, quiet moment, they held each other as the waves rolled softly in the distance.

"This... feels surreal, doesn't it?" Liam whispered, his voice barely audible over the sea breeze.

Bobby replied, "It feels like how I envisioned it when I cut the clips for my vision board, but so much grander!"

Bobby stared into the distance as the sun started to dip below the horizon, the sky beautifully painted with a tapestry of pink, purple, and orange. She took a deep breath as if trying to take in all the beauty of the moment.

"Feels like the start of something, doesn't it?" Liam whispered as he squeezed Bobby's hand. Both of them are fully present.

They sat in silence, watching the horizon as the waves rolled in front of them until the light faded.

TRANSFORMED LIVES BEGINNING

NOT NARRATED

JFK, the larger of New York's airports, buzzed with its typical chaos, a symphony of hurried footsteps, rolling suitcases, and muffled announcements. The fluorescent lights felt sharp and cold, a stark contrast to the warmth of Italy's golden sun. New York felt like a world apart from the laughter and embrace of the Russo family. Here, faces were turned downward, eyes glued to screens or cast far into the distance, each person absorbed in their own world, oblivious to the lives moving around them.

Liam weaved through the crowd, pulling his carry-on with one hand and gripping a leather duffel with the other. Liam felt drained, the overwhelming noise of the airport and the constant buzz in his mind weighing him down. He was already missing Bobby. Collecting his suitcase from customs, his mind wandered off. For a brief moment, he wondered if he could do as Nonna Giovanni did many years ago and take a leap of faith and live in a country other than his own. The thought scared him and excited him all at the same time.

The familiar airport chill crept through him as he exited the terminal and spotted his Uber pulling up at the curb.

As he reached the curb, a woman's strident voice cut through the air, promoting what she was selling: *"Five dollars, folks! Only five dollars!...*

Get your handmade, unique, beautiful hand-knitted rose for only five dollars! Give this special, unique gift to the love of your life." She was surrounded by people eager to purchase, quickly handing over the roses in exchange for cash.

Liam attempted to flag down his Uber when the woman approached him. *"Sir, can I interest you in a unique rose?"*

Liam looked up, surprised. *"Betsy, it's you! How are you?"*

The woman paused, her eyes widening. *"I remember you, boy. You're Bobby's friend. Ohhh my goodness, how is she?"* Betsy said in delightful surprise.

Liam smiled. *"She's doing great, Betsy. I just came back from seeing her. Here's ten dollars. I'll take two roses, please...and here is a tip...I have to hurry, my Uber is here."*

Betsy, still stunned to have bumped into him, responded, *"Oh, yes, sure, wait! Let me give you my best ones."* She handed him two roses, one red and black rose with gold trimming and one plain white rose.

Liam stared at them curiously and nodded. *"I'm proud of you, Betsy ...Bobby will be stoked when I tell her you started a business and it's thriving. Keep up the good work!"*

Betsy, taken aback by his words of encouragement, smiled softly. *"Thank you... Have a good day, boy."* With that, they parted ways. Liam started to walk towards his Uber, and Betsy yelled out, *"Hey,*

Boy!" Liam turned around and looked at her and called back, *"Yeah, Betsy? "She changed my life, you know."* Betsy responded with a serious tone, frozen with her roses in her hand as she looked at him.

Liam smiled at her and nodded softly in acknowledgement. He then whispered to himself, *"She has changed mine too."*

Liam walked to a less crowded spot to order a new Uber as the one he was supposed to catch impatiently took off.

Glancing at the knitted roses in his hand while he was waiting, he sniffed the white one out of curiosity.

He immediately threw his head back in disgust and shock as the rose reeked, the white rose accidentally falling on the ground meters away. Liam got up from his seat to pick it up, and before he knew it, an old, derelict man picked it up and placed it in his suit pocket, none the wiser.

Liam looked at the other rose Betsy gave him that was red and black with gold trimming.

He gathered his courage and cautiously leaned in to take a sniff. To his surprise, instead of the vile scent that he had anticipated, his senses were met with an invigorating aroma, a blend of crisp, uplifting chic fragrance and fresh fabric softener. Liam stuck it almost right up his nose.

He tucked it into his pocket with a smile, unbeknown to him, the rose had been knitted from the underwear Betsy had stolen from Bobby's suitcase.

Betsy's words echoed in his head: *"You're Bobby's friend."*

The title didn't sit well with Liam, it didn't feel right. He wanted to be much more to Bobby, but at this moment, they were in limbo. Frustration immersing his whole body.

He tossed his bags in the back of the Uber, slid into the seat, leaned his head back with a deep breath, and shut his eyes.

He wished the car could somehow reverse time, driving him back across oceans and continents, back to the sound of waves and the laughter of family on the Italian shore.

A part of him wasn't ready to be back home, to leave behind people he truly belonged to.

Just as he was settling into a bittersweet quiet, the driver's voice broke through his thoughts.

"Long trip?" The voice held a certain warmth, a friendliness that felt oddly out of place amid the hustle and bustle of New York.

Liam opened his eyes, glancing at the driver.

"Yeah, it's been a trip, alright," Liam replied with a grin. *"Spent some time in Italy with a family from Australia, a girl I met right here in New York, actually. Her family welcomed me like one of their own."*

Timothy's eyes lit up. *"Australia? Man, I've driven a lot of Aussies over the years, but there's one young woman I'll never forget. She had this mountain of board games with her, and I helped her load 'em up. She even gave me one as a thank-you, and it ended up being a real game-changer for me and my teenage sister."*

Liam's eyes widened. *"No way, you're talking about Bobby Russo, right?"*

"Yeah, that's her, Bobby Russo. Oh my god, do you know her!" The driver chuckled with delight, introducing himself. *"My name's Timothy, by the way."*

Liam shook his head in disbelief and thought to himself, *"Wherever I turn, I'm haunted by Bobby. What is the universe trying to tell me?"*

Timothy continued, *"What a small world! Are you for real... you really know her?"*

"Yes," Liam responded, *"She's my... um..."* it hit Liam like a tonne of bricks as he thought to himself ... *"I can't even label our relationship!!"* *"If she were my girlfriend, I would be with her, right????"* Liam was more confused than ever about what to do from there. His face gaunt.

Meanwhile, an excited Timothy was talking a hundred miles an hour saying,

"It was a memorable night. I still have that original game she gave me. Now I see it everywhere in stores, but this one, " he tapped his chest proudly, *", this one's the real deal from her first trip here. Someday, I'll be bragging that I have one of the originals, straight from the game maker herself."*

"Wow," Liam murmured, processing this new layer of Bobby's journey. *"Bobby never told me about that day."* Liam thinks 'typical mysterious Bobby'

Timothy's tone softened. *"My little sister... she'd been going through a rough time, and we couldn't connect with her. But I brought home that game Bobby gave me and told her Bobby's story, coming from Australia to share her dream with the world. It sparked something in my sister. She played with me that night, and we've been at it every chance I get between driving and my pilot classes. Honestly, it's done wonders for both of us."*

"Classes?" Liam asked. Something about that word, combined with driving an Uber in New York, sparked Liam's curiosity.

Timothy grinned sheepishly. *"Yeah. Thanks to Bobby's game, I went back to college, man. My dream is to be an airline Pilot. That board game really inspired me. But it's my sister, she's really come around. That game's helped her work through stuff, you know, teenage challenges and emotions I never understood. She even brings it to game nights with her friends now."* Timothy chuckled.

Liam beamed with pride and excitement. He realized he felt like he was part of Bobby's story. Like her story was his too.

Timothy continued, *"Every time she goes out with that board game, I remind her, 'That's an original. Don't you dare lose a piece or spill anything on it!"*

"Great advice!" Liam said with a smile. He could almost see it, the way Bobby's game had quietly found its way into people's lives, shifting things in small but powerful ways.

Timothy nodded. *"Actually, you know what, thanks to this conversation, I'm heading over to Barnes & Noble later to buy her a copy of her own. No way am I letting her keep the original. It's priceless to me."* He laughed, then shook his head, recalling the night he helped Bobby.

"That night, we nearly broke our backs lugging her games out of her hotel and into this rundown building. I'm telling you, the whole time

I was thinking, 'Why here? We couldn't find a decent enough bathroom that night, and she settled for that one. Why was she looking for a bathroom for her board games? Never figured it out!" Timothy shook his head with an expression somewhere between admiration and mystery.

"Yeah, I imagine that would be perplexing," Liam responded, realizing he hadn't heard this story before.

"But the next day," Timothy continued, *"I saw in the news that the toilet block I dropped her off in had caught fire. I was worried she'd lost everything. But she knew my number, and I knew if she needed to haul the games again, she'd call me. But she never did. Now her game is big and all over!"* Timothy took the last turn into Liam's Street.

"I can't believe it, man! I was lucky to have been her driver that day."

"Oh yeah, by the way, did a publisher from LA contact her?" "Yes, she did say someone contacted her from LA. Did you have something to do with that, Timothy?" Liam asked inquisitively. *"Yeah, I drove him to Times Square and we had a chat. Turns out he was a game publisher, and I immediately gave him Bobby's number. I told him to work out the country code as I had no idea how to work it out. Please give Bobby my regards, ok."*

Finally, Timothy shut up.

Liam was silent, taking it all in. He remembered when he met Bobby, her rough beginnings, her relentless spirit. What Timothy said brought him back to seeing Bobby for the first time, with her backpack and a board game sticking out of it with a burnt edge on its corner. *"Now I know why it's got a burnt edge and why she said it was special."* He thought.

"Yeah, Bobby is something alright... By the way, thank you for sending the publisher her way, you have made a difference in her life. Your enthusiasm must have really sold it to him," Liam said, a mixture of admiration and appreciation in his voice.

As Timothy pulled up to Liam's apartment, he leaned back, looking at Liam in the mirror. *"Keep good friends close. People like Bobby, they do not come around often."*

"Thanks, Timothy. For the ride and... the reminder."

Once inside his apartment, he dropped his bags, turned on his radio, and the song "By My Side" by INXS was playing, and Liam's heart sank. The words in the song expressed exactly how he was feeling, a pang of deep sadness and frustration came upon him,

By My Side - INXS

Play when Liam has just got back from Italy and put his Radio on and throws himself on his couch

Die With A Smile - Lady Gaga ,Bruno Mars
Go to www.ritamontalto.com/songs to scan song
Play when Liam Wakes up in the middle of the night from a bad dream and hears that song on the Radio he left on when he fell asleep on couch

and just dropped heavily on his couch from exhaustion. He didn't expect to fall asleep there and then, but he did.

He was plunged into a deep, vivid dream...

It was of the breathtaking waterfall in Sunflower Springs. From the cascading water emerged the mysterious arm of a woman, reaching out for him. He lunged forward to pull her from the torrent, only to find it was Bobby. She gave him a tender smile and whispered, *"To rise stronger, laughing louder,"* Liam then added *"and loving deeper!"* He leaned in to kiss her gently, but she retreated, her eyes glistening with tears. *"Goodbye, Liam. I'm sorry... I'm sorry,"* she murmured, before vanishing into the waterfall's embrace once more.

He turned around, and he was in a bustling airport. Suddenly, he saw Timothy the Uber driver in a pilot suit, demanding his one-way boarding pass to Australia. Liam hesitated, his heart pounding as he slowly stepped inside the plane.

Timothy's voice echoed with finality: *"Once airborne, there would be no return."* Still locked in a stare with Timothy in his pilot suit, the voice thundered, ***"Decide... Decide, boy!"*** Yet it was Betsy's voice erupting from his lips. Spinning around, he saw Betsy, almost unrecognizable. She was clothed in a sharp red and blue air hostess outfit, her hair impeccably styled, her hand-knitted roses artfully arranged around her neck, clutching a real koala.

Betsy surged toward him with ferocity, her face inches from his. She grabbed a hold of him, delivering a brutal punch to his nose, blood gushing forth. He flung open the airplane door to run away, exiting the airplane and plummeting without a parachute, he saw

Sunflower Springs below. He stretched his arm out desperately, screaming, *"Bobby, goodbye goodbye, Bobby!"* Certain of his death as she saw her running into the field to catch him, yelling out his name. But she couldn't reach him, and he hit the ground hard and felt himself starting to die.

Liam jolted awake at 2 a.m., drenched in a cold sweat on his couch.

Bruno Mars' song *'Die with a Smile'* played faintly through his radio. He thought it was very odd that the words were so describing how he felt.

He stared blankly at the ceiling, yearning for the solace of an empty mind, but the turmoil inside him was suffocating. He felt like he was drowning in his own emotions, gasping for air. Sleep eluded him for the rest of the night.

Daylight finally came.

He was drawn to go look for the board game Bobby gave him that day in the diner. The one with the charred edge. Liam leaned forward from his ladder and. whispered, *"You're the one who survived the fire."*

Memories flooded back, stories Bobby had told him about how she held that very game with the burnt edge in the spirit realm when she teetered between life and death, her body lying lifeless for days in the hospital.

He called his friends...

This moment felt surreal, like all of Bobby's journeys converging at this one point as he stared at the board game.

Liam climbed up the ladder, the worn steps creaking under his weight as he reached for the dusty top shelf. His heart thudded in anticipation, a strange pulse of warmth seeming to emanate from the game. He stretched out his hand to grab it, but couldn't quite reach it.

Just as he pulled closer, he saw her face on the cover.

"Oh, Bobby, I love you," he softly whispered, placing his fingers on his lips, realizing how naturally and wholeheartedly it came out.

He froze. *"Oh my god, I never told her those specific words … when I was in Sunflower Springs or in Milan! How could I be so stupid?!"*

He whispered to himself, *"I don't know what to do. We live worlds apart. How can this work? I can't keep living like this! And she has been patient. Should I just end it?"* The sheer thought of that completely shattered him.

He was overcome by sadness and in need of someone to talk to.

He FaceTimed his friends in LA on the group chat. They all answered eagerly, putting themselves on camera.

"Hi, guys, so good to see your faces! How are you all? I miss you!" Ava said.

"Doing great! Liam replied enthusiastically.

"How was Italy?" Kizzy asked. Liam replied, *"Oh my gosh, it was even prettier than I imagined. It felt so surreal, I loved it. Listen, guys, I'm calling to invite you here. It's been a while since you were here. And we need to play Bobby's game together. Shame on me, I haven't played it since I promised her I would."*

Ethan eagerly chimed in, *"I love board games, and I am excited to get together again!"*

"We are so there!" Kizzy said, beaming with a huge smile.

"Alright, guys, we're on!" Liam said with a smile, and everyone agreed, cheering.

"I'll put in for time off at work," Ethan added.

Liam replied, *"Are you still working at that shitty place? I thought you hated it?"*

"I do, I feel very stuck," Ethan replied.

"Well, when you play the game, Bobby just might have the answer to unstick yourself," Liam said with a smile. *"Is that even a word?"* Ethan replied, smiling.

"How is Bobby, Liam? What's going on? Are you any clearer about her?" Ava asked.

Liam paused for a moment and said, *"I've never been clearer about anything in my whole life. I know that no matter what girls I meet from this point on, no one will ever measure up to Bobby.*

Ethan asked, *"Do you want to meet other girls?"*

"No, I don't!" Liam replied with a desperate look on his face.

He paused again and said, *"Look, the outback is her life. She's made it clear she won't move, which I totally don't blame her and you would understand too if you see how and where she lives... Anyway, all I have created is a difficult situation for her; she deserves better. My logical mind says just cut the emotional cord and say goodbye. Then there's another part of me that's much louder, which is my heart, and it says, 'For God's sake, work something out!' Then I go full circle again and go back to my logical mind, and it says, 'I have no clue HOW it can work; I love my country too."*

His friends went quiet, unable to offer any resolve. There was a pause of concern for him.

Liam added, *"When we were in Milan and Grandma Giovanna showed us where her husband proposed to her, I wanted nothing more than to do the same for Bobby on the exact spot. And as if the distance isn't enough of a problem, I have nothing to offer her anyway, she has a multi-million-dollar farm with her father, not to mention her successful board game, and I have Jack diddly squat. I must find a way to become more than I am."*

There was another pause. Kizzy said softly, *"Liam, you'll lose her if you wait too long. From what I can tell about her strong persona, you are bound to work something out."*

Kizzy's words seemed to fall on deaf ears.

"Anyways, on a lighter note," Liam said, trying to shift the mood, *"I can't wait to see you all. Let me know when you can get here. But meanwhile, I'll show you the game Bobby gave me. I put it up at the top of my wardrobe, but bear with me, I can't seem to reach it."*

Liam climbed up the ladder higher to show his friends the board game on camera. Ava called out, *"Be careful, don't fall, Liam!!*

"Oh yeah, I can see it, I remember what it looked like now. I saw it at the diner that day," Ethan said.

"Is that a burnt bit in the corner?" Kizzy asked curiously.

"Long story, Kizzy," Liam replied.

"How many players can play?" Ava demanded, her voice brimming with an impatient curiosity.

"I'm pretty sure it's four players... let me check," Liam replied, stretching precariously from the top of the ladder to grab the game. His friends stood below, their eyes glued to him, tensed with anticipation.

Suddenly, an intense jolt, as if lightning itself had struck, surged through his hand. With a thunderous crackle, the electric charge exploded, unleashing a fiery cascade of sparks that violently hurled Liam backward off the ladder. His friends screamed in terror, their cries slicing through the air as they witnessed the chaos unfold.

Liam slammed onto the ground with a bone-jarring thud, the impact jolting through his body like an electric shock, as if the very game itself had struck him. For a moment, there was only silence, an eerie pause, as though the world itself was holding its breath. When his eyes opened wider, he realized he was no longer looking at his own world at all.

Then it came, a surreal sound that sent shivers down his spine. Applause. Gentle at first, then swelling into waves, as though invisible forces welcomed his arrival. Distant, eerie voices followed, rising and falling in strange harmony, as though the maze itself was speaking.

And then, impossibly, he felt it. An unseen hand lifted his body up, not gently but with a strange weight that filled him with fear and uncertainty, as though he was no longer in control of what was happening to him.

He pulled himself upright, gasping, his heart pounding in his chest. And that's when he saw it. Stretching before him was a surreal garden maze of wonder, glowing with a light of its own making. Emerald hedges soared high, their leaves shimmering like jewels under starlight. Blossoms larger than his head swayed gently, their petals dusting the air with golden sparkles that drifted like fireflies. The maze paths twisted endlessly, lined with picturesque fountains that poured liquid light, and beautiful lanterns floated freely above, casting a soft, celestial glow.

Yet as his eyes adjusted, he realized the maze wasn't uniform. One half shimmered like a surreal cosmic garden of light, but the other half twisted into something much darker. Gothic towers clawed at a storm-filled sky, thorned hedges stood jagged like blades, and shadows slithered around in a predatory, sinister way, as though they longed to claim his soul.

And far in the distance, rising above the endless hedges, stood a luminous Four Pillar Pavilion. Its golden spires shimmered with an otherworldly brilliance, not gaudy or loud, but elegant and mysterious, radiating quiet power as though it had always been waiting for him.

His breath caught in awe of his surroundings, his emotions tangled between excitement and unease. *"Holy shit… this is freaky. Am I dead?!"* His horrified words tore from his throat, echoing back as though the maze itself had heard him.

Then, suddenly, light burst at his side. His phone lay on the ground, glowing brighter than ever before. From its screen came the voices of his three friends, urgent, alive, and closer than he could have imagined. Their words carried across the maze, weaving through its corridors like music.

The glow wrapped around him, a cosmic storm of light and color. Liam's chest thundered as the truth struck. He wasn't gone. He wasn't dead.

The game had pulled him inside, into the surreal garden maze Bobby had once sketched by moonlight, the very scorched board the man in the white cloak had once touched.

And now, it was reaching for his friends.

LAST WORDS

From Nonna Giovanna

I am no different to anyone else. I had my fair share of pain but also my share of immense joy beyond anything I ever imagined. But let me share something with you about Adversity and pain.

Pain is inevitable. Sometimes it crashes into you like a storm, other times it lingers in the shadows, barely noticeable. But no matter its form, it's always there, woven into the maze of life, much like Bobby's game. It's not what happens to you that defines YOU it's how you deal with what's happened that shows your true colours. Like all of Us Bobby had many choices, but she chose the road least travelled. The world is better because she followed the path least travelled. Most people don't realize that's where your inner joy and magic are awaiting you".

Pain has two purposes: it teaches, and it reminds you that you're alive. Then, just as suddenly as it arrives, it fades, leaving you changed. Adversity is no different. It shapes you, carves into you, and leaves its mark. It makes you wiser and stronger. But one way or another, it transforms you. And the truth is, every defining moment in life will demand its price in pain.

Most failures could have been converted into success if someone had held on and made more effort.

When you have the potential for success within you, adversity or temporary defeat only helps you prepare to reach greater heights of success. Without adversity, you would never develop the qualities that are essential to ensuring success.

Adversity and temporary setbacks are crucial for those who seek success, as they help prepare you to achieve even higher levels of great results. Without such challenges, you would never cultivate the essential qualities needed to ensure a lasting, successful life.

When you make every mistake possible in a maze but keep moving ahead consistently and learning from errors, it's only a matter of time before you discover the path to your destination. Success is no different.

Nonna Giovanna

"YOUR REALITY WILL ALWAYS
DIRECTLY REFLECT
WHO YOU BELIEVE YOU ARE——-----
----NOTHING MORE, NOTHING
LESS."

Bobby Jo

I hope you have enjoyed Adversity Gift...

Part 2 coming soon

Rita

Audio of Author summerizing
success principles in this book

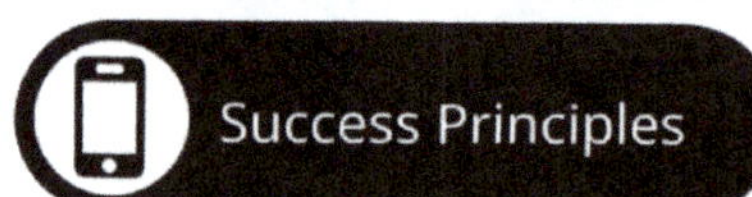

Success Principles

"Curious what Bobby Jo's game looks like inside
Scan the code and step in... if you dare "

SCAN ME

"One scan can change everything."

"Don't let this be
the end 😢...step
through the magical
door.!
I'LL BE WAITING TO MEET YOU
ON THE OTHER SIDE."
RITA MONTALTO

www.ingramcontent.com/pod-product-compliance
Lightning Source LLC
Chambersburg PA
CBHW070340170726
48291CB00001B/116